ORIENT

The third sweeping novel
in the best-selling series
about a great family
**THE RAKEHELL DYNASTY**
From the producer of
The Kent Family Chronicles,
The Australians,
and the Wagons West series.

## IN THE MYSTERIOUS EAST, AN EMPIRE TREMBLED...

*Jonathan Rakehell*     whose clippers had changed the course of history, now grieves for the wife he has lost. The company's leader must reclaim the power he once held and learn to love anew.

*Elizabeth Boynton*     the adopted cousin of Jonathan, long secretly in love with him, yearns to fill the role of the beautiful Lai-tse lu in his life.

*Charles Boynton*     Jonathan's cousin and partner, whose keen business sense and appreciation of pleasure sent him across the Orient and into many a slave woman's arms, now finds a new ally—his own wife.

*Molinda*     the Balinese beauty and Rakehell lieutenant in Hong Kong, strives to keep the dragons from their door.

*Dr. Matthew Melton*     sent by Jonathan to serve China in the Rakehell name, must face the enmity of China's native physicians.

*Dom Manuel Sebastian*     plans to crush the Rakehell dynasty
*Marquês de Braga*     as his trained elephants have trampled his enemies' bones.

*Erika von Klausner*     German baroness and skillful courtesan, is on assignment: to trade her body for trade contracts—and marry the most influential shipping magnate of them all—Jonathan Rakehell.

Books by Michael William Scott

*Rakehell Dynasty #1*
*Rakehell Dynasty #2: China Bride*
*Rakehell Dynasty #3: Orient Affair*

Published by
WARNER BOOKS

# The Rakehell Dynasty
## Volume III

# Orient Affair

## MICHAEL WILLIAM SCOTT

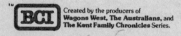

**BCI** Created by the producers of
Wagons West, The Australians, and
The Kent Family Chronicles Series.

**Executive Producer: Lyle Kenyon Engel**

WARNER BOOKS

A Warner Communications Company

**WARNER BOOKS EDITION**

Produced by Lyle Kenyon Engel.

**Copyright© 1982 by Book Creations, Inc.
All rights reserved.**

*Cover art by Tom Hall*

Warner Books, Inc., 75 Rockefeller Plaza, New York, N.Y. 10019

 A Warner Communications Company

Printed in the United States of America

**First Printing**: August, 1982

10 9 8 7 6 5 4 3 2 1

For
**My Daughters**

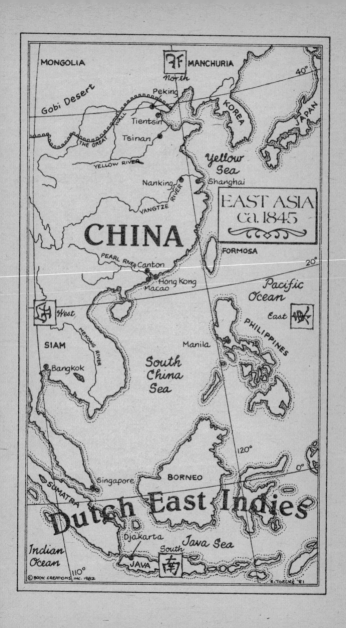

HONG KONG ca. 1845

# Book I

Book I

# I

At the peak of the second highest eminence in the ancient Chinese city of Canton, just inside the inner city walls, stood the handsome estate of the late Soong Chao, Cantonese merchant and shipping magnate, who had died three years earlier, in 1841, during the hostilities between the Middle Kingdom and Great Britain. Scattered on the estate, behind high brick and stone walls that protected the privacy of the inhabitants, were buildings of various sizes, all of them with pagodalike roofs, and here the present inhabitants ate and slept, worked and played. Connecting these structures of various sizes were formal gardens complete with streams and lily ponds, bewildering varieties of flowers, and carefully pruned trees.

There was also a large stretch of level ground on which green grass was growing, and here Kai, majordomo for the late Soong Chao and now similarly employed by his son-in-law, Jonathan Rakehell, stood with his feet apart, a mock ferocious smile on his face as he beckoned, one at a time, to the three children who awaited their turns to be instructed in the martial arts.

The first in line, as was appropriate for a boy of eight years, was Julian Rakehell, the son of Jonathan and his first wife, Louise, the principal heir to the Rakehell dynasty, clipper builders extraordinary to the world.

A low growl emanated from deep within Kai, and most

Chinese hearing the sound would have flinched. Kai was known to be fierce and unscrupulous, a leading member of the secret Society of Oxen, and as such he was a dangerous foe.

But Julian displayed true Rakehell courage and hurled himself at the man as he had been taught, throwing himself directly above Kai's knees. The boy knew that if he landed in precisely the right place, Kai, in spite of his vastly greater weight and bulk, inevitably would collapse to the ground.

Watching with keen interest was David Boynton, the seven-year-old son of Jonathan's first cousin, business partner and heir to the English end of the Rakehell and Boynton commercial empire. David was Eurasian, the son of the English Charles and a Cantonese prostitute who had given her life for him. At the age of seven David was already an accomplished mimic, and he watched Kai as closely as he observed his cousin. When his turn came he would glower as fiercely as the burly majordomo was doing, and he would somehow manage to imitate the growls that caused Kai's barrel chest to heave.

Relegated to third place in line and scarcely able to wait for her appropriate turn was a very small girl of four years. Jade was the daughter of Jonathan and his dearly beloved late wife, Lai-tse lu, the daughter of Soong Chao. Ordinarily females did not participate in the martial arts, but Jade Rakehell was no ordinary girl, by any stretch of the imagination. She had inherited her mother's dazzling beauty, as well as the keen intelligence of both her parents. She had also acquired a mind of her own, and what Jade wanted, Jade usually got. In this instance Jade insisted that she join the boys in their martial arts lesson, and she refused to be denied. Granted that she paid scant attention to the proceedings and devoted her time to her black chow dog, Harmony, who was leaping and frolicking with her, wagging his tail furiously. There would be ample time to concentrate on the martial arts when her turn came, and she was supremely self-confident of her ability to do well.

Jonathan Rakehell, tall and slender, his build still athletic although he was well into his thirties, emerged from the main house and paused, unobserved, to watch the children for a few moments. He approved of Julian's efforts and smiled slightly as he nodded. The boy was quick, agile, and fearless, and even more important, was showing that he was capable of thinking clearly under duress. As a father, Jonathan could ask no more.

David's turn came, and Jonathan's grin broadened. The boy was impetuous, much like his own father, Charles Boynton, and he tried to compensate for his small size by hurling himself violently into the fray.

Jonathan's smile faded when his gaze fell on Jade. Her resemblance to her late mother was so marked that he felt a pain deep in his chest, and without thinking he reached beneath his shirt to touch the jade Tree of Life medallion that Lai-tse lu had presented to him long ago, and that somehow had come to stand for all they had meant to each other. A flag bearing the same symbol with its three prominent branches flew from the masthead of every Rakehell and Boynton ship afloat, and just touching it now reminded Jonathan anew how badly he missed his wife.

Jonathan had no time today to dwell on the antics of the children, so he turned away abruptly and walked down a pebbled path to a pagoda that stood beyond the other buildings, surrounded by a small grove of stylized trees. Pausing inside the entrance, he took two joss sticks from a container, lighted them with the flame from the oil lamp that burned day and night in the little temple, and then put them into their holders. As the scented perfume of the burning incense filled the interior, Jonathan crossed the polished marble floor and then stood in silence before the crypt of Lai-tse lu. At moments such as this, he felt totally forlorn, not caring what might happen to him, but he knew this attitude was wrong. Lai-tse lu had told him herself with her dying breath to persevere—for his own sake as well as for the sake of the children. He knew her advice was sound: someday Julian would replace him as active head of the company, and Jade would benefit, too, from the security that Rakehell and Boynton ships would provide.

Jonathan's memories were so painful that he could not remain in the pagoda for long, and when he emerged again into the open he heard once more the shouts of the children and the barking of Harmony. As much as he wanted to play with them, perhaps joining Kai in giving them an exhibition of real combat in the martial arts, there was no time for such frivolity today. Instead he made his way directly to the pavilion that served as his office on the grounds of the estate.

An extraordinarily handsome woman with flowing black hair cascading down her back, her kohl-rimmed eyes huge, rose to her feet from the three-legged cushioned stool on which she had been sitting, and smoothed her simple, bare-shouldered Indonesian gown, which did ample justice to her superb figure. Molinda was the daughter of a Balinese woman and a French physician whom she had never known. She had been a handmaiden on the extensive staff of the Fat Dutchman, the business associate of Jonathan and Charles, in Djakarta, the capital of the Dutch East Indies. She had eventually won her freedom, and since that time she had more than lived up to her potential, becoming the head of the Far Eastern offices of Rakehell and Boynton. She, too, was recently widowed; her husband, Shaong Wei, a cousin of the emperor, had been killed by persons unknown, and Jonathan suspected that the blow had been intended for him rather than for the Chinese man. Only the delicate shadows beneath Molinda's eyes indicated that she had also been under a great strain of late.

"If Charles is here, we can start the meeting," Jonathan said.

Molinda shook her head. "He's been visiting the new clipper that just put into the harbor at Whampoa, and he hasn't yet returned," she said. "I suppose that, as usual, he's made too little allowance for the crowded conditions of the streets of Canton during the noon hour."

Jonathan smiled fleetingly. Molinda, who had once had a

brief affair with Charles, understood him well. "Just as long as he doesn't tarry," he said. "I'm anxious to begin this meeting and come up with some solutions to our problems."

As he took a seat behind a polished desk, Molinda sank back onto her cushioned stool and sighed. She well knew that the problems Jonathan referred to involved the overextension of Rakehell and Boynton funds to construct new clipper ships, as well as the enormous financial loss from a loan that she herself had made. "I take full responsibility for our current predicament," she said, looking down at the floor.

"Please stop blaming yourself," Jonathan replied briskly. "You had no way of knowing that that damned Scotsman Owen Bruce has hated me for years, and that he was in league with my late brother-in-law, Bradford Walker, who would do anything to destroy the Rakehells."

"You're very kind, Jonathan," Molinda said, "but I still think I was naïve to have advanced Bruce and Walker more than a quarter of a million dollars with only their word to support the loan. I only did it because they had promised to pay such high interest rates, and I thought Rakehell and Boynton would profit enormously." She sighed again, then looked at Jonathan. "Is there any way we can insist on being recompensed?" she asked hopefully.

He shook his head. "Bruce owns a warehouse and is allegedly in partnership with the Marquês de Braga, the Portuguese governor of Macao, in various shipping enterprises, but I'm afraid we have no proof other than your word—which alone is useless in a court of law—that we actually advanced him such a huge sum of money. Besides, his association with a high-ranking Portuguese official makes him almost untouchable. Even if we were to apply to the British courts in Hong Kong, and even though British justice is supposedly austere and impartial, no judge is going to willingly involve the governor-general of Macao."

"I see," Molinda replied, and stared gloomily out the window at the pond in which carp were swimming.

Both were lost in thought, and in the silence that followed, Charles Boynton bustled into the room. Dashingly handsome, almost as tall as his cousin though a bit stockier, having put on some extra pounds over the years, Charles was endowed with seemingly inexhaustible energy. He was one of the rare men who could work for eighteen to twenty hours at a stretch and appear as fresh at the end of a grueling stint as he looked at the beginning. "Sorry I'm a little late," he said, "but I needed more time than I realized to go over the manifests of the captain who just put into Whampoa today. His profits from his voyage should bring us a pretty penny."

"I estimate," Molinda said, "that we'll make about twenty thousand dollars on his cargo. It's not a sum to be sneezed at, to be sure, but in our present predicament it will do little to help."

Charles preferred to remain on his feet when engaged in deep thought, and jamming his hands into his trouser pockets, he began to pace the office restlessly. "Jonnie," he said, "I want you to be completely honest with me, if you will. I've often heard it said that Soong Chao was one of the wealthiest men in the Orient."

Jonathan nodded. "There's no doubt of that," he replied mildly.

Charles became aggressive. "Lai-tse lu was an only child and inherited a vast sum from her father. Now that she's gone, that fortune has come to you. I can understand that you want to save as much of it as possible for your children, but Rakehell and Boynton face an unprecedented emergency, and we're desperately short of cash. Surely you could advance the company some of your fortune and not even feel the strain."

Jonathan exchanged a significant glance with Molinda and then sighed. "I thought you knew, Charles," he said. "When Lai-tse lu died, I donated the fortune that she had inherited to the Society of Oxen to help the people of China."

"I see," Charles said. "Trust you to give in to your idealism and to cause the company to suffer as a result."

Jonathan bristled, but Molinda intervened quickly. "Jonathan did what he thought best for the good of China," she said, "and having been privileged to know Lai-tse lu myself, I know that she rests in peace because of his unselfish gesture."

Charles nodded gloomily but said nothing. Molinda reached for a bell rope that summoned a servant, and there was no need to tell the middle-aged woman who appeared what she had in mind. She had lived on the estate for a considerable time, and the servants were familiar with her ways. So, soon thereafter, a tray of tea appeared, and Molinda took charge, ceremoniously pouring the steaming, fragrant brew into small lacquer cups.

"I find it hard to believe," Jonathan said, "that we're on the verge of bankruptcy. We're turning out four clipper ships a year from our New London yard, and ships of the Rakehell and Boynton fleet are sailing the seven seas." He sighed deeply. "But it takes cash to operate a large company, just as strong winds and fair seas are needed for a clipper to race through the water. Our problem is simple but nonetheless pressing. We have a shortage of cash."

Charles sipped his tea, which he found too hot for his liking, and began walking around the room again. Suddenly he surprised his companions by laughing aloud.

They saw no humor in the situation they were facing, and stared at him in surprise.

He chuckled again. "You Yanks have a descriptive phrase that applies to our present situation, Jonnie," he said. "I think it's 'There are many ways to skin a polecat.'"

Charles was so inventive that Jonathan was not surprised. "You have something in mind, I take it."

"You bet I do," Charles replied. "Molinda, you worked for the Fat Dutchman for years and were far closer to him than either of us has ever been, so listen carefully and tell me of any flaws you see in what I'm going to outline. I think the answer to our problems lies in black gold."

"In pepper?" Molinda asked in surprise.

"In pepper," Charles replied emphatically. "As luck would have it, there are six Rakehell and Boynton ships currently in this part of the world. There are two at Whampoa, three at our dock in Hong Kong, and another has either just arrived in

Java or is about to dock there momentarily. I propose that we scrape together every penny that we can find and buy six shiploads of pepper."

Jonathan whistled softly under his breath. "I'm not necessarily doubting your wisdom, Charles," he said, "but I'm not sure we can make a profit on six shiploads of pepper large enough to justify—"

"Hear me out," Charles interrupted. "Immediately after we buy the pepper and it's loaded on board our ships, the Fat Dutchman uses his unlimited connections with the government of the Dutch East Indies to make the sale of pepper—to anyone, for any reason—forbidden for a time. The embargo won't be permanent, of course, but will last long enough for us to name our own prices on the world market in London and to make a great killing on pepper."

The scheme was so audacious that Jonathan had to laugh. "It's a unique idea," he said tentatively, "but I can think of all sorts of reasons why it won't work."

"Think positively, Jonnie," Charles said, and turned to Molinda. "Well?" he demanded.

With her hands pressed together as she sat deep in thought, Molinda resembled a Balinese statue. "You have projected a fascinating concept, Charles," she said. "Let me ask you just one question. Why should the Dutchman be inclined to follow your wishes in this matter?"

"We've been doing business together for quite a time," Charles replied, "and he's never forgotten that Jonnie provided him with a clipper ship at a time when the whole world was clamoring for them. For that matter, he's bought half a dozen clippers from us by now, and we've always kept his requests at the head of the list."

Molinda shook her head. "The Dutchman is very grateful for the favors of his friends," she said. "He will make you a gift of a slave girl or of a parrot. He will provide you with Indonesian silks and ivory to take home to your wives and your mothers. What you are proposing, however, is something that would require him to perform a major deed on your behalf."

"I'm hoping that his vanity would impel him to act," Charles said.

Jonathan was quick to grasp his meaning. "Yes, I see what you mean," he said. "The Dutchman is vain, and we'd be asking him to do something that he alone—in all the world—could do. But I doubt that his vanity would be a sufficient motive. It's too bad, because your scheme is legal and foolproof. We'd undoubtedly earn a fortune if we had the only pepper for sale anywhere. I'm not losing sight of the fact that the only source of pepper in the world is the Dutch East Indian Islands, and we'd be taking advantage of a natural monopoly, but as I say, I don't think we've yet found the key to inspiring the Dutchman to act on our behalf."

"You have not found the key," Molinda said, "but you have not searched diligently for it." All at once she smiled and looked ravishing. "I cannot blame you, however. The solution is so simple that you have overlooked it quite naturally."

Jonathan raised an eyebrow. "Simple?" he asked.

"Indeed," the young woman replied emphatically. "You know the Dutchman as a trading partner, and as a generous host and friend. You have not sat beside him day after day, month after month, as he does business. I have, and I tell you flatly that what motivates him beyond all else is greed."

Charles stopped pacing long enough to stare at her thoughtfully. Jonathan was attentive, too.

"The Dutchman," Molinda said quietly, "trusts both of you, so your battle is already half-won, as there are few people on earth whom he trusts sufficiently to enter into a deal or bargain without a written contract, which in this case would be impossible. I am sure, however, that all you need to whet his appetite is a promise of a percentage of the profits that you'll obtain."

"How much?" Charles demanded.

Again Molinda thought hard. "If you offer him too little, he will reject the deal outright and will be inclined to put it into effect himself. If you offer him too much, his greed will get the better of him and he will demand still more. I suggest you offer him ten percent, which is very fair, and no matter what he says, refuse to budge from your position. I'll be very much surprised if he doesn't give in eventually.''

"I assume that both of you will come to Djakarta with me," Charles said. "Then you can supervise the day-to-day strategy yourself, Molinda."

The young woman shook her head. "My presence would remind the Dutchman that I once served him. He would feel that I was taking advantage of him, and he would feel insulted, too, because a mere woman would appear to be outsmarting him. It is far preferable, I think, if I remain quietly in the background."

"From what I know of the Dutchman," Jonathan said quietly, "I quite agree with you, Molinda. We'll do it your way."

"What about you, Jonnie?" Charles asked. "You'll sail to Djakarta, too?"

"I'm afraid," Jonathan replied, "that I am not able to budge from Canton at the moment. You forget that I am not my own master at present. I sailed here from the United States, bringing Mr. Caleb Cushing as a special envoy from the President, to negotiate a trade treaty between America and China. I am expected to remain here until Mr. Cushing completes his negotiations, and then I am obliged to sail him and the members of his commission back home again. So I'm afraid you'll have to act alone in all of this, Charles."

"If I must," Charles said, "I shall. I'll take David with me, naturally, since I'll be sailing home to London from Djakarta, and I'll write to both of you about the results of our little pepper scheme. Wish me luck."

Before either of the others could reply, the children streamed unexpectedly into the pavilion, accompanied by an excited, barking Harmony.

"Papa, Papa!" Julian shouted exuberantly. "Come and watch. I can bowl Kai over."

"Me, too!" David asserted at the top of his lungs. "Come and see, Papa."

Jade, as always, had a practical turn of mind. "I can't beat

20

Kai," she said, "because he's a man and he's too big, but I can beat David, and I can almost beat Julian."

Kai's bulk filled the entrance to the pavilion, and his tone was apologetic as he said, speaking in the Cantonese dialect, "A thousand pardons for the interruption, but I could control the young devils no longer. They insisted on seeing you."

"I quite understand," Jonathan replied, "so don't give it another thought, Kai." He picked up his daughter, hugged her, and still holding her in one arm, draped his other around the slender shoulders of his young son.

Molinda felt compelled to intervene. "You were practicing the martial arts, were you not?"

The children's clamor assured her that she was right. She turned to Jonathan with a frown. "It is well for your son and the son of Charles to become adept in the ancient arts of self-defense that are practiced in the East, but it is not seemly for Jade."

Jade promptly pouted.

"You will grow to be a lady, like your mother," Molinda told her firmly. "I do not think she familiarized herself with the martial arts. I certainly do not know them. I am acquainted with no member of our sex who knows them."

What Kai alone of those present knew was that Lai-tse lu was, indeed, adept at the martial arts, having been taught by Kai himself when he was in her father's service. But the huge majordomo felt it was not his place to interfere, and he kept silent.

Jonathan, however, felt compelled to come to his daughter's defense. "All the more reason, then, for Jade to be familiar with the martial arts," he said. "The knowledge can't hurt her, and I could see where it would benefit her."

Jade didn't understand the adults' dispute and decided to settle the question in her own way. Wriggling out of her father's grasp, she shouted, "C'mon, David, I challenge you."

"You do, eh?" David cried. "Very well, I'll show you a thing or two!"

Suddenly the two children were hurling themselves at each

21

other with a violent enthusiasm. Molinda's deep frown indicated her displeasure, and she tried to intervene, but neither David nor Jade paid the slightest heed to her. The dog, in the meantime, became wildly excited and added to the noise by barking wildly and circling the children, who were trying to knock each other down. Kai restored order by the simple method of reaching out with two huge hamlike hands and picking up David with one and Jade with the other. He held them at arms' length while they struggled. Molinda quickly took charge.

"Jade, David," she said severely, "behave yourselves this instant."

Something in her tone told the youngsters that they could not trifle with her, and they fell silent and stopped their struggles. "You are in the office of Mr. Jonathan Rakehell," she announced severely. "He is your father, Jade, and he is your uncle, David. He also is a senior partner in one of the largest and most successful shipping companies on earth. It is thanks to his efforts that clipper ships now sail every sea known to man. You will not conduct yourselves in this manner ever again in the office of Mr. Jonathan Rakehell. You will treat him with the respect that he deserves."

Her tone was uncompromising. The children stared at her, then looked at Charles and at Kai, who were equally sober-faced. Jonathan wanted to laugh and comfort his daughter, but he knew that Molinda, with her Eastern concept of the respect that children owed their parents, was right. He would only serve to undo the good that she had accomplished if he interfered, so he, too, remained stone-faced.

David was abashed. "I'm sorry, Uncle Jonnie," he whispered.

Jonathan reached out, ruffled the boy's hair, and forgave him with a quick smile.

Now Jade stood before her father and held out both arms to him. He could resist her appeal no longer and, lifting her up, kissed her. "There's no harm done, children," he said, "just remember what Molinda has told you, and always heed her word when she speaks."

The thought occurred to Charles that it would be helpful in

the rearing of Julian and Jade if Jonathan saw fit to marry Molinda. The idea of such a union was beyond the understanding of most British aristocrats, for the West and East never mixed, at least publicly, but Charles looked at the world differently. He had greatly admired Lai-tse lu, and for his own part he would have given serious thought to marrying David's Chinese mother if she had not been killed. Still, he believed people had to sort out their own lives, and he would not advise his cousin, instead leaving well enough alone.

"I'll set sail tomorrow morning," he said, "stopping in Hong Kong to add the ships there to my flotilla. I'll keep you informed as to how I make out." He took his son by the hand and left the pavilion hastily. A morning sailing meant that he would be obliged to return to Whampoa immediately to make certain that his ships there were ready in time, and having decided on a course of action that would fill the depleted coffers of Rakehell and Boynton with vitally needed cash, he was proceeding with all haste to put his scheme into operation.

A half-dozen covered porcelain dishes stood on the table in the dining pavilion, among them chicken with ginger and shredded beef with bean curds, cooked with hot peppers, both of them among Jonathan's favorites. He ate easily with his chopsticks and discovered that for the first time since Lai-tse lu's tragic death, he had an appetite. He looked at Molinda, who sat opposite him at the table, eating demurely and efficiently with her own ivory chopsticks, and he smiled at her. "You amaze me on occasion," he said. "You're not only a first-rate businesswoman, but you have a real flair for the domestic. How you remembered dishes that I enjoy is beyond me."

"It's no great secret," Molinda said. "The training I had at the Dutchman's makes such things second nature to me."

He nodded and reflected that Shaong Wei had been the most fortunate of young men during the short time he was married to Molinda. It was small wonder that he had been rehabilitated and had completely conquered the drinking problem that had plagued him for years. "I thank you for it,"

Jonathan said, "just as I thank you for the control you exerted over the children. I'm inclined to be too lax, particularly with Jade." He changed the subject. "Are you intending to stay on in Canton for any length of time after I sail back to the States?"

Molinda's long blue black hair swayed and bobbed as she shook her head. "No," she said, "I'm needed more at the headquarters that I've established at Hong Kong. The town is growing so fast, you know, that it will soon become the trade center for the entire Orient, and I'm a little out of the mainstream here."

"That's strictly up to you," Jonathan told her. "You're free to live and work where you please."

"If I may," she said, "I'll certainly maintain an office here and keep a full staff on duty at this house. Fortunately, hired help is so inexpensive that I'm sure the company can afford that much, no matter how shy of cash we may be."

Jonathan nodded and helped himself to more chicken and ginger. "If it's all right with you," Jonathan said, "I'm thinking of taking Kai back to America with me. He was so devoted to Lai-tse lu that he's transferred his devotion to the children, and he's good for them. But Lo Fang, of course, will continue to be in your employ."

"I don't know what I would do without him," Molinda said, and meant it. Lo Fang, the head of the secret Society of Oxen, had served as majordomo to a succession of viceroys of Canton, but he had broken with the authorities during the Opium War that had ended two years earlier, in 1842, and had led the members of his society in guerrilla warfare against the British. Jonathan had served with Lo Fang and consequently knew and appreciated the man's great talents.

"I'll feel quite at ease knowing that Lo Fang is on hand to protect you," he said. "With Lo Fang to guard you, I know that you won't be molested."

"You're very kind," Molinda said.

"So are you!" he retorted. Their eyes met and held for an instant, then they both quickly looked away. They suddenly

24

felt awkward and uncomfortable with each other, and they now ate their food in silence.

When they finished their meal, Jonathan suggested a walk. Molinda nodded, and with one accord they rose, left the table, and wandered outside. The weather was mild, and the stiff breeze from the mountains that lay to the west dispelled the heavy dampness that ordinarily enveloped Canton. They strolled down a pebbled path, pausing occasionally to look at the shadows cast by the three-quarter moon on various parts of the garden, and eventually they came to a stone bench supported by four sturdy feet that resembled dragons. There they sat. Jonathan was very conscious of Molinda's femininity, and after a long silence he forced himself to speak. "It occurs to me that you and I have developed a very complex relationship," he said.

Molinda smiled gently. "Being realistic," she said, "we are both very attractive people. We are thrown together by business into each other's company for most of our waking hours. It's only natural that we should have strong desires for each other. The death of your wife and of my husband have not killed those urges within us."

No American or English woman would have spoken in that manner, Jonathan reflected. Only a native of the East who had the objectivity peculiar to her part of the world could have seen their situation so clearly, and only someone as honest as Molinda could have spoken with such fearless candor.

"I reckon you're right," he said. "I never thought of life in those terms. I had the feeling that I'd betray Lai-tse lu's trust in me if I were unfaithful to her memory. But that's nonsense, of course. Life must be lived by and for the living with the living."

She folded her hands in her lap and looked demurely across the gardens, where flowers were planted in clusters of colors, pinks together, blues in one place, yellows massed near each other. She did not speak, and the silence between them grew long and heavy.

Jonathan realized that Molinda was wisely giving him

complete freedom of choice: he could either pursue a closer relationship with her, if that was what he wanted, or he could back off without loss of face. She was not losing sight of the fact that he was her employer as well as her close friend and confidant. Pondering the problem, he knew he could not keep his grief for his departed wife alive within him indefinitely. Someday he would be forced to readjust his sights, put her in a proper place in his life, and go on from there. It was healthier, in all probability, to begin that process now rather than later.

Steeling himself, he reached for Molinda's hand.

Her slender brown hand willingly became entwined with his brawny fingers. They looked at each other, and there was no need for further words between them. They stood and walked to the pavilion that Molinda used as her bedchamber. Jonathan followed her inside and slid the door closed behind him.

She braced herself, then unfastened her single garment and let it slither to the floor as she proudly faced him in the nude.

This was not a time for thinking. Jonathan swept her into his arms, and they embraced, kissing hungrily. In a remote corner of his mind he was vastly relieved because kissing Molinda in no way reminded him of the countless times he had kissed Lai-tse lu.

It occurred to both of them, as their lovemaking progressed, that what they were experiencing was valid unto itself and had no connection with the relations they had enjoyed with their respective spouses. Precisely as Molinda had indicated, she was a woman, Jonathan was a man, and they developed a chemistry of their own as they responded to each other. What they shared belonged to them alone, and had no bearing on anything either of them had known previously.

They found the release they sought, and then, as their ardor cooled, they relaxed, still wrapped in a close embrace. Many thoughts crowded Jonathan's mind now. He knew that Molinda was lovely, to be sure, but far more important than that, here was a woman he could trust implicitly, just as she could trust him. Neither would betray or willingly hurt the other, and

26

they could let themselves go, knowing they would emerge from the experience unscathed.

Jonathan was relieved beyond measure when he discovered that the jade Tree of Life medallion suspended from his neck remained cool to the touch. He would never forget that, at the moment that Lai-tse lu had expired, the medallion suddenly had burned with a terrible intensity. He was in no way superstitious, but having spent a number of years, on and off, living in the Orient, he well realized that much here was inexplicable and impossible to comprehend by Western standards. All he felt for certain was that the spirit of Lai-tse lu knew of his intimacy with Molinda and did not disapprove. The medallion gave off no heat of anger.

"Thank you, my dear," he murmured, "I shall never forget you for this."

"I shall always be grateful to you, too," she replied in a half-whisper.

After a time they stirred, and Molinda reached for an ankle-length robe of embroidered silk, handing to Jonathan a shorter robe that had belonged to Shaong Wei. They donned the apparel, then moved into the sitting room, and the young woman busied herself making tea.

Jonathan realized that for the first time since his wife's death, he was at peace within himself.

Molinda knew how he liked his tea and added sugar and a squeeze of lime to it without being asked. Then, stirring her own tea, she became thoughtful. "It is good for both of us, I believe, that you will return soon to the United States."

Jonathan grasped her meaning instantly and nodded.

She looked out the window, and as she sipped her tea she remained ruminative. "We are both lonely," she said. "We create sparks when we are together, and it would be easy—far too easy and far too dangerous—to mistake these sparks for love."

"I don't necessarily say that we'd be wrong for each other on a permanent basis," Jonathan told her. "It might be that we'd be right, it might be that we'd be making a grave error, but I do know that it's far too soon to determine such things."

Molinda nodded and smiled. "I ask only one thing of you," she said.

"You know I will grant any favor that's in my power to give," he said quickly.

"What I ask," she said, "is not a favor for me. I ask it for your children because it is their right. Had Lai-tse lu lived, they would have grown to manhood and womanhood with an understanding of the East ingrained in them. The Orient is important to them, now and always. I want you to promise me you will bring them with you to Hong Kong from time to time so that I may see them and do what I can to instruct them in the ways of the Orient."

"I can't thank you enough," he said, overwhelmed by her offer.

"No," she said, "it is wrong to thank me. I am only doing what must be done—for the children, for the company, and for the memory of Lai-tse lu."

# II

Macao, the Portuguese colony located at the mouth of the Pearl River below Canton, was a strange blend of two cultures, two ways of life. Here the pagodas of the Orient stood side by side with pastel-painted houses that looked as though they had been transported to the East from the Mediterranean Sea. Here, Chinese scholars in traditional ankle-length gowns of black silk mingled with equally traditional mid-nineteenth-century European businessmen wearing swallow-tailed coats, high-crowned beaver hats, and tight-fitting trousers. Portuguese was universally understood, if not spoken, but the Cantonese dialect remained the predominating language.

On the waterfront, to be sure, where the British and American clippers, brigs from France, Spain, Holland, and the Scandinavian countries mingled with the junks of China and the dhows from the Arabian Sea, a dozen languages filled the air. Here, the proprietors of the taverns, inns, and brothels of the waterfront district insisted on being paid in pounds sterling for their wares. A consciousness of money certainly permeated all of Macao, which existed only because it had been the first European foothold in the Middle Kingdom, and as such had brought great prosperity to the Portuguese.

No one earned more or was more alert to the opportunities offered by Macao than the already wealthy governor-general, the wily and brutal Dom Manuel Sebastian, Marquês de Braga. He sat now in a private sitting room of his inner suite in the huge palace to which his rank entitled him, and as he sipped a glass of wine to which various fruit juices had been added, he looked coldly at his partner. Owen Bruce was abnormally tall and husky and had a Scotsman's typical high coloring and red hair. Those who had known him best during the many years he had spent in the East claimed that he had no emotions and remained cool at all times. But his present appearance belied these stories. Color burned in his cheeks, his eyes flashed, and when he spoke, his voice trembled with anger.

"We are partners, Your Excellency," he said hotly. "Is that correct?"

Dom Manuel nodded sleepily and folded his pudgy hands over his expansive paunch, the diamond rings on his fingers glittering in the afternoon sunlight that streamed in through the palace windows.

"It seems to me," Bruce declared, "that I do all the work and take all the risks. I deal with the exporters in India for the purchase of quantities of opium disguised as tea; I provide the ships that carry the drug from India to China; I make arrangements with the Chinese smugglers who purchase the opium from me; and I supervise the actual transfer of the cargo on one or another of the unoccupied islands in the Pearl River estuary. And what do I get for my efforts? Forty percent of the profits, while you, Your Excellency, take sixty percent. It doesn't seem fair to me."

The Marquês de Braga chuckled. "Life itself is unfair, my dear Bruce, and you've spent enough decades on this earth to know it. The only reason that our opium traffic succeeds is because I give the ships carrying the drug sanctuary here in my harbor until you complete your deals with the smugglers. Without me, you'd fail completely."

Bruce had to concede the validity of Dom Manuel's statements, but still felt aggrieved. "What you say may be true, Your Excellency," he replied, "but all the same, I believe a fifty-fifty split would be far more equitable."

The marquês sighed very gently and sipped his cool drink. "Ah, how soon we forget," he murmured. "Your

American colleague, Bradford Walker, was greedy, you recall. He couldn't contain his greed."

Bruce stirred uneasily. Brad Walker had been executed by one of the governor-general's trained elephants, which had stepped on his head and crushed him to death.

A malicious gleam appeared in Dom Manuel's eyes. "Ah, so you do remember Walker! Good! Let me assure you that you don't want to experience the fate that he met."

Owen Bruce was ruthless, a man totally lacking in conscience, but he had the sensitivity to realize when he was going too far, and he decided to relent. "I meant no harm, Your Excellency," he said, "I'm well satisfied with our partnership, and we're just having a friendly little discussion."

The marquês smiled indulgently. "I'm glad you brought it up, because I'd intended to raise the subject myself. I've decided to realign our percentages. Hereafter, I'll take two-thirds of all that we make, and you will content yourself with the remaining one-third." His smile was bloodless.

Bruce swallowed hard. He knew he was being punished for his temerity, and his harsh lesson was not lost on him. "Very well, Your Excellency," he muttered, "you're the final judge, as you are in all things."

His vanity restored and his purse enlarged, Dom Manuel immediately showed a much-improved mood. "We have other business that requires our attention," he said. "Have you been in touch with Ling Ch'i?"

"Yes," Bruce said. "It took me some time to reach him, but I finally got in touch with him and held a highly satisfactory meeting with him." Ling Ch'i, the most notorious of living pirates currently marauding the innocent in the South China Sea, trusted no white man, and Bruce had to go to great pains to establish his credentials with the go-betweens. Thus, his meeting with the pirate was no mean achievement.

The Marquês de Braga refolded his hands across his paunch and leaned forward eagerly in his chair.

Owen Bruce worded his recital with great care. "I told Ling Ch'i," he said, "in detail about the American clipper ship known as the *Lai-tse lu*. I told him she is currently docked at Whampoa and intends to sail for the United States as soon as a Caleb Cushing, who represents the American President, completes his current discussions with the representatives of the emperor. I suggested to Ling Ch'i that he lie in wait for the clipper ship, and that there would be a vast sum of money in store for him if he should capture Cushing and hold him for ransom. The U.S. government will be so mortified it will pay handsomely for his release.''

"Did you also inform the pirate of my own—ah—involvement?''

"I did, indirectly," Bruce replied. "Ling Ch'i was reluctant to contemplate the idea of making such an assault because he was rightly afraid that units of the British and American Navies stationed in these waters might interfere and send him to the bottom. But I made it clear, without mentioning Your Excellency's name, naturally, that certain highly placed persons in Macao were interested in the abduction of Cushing, the destruction of the clipper ship, and the death of her owner. Consequently, I made clear to him that, as he sails to his hidden rendezvous on one of the safe islands in the Pearl River estuary, he can put into the port of Macao for up to forty-eight hours, and he'll be completely free from molestation by British or American warships here. I also mentioned that he would be paid handsomely in gold.''

"What was his reaction?" the Marquês de Braga asked.

"Ling Ch'i," Owen Bruce said slowly, "is nobody's fool. It was obvious to him that I was speaking as an implacable enemy of Jonathan Rakehell, and that I wanted him out of the way. It was also plain to him that my unnamed highly placed sources in Macao feel toward him just as I do. If there were any doubt in his mind, the fact that we demand no share in the ransom he obtains for Cushing was enough to confirm his suspicions.''

The governor-general rubbed his hands together briskly. "You are quite sure that Ling Ch'i understood what we expect of him?''

"I'm positive!" Bruce replied firmly.

A slow smile of deep satisfaction spread across Dom

Manuel's pudgy face. "I care nothing about disgracing the United States," he said. "The government of their newly elected President, James Polk, means nothing to me, but the death of Jonathan Rakehell is of primary importance. I have lost very large sums of money in trade since he first came to Cathay with his accursed clipper ships, and the sums get larger and larger, year by year. You are quite certain that his company will be crippled badly once he's out of the way?"

"There's no question of it, Your Excellency," Bruce replied emphatically. "I had many talks with Bradford Walker on the subject, and I'm convinced that young Rakehell is the hub of the wheel that makes Rakehell and Boynton spin. Young Boynton can be distracted far too easily by a pretty face, an evening's entertainment, or a sumptuous meal. Rakehell's father is quite elderly, and so is Boynton's father. Jonathan Rakehell is the man who is personally responsible for the enormous success his company has been enjoying."

Dom Manuel nodded complacently. "That brings up another question," he said. "What are you doing about the large loan that the Rakehell and Boynton manager for the East made to Walker?"

Bruce shrugged indifferently. "I'm doing nothing about it. The loan was made by the woman called Molinda to Walker, not to me. Of course I cosigned the loan agreement, but I made sure my signature was illegible."

The Marquês de Braga frowned slightly. "But the money—more than a quarter of a million dollars—ultimately found its way into your pocket and mine."

"Before anyone could collect a penny from me," the Scotsman said vehemently, "they'll have to prove that I profited personally from the loan, and they can't do it. No one can. After Walker unfortunately—um—vanished on a journey to Macao, his personal records happened to disappear from our Hong Kong office. No one knows what became of the loan money."

"But didn't I understand correctly," Dom Manuel persisted, "that the woman named Molinda sent a letter to you requesting repayment?"

Bruce's expression became insolent. "That she did," he said. "But I've paid no attention to the letter, and I shall continue to ignore it. I see no reason to be operating a charitable enterprise, and the fact that she loaned a sum that large to Walker without obtaining any collateral in return is strictly her problem and that of her employers. It has no connection with me."

"You're quite sure," Dom Manuel persisted, "that the funds can't be traced to either of us? It would be embarrassing, you know, if Rakehell and Boynton obtained the help of the United States government and a complaint were made to my own superiors in Lisbon."

"You can put that fear out of your mind for all time, Your Excellency," Bruce assured him. "No human being can trace a penny of that money to you or to me."

Dom Manuel drained his glass, then wiped his mouth with the back of the sleeve of his silk jacket, paying no attention to the spots that he left on the delicate fabric. Ever since Jonathan Rakehell had married Lai-tse lu, the governor-general had vowed revenge, since it had been his intention to marry the beautiful Chinese woman himself. That desire for revenge had grown now to the point of an obsession: Jonathan Rakehell had not only taken the woman he wanted but had also taken much of the governor-general's trade, and thus his power and influence. Yes, more than ever, Dom Manuel wanted Jonathan Rakehell dead, and it appeared his wish was now coming true. Filling his glass again, he looked at Bruce and smiled evilly. "I look forward," he said, "to the events of coming days."

The few Americans living in Cathay or on its perimeter rejoiced when the representatives of the Tao Kuang Emperor and Caleb Cushing of the United States reached a final agreement. The terms of the treaty were eminently fair to both sides. Americans were granted the same rights as those accorded the British and French, and five ports were opened to American trade. The treaty carried a codicil that was unique: Cushing, on behalf of the United States government, deplored, as did the emperor's representatives, the opium trade that continued to flourish in China in spite of the vigorous attempts of the emperor's subjects to suppress it. The codicil was regarded in diplomatic circles as a slap at the British, who had fought a war and defeated the Chinese in order to maintain the lucrative opium trade.

The condemnation of the traffic in opium was included because of the natural repugnance of Americans to the debilitating drug. The fact that anything was known in the United States about the opium trade was due in large part to Jonathan Rakehell's efforts in educating the President and members of the Congress. Jonathan realized that the inclusion of the codicil was something of a triumph for him, and he knew that Lai-tse lu would have been delighted. She had hated opium and its effects on her people with an all-consuming passion.

The imperial viceroy in Canton gave a farewell reception for Cushing, and Jonathan, who was invited to attend the event, escorted Molinda, who looked even more ravishing than usual. She was the center of attention from the moment of her arrival in a glittering, figure-hugging cloth-of-silver gown, and she was well satisfied with the results.

"Every foreigner in Canton has noticed me tonight," she whispered to Jonathan, "and every one of them knows that I work for Rakehell and Boynton. We should enjoy an appreciable increase in our business as a result."

There was no doubt in his mind that she was the right representative for his company in the Orient. Surely she was the only woman he had ever known who had shared his unflagging devotion to business.

Thereafter, he spent the better part of his time in Whampoa preparing the *Lai-tse lu* for her return to the United States. As was customary for a shipowner, he would not take command of his own vessel, and had given the post to Elijah Wilbor, but Jonathan alone knew the Middle Kingdom sufficiently well to obtain the best meats, fish, and vegetables for his crew and passengers and to ensure that preparations for the vessel's departure went smoothly.

He returned to the house on the Canton heights in time to

spend his last night ashore with Molinda, and their relationship was such that he felt no guilt, even the following morning when he went to the pagoda that served as Lai-tse lu's mausoleum in order to pray at her crypt. He was joined there by his children, and all three emerged sober-faced, with Jonathan's arms around the shoulders of the youngsters.

Molinda waited discreetly for them, some distance from the pagoda, and intended to accompany them to Whampoa for the sailing of the ship.

Julian looked sad, and Jade, already bewildered by the loss of her mother, was stricken. "We're going to miss you awfully," the little girl declared solemnly.

Molinda picked her up and hugged her, then slid an arm around Julian to include him in the conversation, too. "Never fear, children," she said. "We shall meet again. Your father has promised to bring you back to the Middle Kingdom to visit me."

"Really, Papa?" Julian demanded eagerly.

"You promised?" the impressed Jade wanted to know.

Jonathan nodded and saw that both of his children were satisfied. They knew that he always kept a promise, no matter how difficult it might be for him, and therefore they took him at his word.

Kai already had arrived in Whampoa and awaited the children on board the clipper, taking charge of them the moment they set foot on the ship. Jonathan remained on shore, waiting to greet Caleb Cushing when he arrived. He was pleased to note that the gigantic Lo Fang, the head of the secret Society of Oxen and his former comrade-in-arms, had arrived from Hong Kong, where he was employed as foreman of the newly built Rakehell and Boynton warehouses. He now stood near Molinda and watched her carefully. He was a perfect bodyguard for her, and Jonathan knew he need have no qualms about her safety as long as Lo Fang was near her. He went to the Chinese giant and clasped him by the shoulder.

"Lo Fang," he said, speaking in the Cantonese dialect, "I

depend on you to keep watch over Miss Molinda, and see that no harm comes to her."

Lo Fang nodded slowly. "She will be safe," he said. "All will be well with her. Jonathan need not fear for her safety or her well-being."

They grinned at each other, and Jonathan knew the man was making a sacred commitment that he would be certain to honor. He turned to Molinda and said, "The time has come for us to part."

"I know," she replied. "May your God sail with you, and may you enjoy fair winds on your voyage."

Jonathan bowed his head and then replied, "May you find true happiness and contentment in the life you plan to lead in Hong Kong."

There was much that both left unsaid, but they understood each other so well that no further words were necessary. Jonathan bowed, Molinda inclined her own head in parting, and then she turned away abruptly. Rather than wait until the ship sailed, she walked quickly up the dock and headed for the nearby offices of Rakehell and Boynton, formerly the headquarters of the Soong Chao business. A pace behind her walked Lo Fang, his eyes darting first here then there as he took in everything within view.

Caleb Cushing, a lean, thickly bearded New Englander, arrived at the pier with the three members of his entourage who had accompanied him on his long journey from Washington, and he shook Jonathan's hand as they greeted one another.

"I understand," Jonathan told him, "that a crate of delicacies, mostly fresh fruit, arrived for you in the last hour or less, and that it's been stashed in your cabin already, Mr. Cushing. So if you're ready, we'll set sail right off."

"I'm ready," Cushing assured him. "I can scarcely wait until we reach Washington so I can tell the President of the success that we've enjoyed here."

They went on board the vessel, and Jonathan, as always, took great pride in the *Lai-tse lu,* the most luxurious clipper ship that Rakehell and Boynton had ever built. Her teakwood decks gleamed, her copper, which had been polished that very day, shone brightly in the late morning sunshine, and high overhead in the rigging were the clouds of canvas, soon to be unfurled, thousands of square feet of sail that would transform this sleek vessel into a greyhound of the sea, a ship capable of attaining speeds greater than those ever before achieved by a sailing vessel. Jonathan well knew that his clippers, which had literally clipped many days off voyages across the world's oceans, had transformed the entire industry. Granted that cargo space was relatively limited aboard a clipper, which necessitated exercising great care in what such a vessel carried, the clipper was still undoubtedly instrumental in the opening of the Middle Kingdom to international trade, just as clippers gave a boost to traffic with other places remote from the United States and Europe.

Even as Jonathan slowly made his way to the quarterdeck, Captain Wilbor shouted commands; the crew cast off, sails were set, and the sleek vessel edged away from her Whampoa berth, then gradually began to gather speed as she headed down the Pearl River estuary toward the open waters of the South China Sea.

At this moment, Jonathan felt very much alone. Standing at the aft rail, he peered back at the land he was leaving. Here he had met the one woman he had ever loved with all his heart and had, after many vicissitudes, taken her back to New London, Connecticut, as his bride. Now he was leaving her in a silent crypt near the bier of her father. He was tempted to give in to the waves of anguish that swept over him, but he refused to become a victim of self-pity. He had work to do—important work—and the company faced a crisis that had to be overcome. Julian and Jade needed him as they had never needed him before. Regardless of how lonely he might feel, regardless of how empty might be the life that loomed ahead for him, he had to face the future resolutely, with courage and with good humor. Too many people depended on him for him to give in to his natural feelings.

He now walked to the quarterdeck, where he lingered for a time without calling himself to the attention of Elijah Wilbor and the Chinese pilot who was guiding the ship through the traffic-laden waters of the Pearl River. Long experience had taught him that it didn't pay for a ship's owner, particularly one who himself held a master's license and was responsible for setting speed records in both the Atlantic and Pacific oceans, to make himself overly visible in the presence of his vessel's captain. Wilbor would be self-conscious enough with Jonathan traveling on board the *Lai-tse lu* as a passenger, and there was no sense in adding to his burdens.

Aware that his depression would grow worse if he continued to stare at the land, Jonathan busied himself, making certain that Caleb Cushing and the members of his staff were comfortably ensconced in their cabins, and then he went to the quarters reserved for his children and Kai. To his astonishment, he found the trio at the aft rail with Harmony sitting alertly nearby. The day was very warm, and the dog was panting; as Jonathan patted him he noted, certainly not for the first time, that the chow's tongue and the roof of his mouth were as black as his fur. The Chinese chow was a rare and unusual breed.

"What are you youngsters up to?" he demanded.

Jade giggled, and Julian looked dubiously at his father.

Kai had to explain and gestured toward several lines, tied to the rail, that drooped and fell into the water not far from the ship's rudder. "We are fishing," he said, trying in vain to retain his dignity.

Jonathan looked at him incredulously, then glanced at the children. "You're joking," he said.

All three shook their heads. He couldn't help laughing, and Harmony happily wagged his tail. "At the very most," he said, "you will pick up an eel from the bottom of the river. But I can't imagine any self-respecting fish inhabiting these waters."

Kai shrugged. "The children wished to go fishing," he said.

Jonathan curbed his urge to laugh again. "If I know Julian," he said, "he's responsible."

"I like fishing, Papa," the little boy said defiantly.

Jonathan nodded. "Yes, you'll have ample opportunity to catch your share and more on this voyage," he said, "but you'll have to be patient. You won't have any fish biting at your bait until we reach open salt water sometime tomorrow."

Julian tried to hide his disappointment, and Jade looked crestfallen.

"I think that the cook probably has your dinner for you in the saloon right about now," Jonathan said. "I know what he's fixed for you, and you'll like it."

"What is it, Papa?" Jade wanted to know.

Jonathan looked at her solemnly. "It's a surprise, but if I tell you it won't be a surprise any longer."

His reply seemed to satisfy her, but Julian lingered behind. "May Harmony come with us to eat his dinner, Papa?" the little boy wanted to know.

Jonathan had to make a decision and act swiftly. "Yes," he said, "Harmony can be fed his meals when you have your meals, provided that no adults are in the saloon at that time. I don't know how Mr. Cushing feels about animals, and since he's the personal representative of the President of the United States, we've got to defer to him, so anytime that he comes to the saloon, Harmony will have to wait."

Jade ran to the dog, threw her arms around his neck, and hugged him. "Don't you fret, Harmony," she said. "If you have to wait for a meal, Julian and I will wait, too."

They trooped off together down the deck, with the dog frolicking and running between them. Kai, Jonathan thought, would earn his pay by the time the voyage ended.

The clipper was doing about ten knots an hour now, Jonathan estimated as he made his way forward and glanced up at the sea of canvas above him. Had he been in command he might have given the clipper a bit more sail, but the question was academic. The truth of the matter was that he was not in command, and he warned himself anew not to interfere.

Time passed quickly, and when Jonathan heard the boatswain's mate striking a gong, he knew that the time had come for him, for Caleb Cushing and his associates, and for the ship's officers to repair to the saloon for their own dinner. There he found that the cook had outdone himself, not only baking chickens, but preparing a half-dozen vegetables as well. As everyone who went to sea well knew, vegetables did not keep, and Jonathan was particularly appreciative of the bowls laden with Brussels sprouts, bamboo shoots, Chinese cabbage, and a delicacy of the Middle Kingdom known as tomatoes. These were a red fruit, called love apples in the United States, where they were regarded as poisonous, and whenever Jonathan ate them he marveled at the ignorant who were slaves to their own customs. Not only were tomatoes delicious when boiled, as the cook had prepared them, but when served in a paste form, as the Chinese so often did, they concealed the taste of meat that was on the verge of spoiling. No foreign ship ever visited Cathay without taking quantities of the substance known as *ke-tsu-up* with them for their return voyage.

The guests and the two ship's officers not on duty ate heartily, and Jonathan was surprised when his twelve-year-old nephew, Brad Walker, Jr. came into the the saloon and stood beside him. Brad, who was in training as a deck officer, had recently arrived in the Orient on a Rakehell and Boynton clipper, and it was a great source of pride to him to be returning home, serving on a ship with his uncle on board.

"Sir," Brad now said to Jonathan, "Captain Wilbor's compliments, and he'd like to see you on the quarterdeck."

The request was so unusual that Jonathan, saying nothing to his dinner companions, hastily excused himself and hurried up to the deck. He found Elijah Wilbor, with a long glass up to one eye, studying the river ahead. "Look at this, Mr. Rakehell, and tell me what you think." He handed the glass to Jonathan, who raised it and held it to one eye. Directly ahead, in the path of the clipper ship, was a large, ungainly Chinese junk with the inevitable human eye painted on it near the prow in order to ward off supposed evil spirits. A half-dozen small cannon, were emplaced on her deck, and instead of being covered with tarpaulins, all of them had been unlimbered. Furthermore, her deck was crowded with men in motley attire, all of them Chinese and all of them armed with double-bladed swords and other weapons. "I don't like to be an alarmist, Mr. Rakehell," Elijah said, "but that ship looks too blame much like a pirate, for my fancy."

"I'm afraid she does," Jonathan agreed, and glanced up at the masthead. The Stars and Stripes floated there, and below the national flag was the Tree of Life pennant flown by all Rakehell and Boynton ships. "There's one way to find out," he said. "Query her."

Wilbor nodded, then ordered signals made inquiring as to the identity of the other vessel. There was no reply as such from the junk, but figures could be seen scurrying to and fro on her deck, and suddenly one of her short, squat cannons belched, making a loud report that sent a number of seagulls perching on the lines of the clipper to ascend high into the air, flapping their wings wildly. "I'll be damned," Elijah muttered, "if she hasn't shot at us."

Jonathan was grimly amused. "Her shot," he said, "fell short by at least a hundred yards, and if that's any criterion of her marksmanship, we don't have anything to fear."

Wilbor looked worried. "You know this part of the world a heap better than I do," he said. "What do you suggest I do?"

Jonathan's reply was prompt. "Send your gun crews to their stations," he said, "and teach these devils a lesson that they won't forget in a hurry. The Pearl River is infested with pirates, but this is the first time I've seen one with the courage to attack a clipper."

Wilbor nodded and summoned all hands to their duty stations.

The *Lai-tse lu* carried four six-inch guns, equally divided fore and aft, and in her arsenal were two nine-inch guns, which could be moved from place to place. Her gun crews immediately became busy, and it was clear that a duel was about to take place. There was no question that the cumbersome junk was blocking the path being taken by the clipper, and Jonathan deemed it expedient to offer the ship's master a word of advice. "Don't slow your pace unless you absolutely have to," he said. "Keep moving at any cost. Either you'll blow her out of the water or you'll have to veer at the last possible minute to avoid a collision, but keep moving."

"Yes, sir," Wilbor said, automatically assuming the role of a subordinate. "Would you take charge of our gun crews, Mr. Rakehell?"

"Certainly, if you wish," Jonathan replied, and hastened to the main deck, where Kai suddenly materialized beside him.

"That junk," Kai told him, "is the ship of Ling Ch'i, the worst of the pirates who kill innocent travelers on the river. He has been lying in wait for us."

"You think so?" Jonathan asked as he directed the emplacement of the two nine-inch guns.

"I know it is true," Kai replied grimly. "I knew it the instant I saw the junk appear from behind an island that I happen to know is used as a headquarters for stolen goods."

"I see," Jonathan said, and didn't bother to puzzle out why his ship had been chosen as a target for the band of Chinese brigands. He was mindful of his responsibilities to the personal representative of the President of the United States, and all other problems promptly vanished from his mind.

The junk's guns fired a salvo in unison, but it was instantly apparent that the cannons were inadequate and the gunners themselves inexperienced. Not one shot came near the *Lai-tse lu*.

Jonathan ordered the crew of his starboard six-inch cannons to fire a shot that would establish the range. The cannonball rose high into the air and dropped into the river about seventy-five feet short of the junk. Jonathan promptly ordered the trajectory of all of his cannons changed and then directed that the guns be fired one at a time.

He had taken great care in the selection of his crew before he had sailed from New London, and that caution paid unexpected dividends now. Of the twenty men assigned to gunnery duty, at least half were U.S. Navy veterans who were familiar with cannons, and their experience was invaluable. A six-inch iron ball slammed into the port hull of the junk, and a nine-inch iron ball plummeted to her deck, where it dug a deep furrow. The range had been found.

"Fire at will!" Jonathan ordered. His men responded with vigor and enthusiasm, and shot after shot found its mark, digging deep ruts in the wooden planks of the junk's deck, splintering her hull, and utterly destroying her superstructure.

The Chinese crew fought courageously, but they well realized their cause was hopeless. Just as they had been notably unsuccessful in combat with British warships during the Opium War, so their antiquated cannons, some of them two and three hundred years old, were inadequate for the task they were being required to perform now.

Ling Ch'i was not lacking in valor, however, and did not break off the contact with the more modern vessel and her expert gunners. He had been promised a rich reward if he captured the American envoy on board the clipper ship, and he was determined to achieve his goal in one way or another.

He resorted at last to a daring maneuver. Buckets of pitch, used for caulking seams on the junk, were set on fire, and soon the flames spread to the sails, then to what was left of the superstructure. Drifting with the tide, the junk began to bear down on the clipper ship. Elijah Wilbor was mesmerized by the burning apparition sweeping across the water toward him.

Only Jonathan, long accustomed to the Chinese mode of fighting, realized that action had to be taken instantly. He raced to the quarterdeck and superseding his captain, gave terse instructions to the helmsman.

The *Lai-tse lu,* as sensitive as the lovely woman for whom she was named, responded instantly, and veered delicately to starboard. The burning junk passed near to her, but there was no direct contact, and the flaming ship left the clipper totally unscathed.

The unequal battle was ended no more than a quarter of an hour after the hostilities had commenced.

As Jonathan and his crew watched, the junk went aground on the mud flats near the bank of the Pearl River, and there she burned out of control, down to the waterline. Her boats were lowered, enabling part of her crew to escape, and the others jumped overboard, even though they couldn't swim, and consequently were drowned. A greater and greater distance separated the combatants, and the clipper ship was completely out of danger again.

Caleb Cushing came to the quarterdeck and approached Jonathan.

"Mr. Rakehell," he said, "I'll be obliged if you'll tell me what that was all about."

"I found the incident rather strange, myself," Jonathan said. "Bandits are common on the Pearl River, to be sure, but they rarely attack foreign vessels of our size, particularly those that may be armed, as we are. I'd say that the commander of the bandit ship showed poor judgment, but he certainly has paid now for his mistake. He's lost his ship and the better part of his crew."

"I can't pretend that I'll be sorry for him," Cushing replied.

The pilot, Jonathan noted, was deep in conversation with Kai at the opposite end of the quarterdeck. Both Chinese men were speaking in a low undertone, even though only Jonathan, of all the men on board, was capable of understanding their language.

Ultimately, Caleb Cushing rejoined his companions below, and the pilot returned to work, taking his place near the helmsman, where Captain Wilbor joined him.

Jonathan wanted to hear what Kai had been talking about. Only his extensive experience in the East enabled him to realize that the majordomo had been engaged in no ordinary chat. Most Occidentals would not have noticed that taut lines were formed around his mouth, and his eyes glowed with a suppressed inner excitement.

Taking his time, Jonathan moved to a place beside Kai, and then they descended together to the main deck, where they sauntered to the aft rail. There they stood in silence for a time, staring at the green white waters of the clipper ship's wake.

Jonathan knew that Kai would reveal what was on his mind

in his own good time, but he couldn't help initiating the conversation. "I find it odd," he said, "that a pirate with Ling's experience would show the poor judgment to attack a Western ship as large as the *Lai-tse lu*. He must have guessed that we carry arms."

"The attack was no accident," Kai said. "Ling Ch'i had been lying in wait for you and had been awaiting your journey down the river for many days."

"All the more reason, then, for his exercise of greater caution," Jonathan declared.

Kai shook his head. "He hoped to take you by surprise; in fact, that was his only hope of victory."

Jonathan realized he would have to dig for details. "What did he intend to accomplish?" he wanted to know.

Kai spoke so softly that Jonathan had to strain to hear him. "He wanted your head on a pike," he said bluntly, "and he wished to take as a hostage the gray-haired one who represents the President of the United States."

Jonathan absorbed the information in silence. "How does it happen, I wonder," he mused aloud, "that a Pearl River bandit like Ling Ch'i has ever heard of the United States of America, much less the identity of Mr. Cushing as the President's envoy? I wonder, also, what earthly use my head would have been to him? To the best of my knowledge, I never met him and we weren't enemies."

Kai's expression was grim. "Ling Ch'i was not the natural foe of Jonathan," he said. "But he was in the pay of men who have reason to wish Jonathan dead."

Raising an eyebrow, Jonathan awaited a fuller explanation.

"The pilot on the *Lai-tse lu*," Kai said, "is a member of the Society of Oxen."

The majordomo was not digressing from his theme, Jonathan knew, but was going to great pains to explain that the credentials of the pilot were impeccable, and that his word could be accepted. The American nodded to show that he understood.

"The pilot came to us," Kai said, "from Macao, where he had just guided a large Portuguese trading ship. In a tavern in

Macao he saw Ling Ch'i dining one night with the Scotsman who owned a factory-warehouse at Whampoa and who now makes his shipping headquarters at Hong Kong."

"You refer," Jonathan said, "to Owen Bruce."

Kai nodded slowly.

"I am grateful to my friend for this information, but it does not surprise me," Jonathan declared. "Bruce has been my enemy long before he became involved in business with my brother-in-law. He has hated me because I achieved a success greater than he in his chosen field, and I did so without dealing in opium."

"That is so," Kai replied, "but Bruce was not your only enemy."

Trying to conceal his tension, Jonathan raised an eyebrow and waited.

"Years ago," Kai said, "Soong Chao prospered mightily when he was one of the few merchants in the Middle Kingdom who was permitted to trade with the West. He amassed great wealth, and there were many who sought the hand of his daughter in marriage. Lai-tse lu was not only wealthy, but she was beautiful and intelligent beyond compare, so she had many suitors. But she had no interest in them and rejected them because she had given her heart to an American, and she waited for him to return to Cathay to claim her as his bride."

Jonathan had no idea to what Kai was leading. "I returned," he said. "I claimed my bride, and we were married. What is the connection with—"

Kai raised a callused hand to silence him. "Among those who yearned for Lai-tse lu was a great and powerful man, the first lord of Macao."

"You mean the Marquês de Braga," Jonathan interjected.

The majordomo nodded. "It was said that he would give a considerable portion of his own vast fortune to have her for his bride. When she married elsewhere instead he became the enemy for life of her husband, Jonathan Rakehell. He is even more the foe of Jonathan than is Bruce."

Jonathan was already well aware of the Marquês de

Braga's deep resentment, and was tired of the indirect game that the Chinese played instinctively. "Are you trying to tell me," he demanded, "that Dom Manuel Sebastian, the governor of Macao, was involved in some way with this?"

Kai's tone did not change. "It is so," he said. "The arrangements were made by the Scotsman, Bruce, but the gold that was paid in advance to Ling Ch'i and the greater sum he would have been paid when your head was presented to him on a pike was the Marquês de Braga's."

Jonathan had no reason to doubt the word of Kai, and he accepted the situation that had just been outlined to him as the truth. He knew now that he had two terrible, implacable enemies who were prepared to go to great lengths to do him harm, and he hurried to his cabin, where he wrote a letter to Molinda in which he explained the situation to her with great candor. He would send the communication to her via the pilot, who would go ashore when the ship reached the open sea. It was essential that she be warned.

# III

Visitors to New London, Connecticut, who had business dealings with the one-hundred-fifty-year-old Rakehell and Boynton Company and were fortunate enough to be invited to the home of Jeremiah Rakehell, the present head of the firm, were surprised by the way he lived. In New York, Philadelphia, or Charleston, the man who was responsible for making most of the clipper ships that his country produced and, in addition, ran an international trading empire that extended to the seven seas of the earth, would have lived in a grand mansion. As a matter of fact, the English Boyntons, Jeremiah's sister and brother-in-law, the parents of Charles, owned precisely such a home in one of the more fashionable districts in London.

But New Englanders were known for their modesty and reticence, and there were few less obtrusive than the gray-haired Jeremiah Rakehell, the fifth in a direct line of descent to be the chief operating officer of the concern. His home was spacious, it was true, rooms having been added to it generation by generation, but it was made of white clapboard, and anyone unfamiliar with its ownership wouldn't have dreamed that someone as prominent and powerful as the head of the house of Rakehell lived in the dwelling, located not far from a shipyard that faced the waters of the Thames River estuary, a short distance above the place where the river flowed into Long Island Sound.

It was customary for Jeremiah to come home for his noon dinner, and his wife, Missy Sarah, his bride of only a year, saw to it that she was always on hand when he came home. Also present today were Jeremiah's daughter, Judith Rakehell Walker, and her fiancé, Homer Ellison, a former Rakehell and Boynton sea captain who had been promoted to an executive position at the shipyard.

Jeremiah was not one to linger over the noon meal when there was work awaiting him at the office, and today was no exception. "Judy, Homer," he said, as they took their places in the dining room, "I asked you to join Missy Sarah and me today for a specific reason. I received a letter from Jonnie that was delivered by clipper this morning." He looked at his daughter and then smiled. "You two have exercised great forbearance," he said. "You've waited patiently for the day when it might be possible to have Judy's marriage to Brad Walker annulled. Well, I'm pleased to tell you it won't be necessary. Brad is dead."

There was a moment of stunned silence, and then Homer's and Judy's hands crept toward each other beneath the table.

"It isn't seemly to rejoice over someone else's misfortune, I know," Homer said somberly, "but I thank the Almighty for His great mercy. He's giving us a chance to find happiness together."

"I won't pretend I'm sorry that Brad has passed on," Judy said quietly. "He was a vicious criminal and unscrupulous schemer who deserved the very worst."

"The very worst happened to him, I can assure you of that," her father said. "He was crushed by a trained elephant in the menagerie of a prominent Portuguese official whose enmity he had incurred."

Judy shuddered involuntarily.

"Don't take on so, child," Missy Sarah told her. "Things happen for the best."

"Indeed they do," Homer said. "Now there's nothing to stand in the way of our wedding in the immediate future."

"You may or may not want to delay your plans," Jeremiah said, as the serving maid brought in a platter of pot roast and

Missy Sarah began to serve it. "Jonnie has also told us that our worst fears for Lai-tse lu's well-being have been realized. She passed on, and he's buried her in a crypt beside her father at their ancestral home in Canton."

Sarah Rakehell's hands did not falter as she continued to serve the pot roast with potatoes and vegetables that had been cooked with it, but her eyes filled with tears, and she had difficulty in blinking them away.

"I'm sorry, my dear," Jeremiah told her gently, "I know how close you were to her."

Missy Sarah could only nod. As a young widow of a sea captain stranded in China, she had become governess to the motherless Lai-tse lu and spent the next twenty years with the girl. She knew that she would grieve for the rest of her days. But she never forgot her New England upbringing, and when she spoke her voice was firm.

"I've been prepared for this for the past two weeks," she said, "ever since I received Lai-tse lu's last letter and the covering note that Jonathan wrote with it. She was in great pain, suffering from an incurable illness, and the Lord took pity on her. How are the children reacting, Jeremiah?"

"Julian and Jade are being well looked after and are not grieving too deeply, which is fortunate. I'll give you Jonnie's letter to read. He's bringing them home as soon as Caleb Cushing is ready to sail, and I daresay they're on the high seas right now, which means they'll be arriving here in about three months, perhaps a little less."

Missy Sarah nodded, and it was apparent from her attitude that she had a new goal in life: she would take charge of Lai-tse lu's motherless youngsters, just as she had sheltered Lai-tse lu herself.

"I see what you mean, sir, about postponing our own plans," Homer said quietly. "This news does alter the situation quite a bit."

Judy gulped, dabbed at her eyes with a handkerchief, and hastily drank some water. "I was as fond of her as if she'd been my sister, rather than my sister-in-law," she murmured.

Missy Sarah sat, her back ramrod straight, and looked first

at Judy and then at Homer. "I was close enough to Lai-tse lu," she said slowly, "that she might have been my own daughter rather than my ward, but she is gone now, and none of us can pretend surprise. She was ill for a long time."

They nodded, and Homer's square, blunt jaw became set. He was bracing himself for whatever might be forthcoming.

Judith Walker was first and foremost a Rakehell. She bore a sufficiently striking resemblance to her father and brother to be attractive rather than pretty, and when she clamped her teeth shut, her lower jaw jutted forward. She, too, was ready for anything that Missy Sarah might have to say.

Sarah Rakehell set an example by stoically picking up her knife and fork and beginning to eat. "No matter how much we grieve," she said, "we cannot bring Lai-tse lu back to life. Therefore I urge you two—who have waited so long for your own happiness—to wait no longer. I see nothing to be gained by postponing your marriage until Jonathan returns home. You will only succeed in delaying for three more months."

"I suppose that's true," the troubled Judy replied, "but I'm not forgetting that young Brad is on board that clipper ship. I'm wondering if we should wait until he can be present at the ceremony before we marry."

Her father shrugged. "That's a matter of your own choice, Judy," he said. "Sarah and I wouldn't dream of advising you or of interfering."

"Maybe you'd rather wait until we're alone and can hash out the question," Homer suggested.

Judy shook her head. "I'd like to settle it right now. What's your thinking, Homer?"

"Well now," he replied. "I think I've established a good rapport with both young Judy and young Brad, and I aim to be as good a stepfather to them as I can. Whether we should wait until Brad can be here to attend our wedding strikes me as a matter of strictly personal preference, and as you're the children's mother, I defer to you on it, Judy. I'm not sidestepping the question, mind you; I just don't feel it's my place to make the decision."

Judy picked at her food in silence, her mind in a turmoil. "Homer," she said at last, "you and I often have despaired of ever finding happiness together. Every time we heard that my husband was alive and was living somewhere else, we realized that our hands were tied and there was nothing we could do. Now, suddenly, we're free to marry, free to follow our own desires."

Homer nodded. "Yes," he said, "it's a miracle. It's just like what happens at sea when the winds die away after a gale and the sun comes out. You're sure—just as I'm sure now—that a miracle has taken place."

"Exactly," Judy said. "There has been a miracle, and I want to take full advantage of it. If that's being selfish, so be it. We'll go into town and pay a call on the minister as soon as you can find the time."

Homer couldn't resist grinning as he looked at his future father-in-law. "I reckon the business won't collapse," he said, "if I take an hour after dinner to get things straight with the minister."

Judy had a typical Rakehell's organized mind. "We'll have a very small wedding with only our few relatives and a very few close friends on hand," she said.

"Your father and I," Missy Sarah declared, "will be insulted if we're not allowed to give the reception for you."

"All right," Judy replied, "I accept gratefully—provided that the reception is simple. I'm not for a moment forgetting that Lai-tse lu is gone, and I can guess how you must feel, Missy Sarah."

The older woman bowed her head but said nothing.

"There's one favor I'd like to ask of you," Judy said hurriedly.

The older woman raised her head.

"Homer," Judy asked, "will you be able to take the time away from work for a wedding trip?"

His grin became broader. "Naturally," he said.

"I've sailed to England and the continent of Europe," Judy said with a laugh. "I've visited a dozen Caribbean islands and several South American capitals. I guess that what happens in a seafaring family is that there are no thrills left in the world of voyages. But I've always wanted to see Niagara Falls—"

"Then that's where we'll go," Homer cut in.

Judy nodded happily. "All that needs to be settled, then, is what to do with Judy when we're gone. Would you and Papa look after her while we're away, Missy Sarah?"

The older woman sniffed and looked hurt. "Of course," she said in an aggrieved tone. "I'm surprised you would even ask."

And so the future of Judith Walker and Homer Ellison was settled. That afternoon they made arrangements with the Anglican clergyman who traditionally conducted Rakehell weddings, and with only a handful of people invited to the ceremony, they were married quietly the following Saturday. They returned to the Rakehell house for a modest reception and then took the railroad train to Hartford, from which they would travel to Niagara Falls by way of Albany, New York. The festivities had been quiet, and that evening Jeremiah and Missy Sarah dined alone, joined by his second oldest grandchild, young Judy Walker, who would soon celebrate her twelfth birthday.

Ordinarily a vivacious, talkative child, Judy was subdued and showed no enthusiasm even for the chocolate cake with apricot preserves between the layers, long one of her favorite desserts, which her grandmother had ordered for her benefit.

Jeremiah stared down at her from his place at the head of the table. "Got a tummyache, Judy?" he asked.

She nodded. "I guess," she said. "Something like that, Grandpa," she said.

Missy Sarah studied the child but made no comment.

"Well," Jeremiah said, "I can't say as I blame you. It's been a big day."

"Big for some people," Judy replied, choosing her words carefully, "but not so big for others."

Jeremiah looked confused. "What's that supposed to mean?"

His granddaughter shifted uncomfortably in her seat. "Oh, nothing," she muttered.

Missy Sarah was not one who would willingly tolerate any nonsense. Pushing a stray wisp of gray hair into place in the bun at the nape of her neck, she said severely, "Something is troubling you, child. What is it?"

Judy's embarrassment deepened and verged on panic. "It—it isn't important, Grandma," she sputtered.

"Out with it," Missy Sarah commanded.

Jeremiah put down his knife and fork and stared at his granddaughter as though seeing her for the first time.

"Oh, all right," Judy said, and her sigh was long-drawn and pained. "I've known for a long time that Mama and Homer were sweet on each other," she said. "I'd be awful silly and dumb if I didn't, because he's had dinner at our house just about every night for months. But you'd think they'd show more respect for my father than to get married as soon as they'd heard that he isn't alive anymore." She spoke forcefully, and seemed very certain of her ground.

Jeremiah could cope with a mutinous board of directors, with labor difficulties at his plant, or with a raging gale at sea, but he had no idea how to handle a grandchild under the present circumstances. He muttered something incomprehensible and transferred his gaze to Missy Sarah, mutely appealing for her help.

His wife had already decided she would handle the problem in her own way. "So you think, do you, child, that it was wrong of your mother and Homer Ellison to marry so soon?"

The little girl swallowed hard and nodded.

"Just how much do you know about your father's departure from New London?"

"Careful, Sarah," her husband muttered. "I don't rightly think that Judy went into any detail with the youngsters."

There was an air of defiance in Judy's reply. "Everybody in this family is always traveling," she said. "Uncle Jonathan goes traipsing off to the Orient, Cousin Charles goes all over, so why shouldn't my father have gone?"

Missy Sarah took a deep breath and glared at her husband, her expression instructing him to remain silent and leave matters to her. "Your father," she said succinctly, "sneaked into Grandpa's office the day he left, and stole fifty-two thousand dollars in cash that didn't belong to him, from Grandpa's safe."

The child gasped and turned to her grandfather. As much as Jeremiah regretted the circumstances of the revelation, he was too much a Rakehell to deny the truth. He nodded slowly. "I'm afraid that's right, Judy," he said. "You and your brother were too little to be told at the time."

"Your father," Missy Sarah went on dryly, "led your mother a dog's life, long before that. He was too ambitious for his own good, you see. He wasn't satisfied to be a high-ranking executive in the company; he wanted to take Jonathan's place as the principal heir, and the success of Jonnie's clipper ships made that impossible for him. He went off to the Orient, and there he formed associations with some very questionable characters, including people who were known to be enemies of Rakehell and Boynton."

Judy Walker returned her grandmother's stare, then her head dropped and she covered her face with her hands.

Jeremiah was on the verge of speaking, but his wife silenced him with a look. Rising from her chair, Missy Sarah went to the girl and put her arms around Judy's narrow shoulders. "I'm sorry, child," she said, "to have to tell you things that pain you, but you're big enough and strong enough now to know the truth."

Judy clung to her, burying her face in the folds of Sarah's bombazine dress.

Sarah stroked the back of her head but said nothing, letting silence work its own healing powers.

"I—I guess I kind of knew it all along," Judy muttered at last. "I sort of guessed it, and so did Brad, but we didn't like to think ill of Papa, even though he was always so busy that we never saw him. Were Mama and Homer ever going to tell us the truth?"

"I reckon they were," Jeremiah replied, "when they thought you were old enough."

"I knew," Sarah said distinctly, "that you had to be told

56

now, or you'd resent your mother or you'd hate Homer for things that are certainly not their fault."

Judy raised her head and looked thoughtfully at the older woman. "I guess," she said, "things sometimes work out for the best. I have a stepfather now who likes me—I know he does. I can tell it from the way he looks and the way he talks to me, and Mama is happy for the first time. I shouldn't say this, I suppose, but while Papa was still living at home I used to hear Mama crying at night sometimes."

"Those days are behind you now," Sarah told her. "The only way to look is upward and ahead. I always told Lai-tse lu, never look back over your shoulder at what might have been. Concentrate instead on what can be."

The child nodded gravely. "I guess Brad and I are luckier than we know," she said. "We have you and Grandpa, and we have a happy mother and a stepfather who will help us." Suddenly she thrust out her chin and said, "You know what? I'm not going to feel sorry for myself now or ever. I absolutely promise myself that."

Sarah nodded and patted her on the shoulder. "Good girl," she said.

"I'm astonished, as the years go by," Jeremiah said, "to find the Rakehell traits coming out in one generation after another. Judy, you have something priceless in you, something that money can never buy. You have real courage."

The child nodded in embarrassment, and then grinned. All of a sudden she said, "I have an appetite for that chocolate cake with apricot preserve filling. Do you suppose I could have a great big slice, Grandma?"

With due ceremony, Sarah cut her a slab of the cake and presented it to her. "What you don't eat tonight, you'll get tomorrow," she said. "This cake is all for you."

Judy's smile was beatific as she dug her fork into the rich cake.

Tradition was all-important in the fashionable town house located in London's Belgravia Square. Just as the house

57

itself, painted white with stately Georgian columns, resembled the equally large dwellings on either side of it, so the inhabitants followed certain rules that they regarded as inviolable.

Principal among these was the hour devoted to predinner drinking of sack in the family sitting room. Sir Alan Boynton, head of the English branch of Rakehell and Boynton, was the first to arrive, and promptly poured himself his customary two fingers of Scotch whisky to which he added a dash of water. Moments later his wife, Jessica, who was Jeremiah Rakehell's sister, entered the room, already attired in the dinner dress that she would wear to the first-floor dining room. Sir Alan had seen her only moments earlier when he had paused briefly in her dressing room, but he nevertheless bowed to her gravely and then poured her a small glass of dry sack.

Jessica took it from him but made no attempt to drink it, and placed it on a table beside her usual chair. Obviously she was deeply troubled.

"You'll forgive the observation, Jessica," her husband said, "but you'll accomplish nothing by getting yourself upset over the death of Lai-tse lu. You must try to see these things in perspective."

"What do you mean by 'perspective,' Alan?" she said, challenging him.

"She had already passed away at least two weeks before Jonathan wrote to Charles in Djakarta, and I daresay it took the better part of a week for the news to reach Charles. He wrote to us a full month after Lai-tse lu's death, and it took—let me see—almost five months for the clipper carrying Charles's letter to reach us here. So although the news is fresh to us and therefore shocks us as though it referred to some very recent event, keep in mind that a half-year has passed since Lai-tse lu died."

"That's just what I've been telling myself," someone said from the entrance, and Ruth Boynton, Charles's wife, came into the room. Not waiting for her father-in-law to pour her the customary glass of sack, she helped herself to it and then raised her glass. "If I knew Lai-tse lu," she said, "she'd blister us for moping. She led a rich, full life, and although she died young, I'm sure she wouldn't want anyone to grieve for her.''

Sir Alan looked appreciatively at his daughter-in-law as he sipped his whisky. She was bright as well as attractive, with her brown eyes and neatly coiffed brown hair, and he sometimes wondered how his son, who had long been inclined toward wildness, had managed to persuade such an intelligent girl to become his wife.

Had he known the truth he would have been shocked. Ruth was a native of New London, and had virtually grown up at Rakehell and Boynton, where her father had served as head carpenter. For years she had nurtured a secret: she had been hopelessly in love with Jonathan Rakehell, but realizing at last he had no intention of marrying her, she had accepted Charles's proposal. At least she was a member of the same family, and her marriage had brought her financial security.

It had also earned her great unhappiness. She had been able to swallow her pride and accept the fact that little David was another woman's child; she had come to love the boy as her own and was devoted to him. His father, however, remained an enigma to her. All too often she learned that Charles had engaged in another affair, and even though she had tried to steel herself, such revelations invariably hurt her. Now, however, the shoe was very much on the other foot. The information that had been contained in Charles's letter delivered that same day had excited her almost beyond measure. The passing of Lai-tse lu meant that Jonathan was a widower for the second time in his life, that he was free and unencumbered. Therefore, almost in spite of herself, Ruth could not help giving in to the fantasies of her youth and imagine that Jonathan was making love to her.

Somehow she could almost understand now why Charles had extramarital affairs. They were exciting, but they had no connection with his real life. He had sworn that he loved her, just as he loved little David, and she was convinced that at the time of his assurances, at least, he had been telling the truth. Well, she could imagine that Jonathan was making love to her, and in a sense she was enjoying a "safe" affair with him, but in no way was she jeopardizing the security of her marriage, nor was she harming the genuine love that she bore Charles.

All she knew for certain was that she was playing a dangerous game. Under no circumstances could she throw herself at Jonathan, so she knew she would be wise to begin curbing her daydreams.

"What arrangements do you suppose Jonathan will make for the children?" she asked her mother-in-law. "I mean, I'm wondering whether he'll hire a governess for them."

Jessica shook her head. "If I know Sarah," she said, "she wouldn't tolerate having a younger woman around directing the lives of Julian and Jade. Unless I'm very much mistaken, she'll take charge of them herself."

Ruth nodded thoughtfully. "Yes," she said, "I suppose you're right. Sarah certainly isn't the type of woman who will stand for any interference."

Neither they nor Sir Alan realized it, but a newcomer was listening avidly to their conversation. Elizabeth Boynton, the nineteen-year-old adopted daughter of Sir Alan and his wife, was standing in the doorway, taking in every word of the conversation. Recently returned from a finishing school near Paris, Elizabeth had changed from a gawky adolescent into a ravishingly beautiful young lady. Her straight wheat-colored hair hung down her back to her hips, her blue eyes were as intense as they were large, and she carried herself with an air, conscious of her slender but sensual figure, her height, which was greater than that of most women, and her natural grace, which made her every move a joy to watch.

Elizabeth had disappeared into her own bedchamber immediately after hearing of the death of Lai-tse lu, and she had remained in seclusion for hours. It was easy enough for her mother and her sister-in-law to guess her reasons. She had imagined herself in love with Jonathan Rakehell—to whom she was not related by blood—ever since she had been a very little girl. The subject hadn't been mentioned at home for some time now, but that in no way meant the young woman had abandoned her dream. On the contrary, she thought of Jonathan frequently, at all times of the day and night.

Here, in the bosom of her immediate family, she felt she could speak freely. "Just think," she said in her high, clear soprano voice, "of all the women who are going to snare Jonathan by paying attention to his children. Those youngsters will be pampered and spoiled half to death."

The others looked up at her. Sir Alan poured her a glass of sack, and Lady Boynton looked reprovingly. "I think you'll find that Jonathan is smart enough to see through such maneuvers," she said. "After all, he is a man of vast experience, and I'm sure he can catch the scent of any woman who is seeking the protection of his name."

"Perhaps, perhaps not, Mama," Elizabeth replied jauntily. "The stakes are exceptionally high, you know, so you can expect a great many women to act with cunning as well as caution. Jonathan is not only the most handsome man in New England, but he's probably the wealthiest as well."

"He was the wealthiest, perhaps," Sir Alan interjected dryly. "He stupidly gave all of his late wife's great fortune to help the poor of China, and in the meantime, the company faces a very uncertain future, due in large part to the expansionist policies that Jonathan and Charles insisted on. I was always opposed to them, but I was outvoted, and no one has paid any attention to my forebodings."

Jessica was uncertain whether her husband was speaking the truth or was exaggerating. She found it difficult to believe that a business enterprise as solid as Rakehell and Boynton could be in financial difficulties, and in the absence of Charles she decided that she would write a brief, confidential note to her brother asking him the actual circumstances.

"I think you'll find that most women will keep their distance from Jonathan Rakehell," Ruth said. "He's quite expert at holding them at arm's length, and he obviously has a great deal on his mind these days."

"So much the better," Elizabeth said blithely. "I'm certain I can beat any competition that may materialize, but it's so boring and such a waste of time."

Her mother was scandalized. "Really, Elizabeth!" she exclaimed.

Sir Alan's thoughts were mired in the details of the financial crisis in which Rakehell and Boynton found itself, but he could not allow his daughter's outrageous comments to remain unchallenged. "Elizabeth," he roared, "I forbid you to engage in such unseemly talk."

The beautiful young woman looked at her red-faced father, and could not resist giggling. Even Ruth could not help smiling behind her hand.

"When I was a child," Elizabeth said, "you taught me to tell the truth no matter how embarrassing or painful it might be. Well, that's exactly what I'm doing. It's no secret to any of you that I've been in love with Jonathan for many years."

"Puppy love!" Sir Alan thundered. "Certainly you don't expect that kind of an emotion to be taken seriously by serious adults."

"I regard it strictly as a matter between Jonathan and me," Elizabeth replied coolly. "I'll grant you that he has no idea of the extent or depth of my feelings for him, because circumstances were such that I couldn't reveal myself to him. Now, however, the picture is changed, and he's as free to marry as I am."

Sir Alan stared hard at her and then turned to his wife in amazement. "My God, Jessica," he muttered, "the child means every damn word of it."

Lady Boynton remained unshaken. "Of course she does," she replied comfortably. "But I wouldn't worry about it if I were you. I honestly can't see a man of Jonathan's age and stature engaging in a romantic liaison with someone who's just completed school."

Elizabeth drew herself up to her full, considerable height. "I didn't think that my feelings would be such a cause of concern to the entire family," she said stiffly. "If you don't mind, I prefer to change the subject."

"Quite right," Jessica said sweetly, "we're dealing with a purely hypothetical situation, and we're wasting our time and our substance." She smiled, then deliberately began to discuss with Ruth a new gown that she had just ordered made by her dressmaker.

Elizabeth fumed in silence.

Sir Alan referred obliquely to the subject at the dinner table when he remarked, "I wish that Charles and Jonathan would stop lolling in the Far East and would come home. They're badly needed to help straighten out the terrible financial mess we're in."

Ruth immediately leaped to her husband's defense. "Charles is not only aware of his obligations, Papa," she said, "but if you'd like to read his letter again, he wrote in so many words that he was concluding a business deal with the Fat Dutchman in Java that would help solve Rakehell and Boynton problems."

"I'm well aware of what he said," Sir Alan replied, "but I don't believe him. I fail to see how any deal could provide the huge sums of money that we require."

"I have complete confidence in Charles," Ruth said quietly.

Her mother-in-law looked at her and beamed. Here was the perfect daughter-in-law, almost too good to be true, and Jessica Boynton well knew that the loyalty Ruth displayed to Charles was difficult for her to maintain in view of his frequent infidelities. She could only hope that Ruth would continue to stand by him until he matured and devoted himself to her with the loyalty that she so richly deserved.

Before the sweet and coffee were served, Elizabeth asked to be excused. "I'm going to the ball that Lord and Lady Visdale are giving tonight," she said, "and I want to wear a more head-turning gown."

"Oh, yes, so you are," her mother replied. "Who's escorting you?"

"Ronnie Weybright," Elizabeth replied, her face as expressionless as her voice.

Jessica immediately brightened. "Well!" she said. "Sir Ronald is a rather exceptional young man and quite good-looking, too. How do you happen to be going with him?"

Elizabeth shrugged. "Our hostess assigned him to me as an

63

escort, as nearly as I could make out," she said. "Besides, I don't see what difference it makes. He's just a young man taking a girl to a party."

Sir Alan cleared his throat. "He happens to be well connected financially," he said. "The Weybrights own coal mines and a steel mill."

Elizabeth's long-drawn sigh was exaggerated as she rose from the table and went off to her own chamber.

Ruth and her mother-in-law made small talk over the peach trifle until eventually the younger woman said, "If you think it would do any good, Mama, I'll have a word in private with Elizabeth on the subject of Jonathan Rakehell."

"Please do, by all means!" Jessica urged her. "It was all very amusing when she was smaller to hear her talk about marrying Jonathan someday. Now that she's a grown woman, however, I find such talk mortifying."

"Well," Ruth said, "I don't know that I'll do any good, but the way I see it, I can't do any harm, either."

When they left the table she went at once to the chamber at the rear of the third floor, adjoining her own bedchamber, which was Elizabeth's domain.

The younger woman had not yet donned her dress and sat in front of her dressing-table mirror, where she carefully but skillfully was applying subdued makeup, which enhanced her already great charms.

Ruth admired her and couldn't help studying her. Elizabeth's figure was virtually perfect, she thought. Few women anywhere were endowed with such high, pointed breasts, such elegant shoulders, and such a tiny waist. She had virtually no stomach, and her thighs were as long as they were firm.

"If it's all right," Ruth said, "I stopped in for a private word with you."

"If you don't mind my continuing to get ready for tonight's party," Elizabeth replied, "fire away. Obviously you've come to lecture me."

"How could you tell?" the startled Ruth asked with a laugh.

64

"It's the way you carry yourself," Elizabeth said. "We had a teacher at the French school who was the same way."

"Sorry to be so obvious," Ruth said as she sat on a chair near the dressing table. "But I did think I should warn you not to make a bloody jackass of yourself over Jonathan."

Elizabeth was startled. Ladies never used the word "bloody" in conversation, and it seemed quite out of character for Ruth. Perhaps she had said it because she was an American and therefore was unfamiliar with British customs.

"Jonathan Rakehell," Ruth said, "is fifteen or sixteen years older than you. He is not only the father of two children, but he's been married twice and has lost both wives. Furthermore, he's about as busy as any man can get. He's not only active in the China trade for the company, but he builds clippers that he's designed himself. He'll regard you as a silly, flighty little girl if you throw yourself at him."

Elizabeth busied herself with a rouge pot and a small brush, and only when she had daubed her cheeks to her satisfaction did she put down the pot and stare at her sister-in-law. "Honestly, Ruth," she said. "You seem to think that I'd actually blurt out my feelings to Jonathan. I'm not that naïve, and I'm not that big a fool."

"I'm very glad to hear it," Ruth replied, "and I must say, I'm very much relieved. He and Charles are very close, and he's also in business with your father, so I'm sure he'd be polite to you under any circumstances. That's the sort of man he is, but you'd embarrass him dreadfully if you told him the truth about your feelings."

"That truth," Elizabeth said, taking a dress of pearl-colored satin from a hanger and slipping into it, "will have to emerge in its own way in its own good time. I don't mind telling you, Ruth, that I suffered a terrible setback when Jonathan was married to Lai-tse lu. Now she's gone, and even though he may revere her memory—as I am sure he does—she can no longer compete with a live flesh-and-blood woman. I'm not being vain, Ruth," she continued as she stood and examined herself critically in the dressing-table mirror, "but I've had enough men making a fuss over me to realize that I have certain assets."

"Indeed you do," Ruth murmured, and again envied her the radiance of her youthful beauty.

"I am confident that Jonathan will notice me," Elizabeth concluded. "Would you hook me up?"

"Of course," Ruth replied, and stood behind the younger woman as she closed the fastenings on the off-the-shoulder gown. "The point I'm trying to make is that Jonathan will not notice you in the way you hope and expect."

"You think not?" Elizabeth raised a slender eyebrow.

"I'm sure of it," her sister-in-law replied firmly. "I've known Jonathan all our lives. We attended school together at the age of six. I've seen him through two marriages, and he's seen me marry twice, too. He's my good friend—you might almost say he's been like a brother to me." She refrained from adding that she was eternally sorry that he had never taken note of her as a woman, either. "I'm trying to save you from disappointment."

"I know what you're going to say," Elizabeth declared. "You're going to tell me that I'm badly spoiled, that I'm so accustomed to getting what I want that I'm incapable of realizing that Jonathan is beyond my reach."

"Precisely," Ruth agreed.

"It may be that you're right," Elizabeth conceded. "I don't know that I'm able to view the whole matter sufficiently dispassionately to be a good judge. Laugh at me if you will, but I've loved Jonathan for a very long time."

"I'm not laughing, I assure you," Ruth said earnestly. "He is very easy to love."

The younger woman stared hard at her for a moment, and suspicion flicked through her mind. But knowing Ruth's devotion to Charles, she immediately dismissed it. "I know the meaning of disappointment in life, and I'm prepared, if need be, to face the probability of failure. I talk confidently to keep up my spirits, but between us, Ruth, I live in mortal fear that Jonathan will never know that I exist, and will select someone else as his new wife."

"That's very wise of you," Ruth said somberly. "The odds are definitely not in your favor."

"I shall do what I can, and beyond that I'll have to trust to good luck, or coincidence, or whatever it is that draws a man and a woman to each other and binds them together for all time. Do you know what that is?"

Ruth shook her head as she rose from the chair. "To be honest with you, I don't," she replied, and couldn't help thinking that whatever that elusive quality might be, it certainly was lacking in her own marriage to Charles. Then as she departed, she said, "Thank you, dear—for not taking offense at my bluntness."

Once Elizabeth was alone, she sat at her dressing table and slumped dispiritedly. Ruth was right, she realized: she would be battling overwhelming odds in her attempt to make her lifelong dream come true, and she would be far wiser to put Jonathan out of her mind and get on with her life. She stared hard at her reflection in the mirror, then thoughtfully added a touch of kohl to the ring around her eyes, dabbed additional rice powder onto the tip of her nose, and applied another coating of rouge to her full lips. Standing again, she scrutinized herself with great frankness. There was no question in her mind about her appearance. She had grown into what people of her parents' generation called "a great beauty," and she knew that many members of the opposite sex found her irresistible. So she was stupid to cling to a concept that she had held since earliest childhood, and she knew that it would be sensible to seek happiness wherever she could find it. She had been sheltered all her life, it was true, but she was sensitive enough to observe the lives that others lived, and she well realized that she alone had the power to find contentment if she tried hard enough.

She picked up her cape of rich silk, embroidered with pearls, its collar a lush halo of fox fur, and she went to her parents' sitting room to bid them good night.

Sir Alan was frowning as he checked over a long, complicated financial statement, and Lady Boynton looked up from the novel by Sir Walter Scott that she was reading. Both smiled at their daughter. "Well," Sir Alan said, "you look very pretty." Coming from him, that was a great compliment.

"Very pretty, indeed," his wife said with a sniff. "You look positively gorgeous, and I'm sure you'll bowl over Sir Ronald."

Dutifully kissing her mother, then her father, Elizabeth refrained from saying that she had no interest in bowling over her escort for the evening. She went to the formal parlor, where she awaited his arrival. He was punctual to the minute, resplendent in his blue and white dress uniform as a captain of the Grenadier Guards, a household regiment charged with the protection of Queen Victoria.

Sir Ronald was one of the score of young men whom Elizabeth had always taken for granted. The second son of an earl, a baronet in his own right, he was strikingly handsome, charming, and an eminently suitable escort for a social occasion. Now, seeing the admiration in his eyes as he gazed at her, Elizabeth recklessly decided to test her powers. She and her classmates had held endless discussions on the matter, and she well knew that flirtations were regarded as beyond the pale for young ladies, but she was imbued with a restlessness that seemed to fill her entire being, and she smiled steadily at Sir Ronald as they left the house, her eyes fixed on his. He followed her into the waiting carriage and then sat somewhat closer to her than propriety decreed.

Elizabeth made no protest and did not try to enlarge the distance between them by sliding farther to her own side of the carriage. She was encouraging Ronnie Weybright, as she well knew, and she was playing a game in which the risks were enormous. If she slipped, if she became careless, she could ruin her good name and never recover it. But, in a sense, she didn't care. Ruth's advice to her was good. She knew it was the better part of wisdom to put Jonathan Rakehell out of her mind and out of her heart. One way to do it—the best way, perhaps—was to live a little dangerously.

# IV

So little was known about China in the West that few people realized that Peking was the largest city on earth, with more inhabitants by far than lived in London or Paris or New York. Peking was a most unlikely recipient of its honor, and most residents of the metropolis, being unable to read or write, had no idea that they lived in such a large community.

Located ninety miles from Tientsin, its outlet to the sea, Peking was protected by the Great Wall, built to keep out the Mongol invaders who periodically were bent on conquest. The Tao Kuang Emperor was the direct descendant of the last of the Mongols to subdue the Middle Kingdom, and his family had been ruling Cathay since the early seventeenth century. China was so vast and had such an enormous population that such rule was not easy. The very architecture of Peking told its own story. On the outside, stretching for miles across the arid, hilly country beneath the perennially porcelain-blue sky, stretched the simple one-story dwellings of the poor. These houses were little more than huts, and their monotony was relieved here and there by a temple with a graceful pagodalike roof, where the faithful prayed to their ancestors.

As one penetrated deeper into the metropolis, one came at last to the vast walled enclosure known as the Imperial City. Here lived the almost countless bureaucrats who made up the government of the Middle Kingdom. Here, in vast buildings of stone, were the tax collectors and the clerks, the lawyers and the law enforcement officials, the high-ranking officers of the Royal Navy and the even more outmoded Royal Army. Here, also, were the offices and dwellings of those who, it was claimed, were the real rulers of the land, the corps of eunuchs. Their numbers were constantly swelling as the brightest and most promising boys in the land were plucked from their homes in villages and towns, subjected to an operation that removed their manhood, and then given years of rigorous training in the disciplines that enabled them to govern a vast, sprawling nation that many in the West considered ungovernable.

At last, in the heart of the city, was a walled enclosure inside which stood the Forbidden City. Here lived the Tao Kuang Emperor, his wives, and his children. Here, too, lived his sister, the Princess An Mien, perhaps the most vigorous single force responsible for the modernization of the ancient realm that seemed to resist modernizing. Here dwelled the highest judges of the land and the chiefs of cabinet departments and bureaus, all of them subject to the will and whims of the all-powerful Tao Kuang Emperor.

The Forbidden City was a world unto itself. No one knew this better than the woman, now in her early twenties, known as Wu-ling. The product of a Canton slum, she was the aunt of little David Boynton. Her experience, thanks to the intervention of Lai-tse lu Rakehell and Ruth Boynton, had been extraordinary. She had lived in New London and in London, England, and consequently had learned to speak, read, and write English. Lai-tse lu and Missy Sarah had taught her to write in Chinese, and she now spoke the Mandarin dialect of the ruling class as well as the simple Cantonese dialect of the slums from which she had risen.

Thanks to the efforts of Lai-tse lu and Jonathan, Wu-ling now held a post of great and unique importance in the Forbidden City. She served on the staff of Princess An Mien, and was regarded by the armies of palace servants as An Mien's personal protégée. Her actual duties were twofold. First, as had been planned, Jonathan and Lai-tse lu had been providing the emperor with a steady stream of books and periodicals on a wide variety of subjects, all of them pertinent to the growth, development, and modernization of the Middle Kingdom. Wu-ling was charged with translating these works from English into Chinese and was encouraged to use her own judgment regarding priorities. Second, the young woman was responsible for teaching the English language to both An Mien and her illustrious brother. Consequently, although she was unknown to the public at large, she held a position of importance and influence in the royal household.

Certainly she never stopped marveling at the intricacies of life in the Forbidden City. Here there were vast palaces for members of the royal family and the highest-ranking nobles and officials. Here, also, were museums containing priceless works of art extending back through the long ages of Chinese history, and here, too, were the guesthouses for those visitors who were fortunate enough to be seen by the emperor.

The whole of Cathay was in awe of the Tao Kuang Emperor, who was considered divine by his subjects. Even the highest-ranking of his subjects were required to kowtow before him and to address him in circumlocutory language that made ordinary conversation impossible. In order to circumvent tradition, the Tao Kuang Emperor, a mild-mannered, gentle man in his early fifties, had devised a system that he regarded as foolproof. Indeed, it worked effectively as long as others understood the rules of the game. He enjoyed wandering into a room where one or more persons were gathering, and then pretending that he was invisible. This meant that they were able to ignore his august presence, and when they addressed him they made general remarks to which he replied in kind.

Certainly Wu-ling had grown accustomed to having the emperor drop in on her in her modest office, where books were piled high in wall cases and overflowed tables. He formed the habit of strolling in unannounced, perching on the edge of the desk or a convenient table, and when his sister, An Mien, was present, addressing his remarks to her when he wished to speak with Wu-ling. Similarly, during their daily English lessons, the emperor spoke only to his sister when he had a question regarding grammar or pronunciation.

The girl rapidly learned to adapt herself to the strange technique, and she answered in kind, being careful to address her remarks exclusively to the princess. In this way she could carry on long, informative discussions with the Tao Kuang Emperor without resorting to stultifying formality.

Every day of her life, Wu-ling was aware of her extraordinary good fortune. Instead of being condemned to life in a Canton slum, where all the members of a family were forced to dwell in one room, she had a spacious, handsomely furnished suite of her own in one of the marble buildings of the palace, and had an army of servants, including two assigned just to wait on her. Her cheongsams, the traditional tight-fitting Chinese dress, with a high, stiff collar and slit skirt to permit freedom of movement, were fashioned of pure silk, and were woven by the imperial silkmakers who worked exclusively for the court. She ate rare and wonderful foods, including a wide variety of foreign dishes that were completely alien to most of the emperor's subjects. Aside from the afternoon English lessons, she was responsible only to herself, and hence was forced to keep no regular hours. Being conscientious, however, she arrived at her office early every morning after a pleasant stroll through the imperial gardens.

Her existence was not as isolated as it appeared on the surface. Certainly the officers of the household guard, who were stationed in the gardens and at the entrances to all buildings, were well aware of the tall, slender girl with the elastic figure, a classically beautiful Oriental face, and long, blue-black hair that matched her glowing eyes. Wu-ling was equally aware of the officers' interest in her, but did not show it by as much as a flicker of an eye. She was always demure, seemingly serene, and she carried herself with the dignity of one who was privileged to serve the highest forces in the land.

This morning, like so many others, she took her time wandering through the gardens, where she enjoyed looking at the spectacle of huge masses of flowers growing in ordered profusion. Their colors covered every spectrum of the rainbow, and their scent was sweet and almost overpowering. When she reached her office she was promptly served fragrant hot tea in a porcelain cup so thin that it was semitransparent. With it she was given a bean-curd cake, which served as her breakfast. Within minutes she was lost in her work, and her pen-brush flew as she translated a work on agricultural experiments being made in the United States.

She was so engrossed in her labors that she failed to hear the door open as Princess An Mien slipped quietly into the room. There were many among the highest-ranking officials in the land who felt privately that the princess, rather than her brother, should be sitting on the Celestial Throne, but of course they kept their opinions to themselves. As it happened, however, An Mien had the best of two worlds. Without suffering the innumerable personal restrictions placed on the absolute ruler of the Middle Kingdom, she had, for all practical purposes, the powers of the emperor very much in her grasp. Her brother made no major decisions without her advice.

In her late thirties, slightly overweight, An Mien had strong features and a personality to match. Caring little about clothes or jewels, she dressed in a plain, black, ankle-length cheongsam, and rarely bothered to wear any of the many gems from her priceless collection. Her absorbing interest was the welfare of her people. She had seen China defeated by the British in the humiliating Opium War, and although the Middle Kingdom had been forced to open five ports to foreign trade as a consequence, she did not really regret this development. Cathay, as she knew all too well, lagged hopelessly behind the great powers of the world in its attempts to modernize. She was doing all within her power to speed that process, and in so doing to alleviate the poverty and ignorance that had cursed the poor citizens of Cathay for so many centuries.

Humor gleamed quietly in her dark eyes now as she watched Wu-ling diligently writing her translation of the book, and she could no longer refrain from speaking. "I wonder," she said, "if the topic is as fascinating as it appears?"

Wu-ling started, dropped her brush, and began to rise to her feet.

"Stay where you are, my dear," the princess ordered.

"I'm so sorry, Your Imperial Highness," Wu-ling said, "I didn't hear you come in—"

"That was obvious to me," An Mien replied. "I won't disturb you for too long, but I want you to tell me whether you've found anything new on the construction of steel plants. The book that you translated was absorbing, but we require more technical information if our own engineers are to build such a plant themselves."

Wu-ling shook her head. "I knew of Your Highness's interest in the subject," she said, "so I asked for more material on it. When I last wrote to Jonathan Rakehell, who was still in Canton following his wife's passing, he replied that he knew of no books, but that he was acquainted with the members of the family who built the mills. When he returns to the United States—as he's doing currently—he's going to try to obtain a set of the actual blueprints for a new steel mill."

An Mien's face became wreathed in a broad smile. "That will be wonderful," she said. "If he's able to obtain the blueprints, perhaps we can then build such a plant without being forced to call in outside engineers to supervise the task."

Wu-ling hesitated, was on the verge of speaking, and then changed her mind.

"Say it, my dear," the princess urged.

"I can't help wondering, Your Imperial Highness, why there is such great reluctance on the part of those in the highest places to import foreigners who can supervise and direct so many projects that we badly need. Please don't take offense at my question."

"Your question is very sensible, and I certainly am not offended by it," An Mien replied emphatically. "I am afraid that here we are our own worst enemies. We have a national phobia against foreigners. We are so unaccustomed to seeing people whose skins are another color and whose customs are unlike ours that we automatically mistrust and dislike them. My brother, I am sorry to say, feels as the most ignorant of our peasants feel on the subject. I am to blame, too. I find I shy away from contact with outsiders.''

"That isn't true, Your Imperial Highness,'' Wu-ling protested. "You've granted many privileges to Jonathan Rakehell and treat him as though he were a high-ranking Chinese noble.''

"It is true,'' the princess said with a smile, "that I no longer regard Jonathan as a foreigner, nor does my brother. His marriage to Lai-tse lu was partly responsible, of course, but he created his own aura of trust. I know that you are going to tell me that there are countless other foreigners who are honest, sincere men, and can be trusted, too.''

"Exactly,'' Wu-ling replied.

"I must learn to accept them when necessary, and I must counsel my brother to do the same.''

Wu-ling took a deep breath. "Should it be advisable to import a Western engineer to supervise the building of a steel mill, I urge you to consider such a plan,'' she said.

An Mien nodded cheerfully. "Oh, you are absolutely right,'' she replied, "and anytime you find me hesitating, please feel free to talk me out of my complacent mood.''

"I'll try, ma'am,'' Wu-ling murmured.

The door opened, and Wu-ling had difficulty in controlling her desire to leap to her feet and then prostrate herself on the marble floor. Sauntering into the room was the absolute ruler of more millions of subjects than had ever been counted, the Tao Kuang Emperor. A pale man who wore thick eyeglasses, he more nearly resembled a scholar of the first-level mandarin class. Insignificant in appearance, he habitually wore a dusty ankle-length gown of black silk, and his feet were shod in felt-soled carpet slippers of the sort that the meanest of his subjects wore. On his head was a pearl-studded cap, the symbol of his exalted rank, that was a duplicate of the one he had impulsively given to the little daughter of Jonathan

75

Rakehell the previous year. It contained thousands of pearls, the largest of them the size of his thumbnail, and the headgear certainly was worth a small fortune. But it gave him a headache, or so he said, so he pushed it to the back of his head, where it wobbled precariously when he walked. No one had ever seen it fall to the ground, which was a good omen, but the courtiers were perennially prepared for the worst.

It was immediately apparent that the Tao Kuang Emperor intended his visit to be informal and unofficial. Greeting no one, he perched on the corner of the desk, where he swung his legs idly as he picked up several books lying within reach. He pretended to study them, but not knowing how to read English, he soon dropped them.

"Where were you this morning?" he demanded of his sister in an aggrieved tone. "I wanted to have breakfast with you, but you were already gone."

"I had my usual tea in my own apartment," An Mien replied. "If you had told me you wanted to have breakfast with me, I would have come to your dining room, naturally." She refrained from adding that she was relieved that she had not been required to have breakfast with her brother. He enjoyed eating leftover rice, which was served cold with sugar and cream, and she found the dish virtually inedible.

The Tao Kuang Emperor was not mollified. "I had a horrid session," he said. "One of my wives and the new little concubine from Kwangsi Province got into a shouting match and threatened to pull each other's hair out by the roots. It was very unnerving."

The princess tried without success to control the laugh that bubbled up within her.

Wu-ling hastily averted her own face so the Celestial Emperor would not see her smile. Everyone at the court knew that his new concubine was a troublemaking spitfire, who hadn't yet learned her lesson. After a few more exhibitions, she was certain to disappear from the court.

"No one knew where you were," the emperor continued, "but I suspected that I'd find you here." He sighed plaintively.

"However, it's just as well, I suppose. What I wanted to discuss with you concerns Wu-ling."

The young woman could not hide her astonishment. She could imagine no reason why she should become a subject of discussion between the Celestial Emperor and his sister.

An Mien was surprised, too. Instead of replying, however, she looked at her brother inquiringly.

He seemed ill at ease and ran a tentative forefinger around the inside of his shabby, high-standing collar. "I wonder," he said, "if Wu-ling happens to be acquainted with Chen Wen-lo?"

Here was the Tao Kuang Emperor's system of making himself invisible operating at its best. Only Wu-ling herself could answer the question, but she had to pretend that the princess had asked it.

"I wouldn't go as far as to say that I am acquainted with Chen, Your Imperial Highness," she replied, "but I have seen him on occasion at the court. He's fairly tall and wears his gray hair in a very long pigtail. If I remember correctly, he walks with a slight stoop."

The emperor was delighted, and slapped his thigh. "That's it," he said, "that's the fellow!"

"Unless I'm mistaken, Your Highness," Wu-ling went on, "he also serves the Celestial Emperor as minister of transportation."

The Tao Kuang Emperor rubbed his hands together. "That's very accurate and very observant," he said. "I like that."

Wu-ling made no reply.

"It so happens," the emperor said, again addressing his sister, "that Chen Wen-lo has taken note of the presence of Wu-ling at the court and desires to make her his wife."

The girl was stunned. The possibility that she might someday become married to a high-ranking noble and cabinet member had not crossed her mind.

The princess, however, remained totally unimpressed, and her lips formed a thin, straight line. "I refuse to release the maiden from my service for the purpose of marrying Chen," she said flatly.

Wu-ling's confusion was so great that she did not know whether to feel disappointed or not.

The emperor, however, was quick to take offense. "You preach enlightenment as the cure-all, my sister," he said. "I think you should practice what you preach and give Wu-ling the opportunity to speak for herself."

An Mien remained undisturbed, but behind her calm façade there was rock-hard determination. "Very well," she replied, "feel free to express yourself, young woman."

Wu-ling thought as rapidly as she could, and her reply was tentative. "I know very little about Chen Wen-lo, as it happens," she said.

"Then you're one of the few people in the Forbidden City who are ignorant of his private life," the princess replied dryly. "It is no secret that he has long preferred the company of handsome young men to women, and those who have visited his palace report that they wear women's clothes and have been known to bind their feet."

The emperor saved Wu-ling the necessity of replying. "Chen has some personal tastes that are rather odd," he said. "I'll grant you that. But the fact remains that he's a very competent minister of transport, the best I've had in more than twenty years. The army and navy are making all sorts of threats against him because of his personal tastes, and it occurred to me that a marriage to a young lady as attractive as Wu-ling would silence his critics in the army and navy, and would smooth the ruffled waters."

His sister glared at him openly in a way that no one else in the Middle Kingdom dared to do. "You would sacrifice the happiness of a lovely young woman by marrying her to a known pervert, would you?" she inquired acidly. "Just so you wouldn't be forced to dismiss him from your cabinet. Shame on you, Kuang. Our Manchu ancestors were men of courage who never faltered in doing what they believed right. If you lack the backbone now, I do not, and I tell you flatly that I will not allow you to jeopardize Wu-ling's happiness. That's final!" She rose to her feet, went to the young woman, and placed a protective arm around her shoulders. The emperor looked first at his sister and then at Wu-ling, moistening his lips repeatedly.

Wu-ling felt certain she would be condemned to death, or at the very least she would be sent far to the interior to a place of permanent exile. To her amazement, however, the Tao Kuang Emperor spoke meekly when he found the voice with which to reply.

"Very well, An Mien," he said. "You're right, as usual. I was choosing a lazy way out of my dilemma."

"If you wish," the princess declared, "I shall speak to the principal eunuch myself this very morning, and obtain his recommendations for the three best candidates for minister of transport. I shall tell him to keep the matter strictly confidential and to have his report ready for you by midafternoon today. Then you can take your choice of candidates, knowing that they're competent, and you can end the furor of the generals and admirals by dismissing Chen Wen-lo at once."

The emperor sighed and nodded. "It's the best way, really," he muttered. "I hope I didn't upset you too much, Wu-ling."

The young woman forgot she was not supposed to reply directly and shook her head vigorously. The emperor grinned, reached out, and patted her hand. "Then there's been no real harm done, has there?" he asked brightly.

Again Wu-ling shook her head. The emperor dragged himself to his feet with an obvious effort and started toward the door. Pausing with one hand on the latch, he called over his shoulder, "If I should want to see you at breakfast tomorrow, An Mien," he declared, "be good enough to leave word where you've gone." He left the chamber, softly closing the door behind him.

Wu-ling breathed a trifle more easily.

"That was a narrow escape, Wu-ling," An Mien said. "But never fear, the work you do is vital to the future of the Middle Kingdom, and therefore you are under my protection. No harm will come to you while I stand near the throne!"

Halfway around the world from Cathay stood the community known as the Free and Hanseatic City of Hamburg, an independent city-state, which ranked among the most important of the German principalities. By far the largest seaport among the German states, and for that matter the most prosperous in Europe, Hamburg was located on the Elbe River, a short distance from its estuary, where it flowed into the North Sea. A second river, the Alster, also contributed to the community's prosperity, and it was said that nowhere in Europe were there wealthier or more prominent shipping men.

Consequently, the building that stood on the bank of the Binnenalster, one of the city's two lakes, was of great importance in the world shipping industry. Resembling an early Renaissance castle, it was the headquarters of the von Eberling shipping interests, and from the upper floors of the headquarters could be seen a dozen or more von Eberling ships riding at anchor in the port, among them brigs and two very modern vessels that were propelled by steam.

Although everyone in Hamburg knew the von Eberling ships, and many had relatives who were employed in the dockyard as crew members of various vessels, very little was known of the operation of the company and of the men who controlled the corporation. That was because Baron Rudolph von Eberling, the head of the firm, shied away from publicity. As he so often remarked to his close associate and fellow board member, Colonel Graz, "The beaver does not advertise his building of a dam. He goes to work quietly and builds it."

The members of the board of directors knew that Rudi von Eberling was inordinately ambitious, and they were not surprised at a meeting one day when he unfolded a new plan to them.

"Gentlemen," he said, "I have watched with great interest as the Anglo-Saxons have snatched the juiciest plums from the table of Far Eastern commerce. It appears that America and particularly Great Britain have obtained a near monopoly on the China trade. We cannot hope to compete with them, however."

80

"That," Colonel Graz interjected, "is because we have no clipper ships in our fleet, and they are so exorbitantly expensive that we intend to buy none."

"Nevertheless," the baron continued, "I have watched our neighbors in Holland and France growing fat on trade with the Orient. I have even known huge fortunes to be made in the little nation of Portugal, which is impoverished and of secondary importance. I wish to see the von Eberling company enter into this profitable trade. On the other hand, we cannot afford to lose a vast fortune while injecting ourselves into the business of the Orient."

"That is an important point, and I am glad that you remember it, Herr Baron," one of the board members declared. "We prosper although our funds are limited. We rely on our native Germanic cunning and shrewdness to achieve for us what other nations spend vast sums in gold and silver to accomplish."

"Precisely," Baron von Eberling said. "So with the assistance of Herr Graz, I have worked out a plan that is virtually foolproof."

The tension in the room increased, and the members of his board of directors listened carefully as he outlined the scheme he had in mind. When he was done, there were nods of satisfaction.

"I warn you, gentlemen, it will not be cheap to put my plan into effect. If it is to be done at all, it is to be done properly, with a certain flair."

"However," Colonel Graz said with a bloodless smile, "the cost to us will be but a small fraction of what we would otherwise spend, and our success is virtually guaranteed."

"I must ask the board for its formal approval of the plan," Rudolph von Eberling declared. "It is just a formality, of course, but it is necessary."

The scheme was adopted unanimously without further discussion. A short time later, the meeting came to an end, and the baron returned to his own tower suite, accompanied by Colonel Graz.

"The lady should be here shortly," the baron said. "I anticipated the approval of the directors, so I sent for her."

"Unless I am mistaken, she is already making herself at home in your office," the colonel muttered.

The baron peered over his associate's shoulder into his private room, and then chuckled indulgently. "Well, why not?" he said. "I cannot really blame her, you know; it isn't as though she was a total stranger to these surroundings. How long was I involved with her, Colonel?"

"For three months and eleven days, Herr Baron," Graz replied carefully. "Then, when you and she had a falling out, I—ah—relieved you of the burden, and my close association with her lasted for another sixty-seven days."

Half sitting and half reclining in an overstuffed chair in Baron von Eberling's private office was an extraordinary young woman, who watched the approach of the two men with an ironic smile on her full scarlet lips and an expression of deep irony in her green eyes, whose color and size were enhanced by the artful use of cosmetics. Her flaming red hair tumbled below her shoulders in what appeared to be a wild tangle but actually was a careful arrangement. Her gown showed off her lush feminine figure to full advantage, and she didn't seem to mind in the least that her breasts were half-exposed or that a slit in her skirt showed more than was proper of her magnificent legs.

Her long, tapering fingernails were painted with a scarlet lacquer that matched her lip rouge, and on her hand glittered a number of large diamond and ruby rings. In her graceful fingers she held a long tube of carved ivory, in one end of which was inserted a strong, Turkish cigarette. She was one of the few women in all Europe who smoked, and had let it be known that she had acquired the habit during a visit to Constantinople, where she allegedly had been the favorite of the sultan of the Ottoman Empire.

No one knew just what stories told by the Baroness Erika von Klausner were true and which were products of her fertile imagination. It mattered little, to be sure. She was fascinating, and many men found her charms irresistible. A few of the many who paid court to her realized that she was an adventuress with a ravenous appetite for money, power, and position. Her father had been an impoverished nobleman, but she lived in comfort and style, thanks to her own efforts. Her judgment of men was unerring.

As Rudolph von Eberling and Colonel Graz came into the office, she smiled lazily and, making no effort to rise, extended her free hand for them to kiss.

They dutifully bent low over her hand, clicking their heels in the approved manner.

"How very nice to see you again, Rudi," she said, "and you, too, Philip. And how convenient to find you together."

They did not rise to the bait of her prodding.

"Don't tell me that you were so lonely for me that you had to see me—or that you were so afraid of me that you decided there was strength in union."

"We have not brought you here out of nostalgia, my dear Erika," Baron von Eberling replied briskly, "and I assure you we intend to waste neither your time nor our own." He closed the door of his office and went straight to his desk.

While he spoke, Colonel Graz went to a bookcase and opened it, revealing a well-stocked bar located behind several shelves. Without waiting to be bidden, he poured a quantity of white wine into each of three glasses, and when Erika von Klausner gestured imperiously, he added a generous amount of water to the wine he had poured for her.

"The opportunities that exist in Hamburg and elsewhere in Europe for someone endowed with your unique and rather remarkable talents are limited," the baron said. "So I am giving you the opportunity, enthusiastically endorsed by my board of directors, to expand your scope to a worldwide scale. You have read the documents I sent you?"

"With great interest," Erika replied in her deep, husky voice. "The Fat Dutchman, in Djakarta, appears to be a man of great wealth and power, and the Marquês de Braga in Macao is as important as he is rich."

"Both of them, I think, are suitable for the exploitation of your talents, my dear Erika," Baron von Eberling replied succinctly. "The Fat Dutchman, according to information for which we have paid a pretty penny, surrounds himself with beautiful native women in large numbers. I daresay he could be persuaded to forget the natives for a special member of his own race. Similarly, Dom Manuel Sebastian often pays substantial sums for the importation of comely young women."

"I am sure I can interest them in me," Erika replied with just a hint of ruthless impatience in her voice, "but for what purpose? You've neglected to tell me."

"It should be rather obvious to you," the baron said in a mocking, reproving tone, "that the von Eberling shipping interests are desirous of forming alliances with the Fat Dutchman and with the Marquês de Braga. I might also add another tidbit of information that is not contained in the files I sent you to read. The marquês is susceptible to bribes, provided they're discreetly handled."

Erika sat up slowly, and moved the foot curled beneath her to the floor, not bothering to close the slit in her skirt. "To what extent does the von Eberling company wish to become involved with these gentlemen?" she demanded.

"Obviously," the baron told her, "we are interested in making very large contracts. We have no business interests in the Orient, and we are anxious to gain a strong foothold there."

Erika's luminous eyes narrowed. "And what do I have to gain?" she demanded brusquely.

The baron spoke soothingly. "For one thing," he said, "we will pay all your expenses, including a complete new wardrobe with jewelry to go with it, and so forth."

"Naturally." Erika sounded very cold, very self-assured. "But I am speaking in terms of contractual percentages."

"How much do you want?" the baron asked.

Her reply was prompt. "Ten percent."

"I will give you five."

She hesitated, weighing the possibility of finding out whether she could gain more from him.

"Five percent, take it or leave it," he said, and suddenly

he smiled. "I neglected to mention yet another matter that would be of greater concern to you than to my company. We have learned that the wife of Jonathan Rakehell has died and that he is a widower. I am sure he is a lonely man, and it should be an easy matter for someone with your charm to—"

"There's no need to spell it out any further," Erika interrupted. "I know the identity of Jonathan Rakehell, I know what he represents, and I am fully conscious of my own capabilities as well."

"As his wife," Colonel Graz said insinuatingly, "you would be sitting rather pretty. You would be one of the great queens of the shipping business, and there would be no need for you to hire yourself out ever again on assignments like the present one."

She pursed her lips, tapping her long fingernails on the side of her glass. "Where is Jonathan Rakehell at present?" she asked.

The baron consulted a sheet of paper on his desk. "According to our information, he is currently on the high seas en route home to New England from the Orient."

The young woman remained thoughtful. "Clearly," she said, "you have given this a great deal of thought. There is one element that is missing, however. I have no doubt that I can arrange to meet people like the Fat Dutchman in Djakarta and the Marquês de Braga in Macao. Such arrangements are simple. In the case of Jonathan Rakehell, however, I am going for much bigger and much more lucrative game, so I need to exercise far greater caution. Do you have any idea how I can arrange a meeting with him?"

Baron von Eberling chuckled. "You're not thinking, my dear Erika," he replied. "You attended a finishing school in France, did you not?"

She nodded impatiently.

"Attending school at the same time was a girl several years your junior," he went on, and glanced at the paper on his desk. "Her name is Elizabeth Boynton, and she is the daughter of Sir Alan Boynton, the head of the English branch of the Rakehell interests. In other words, she is Jonathan Rakehell's first cousin, or she would be if she were actually the daughter of the Boyntons."

Erika nodded, and a slow-spreading smile of satisfaction appeared on her face. "I remember Elizabeth Boynton, although I haven't thought of her for several years. As I recall her, she was developing into a rather attractive young woman, but no matter. I shall start my travels with a visit to England, and I shall write a letter this very day to Elizabeth."

Von Eberling shook his head. "That's all very well, my dear, but your first field of operations lies in the Far East. Before you—ah—set your snares for Mr. Rakehell, you have to fulfill your contractual obligations to the von Eberling company."

Erika had no intention of allowing herself to be dictated to by von Eberling, and she said sternly, "My contractual obligations, as you call them, make no mention of how or when I'm to go about securing business for your company, and I will do things as I see fit." She smiled confidently. "So I will first spend a little time with the Rakehell family, then I will go to the Far East."

"What I have always admired most about you, my dear Erika, is your independent spirit," the baron said. "It is a positive pleasure to watch you in action—provided that I am not your intended victim of the moment." He smiled. "Of course you may do things the way you see fit. Certainly your ingratiating yourself with the Rakehell family will do the company no harm, either."

Colonel Graz coughed delicately behind his hand. "Begging your pardon, Herr Baron," he said softly. "Braun."

"Ah, to be sure," Baron von Eberling replied. "It is not safe for a young woman to travel alone, especially in the Far East. We have decided to send an employee of the von Eberling company with you in the guise of a manservant."

"Who?" she wanted to know.

He paused almost imperceptibly, then said, "Reinhardt Braun."

"He's a nasty little person," Erika said.

"He happens to be very efficient with a sword, pistol, or knife," the baron told her. "He is very loyal to me and my company, and at my direction he will transfer that loyalty to you. With him to watch over you, I know that no harm will come to you."

She pondered for a moment or two, then shrugged. "Very well," she said.

Baron von Ebeling sealed the bargain by handing her a silk bag filled with silver Hamburg marks.

Erika was all business as she tested the bag in her hand, weighing it. She found the sum of money it contained to her liking, and her nod of acceptance indicated that she expected more to be forthcoming on a regular basis thereafter.

A carriage bearing the seal of the von Eberling company took Erika to her home in the still-fashionable district on the opposite side of the lake. The house that she had inherited was one of the few belongings other than her title that had been passed down to her by her father, and she had almost been forced to sell the dwelling in order to pay off her father's insurmountable debts. But she had found other methods of obtaining money, and the house was a secure base of operations as well as a respectable façade.

As she approached the front door, a small but solidly built swarthy man stepped out of the shadow of a large plane tree in her front garden, and she immediately recognized Reinhardt Braun, who removed his hat, clicked his heels, and bowed to her. "I have been awaiting the Fräulein Baroness for some time," he said.

Erika had to conceal a desire to laugh. Rudi von Eberling had been so sure of her reaction that he had assigned Braun to her before he had even obtained her consent to the deal.

She invited the man into the house with her, and he followed her into the parlor.

Erika frowned when he chose to sit beside her on a horsehair-stuffed settee, but he did not take the hint. "I expect," she said, "that we will begin our journey in about two weeks. We will go first to England, and ultimately to the Orient. Whether we stop in the United States remains to be seen. In any event, have sets of servant's livery made for yourself, one in black, and another, I think, in maroon with silver buttons.''

Braun frowned, his face darkening. ''Is it necessary to pose as a manservant?'' he wanted to know.

''I know of no other way that we could possibly travel together,'' Erika told him flatly. ''Whether I can present you in the Orient as a business associate will depend on circumstances, but as my visit to England is going to be strictly social, the only possible excuse I will have for your presence is as a rather glorified majordomo.''

He smiled at her insolently. ''I could be useful in many ways,'' he said, and reaching into his breast pocket he removed a small wooden doll. Then, taking a folding knife from a pocket, he opened it and touched the doll's throat with it. ''This is a trick I learned in the West Indies,'' he said. ''When it becomes necessary for me to kill an enemy, I first mark a spot on the doll where my bullet or blade will enter the unfortunate being's body.''

''To my knowledge,'' Erika replied coolly, ''there will be no need for you to commit any murders. I could prove mistaken in that, of course, but your principal function will be to protect me from the sinister forces that abound in the Orient.''

''I would be much better able to perform that function,'' he said, ''if I really did assume the role of your protector.'' Dropping the doll and knife into his pocket, he suddenly reached for her.

Erika had been anticipating just such a move. Scarcely moving, she reached into the loose sleeve of her gown and produced a small jewel-handled poniard, which she suddenly held at the man's throat. ''If I were you, Herr Braun,'' she said, her voice becoming almost saccharine, ''I would be very careful to remember my place at all times. I am not one who will tolerate familiarities, particularly from those whom I regard as my inferiors.''

Reinhardt Braun fumed. He had been caught completely off guard.

"I trust we understand each other?" Erika demanded severely, still holding the knife at his throat.

"Indeed we do, Fräulein Baroness," he replied meekly.

Smiling calmly, as though nothing out of the ordinary was taking place, she removed her hand from his throat, and her knife blade vanished up her sleeve again.

Braun now completely adopted a subservient pose. Rising to his feet, he clicked his heels and bowed stiffly. "I shall have the servant's livery made at once, Fräulein Baroness," he said, "and I shall place myself entirely at your disposal. I shall report to you each day."

"Good," she replied, "but do not come around here before noon. I like to sleep late."

He bowed again and was gone. She reached for the purse at her belt, spilled the coins onto the small secretary-desk, and counted the sum carefully. It pleased her to note that she had miscalculated the total amount by only a few marks. Depositing the money in a wall safe behind a small painting, Erika returned to the desk, dipped a quill pen into an ink jar, and began to write on a square sheet of heavy, scented parchment:

*Dear Elizabeth,*
    *I find it necessary to attend to some family business in London, and I thought immediately of you. How good it will be to see you again!*

The Javanese manservant-bodyguard stood at one end of the grove in the lush garden of the mansion that dominated the immediate countryside outside Djakarta and nodded as the small Eurasian boy threw knife after knife at a target attached to a tree about twenty feet away. Throwing the specially constructed lightweight Indonesian knives was an art, and David Boynton appeared to have mastered it with apparent ease. After he struck the outer edges of the target five times in succession, the manservant, who was one of the few employees of the Fat Dutchman who could speak English, called a temporary halt. "You learn the Javanese method of knife throwing very quickly, boy," he observed.

David grinned at him but felt compelled to tell him the truth. "I've thrown knives like these before," he said. "My uncle, Jonathan Rakehell, has a set of Indonesian throwing knives, and he taught me how to use them."

The man brightened and nodded. "Aha! I did not know that you were the nephew of Master Rakehell. That explains a great deal."

David pointed in the direction of the target. "I'm glad that Uncle Jonathan isn't here now," he said. "He'd give me the devil. You notice that I didn't hit the bull's-eye once. Not even once!"

The Javanese manservant was astonished. This amazing child was not only dissatisfied with his efforts but seemed to think he was actually capable of hitting the bull's-eye repeatedly. "Do you really think you can achieve such a feat?" the man asked politely.

David had been taught by his father and Uncle Jonathan never to boast, but he couldn't help showing off slightly. "Sure I can," he said, and hurrying to the tree, he removed a handful of knives. Then he went back to the line that he had made with his heel in the dust, stood behind it, and wiped his forehead with the back of his sleeve. He knew that under no circumstances could he make excuses for his poor performance with the knives. That was strictly forbidden, and the family motto had been drummed into the boy: "Results speak for themselves."

Taking careful aim, David let fly with a knife. To his intense joy, it penetrated the dead center of the target.

The small boy exhaled slowly and then more confidently threw three other knives in quick succession. They, too, landed in the innermost circle. The manservant was astonished. Sure that none of his colleagues would believe that such a small child could demonstrate such prowess, he hailed two of the Fat Dutchman's serving maids, girls who uniformly wore only long skirts, their hair, entwined with flowers, falling down their backs. Two of the girls obediently padded to the grove in bare feet, looked at the target, and appeared unimpressed. "Throw again," the man directed.

David hurled two more knives, both of which found the center of the target. "There," the man declared, jabbing his finger in the direction of the target. "Remember exactly what you've seen, and remember it was the child, not I, who threw the knives!"

Approaching the site through the tangle of plants that grew in seemingly wild confusion were Charles Boynton and the serving maid whom the Fat Dutchman had given him for his pleasure while under his roof. They strolled slowly, with Charles's arm encircling the girl while he cupped a bare breast in his hand. He was long accustomed to the scene at the Fat Dutchman's home but never ceased to marvel at it. Certainly the young women for whom the Dutchman paid large sums of money to serve him as slaves never complained and always seemed pleased when given to Charles as his temporary mistress.

Seeing his young son standing in the midst of a gathering, Charles took care to release his hold on the girl. David certainly had become worldly from his exposure to exotic lands and different cultures, but there still were things that it was not seemly for his son to see or know.

The other scantily clad girls and the bodyguard all began to talk at once. Charles's knowledge of the tongue of Java was rudimentary, and he listened carefully to the babble, trying to make out of it what he could. He gleaned that they were excited by his son's accomplishments. He grinned and nodded casually. "Yes, you've done well, my boy, but I've known you to do better. The knives around the edges of the target indicate that your mind was elsewhere. Just remember this— when it's necessary for you to throw a knife, you've got to concentrate on what you're doing. That's no time for you to let your mind wander."

Another girl, paler skinned than the others, with two white orchids in her coal-black hair, approached rapidly, and Charles's interest was sparked. He hadn't remembered seeing her previously, and decided that she was even more attractive than the wench with whom he had spent the night. "My master will see you now," she said, and not waiting for a reply, turned on her heel and led him back through the labyrinths of the garden.

In a clearing just outside the house, beneath a natural arbor of palms that had been grown in such a way to shade the ground beneath them, the Fat Dutchman sat in his customary wicker chair, with its huge, peacock-shaped back. He was dressed, as always, in an old-fashioned, open-throated shirt and knee breeches of coarse, unbleached linen, and if anything, he was even fatter than he had been when Charles last saw him. Beads of perspiration rolled down his round cheeks and soaked his shirt, which was bulging with rolls of flesh. His overweight body had to be suffering discomforts from the extreme heat and high humidity of Java, but he gave no sign of any distress and seemed to enjoy the gentle breezes created by several of his serving girls, who lazily waved huge palm fans.

As usual, there was the raucous chatter of several multicolored parrots perching on roosts. Just the sight of those parrots irritated Charles, who was reminded of the parrot the Dutchman had given him as a pet and that had been sent to him in London. The bird cursed expertly and at length in Dutch, a fact that had been revealed at dinner one night when the Dutch ambassador had been a dinner guest. Sir Alan and Jessica had yet to forgive him for the incident, and the parrot now belonged to David. If the Dutchman tried to give him another, he promised himself he would refuse it.

The Dutchman was reading a document which he held close to his face. He plainly needed reading glasses but refused to use them. He seemed to sense the approach of his visitor, and as Charles drew near, he put down the paper he was perusing, and his lips parted in a caricature of a smile. "So you're enjoying your little sojourn here, eh? Heh-heh." His laugh, as it always had been, was humorless.

"I'm enjoying myself a great deal," Charles said, and the girl who had been given to him sat on the ground beside him and leaned her head against his knee. Therefore it was only polite that he fondle her bare shoulder.

The Dutchman seemed to have an uncanny ability for

reading the minds of others, and he said, "You've seen a girl that you prefer to this one."

"Well, now that you mention it," Charles replied with some embarrassment, "the—young lady—whom you sent for me just now is exceptionally attractive."

"Ah, you mean Margala," the Dutchman said. "Heh-heh. Unfortunately she isn't available just yet. She's still a virgin, and I'm saving her for a special occasion." It was obvious from the way he spoke that he thought of his girls as commodities, just as he thought of his ships and the enormous trade they engendered in the same light.

All at once the Dutchman's joviality vanished, and his tone became crisp. "You have indicated that you have a business matter of great importance to discuss with me," he said. "What is it?" He leaned forward in his chair and peered hard at his visitor.

Speaking very distinctly and slowly, Charles outlined the scheme whereby he would purchase a considerable quantity of black pepper, following which the Dutch authorities would forbid the exportation of the so-called black gold by any foreigner or any Dutch national. The Dutchman listened intently to his young English friend, his watery blue eyes fixed intently on Charles's face and never wavering. Perspiration poured unheeded down his fat face and chubby jowls, and the slave girls fanned him more vigorously, but it seemed to have no effect.

Charles finished his recital by emphasizing that he and Jonathan anticipated that the Dutchman would be their partner in the venture, and quoting the figures that Molinda had cited, he offered an attractive deal.

The Dutchman's eyes gleamed avariciously, and he rubbed his chubby hands together. "I have always claimed, Charles, that you have a touch of genius in you. Heh-heh. Now I know it."

"You agree to the scheme, then?"

"I think it's brilliant!"

"And you'll go into partnership with us on it?"

The Dutchman leaned back in his wicker chair and smiled

lazily. "That," he said, "is a peculiar circumstance. Heh-heh. The terms you offer me are so attractive that I find them impossible to turn down. As I'm sure you know." He peered intently at his visitor. "I have a strange notion," he said, "that you're acting on the advice given you by Molinda when you make me this offer. She alone would know the terms that I find irresistible."

Charles saw no reason to conceal the truth from him. "Yes," he said, "I did have a rather lengthy chat with Molinda, and she advised me of the best possible way to ensure your cooperation."

"Bless her two-faced, conniving soul," the Dutchman said fondly. "I shall never see her like again, heh-heh. I was wrong ever to make a gift of the wench to you. You turned her free, and she's been making vast sums of money for Rakehell and Boynton that she could have been making for me."

Charles warned himself not to forget for a moment that the Dutchman was very greedy when profits were involved and would not hesitate to take whatever he felt he could get away with. "Do you suppose we need a formal agreement?"

The Dutchman laughed with genuine merriment. "You are sometimes very droll, my young friend. Your overall scheme would be regarded as illegal if news of it ever leaked out. We can't possibly put our agreement on paper. We'd be condemning ourselves to terms in a stinking prison near Amsterdam if word of our understanding ever leaked out. No—heh-heh—I'm afraid we'll have to subsist on sheer, undiluted, mutual trust."

"By all means," Charles said swiftly. "We'll take no risks."

The Fat Dutchman's smile faded, and his voice became metallic. "I never run risks," he said coldly. "That, my dear Charles, is the ultimate secret of whatever success I've enjoyed in this world."

As the Dutchman moved into action, Charles had to busy himself sending messages to the captains of the Rakehell and Boynton clippers that were visiting various ports in the

Orient. All were ordered to proceed without delay to Djakarta.

In the meantime, the Dutchman bought large quantities of pepper from local Javanese growers to whom he paid the usual high fees, minus ten percent because he was buying in such bulk.

Charles began to gain an insight into the man's extraordinary methods. Ten percent was a considerable amount of money, and the Dutchman was already piling up the profits that would accrue to him and his partners.

Within twenty-four hours, carts began arriving at the Dutchman's warehouses near the Djakarta waterfront, and sacks of pepper were unloaded there under the watchful eyes of knife-bearing guards.

Seventy-two hours after the scheme went into operation, the first of the clippers flying the Rakehell and Boynton Tree of Life banner began to arrive, and dropped anchor in the Djakarta harbor.

The Dutchman was ready now for the most delicate part of his operation. Three high-ranking Dutch officials were invited to the estate outside of Djakarta for supper. They included the commissioner of trade for the Dutch East Indies, his deputy, and the personal aide-de-camp to the governor-general. It was a sign of the regard in which the Fat Dutchman was held by his fellow countrymen that all three responded affirmatively to his invitation.

No effort was spared to make the honored guests feel at home. The entire corps of slave girls was on hand, and for the occasion they wore silk skirts and heavy makeup, even rouging their nipples. Dutch gin, which was in perennial short supply on the island, flowed ceaselessly, and the meal was fit for royalty, with special dish after dish being served by the Dutchman's staff. Delicacies from virtually every island in the Dutch archipelago were included, and the serving and eating of the meal required several hours.

Then, one by one, the guests vanished to upstairs bedchambers with the young women of their choice.

Charles noted that the Dutchman had made no mention of the favor he sought from the government officials of Djakarta.

He would wait until the following day, after his compatriots appeared and ate a hearty breakfast. Then and then only would he make it clear to them that he would very much appreciate their placing a temporary embargo on the sale and exportation of black pepper.

The Fat Dutchman was so powerful and so skilled in the fine art of getting exactly what he wanted from those in high places that the scheme went off without a hitch. As the Dutchman had anticipated, the Djakarta officials readily agreed to the plan, since there was currently a glut of pepper on the market and an embargo would ensure that prices remained stable. That same day, the pepper buyers from England, several continental European nations, and the United States who were stationed in Djakarta would be startled to learn that under a new law, signed at noon by the governor-general, the purchase of pepper was strictly forbidden, and all supplies of the condiment previously acquired would have to be removed from Java within the next two weeks. After that time the government would confiscate any stores it found. The delay of a fortnight, the Dutchman privately informed Charles, allowed sufficient time for the Rakehell and Boynton ships to leave Djakarta again.

"What price are you thinking of asking for the pepper in England, Charles?" the Fat Dutchman wanted to know.

Charles frowned. "I've been thinking of little else," he replied. "I'm inclined to triple the price of ten guineas per hundred pounds to thirty guineas."

The Dutchman shook his head. "You surprise and disappoint me, my young friend," he said. "I thought you had the true instincts of a killer shark, but they seem to be sadly lacking in you. You can demand any price you want, and you can be sure of getting it."

"True enough," Charles said, "but I don't want to offend regular clients by raising the prices too outlandishly."

"Nonsense!" the Dutchman roared, pounding on the arm of his wicker chair so forcefully that two of the nearby parrots stopped chattering and gazed at him warily, their beady eyes unwavering. "You're not forcing anyone to meet your terms,

96

Charles," he said. "You'll be offering pepper for a fair-market value, and buyers can either accept or reject your terms. They'll have no reason to feel offended or to bear you a grudge. So I urge you to be sensible."

"What do you mean by 'sensible'?" Charles demanded.

The Dutchman's face seemed to explode in happy creases. "If I were in your boots," he said, "I do believe I would charge a guinea per pound."

Charles was startled. "Good Lord! That's a hundred guineas for a one-hundred-pound sack. No one has ever paid that price for black pepper."

"That's because the market has stayed in existence and the buyers have been able to dicker. Now, however, you own the world's only supply of black pepper, and you'd be wise to act accordingly."

Charles's head spun, but he knew the shrewd Dutchman was right. The profits he would earn for Rakehell and Boynton would be infinitely greater than he had anticipated, and he knew that he'd be staving off the financial disaster that threatened to inundate the company for that much longer a time. He nodded slowly. "I guess," he said, "that you're right. It's worth taking the gamble."

"You don't understand," the Dutchman said with a touch of asperity in his voice. "There is no gamble. You are placing a wager on every horse entered in the race, and they are all going to win."

# V

A supremely happy Homer and Judy Ellison returned to New London from their honeymoon in Niagara Falls and braced themselves for a difficult homecoming. Their principal concern was Judith's children, specifically young Judy, who had made no secret of her unhappiness at their wedding. They had discussed the youngsters at length, and both were sure that they faced a problem of somehow persuading Judy to accept their marriage. They stopped off at Jeremiah Rakehell's house on the way to their own home and were greeted by Jeremiah and Missy Sarah, who happened to be sitting on the front porch, where they were enjoying an unusually balmy evening. Then young Judy emerged from the house onto the porch.

Anticipating a snub, her mother squared her shoulders. Homer realized that he had clenched his fists tightly, so he concealed them beneath the tails of the frock coat he was wearing. Judy, however, astonished her mother and stepfather by unhesitatingly going to them and soundly kissing them in turn. "Welcome home," she cried.

Her attitude was so unexpected that the honeymooners exchanged a covert, startled glance.

Sarah and Jeremiah were aware of their confusion and its cause, and grinned amiably.

"I guess," Judy said, "this is as good a time as any to tell you what I'm thinking. Is that all right?"

Her mother was too tongue-tied to reply.

"By all means," Homer responded.

"I know the whole truth now," the girl announced breathlessly.

Judith Ellison found her voice. "What do you mean by that, Judy?" she wanted to know.

The girl spoke with surprising adult dignity. "Grandma told me about my father's conduct and about the hard time you had, Mama," she said. "I didn't know, so I hope you'll both forgive me for some beastly behavior."

"It wasn't that bad," Homer replied with a grin.

"Oh, but it was," Judy insisted, "I'm going to make it up to you, and I'm sure Brad will feel exactly as I do when he comes home from the Orient and I bring him up to date on everything. There's only one way I know of to show you both how I feel now, and I want to ask a favor of you."

"You shall have everything within our power to grant, naturally," Judith murmured.

"Well, you might not feel like giving me this or giving it to my brother, either," the girl declared. "I want to change my last name to Ellison, and the sooner the better."

Homer drew the child into his arms and hugged her; then it was her mother's turn.

"I'll apply to the court without delay for adoption proceedings," Homer said. "I'm very pleased to welcome you and your brother as my children rather than my stepchildren."

Judith blinked back the tears that welled up in her eyes. "I don't know how you did this, Missy Sarah," she murmured, "but you're really a wonder."

Sarah Rakehell shook her head, and then said primly, "You're mistaken, Judith; I did nothing. I gave your daughter the opportunity to use the good sense with which the good Lord endowed her, and she did the rest all by herself."

Jeremiah was relieved beyond measure. Now at last the stigma of his late son-in-law was being removed, and he knew that his daughter and her family were truly starting a new life with Homer.

Young Judy happily went off to her own home that same night with her mother and stepfather.

The following morning, although no one in New London yet knew it, the *Lai-tse lu* put into port at Baltimore, where Caleb Cushing and his subordinates disembarked, then hastened to bring the news to the President and the members of the Congress that the mission to Cathay had been eminently successful. Though it was President John Tyler who had initiated this mission during the last months of his term in office, it was the newly elected President James Polk who received the news from Cushing that the treaty had been signed with the Tao Kuang Emperor, granting American merchant ships the right to enter the five major Chinese ports for the purpose of trade. A new era in American commercial life was about to open.

Tarrying no longer than necessary in Baltimore, Jonathan ordered Captain Wilbor to set sail again and head for home. The next day, the arrival of the clipper ship in New London was heralded by the booming of a cannon at the Rakehell and Boynton shipyard. This gun was fired only to announce the arrival of company vessels, with each assigned a number of shots. The cannon roared three times in succession, which signaled to the wives and parents of crew members that the clipper *Lai-tse lu* had come home from the Middle Kingdom. Within moments eager relatives were hurrying from their houses to the shipyard waterfront.

Jonathan carried his daughter ashore, holding his son's hand, while Harmony frisked beside them. As he was eagerly greeted by his family, no one spoke of Lai-tse lu or her passing, and, indeed, no words were necessary. Everyone knew what the others felt, and the family shared its grief in silence.

Missy Sarah immediately took charge of the children, her manner making it plain that she alone would determine what was best for them.

Kai was afraid of no man, but he had served under Missy Sarah's direction in the Soong Chao household in Canton, and he greeted her with the respect he would have shown the Princess An Mien.

Sarah Rakehell was more pleased to see the majordomo than she was willing to let on. "I see you're gaining weight, Kai," she said, addressing him in the Cantonese dialect. "We shall have to give you enough work and enough responsibilities that you take off your excess pounds."

Young Brad Walker had matured in far more than appearance on his long journey to the far side of the world. He listened intently to his sister, who spoke to him in private, and then he immediately approached his mother and Homer, who were awaiting them in the family carriage. "Judy has just told me some things that I had long suspected," he said manfully. "I don't want to damn the dead, so I'll keep my mouth shut about certain opinions that I hold. Mama, I'm sorry you were made so unhappy for so long, and I wish I'd known it, although I don't see what I could have done to improve your lot any. Anyway, I'm glad you finally found real happiness. As for you, sir," he continued, turning to Homer and extending his hand, "I have only one thing I want to say. I'd like to ask you a question."

Homer had no idea what to expect, but nodded. "Is it all right with you," Brad asked, his voice suddenly trembling and revealing the intensity of the emotional strain that he was undergoing, "—is it all right with you, sir, if I call you Papa from now on?"

Homer had to fight back the tears that unexpectedly came to his own eyes. "I'd be very proud," he said, "if you would. Nothing would make me happier."

The Ellisons looked and acted like a united family when they appeared at the Rakehell house shortly thereafter for the customary homecoming dinner for Jonathan, and in this instance, for young Brad, too. Julian and Jade were very much part of the scene, and related in detail some of their own experiences in the Middle Kingdom. They were especially eager to talk about their journey to Peking, where they had a wonderful visit in the garden, at the imperial guesthouse in which they were staying, with an elderly man who had given them gifts. "That man," Jonathan revealed dryly, "was none other than the Tao Kuang Emperor himself, and his kindness to the children was virtually unprecedented."

At the insistence of Jonathan and of Missy Sarah, Kai sat at the table, too, and ate with the family. This was the first time that he had ever participated in a formal meal with his employers, but as Jonathan told him, "You're in America now, and we have our own way of life, our own standards here. We'd all be very much insulted if you went off to the kitchen and ate there."

Kai was almost overcome, but the Western foods that were served caused him problems that kept him preoccupied. Using chopsticks, as he had not yet learned how to wield a knife and fork, he was faced with the technical difficulties of eating roast beef, baked potato, and vegetables.

Immediately after dinner, Jonathan retired to the study with his father and brother-in-law for a critical business discussion.

"We're cutting corners wherever we can," Jeremiah told his son. "We refuse to compromise quality, naturally, and that means we've not been able to lay off any of the men who are building new clipper ships. As for our existing fleet, Homer is performing some juggling miracles."

"What I'm doing, specifically," Homer explained, "is to take the clippers off the shorter secondary runs like the North American coastal trade and the Caribbean trade, and I've been reassigning them all to voyages to Europe and to the Orient."

"That's very wise," Jonathan said.

"I'll be grateful to you," his brother-in-law went on, "if you'll give me some idea of when the various clippers that are off in the Orient at the moment will be coming home for reassignment."

"It won't be as soon as you think," Jonathan replied, "because they're already on a special assignment for Charles." He proceeded to describe in detail the pepper scheme that had been devised by his cousin.

"Is it going to work, do you think?" Homer demanded incredulously. "Do you actually believe that the officials of Dutch East Indies will go along with something of the sort?"

Jonathan smiled and nodded. "I know exactly how you feel, Homer," he said, "but you don't know the Fat Dutchman as Charles and I know him. He has a knack—you might even call it a genius—for getting exactly what he wants anywhere in the East. His methods are strictly his own business, of course. As a matter of fact, I had a letter from him myself, just before I sailed home, in which he inquired about the possibilities of setting up a partnership with Rakehell and Boynton."

"I'm against it," Jeremiah said flatly. "It's not that I think that the Dutchman would try to cheat us or be dishonest with us in any way. But he has a habit of becoming the sole proprietor of firms that he enters, and I prefer to hold him at arms' length as long as we possibly can."

"I feel that way, too, Papa," Jonathan said. "If Charles's pepper scheme succeeds, we should gain a few months' breathing spell."

"That would be most useful," Jeremiah replied. "We're not in a unique situation, you know. This sort of thing has happened to a great many companies that have expanded at a faster than normal rate of growth. No one could have predicted that the whole world would be clamoring for your clipper ships, Jonnie."

Jonathan nodded and then said thoughtfully, "One advance leads directly to another these days, it seems. I intend to spend as much time as I can spare on steamships in the immediate future."

Homer was stunned. "You—think there's a future for ships driven by steam, then?" he demanded.

"As a sea captain, I think you know the answer to that as well as I do," Jonathan replied. "Just imagine having a ship that doesn't depend on the wind, the tides, and the weather, but generates its own power and adheres to its own schedules." His face lit up. "That would be truly miraculous, and from what I understand, the British are making great progress with steam in some of their shipyards up in Scotland."

"There's been a considerable expansion on this side of the Atlantic as well," Jeremiah replied. "But so far it has been confined to relatively small vessels on the major lakes."

"I'll be able to discuss the subject more intelligently," Jonathan said, "after I complete my study." He refrained from saying that he intended to throw himself into work to the exclusion of all else. He had noted how empty the house had seemed without Lai-tse lu, and he knew that the only way he would be able to overcome his urgent, obsessive longing for her would be by burying himself in his work.

That is precisely what he did in the days that followed, and he was so busy that he didn't even notice when, early one morning, his stepmother entered the room he used as his office at home, and announced, "There's a Dr. Melton here to see you, Jonathan."

He jumped to his feet immediately. "This is wonderful," he said. "This is the man who can make a long-standing wish of mine and Lai-tse lu's come true." He offered no explanation as he pulled on his coat, then hurried to the parlor, where a young man with curly brown hair and hazel eyes sat quietly, a suitcase on the floor beside him. "Dr. Melton?" Jonathan asked. "I'm Jonathan Rakehell. Welcome, and thank you more than I can tell you for coming here."

"Your letter intrigued me, I must say," the young physician replied. "I'll be obliged if you'll tell me the name of a hotel where I can stay. I simply had the hansom cab bring me straight to your house."

"As he well should. You'll stay here as my guest," Jonathan replied. "You must be tired after your journey from Cambridge, so—"

"Not really," Dr. Melton said, interrupting him. "I stopped off to visit friends in New Haven on the way. I went to Yale as an undergraduate—as I suspect you well know, since I was recommended to you by a fellow Yale alumnus."

"Very heartily recommended indeed," Jonathan replied,

"as you were by the Dean of the Medical School of Harvard, where you've just been made a Doctor of Medicine, as I understand it."

Melton looked even younger than his years as he grinned boyishly. "I've had my M.D. for twelve days now," he said.

"If you don't mind," Jonathan said, "we'll talk now and get as much out of the way before supper, as we can. What are your plans, Doctor?"

Melton waved vaguely. "They're not really solidified, Mr. Rakehell. I've been seriously thinking of going into practice at my home near Hartford, or I might accept a position as an assistant to a diagnostician in New York City. I'm due to see him next week."

"See him, by all means," Jonathan said. "I'd want you to take the post that I have in mind only if you're completely satisfied in your own mind that you want it."

"Why is that, sir?" Matthew Melton asked.

"Because once you're embarked on this venture," Jonathan replied, "there can be no turning back. There's no room for regrets, and you'll be too busy to even think of what might have been."

"May I ask the nature of this position that's opening up?" the young physician wanted to know.

"Rightly speaking, it isn't opening up," Jonathan replied carefully. "I'm aiding in the opening, which will actually be made by the M.D. who takes the post. Let me explain at the outset that I'll provide transportation to the Middle Kingdom free of charge on a Rakehell and Boynton clipper ship, and I'll also guarantee your return passage at any time within a five-year period that you decide that the Orient is not for you. I will also personally guarantee you an income of no less than three hundred dollars per month. I'm reasonably sure that the Tao Kuang Emperor and his sister will want to make their own financial arrangements with you, and in the event that they are willing to pay you at least three hundred per month, I'll be relieved of any obligation to you."

The physician shifted his position on the settee and looked searchingly at his host. "If you don't mind the observation,

Mr. Rakehell," he said, "I find this an exceptionally unusual arrangement."

"So it is," Jonathan agreed. "My late wife, as I wrote to you, was of Chinese descent, and we've both been devoted to the cause of opening the Middle Kingdom to the Western civilization of the mid-nineteenth century. This, believe me, is far more difficult than you might think, since China has been completely cut off from the outside world for thousands of years and most Chinese have never as much as seen a single white man. They know nothing of our language, nothing of our culture. I have a representative at the court of the emperor right now, a young lady who is Cantonese but who lived with us here for a time, and can read and write English. She's translating all sorts of books and articles on industrial and agricultural and other matters. I mention her because she undoubtedly will be a primary contact for you at the imperial court, since she can speak fluent English as well as fluent Chinese."

Matthew Melton nodded soberly. "Now, as to the work itself, Mr. Rakehell. I mean the work that would await me there."

"That will depend on the reactions to you of the Tao Kuang Emperor and his very efficient sister, the Princess An Mien," Jonathan replied. "Western medicine is totally unknown in the Middle Kingdom. I myself was very ill and almost died there after being wounded during the Opium War, and I can tell you flatly that I owe my life to a miracle. There are several kinds of medicine practiced in the Middle Kingdom. One places a great reliance on medicinal herbs and other substances that are taken from various plants. A second is called acupuncture and relies on the insertion of needles at various points in the human body to relieve all sorts of ailments. Both are riddled with a great deal of superstition and nonsense that any educated man will find intolerable. The third type of medicine practiced in the Middle Kingdom, I'm sorry to say, is gibberish that's firmly rooted, nevertheless, in tradition. You'll find little, if anything, that you've learned at the Harvard Medical School, I assure you. In many ways, it's very similar to the practices of the medicine men who administered to the tribes of North American Indians for centuries."

"Would I be welcome to practice there in my own way?" Dr. Melton wanted to know.

"I've been assured by the Tao Kuang Emperor and his sister that you won't be molested and that you would be allowed to do what you deem necessary," Jonathan replied. "That's all I can tell you. It's not a guarantee, by any means, that you'd be given a free hand, but I'd say that a great deal will depend on the trust in your own methods that you can build at the court, especially at the highest level."

The young doctor was silent for some moments as he pondered. "There's little doubt that a challenge exists," he said. "A tremendous challenge."

The mutual friend from Yale who had recommended him had been right, Jonathan thought. Matthew Melton, he had said, would find the challenge of going to the imperial court at Peking utterly irresistible.

"How would I go about procuring medical supplies that I'd need, Mr. Rakehell?"

"I'd advise you to take ample quantities of all that you will need when you first go," Jonathan said. "I will provide you with all funds that you would need for the purpose. Then, as you need replacements for various medicines, simply write to me, and I'll send them to you."

There was a long silence, and the young physician asked, "How soon do you need to know whether I'll take the post, Mr. Rakehell?"

"I don't believe in setting artificial deadlines," Jonathan Rakehell replied. "Obviously this is a matter that I would like to see settled as soon as possible, because I'm anxious that a Western doctor start practicing in China as soon as possible. There's so much to be done there that every day that's wasted is precious. But I realize this is a very big step, and will require considerable thinking on your part."

Matthew seemed, however, to have his response already prepared. "I haven't yet gone into practice here," he said, "and I'm responsible to no one but myself. So, theoretically at least, I could climb on board a ship the moment I acquire my medical supplies and instruments."

Jonathan nodded, knowing that the younger man had virtually made up his mind and required a gentle but firm nudge to start him moving in the right direction. "I have a clipper ship that leaves for Hong Kong and Whampoa in exactly one week's time. That allows ample opportunity to collect the medical supplies. It will also give you time to refurbish your wardrobe and say good-bye to your various relatives."

"I have no relatives," Dr. Melton said. "I'm alone in the world."

It was increasingly evident that he was perfect for the assignment. Jonathan gave him the necessary nudge. "I shall reserve a cabin for you on board the clipper," he said, "and I'll consign to your care various books, magazine articles, and newspaper clippings intended for the Tao Kuang Emperor and his sister. I shall also give you a box containing a variety of newly manufactured tools that will be of interest to them."

The physician grinned and held out his hand. "Either I am an utter fool or the smartest man in Christendom," he said, "but I reckon I won't know which until I've been in China long enough to decide for myself whether I'm wasting my time. If it's all right with you, give me a month in China. That should be enough time to decide once and for all if I should stay on there, or if I should return home to the United States."

"That's fine with me, Doctor," Jonathan said earnestly. "You may or may not like it there, but I can assure you, sir, that you will not be wasting your time. On the contrary, you'll have an extraordinary experience, and you'll do more good for more people than you've ever dreamed possible in your years of medical school."

It was Jonathan's custom in the warm weather to swim off the beach in front of the Rakehell mansion after he came home from work each day, accompanied by his children. Julian and Jade were becoming expert swimmers, and Harmony, taking no chances, always hovered near them in the water, splashing gently as he stayed afloat, and keeping a sharp watch on them. Kai was also always present on these occasions, and after Jonathan enjoyed a swim and a romp with the children, he worked off his tensions by engaging in a combat with Kai in the martial arts.

They were evenly matched, as they had discovered when Kai had first begun to give Jonathan lessons in the ancient martial arts of the Middle Kingdom. Since that time, particularly throughout his long sojourn in China during the Opium War, Jonathan had become infinitely more proficient in the vicious type of hand-to-hand combat that characterized the martial arts. Someone seeing these two giants hurling each other to the ground, using their fists and arms, feet and legs and bodies with abandon, would have wondered how either survived.

Both took great care, however, to inflict no real harm on the opponent. Aware that the damage could be substantial, they were cautious and stopped short of causing mayhem.

The children enjoyed such a session enormously, and even Harmony, once he learned that his two favorite men in all the world were not fighting in earnest, came to enjoy the experience. When the combat was done, Jonathan and Kai ran into the water for a final dip, and when they emerged, Julian stared anxiously up at his father. "Now it's my turn, Papa," he said. "Fight me."

Jonathan hesitated for no more than an instant, and then turned to Kai. "You've been instructing the children, Kai," he said. "Is the boy ready for combat yet?"

"I suggest," Kai replied gravely, "that you try him out and determine for yourself whether he is ready."

Jonathan turned back to his son. "All right, Julian," he said, "let's go."

The words were scarcely out of his mouth when the boy hurled himself at his father, feet and arms flailing in the approved manner.

Even at his age, he could have inflicted considerable

damage, so Jonathan was forced to adopt immediate defensive measures.

The child was undeterred, and continued to attack with enthusiasm and surprising skill. For a youngster of eight years, he had already mastered the intricate principals of the art, and Jonathan was delighted to see that he knew precisely what he was doing when he fought. Jonathan gradually extended his son, putting him through his paces, and ultimately was satisfied that the boy was receiving sound training both in attack and in defense. Certainly he could hold his own with any Chinese boy of his own age, and he had a distinct advantage in a rough-and-tumble or free-for-all with youngsters of approximately his own size and age in the United States. Ultimately Jonathan called a halt. Julian was so intent on the battle he was waging, however, that he was incapable of stopping.

His father threw his arms around him and pinned the boy's arms to his sides. "You've done splendidly, Julian," he said. "That will do for now."

The child subsided and peered up at him anxiously. "You really think I'm pretty good, Papa?" he said. "You aren't just saying it to make me feel good?"

"You should know me well enough by now," Jonathan replied, "to realize that I never issue praise for the sake of making you feel good. When I praise you, son, you've earned it."

Julian was very pleased with himself, and Jade was instantly jealous. "Now it's my turn," she said.

Jonathan was taken aback but tried not to show it. "I'm afraid you'll be hurt, my dear," he said.

The little girl shook her head angrily. "Just you try me," she said, "and you'll find out different." Without waiting for his consent, she hurled herself at him in the approved martial arts manner.

Jonathan had no choice but to defend himself, and was utterly astonished by the little girl's prowess.

Jade was tiny and lacked physical strength, to be sure, but

her martial arts techniques were textbook-perfect. To her father's astonishment, she knew every offensive move, every defensive maneuver, and when to utilize each of them. If she continued to study with Kai she would be unique when she grew older, and would be able to look after herself in any physically dangerous situation that presented itself.

Ultimately Jonathan called a halt, and after he had praised Jade lavishly, the children demanded the right to engage in combat with each other.

Kai intervened and announced that this was strictly forbidden; they could fight him at any time, he made clear, but if he ever caught them engaging in combat together, their lessons would come to an end.

Jonathan was grateful to the majordomo for his thoughtfulness. It was clear that he knew the youngsters well enough to realize that if they fought each other they would be carried away by the spirit of combat and might inflict real harm on each other. They adjourned to the house, and the children, after they were dressed, were summoned to the nursery for their supper, which Missy Sarah would supervise. Jonathan, relaxed at last after his outing, took his time dressing, and then went down to the library to join his father for a presupper drink.

Their talk centered on ships, the shipyard, and trade, as it always did, until Missy Sarah came into the room and joined them.

"There's been enough business talk for one day, I'm sure," she said. "We very much enjoyed your martial arts exhibition, especially the bouts with the children."

"I expect Julian to be growing proficient," he said. "After all, he's a boy. But Jade positively astonished me."

"She's incredibly like her mother," Missy Sarah said. "I wonder if you know that Lai-tse lu was an expert in the martial arts."

Jonathan stared at her. "You're joking!" he exclaimed.

She shook her head. "Kai taught her—with my approval—just as he now instructs Jade. I heartily approve of such training for a girl."

Jonathan shook his head in wonder. "I don't know how I'd get along without you," he replied.

His stepmother exchanged a long, significant look with her husband. "Have you spoken to him yet?" she asked.

Jeremiah shook his head. "I thought we could do it best together," he replied.

Jonathan looked first at one and then the other.

"What's all this?"

His father cleared his throat and managed to look extremely uncomfortable. "There's a matter," he said, "that we've been wanting to discuss with you." He seemed incapable of proceeding.

Missy Sarah intervened and took up the burden of explanation. "You do virtually nothing but work, Jonathan," she said. "You leave here early in the morning, you come home in time to play with the children for a time, and then, after dinner, more often than not you hurry back to your office. By my actual count you have yet to take a single day's holiday since you returned home from Cathay."

"There's a great deal of work to be done," he replied defensively, "and the company needs all the help I'm capable of mustering these days."

"Stuff and nonsense," Missy Sarah replied tartly. "If Lai-tse lu were still alive, you'd be devoting an appropriate share of time to her, and you can't deny it."

"Well, no, I won't try to deny it," he replied. "But the whole point is that I'm alone, and I'm damned if I'm going to fritter away valuable time."

Missy Sarah again exchanged a long look with her husband. "The only way I know to tell you this is to say it right out," she declared. "Jonathan, some men get along just fine as bachelors. You aren't one of them. Aside from the obvious fact that your two little children need a mother rather than just an elderly grandmother to look after them, you yourself must have a wife in order to find real contentment."

"I can scarcely believe my own ears," Jonathan replied. "I don't see how it's possible that you, of all people, having known Lai-tse lu so well all of her life, can possibly suggest

113

that I might find a substitute for her somewhere in this world."

"A substitute?" Missy Sarah asked, and shook her head vehemently. "Never! She was unique, and I know it as well as you do. But you can't and mustn't remain a hermit for the rest of your days. The world is filled with bright, personable young ladies who could lighten your burdens and make life far more pleasant for you, not to mention the good they could do for Julian and Jade."

"I won't argue with you about the youngsters," Jonathan said. "I'll grant you that they'd be better off with the right stepmother, but I have no interest in finding her and no interest in searching for her. I am quite content with my life as it is."

"Rubbish," Missy Sarah replied tartly. "You're overworked and lonely and tense. You don't even know the meaning of contentment."

"Suppose," Jonathan said, "that I admit you're right. Well, I admit it. That still doesn't mean that I could find a new wife or that I would have any desire to find one."

His father entered the conversation for the first time. "I know what you're feeling, and I sympathize with that feeling, Jonnie," he said. "I loved your mother very much, and there was a void in my life when she died. I claimed that I'd never find another woman I could love, and I clung to that view stubbornly—too stubbornly. It took Sarah here to break the mold of my thinking and make me realize that I was missing far more in the world than I was gaining. I'm living proof that a man can love again and can find happiness."

"I'm not very adept at debates," Jonathan said. "I can never think of the clever things to say or when to say them."

Jeremiah was determined to speak his mind and plowed on. "If you were more like Charles," he said, "we'd be less concerned. He's the sort of man who can develop a very sharp and emphatic interest in a woman for a period of time and then can forget her as he takes up with another."

Jonathan's smile was sardonic. "What you're trying to tell me is that since I'm a male animal, I should start engaging in

114

affairs. Well, I'm none too interested in women for that purpose, either. As a matter of fact, I'm too busy to think of women at all. I'm working seven days and seven nights a week, trying to overcome our financial problems, and between the yard and the children, I have no time for women. In fact, even if I found someone that I liked, which is highly unlikely, I'd have literally no time to pay court to her."

His tone of voice and manner suggested that contrary to the belief that he had just stated, he had won a debate and had spoken the final word on the subject.

But Missy Sarah had remained undaunted. "You're quite right," she said. "I did indeed know Lai-tse lu very well. So well, in fact, that I'm going to make a large wager that I'm correct about something. She told me so herself before she sailed off to the Middle Kingdom with you on her last voyage. Knowing her as I did, I feel quite certain that she made it plain to you that she hoped and expected you to marry again, Jonathan."

He looked disconcerted, and his surface poise vanished. "Well," he replied, "I reckon she did say something of the sort, but I didn't take her all that seriously. She was just making one of those unselfish gestures that seemed so natural to her."

"Her gesture was unselfish," Sarah replied, "but you can bet your boots she meant every word of it. She understood you, Jonathan. She knew your needs; she realized that for you to be truly contented in this world, you've got to have a wife. So she meant it quite literally when she urged you to marry again."

He stared down at the floor and shifted his feet. "For the sake of the children, I'd do it," he said. "But I don't know a soul I'd be willing to consider for a moment as a wife, and I can't imagine meeting someone who would qualify. I'm sorry, but I can't change the way I feel."

# Book II

# I

On the hilly mainland facing the South China Sea stood the former fishing village of Kowloon, which the previous residents of the place no longer recognized. Offshore were a number of islands, the largest of them known as Hong Kong. The colony had been ceded to Great Britain by China after the Opium War, and the island was growing at an even more rapid pace than was its sister community of Kowloon. The Peak, approximately two thousand feet above sea level, looked down on one of the world's great natural harbors, and it was this marvelous deep-water shelter as well as the strategic location of Hong Kong that attracted ships from every nation on earth, with the merchant vessels of Great Britain, France, and the United States predominating.

Not even the most optimistic of British chauvinists could have predicted the meteoric growth of the Crown Colony of Hong Kong. London contributed a governor-general, two full regiments of troops, and the skeleton of a constabulary force to keep the peace, as well as establishing a strong Royal Navy fleet in Hong Kong harbor. The merchants and businessmen of the Western world did the rest. They were so anxious to obtain Chinese porcelains, silks, and tea that their ships crowded the harbor, and it was impossible for anyone, British or Chinese, to keep up with their demands for goods or services.

The Royal Navy built a watchtower at the top of the Peak

and from that eminence, naval observers could look down on a minimum of fifty to seventy-five foreign vessels crowding into the port at any one given time. Nowhere on earth—not in London, not in New York, not in Hamburg—was the sea traffic as heavy, as varied, or as lucrative.

Of the many companies that had obtained permanent representation in Hong Kong, none was more prominent than the firm of Rakehell and Boynton, whose three docks always had one or more of the firm's distinctive clipper ships tied up there. Behind the docks stood several massive warehouses, the heart of the Rakehell and Boynton Far Eastern commercial empire.

Ruling this domain from a modest one-story office building of stone, most of whose residents were clerks, was Molinda, who more nearly resembled the bar girls to be found in the seamen's saloons than she did the principal representative of a major company. Nevertheless, she ruled her domain with a firm hand, and her shrewd bargaining sense, enhanced by her previous experience working for the Fat Dutchman, made her a major force in Hong Kong.

Inevitably, she was the object of considerable speculation on the part of the British newcomers to Hong Kong. All they knew about her was that she lived alone, shunning all social life, that she was the widow of an obscure member of the Chinese royal family, and that she actively discouraged all suitors. There were those, too, who marveled at her ability to survive in the rough jungle of the Hong Kong shipping world. Those who held this view were unaware of the existence of the giant Lo Fang, who served as her majordomo. All of the company's sentries and guards, as well as those who loaded and unloaded cargo from ships, worked under his direct supervision and were responsible to him. Anyone who knew Lo Fang treated him with great respect, and no man in his right mind ever tried to fool or cheat him.

Molinda appeared regularly at the docks, greeting all incoming Rakehell and Boynton ships and then seeing them off again. She often ate her noon dinner with their captains in the exclusive waterfront club founded for the owners and managers of docks and of shipping lines, and because she both minded her own business and was professionally competent, she attracted a wide following of admirers.

It was general knowledge on the waterfront that this group did not include Owen Bruce, the known enemy of Jonathan Rakehell. The enmity of Bruce, which spilled over onto Molinda, did nothing to discredit her. Bruce was not popular among his colleagues, largely because he made no attempt to hide the fact that his success to date had come from the smuggling of opium into China, an activity that was strictly forbidden by the Tao Kuang Emperor. Among the English, there was no real stigma attached to those who dealt in opium, but most men had the grace to keep quiet about their illegal activities. Bruce seemed to delight in his ability to ignore the laws of the Middle Kingdom with impunity.

A crisis erupted suddenly and unexpectedly one morning when Molinda was startled by the news that one of the Rakehell and Boynton warehouses had been broken into the previous night, and that silk worth about twenty thousand dollars in American money had been stolen. These bolts of cloth had been acquired from connections of the late Soong Chao, and Molinda was extremely distressed, partly because this was the first business she had done directly with people who had dealt with the legendary Soong, the father of Lai-tse lu Rakehell, and also because she knew that the company, struggling hard to keep its head above water, could ill afford the loss. She sent for Lo Fang, and he came to her office at once.

Wasting no words, he addressed her bluntly in the Cantonese dialect. "I have heard the unfortunate news," he said. "It comes at a bad time, I know, and I grieve for you."

"Be good enough," Molinda said, "to send a runner to Sir Cedric Poole, the deputy commandant of the constabulary. This theft is sufficiently large to call it to his personal attention."

Lo Fang made no move. "Are you sure you want to deal through this Englishman?" he demanded.

"Of course," she said. "His constabulary exists for the

121

purpose of catching thieves and bringing them to justice, as well as returning stolen goods.''

The giant drew a double-edged, bone-handled knife from his belt and turned it over and over in his hand. "Molinda," he said, "sounds like a woman of the West, but she is not of the West. She was born in the East and was trained in the East; therefore she should think as Easterners think.''

"I fail to grasp your meaning," she said, trying to control her impatience.

"There are better ways, surely, to catch and punish a thief, as well as to retrieve the silks that were stolen from under our noses, than by going to the British.''

Molinda thought that she understood. The Society of Oxen had played an important role in the guerrilla warfare waged during the Opium War against the British, and consequently it was only natural that Lo Fang should feel only contempt for his former enemies, so she decided to proceed cautiously. "Hong Kong belongs now to Great Britain," she said.

Lo Fang's face set in stubborn lines. "It was taken from the Middle Kingdom by force," he declared, "and those of my compatriots who live here want only the money of the British. They owe no fealty to the queen of the British, but are loyal to the Tao Kuang Emperor.''

"Nevertheless," Molinda insisted, "this is British territory, and the troops and sailors are stationed here for our protection. Please send a runner to Sir Cedric at once.''

Her tone brooked no arguments, so Lo Fang, in spite of his disapproval, bowed and did as he was bidden.

Less than an hour later, Sir Cedric Poole appeared in person at the Rakehell and Boynton office. Tall, tanned, and with no spare flesh on his taut, athletic frame, he was a veteran of the military and of police work; in spite of his long experience, he was still in his thirties.

Molinda saw a familiar light appear in his eyes as he gazed at her, but she was in no mood for admiration. She outlined the nature and extent of the theft.

Sir Cedric took notes as she talked, then asked a few questions. When she could not answer them all, she summoned the watchman who had discovered the merchandise missing. The man appeared quickly, as did Lo Fang, who said nothing as he loitered as inconspicuously as his bulk allowed in the background.

"I can make no promises that the missing goods will be recovered and returned, ma'am," Sir Cedric said. "We're just getting our constabulary organized here, and we don't have too many lines of communication running into the network operated by thieves. However, we shall do our very best for you."

"I'm very grateful," Molinda replied. "The loss comes at a time when my principals can least afford it."

Sir Cedric chatted about inconsequentials as he prepared to take his leave, and then suddenly he asked, "Are you engaged this evening?"

Molinda stiffened, and her face became masklike. She had thought this Englishman was more of a gentleman than most whom she had encountered, but she was afraid he belonged to the same breed. Because she was attractive and non-Western, they assumed that she lacked morals and treated her like an inmate of a waterfront brothel. "Why do you ask?" she demanded coldly.

"Lord Williamson, the new governor-general, is giving his first reception this evening at Government House, and if you haven't already met him and Lady Williamson, I thought this would give all of you a chance to become acquainted."

He was actually asking her to a formal Hong Kong reception! Hiding her surprise, she remained unyielding. "I'm not English, you know," she said.

"Indeed you aren't," Sir Cedric replied with an amiable smile, "but the Boyntons, who are part owners of your firm, are British subjects, and for that reason, if for no other, you'd be welcome. But I can't imagine a lady of your beauty and stature ever being other than welcome anywhere."

His candor and flattery melted her reserves, and she agreed to accompany him to the reception. The official residence of the governor-general was located high on the Peak, and a large crowd had filled the ballroom and spilled onto the lawns as well as the adjoining rooms by the time that Molinda and Sir Cedric Poole arrived. He looked dashing in a summerweight uniform on which he wore the insignia of a full colonel on his shoulders, and Molinda was even more ravishing than usual in a gown of clinging Indonesian silk.

Precisely as Sir Cedric had anticipated, Lord and Lady Williamson were charmed by the young lady from Bali and held up the reception line for a long time while they chatted with her. Before they released her, Lady Williamson obtained a commitment from Molinda to come to tea the following afternoon.

The unprecedented success guaranteed Molinda's social future in the new British Crown Colony. Her unqualified acceptance by the governor-general and his wife made her more than acceptable; she was someone much to be sought now. Consequently, various couples who heretofore had ignored her existence became very much aware of her, and she and Sir Cedric were constantly surrounded. Then one of the regimental bands struck up a lively air, and Sir Cedric rescued the young lady by escorting her to the ballroom dance floor.

He was unable to dance with her for very long, however. Other gentlemen, one after another, claimed the same privilege, and he yielded to them reluctantly but with good grace.

Among them was a short, slender man whose appearance was far more dapper than most, and as Molinda accompanied him to the dance floor, she recognized him as the Comte de Grasse, the scion of an old and distinguished French noble family, who was serving his government as commercial attaché in Hong Kong. They made several turns around the dance floor, and then the comte asked, "I wonder if I could prevail upon you to stroll with me outside on the grounds, Madame Molinda? I would like very much to talk to you, and it's difficult to have a serious discussion when dancing."

"Of course," she murmured as she took his arm and they headed outdoors.

The grounds at Government House were flower-laden, full

124

and lush, due in good part to the forbearance shown by the architect, who had left the jungle growth standing when he had cleared just enough land to build the mansion and outbuildings.

Molinda was reminded of similar jungles she had known in Indonesia, and she felt completely at home here as they walked down the narrow overgrown paths. The French nobleman, however, was accustomed to the highly cultivated and formal gardens of Europe, and obviously was ill at ease. He seemed relieved when they came to a clearing and could halt. He spread a large silk handkerchief on a rocky ledge so that Molinda could sit, and he took his place beside her. "It has come to my attention that your associates have cornered—so to speak—the market in black peppercorns."

Molinda's heart leaped, but she managed to conceal her reaction. Somehow the Frenchman had learned, even before she had received word, that Charles's mission had succeeded.

"I have just returned this morning to Hong Kong from a journey to Djakarta," the Frenchman said, "and unbelievable though this may appear, there is not one peppercorn for sale anywhere in the Dutch East Indies. I wonder if you happen to know what your firm is charging?"

Molinda smiled blandly. "I am afraid I am unable to cite you any prices, Comte," she said, "because there is no pepper available here. Whatever supplies we've accumulated have been sent to England, and I'm sure that the sales will be conducted there by Charles Boynton."

"I see." He bit his upper lip nervously. "Would it be asking too much to put in a good word for me, Madame? My own markets are crying for pepper, and I'll pay any price for them."

"I urge you to communicate with Charles Boynton in London," Molinda said. "He probably hasn't arrived there as yet, but he should be due any day now."

He nodded. "I shall follow your advice, and I'm very grateful to you." Suddenly he slid an arm around her bare shoulders and tried to pull her to him.

125

Molinda instinctively resisted and drew back. The Comte de Grasse made the mistake of trying to use force and proved to be stronger than he looked.

From somewhere on her person, Molinda drew a short, double-edged knife with a very sharp point, a curved blade, and a jeweled hilt. She unhesitatingly raised it to the Frenchman's throat and delicately pricked his skin with it. "If I were you," she said, "I'd think again. I can assure you I won't hesitate to kill you unless you release me instantly."

He dropped his hand from her shoulders and, shrinking away from her, stared at her open-mouthed. It was plain that she meant precisely what she said, and looking into her calm violet eyes, he knew that if he wanted to live, he would obey her promptly.

"I shall notify Charles Boynton of your interest in our pepper," she said. "For the sake of any future business relationships that we may have, Comte, let me make it very clear that I am not for sale at any price. I tolerate no personal advances of any kind. Now if you will, be good enough to return to the party. I'll follow in due course." She continued to grip the knife as she spoke to him, and she held it raised, ready to strike.

The Comte de Grasse continued to retreat. He had completely lost face with her, as he well knew, and there was no way he could compensate for his blunder. Rather than compound his error, he bowed stiffly from the waist, turned on his heel, and then stalked off through the heavy foliage toward the Government House.

Molinda was startled when she heard a deep, rumbling noise only a few feet from her. She took a fresh grip on the knife.

To her amazement Lo Fang appeared out of the underbrush, and she saw that he was laughing heartily. She stared at him in wonder, shaking her head.

The majordomo managed to control himself. "Lo Fang," he said, "owes a thousand apologies to Molinda. I followed you here, thinking you might need protection. Little did I guess that you are as competent as the deadliest of the female

126

tigers of the deep interior of the Middle Kingdom. Soon all will know what the Frenchman has just learned."

"I hope you're right, Lo Fang," she replied, "and in any event, thank you for your concern."

He nodded amiably. "I wish," he said, "that Molinda were as wise in other ways as she is in protecting herself. But no matter, Lo Fang will continue to watch over her."

There was no time now to persuade him to enlarge on his cryptic comment. She knew Sir Cedric Poole would be waiting for her to return, and she owed it to him to go to him.

The rest of the evening passed without incident. Sir Cedric remained the perfect gentleman, and when, at the end of the evening's festivities, he escorted Molinda to her own home, farther down the Peak, she was genuinely sorry that the evening had come to an end. On sudden impulse, she invited him to dine with her at her house the following week, and she was rewarded by the smile of genuine pleasure that spread across his face. When she was alone, it occurred to her that she was healing from the hurt of widowhood. She was making no premature predictions for her long-range future; she knew too much for that. But she had a right to feel that the evening had been anything but a waste of time.

The following morning, she emerged early from her house to the waiting open carriage, and her driver went directly to the warehouse and office complex of Rakehell and Boynton behind their docks. As she was about to enter the office building, she saw a knot of Chinese workers gathered inside the open door of one of the warehouses, all of them seemingly talking at once. Curiosity led her to them, and she was annoyed because she could not understand what they were saying.

Most of the Chinese who had come to Hong Kong to work came from Kwangsi Province, which lay to the northwest of the Crown Colony. Molinda marveled at the intricacies of Chinese life. Although Cantonese was spoken almost as universally as the upper-class Mandarin, especially in trade circles, Kwangsi—although just across the provincial border from Canton and Hong Kong—was another world, with a language completely its own. As she approached the knot of gesticulating, jabbering men, Molinda wondered how long it would take her to master all of the many tongues of the Chinese language. The written Chinese was one language understood everywhere, as was the Mandarin used by government officials and scholars. To her positive knowledge, however, there were at least nine separate and distinct regional dialects, none of which sounded even remotely like any other.

The workers saw her approaching, and two or three of them tried to stop her. They spoke more loudly, more forcibly, and actually tried to block her progress physically.

Molinda was in no mood for the many nuances of Chinese customs and behavior. She impatiently pushed through the knot of men and entered the building, unexpectedly finding herself in the area from which the bolts of cloth had been stolen.

Suddenly she halted and gasped, her blood congealing in her veins. Directly ahead, resting on a shelf that had contained the bolts of silk that had been stolen, rested a human head.

All she knew was that it was the head of a Chinese male and was smeared with drying blood. Feeling faint, she averted her gaze. All at once she heard someone behind her bellowing commands angrily, and the workers scattered.

Lo Fang came up to her, took hold of her shoulder, and propelled her away from the scene, forcibly directing her toward her office. A secretary brought her a cup of very hot tea, for which she was eternally grateful. She sat behind her desk, sipping the tea, and ultimately recovered sufficiently to ask, "What did I see, Lo Fang?"

The majordomo sounded abject. "The sight was not intended for the eyes of Molinda," he said. "The head of a notorious thief was left on display to teach the many workers who are paid wages by Molinda to remember to curb their greed and to accept their own pay. When they steal, they will lose their lives and their heads."

She discovered her breathing was returning to normal. "But what—"

"If Molinda asks no questions," he replied, "Lo Fang will not be obliged to answer them. Then, when the Englishman who has become Molinda's friend arrives, she will not be able to answer the many questions he will ask her."

"Sir Cedric Poole is coming here?" she asked.

"He has been notified of the death of a thief," he replied.

"How do you know he was a thief?" she demanded.

He remained very calm. "Because the silk stolen from our warehouse was found in the place where he was hiding. It has been recovered, and as soon as the shelves are scrubbed clean, the silk will be returned to its rightful place."

"I—I don't understand," she murmured.

Lo Fang's quiet shrug indicated that he had no intention of offering any explanation of events.

All at once Molinda realized what had taken place. At Lo Fang's instigation, his Society of Oxen had conducted its own investigation and had found the thief or thieves responsible for taking the bolts of silk from the warehouse. So they had retrieved the stolen goods and, in the process, had executed the leader of the band responsible for the criminal act.

Lo Fang excused himself, hurried out of her office, and returning a few moments later, looked much relieved. "All is well now," he said blandly.

"You mean the head is—is no longer in our warehouse?"

He nodded and smiled. "It has been taken to the place where it will do the most good," he said.

She was puzzled, and even though she knew it was unwise to ask questions, she could not resist the temptation. "Where?"

"The thief," Lo Fang replied, "did not act on his own initiative. Bolts of silk mean nothing to a man of that class. He has no use for such merchandise, and he has no way to sell it and acquire money. Why, then, did he steal it?"

Molinda was accustomed by now to Lo Fang's rhetorical questions, and she calmly waited for him to continue.

Suddenly a low, deep chuckle rumbled up within Lo Fang. "The head of the miscreant," he said, "has been taken where it belongs, to the person we know is behind the theft. The head rests now on the desk of Owen Bruce. He will be embarrassed when the constables inquire about his connection with the case. He will deny any connection, to be sure, but the suspicion will be planted in the minds of Sir Cedric and his men. Such taints cannot be easily removed, just as the blood from the severed head of the thief seeps into the wood of Bruce's desk and stains it for all time.''

Sir Alan and Lady Boynton always followed the rules of propriety and polite behavior, so they welcomed the Baroness Erika von Klausner as a guest in their home. Erika wanted to take no chances of having her true purpose revealed, so instead of being accompanied by her "servant," she sent Reinhardt Braun off to a small, inexpensive hotel with orders to remain there until further notice.

So Braun passed his days and nights drinking and wenching, relieving the tedium of his unending orgy only by attending occasional concerts. He was especially fond of the oratorios of George Frederick Handel, the German-born composer who had migrated to England the previous century, and whom the British regarded as their own. Erika, to whom Braun reported weekly, marveled that a merciless killer, a man completely lacking in conscience, should care so much about good music. But she was too busy to concern herself with her associate's affairs. She had matters of her own to attend to.

Aware of the reserve toward her demonstrated by Sir Alan and Lady Boynton, she strove hard to overcome it. Exerting her greatest charm at all times, she succeeded in sweeping away their resistance until both of them became her staunch admirers.

Elizabeth Boynton was far easier to handle. As a younger girl at boarding school, Elizabeth always had admired Erika, and the battle was already half won.

Erika soon discovered that it was absurdly easy to nudge Elizabeth into talking about Jonathan Rakehell. It was obvious, from the first time that his name came up, that Elizabeth was very much in love with him, and she reminded Erika of the schoolgirl she had been as she went on and on about him.

So, saying nothing other than occasionally guiding the

conversational channels, Erika learned all there was to know about Jonathan's two tragic marriages, both of which had ended in the deaths of his wives. She learned his personality traits and his foibles, at least as Elizabeth saw them, and she also gleaned a great deal about his business affairs.

She discovered, too, that Elizabeth, theoretically at least, was eligible to marry him, inasmuch as they were not actually blood relatives. Elizabeth was the daughter of Sir Alan Boynton's partner and his wife, who had been killed in a carriage accident when she had been a very small girl. She had been adopted by the Boyntons, but Sir Alan had scrupulously kept her business interests separate from his own, and as a result she owned a considerable block of Rakehell and Boynton stock. Presumably, when the company prospered again, she would be an heiress of consequence in her own right.

Elizabeth, for her part, found her former schoolmate to be a perfect, sympathetic listener and hence grew very fond of her. Erika was the one person to whom she could pour out her heart about Jonathan without getting a lecture or advice.

The only member of the Boynton family who looked at Erika with critical eyes was Ruth. Having acquired sophistication and poise since she had married Charles and had been living in London, Ruth privately thought that the young German woman used cosmetics too lavishly and dressed too flamboyantly. She might be a baroness, Ruth told herself, but she didn't look like a lady, and she didn't act like one, either.

Sir Ronald Weybright, very much smitten, called at the Boynton house in Belgravia daily to see Elizabeth, and Ruth noted privately that Erika, who seemed bored, was not above flirting with him subtly. It was an unwritten rule, in Ruth's opinion, that no lady ever flirted with a gentleman who was attached to her hostess.

Then, unexpectedly, Charles and little David came home, arriving in London at the head of a flotilla of clipper ships, all of them loaded with as many sacks of black peppercorns as they could carry.

Ruth was delighted beyond measure to see her stepson again, and David made it plain that he had missed her very

131

badly during their separation as well. He tried to be brave, but wept when she embraced him, and Ruth vowed privately that she would not be separated from him again until he became considerably older and could better tolerate being away from home.

Charles was distracted by business, and immediately after his arrival went into a long meeting with his father behind closed doors. They were discussing pepper, as the ladies gleaned at the dinner table, and even before the final course was served, Charles raced off to the Boynton shipyard in Southwark, across the River Thames from London.

Although Charles was completely absorbed in preparing for the sale of his pepper, Ruth still girded for trouble. Erika von Klausner, she knew, was just the type who would appeal to her husband. She was very attractive, her clothes and manner making no secret of her blatant appeal to the opposite sex, and Ruth felt certain that trouble was brewing.

To her astonishment, nothing of the sort happened. Erika was chaste and proper, almost prim in Charles's company, and at no time did she indicate the slightest interest in him as a man. Ruth had no way of knowing the truth of the situation: Erika had sized up Charles at their first meeting, had recognized his weaknesses for the opposite sex instantly, and had decided that she would keep her distance from him. Not only was he already married to a sharp-eyed woman who could cause trouble for her, but he was Jonathan Rakehell's cousin, and as such was to be strictly avoided.

All Ruth knew was that she had been somewhat mistaken in her estimation, and she wondered whether she should completely revise her opinions of Erika. Perhaps she had been too harsh in her judgments, she thought, and she knew that in order to be fair she had to give the young German woman a chance to demonstrate her real worth.

Erika was well satisfied with the results of her strategy. She sensed Ruth's softer, more tolerant attitude toward her, and she was glad that Charles was too busy, too preoccupied at the moment to pay much attention to her. Perhaps she would have her hands full with him later, but she would wait until the problem became acute before she addressed herself to it.

Charles, meantime, was devoting his full attention to the sale of the peppercorns that he had loaded into the holds and other available spaces on the fleet of Rakehell and Boynton clipper ships. He deliberately allowed nature to take its course. Saying nothing about the cargo he had brought with him, he let the word seep out that the sale of pepper was now forbidden in Djakarta, the world's only source of the spice.

Precisely as he had anticipated, the startling news spread like wildfire through London's financial markets. Waiting another twenty-four hours and timing his move as precisely as he would have timed a thrust at an opponent in a duel, Charles waited until after the news leaked out about the unavailability of pepper. Then, but only then, did he reveal in casual conversation that all was not lost, that he had brought back a fairly considerable quantity with him.

He could scarcely curb his excitement when he was inundated with requests for purchases. Some would-be buyers were so eager to obtain quantities of the black peppercorns that they came to his offices on the Southwark waterfront and presented him with bank drafts for impressive sums of money. He refused to accept any of the payments, however, much to his father's consternation.

"Are you mad?" Sir Alan demanded. "You've gone to a great deal of trouble to establish your supply of pepper as virtually the sole quantity available on earth. Now you're refusing to accept very large sums of money for it."

Charles grinned at him. "I think you'll find, Papa," he said, "that we'll earn far more by doing things my way. I'm going to spread the word this afternoon that I'm going to hold an auction and will sell to the highest bidder. I'm going to establish a floor price of one guinea per pound of peppercorns, and anyone who doesn't want to begin the bidding for that figure had best stay home."

Sir Alan whistled under his breath, "Never," he said, "has pepper sold for such exorbitant sums of money."

Charles nodded cheerfully. "Never before has the world supply been limited almost entirely to what we have under lock and key in our warehouse. This is a unique situation, and I want to take full advantage of it."

"Do you think you can?" his father asked dubiously. "Don't you suppose that the potential buyers will rebel and refuse to pay your price?"

Charles shook his head emphatically. "In our own time," he said, "the world's palate has grown accustomed to pepper. I daresay that if you made a tour around Belgravia Square, you'd find pepper mills on every table in every house. I'm sure a survey would indicate that there's pepper on the table in every restaurant and in every boardinghouse in all of London, and we're speaking now of only one city. Pepper has become a staple, a way of life in the Western world, and the Dutch have become very wealthy because they have realized it. Now it's our turn to capitalize on what's become a public habit."

Sir Alan stared at his son for a few moments and then shrugged. "I won't argue with you, because I really don't understand such tactics, Charles. I'm the first to admit that I'm old-fashioned and far behind the times, so I'll stand aside and let you run this operation as you see fit."

Charles happily accepted the challenge. The auction was set for two days later in the boardroom of the Rakehell and Boynton building, and Charles knew that success was assured when so many gentlemen showed up for it that the meeting had to be moved to a far larger room.

Men in top hats of silk or beaver rubbed shoulders with anxious wholesale grocers and with representatives of banks, who were prepared to speculate. A gasp rose from the assemblage when Charles, who was in charge of the auction himself, announced the quantity of pepper for sale. "At first glance, gentlemen," he said, "this may seem like an inordinately large amount. Actually it's pitifully small. This is the only pepper for sale in all the world." With this he produced the document ordering the embargo, and a Rakehell and Boynton clerk passed the paper around the room.

A gentleman wearing a short cloak and carrying a gold-handled cane raised his voice. "May I ask, Mr. Boynton, how long it will be before the Dutch in Java remove their embargo and permit the sale of peppercorns again?"

Charles worded his reply carefully. The embargo would end when he notified the Fat Dutchman that his auction was completed. Until then it would remain in full force. "I'm afraid I can't answer your question, sir," he replied blandly. "The officials of the Netherlands East Indies and of the Dutch East Indies Company don't take me into their confidence. Your guess is as good as mine."

A number of men in the assemblage groaned. A tall man in a handsome beaver hat worn squarely on his head was the next to raise his hand. "Not that it much matters, and not that it affects the practical situation, but I wonder, Mr. Boynton, if you could tell us how it happens that the Dutch decided to prohibit the further sale of peppercorns?"

Charles was prepared for this question, and he was able to answer with the partial truth. "I assume, as many of you have," he said, "that the farmers of Java and other islands in the Dutch East Indies became a trifle too enthusiastic in their growth of pepper and that the market was flooded. The authorities may have decided on this move in order to raise the overall price and to sustain it at a high level. If so, they've certainly succeeded."

"And perhaps you can also tell us," another man in a top hat called out, "how it happens that Rakehell and Boynton ships have acquired all the available pepper."

Charles was skating on very thin ice, but he handled the problem with his typical aplomb. "As you all know, Rakehell and Boynton has had long and honorable business dealings in the East, and has more clippers there and more business contacts than any other shipping company. As a result, we were fortunate to have a number of ships in Djakarta before the embargo was put into effect. I won't deny that Rakehell and Boynton will profit from this situation, but before anyone calls the floor price of one guinea per pound of peppercorns excessive, let me just say that we've had great expenses in

135

extricating the bags of pepper from Djakarta and in transporting them all the way to England in the fastest ships that sail the high seas, so our own expenses have been very much higher than they usually are.'' He saw men in the audience nodding, and studying their faces, he knew they were accepting the conditions he had described.

"If you don't mind, we'll begin the auction," he said. "The pepper has been divided into one-hundred-pound lots, and I'll now hear bids for the first lot." The response was prompt.

"I'll bid a hundred and twenty guineas," someone called.

Charles's heart leaped. Not only had his outrageous floor price been accepted, but the bidding was starting at an even higher figure. Somehow he managed to keep a straight face. Excitement mounted, and the price of peppercorns soared to astronomical heights, as lot after lot of pepper was auctioned off, each one selling for much more than Charles had ever imagined possible. As the *Times* of London would comment in its financial section the following day, a bag of peppercorns truly had become "black gold."

The average price paid for the cargo, Charles told his father after the auction, as he went through the bank drafts and promissary notes he had collected, was close to two guineas per pound, far more than he had dared to hope in his wildest dreams.

Sir Alan was thunderstruck. "It strikes me," he said, "that the buyers lost their wits, but I certainly am not objecting. I can't remember an occasion ever when we earned such a vast sum of money all at once."

Charles was making rapid calculation on a sheet of foolscap. "As I see it," he said, "this should postpone our financial crisis for at least six months. We've won a half-year in our battle to turn the tide."

Sir Alan beamed at him and clasped his hand. "I'm not only grateful, son," he said, "but I'm proud of you. This maneuver will be remembered for a long time to come." His voice became choked, and he blew his nose vigorously. "I've got to go at once to write the good news to Jeremiah

Rakehell," he said, and ducked out the door. He recovered his equilibrium by the time he and Charles returned to the house in Belgravia at the end of the day, but his mood was still euphoric. Before dinner, in the presence of his wife, daughter, and daughter-in-law, as well as Erika von Klausner, he praised Charles lavishly, which was contrary to his lifelong custom. Then, at the dinner table, he insisted that they drink the most expensive of French champagnes to celebrate the occasion.

A festive atmosphere reigned at the dinner table, and afterward, acting on impulse, Charles insisted that they all go to the Drury Lane Theatre to attend a comedy that David Garrick had made a London favorite almost a century earlier. After the play, they stopped at an inn for glasses of wine and a late supper.

This was the first active social life in which Charles had engaged since his return from the Far East, and he was in such high spirits that Ruth dared to hope that a significant change for the better had taken place in his attitudes.

Until now, ever since he had come home, they had been separated by a wall, invisible but impenetrable. Repeatedly, Ruth had tried to climb it or tear it down, but her efforts had met consistent failure. She had been silent when Charles was silent, talkative when he seemed in the mood for conversation, yet nothing seemed to help. Worst of all, there had been no intimacy between them since they had been reunited. They had occupied separate bedrooms for a long time, although prior to Charles's departure for the Orient, he had, for all practical purposes, moved back into Ruth's bedroom. Now, however, he was distant to the degree that they might have been total strangers. He was fully dressed when she last saw him at night and was completely dressed when she first laid eyes on him in the morning. He had made no attempt to enter her chamber, and the few necessary gestures of intimacy in which he engaged—kissing her on arrival or departure, for example—had been perfunctory or strained.

Now, however, she took heart. The Charles who was celebrating the successful sale of the peppercorns was not the preoccupied, harried man who had been so remote. He laughed and chatted with Elizabeth, he was very pleasant if a trifle stiff with Erika, and he joked at length with his mother. His reactions to Ruth were still tentative, to be sure, but at least he seemed to be in a receptive mood.

More determined than ever to put Jonathan Rakehell out of her mind and devote herself to Charles, she went out of her way to be loving and accommodating. She was attentive to him throughout dinner and the evening, she clung to his arm when they went from one place to the next, and she actually flirted with him as though he were some man other than her husband. Charles gradually warmed to her attentions, and as they sat together, squeezed into a corner of the family carriage on the ride home, she dared to hope that the long freeze in their relations had come to an end.

Thus having led herself to believe that the breach between them was healed, she was all the more stunned and hurt by his actions after they arrived back at the house in Belgravia.

They ascended the staircase together to the third floor, but then Charles, instead of accompanying his wife to her own chamber, issued some vague, general good nights and then headed down the corridor toward the room that he had been occupying alone.

Mortified and angry, Ruth retired to her own quarters. There she undressed slowly and then peered for a long time at her reflection in the mirror. Granted that she was a mature woman in her thirties now, but her breasts were still high and firm, her waist remained tiny, and she had no spare, flabby flesh anywhere on her body. She had never regarded herself as a great beauty, but certainly her figure was a match for those of Elizabeth and Erika, who were a half-generation behind her.

Still seething, she attended mechanically to her nightly routines, removing her cosmetics and donning her nightgown. Charles's conduct was inexplicable, and she knew the gulf that separated them would become too wide to cross unless she made a supreme effort. So, on sudden impulse, she donned a negligee and slippers and went through the intervening dressing rooms to Charles's bedchamber, thus avoiding the need to go out into the corridor, where others of the family might see her.

Charles, clad in pajamas and a dressing gown, sat in an easy chair near the windows smoking an Indonesian *cigarro* and sipping a tall drink. He looked up at her in surprise.

"I guess," Ruth said evasively, "I didn't really want the party to end just yet."

"By all means, sit down," he invited her, his tone impersonal. "Would you care for a drink?"

She shook her head. "No thanks," she replied. "I've had my share and more tonight." She lowered herself into a chair opposite him. "I just want to repeat privately what I've already said publicly. Your peppercorn scheme was a truly marvelous idea, and your execution was brilliant. You have every right to be as pleased with yourself as all the rest of us, including your admiring wife, are pleased."

He waved a hand deprecatingly. "I have my reward in pounds sterling, and money talks. As I get older, I realize it more and more. The Dutchman thinks of nothing but money, and I daresay he's right."

Ruth seized the opening that he gave her. "Is money the subject that preys so constantly on your mind?"

Her question startled him, and he shrugged. "I didn't know I was all that obvious about it," he said.

"Something has kept you preoccupied," she said.

He looked as though he didn't know what she was talking about.

"I'll spell it out for you," Ruth said, "although I find it mortifying and degrading to do so. You and I were separated for almost a full year, Charles."

"It was business necessity that kept us apart," he interjected quickly. "Don't think that I deliberately avoided being with you."

"That possibility," she replied, "has never crossed my mind, and even now when you mention it, I reject it totally. No, Charles, I have no doubt whatsoever that legitimate business considerations kept us separated. However, we're

139

together again. You've been home for almost a full week, and during that time, you haven't come to me one night." She had to fight to keep her voice from trembling. "I could have swallowed my pride, I suppose, and come to your bed myself, but I couldn't bring myself to be that forward."

He nodded, his features revealing none of his thoughts.

"As your wife," Ruth said, "I believe I deserve to know whether you want me. If you do, you'll have to prove it. If you don't, let me know, and we can arrange somehow to go our separate ways."

Charles looked stricken. "There's never been a divorce in our family," he declared.

"Divorce—or annulment—are the farthest things from my mind," Ruth said. "I seek neither, and I would accept neither as a solution to our problems. What I'm getting at is that if there's nothing between us anymore, I have a right to know. It isn't fair to be giving love and to be getting none in return."

"You're quite right," he said, "and I agree with the points you're making. What you fail to take into consideration is that I had the whole peppercorn scheme in mind when I came home. I've won a minimum of a half-year breathing space for Rakehell and Boynton, while we try to adjust and put the company solidly on its feet again. My mind was filled with peppercorns to the exclusion of everything else."

"I can accept that," Ruth said, "but I don't see why it should be necessary to remind you that the battle of the peppercorns, so to speak, has ended in a victory for you. It's behind you now, and you have no need to think of it further. I've been hoping your thoughts would turn to me."

Charles struggled for an appropriate reply. "A man of my age is no longer an impetuous young boy," he said. "It's not that my desires are any less than they were, but it takes time to transfer one's thoughts from one subject to another. The battle of the peppercorns, as you call it, has been won so recently that I hope you'll give me ample breathing space to recover my wits and think of what I want next."

It seemed to Ruth that he was being evasive, that his answer lacked substance, and that he had invented it for a lack of anything better to say. Her hurt had been smoldering within her, and suddenly the flames of anger that had been pent up within her burst into the open. "Tell me something," she said, "did you have any affairs during this last separation of ours?" Even as she asked the question, she knew it was a tactical error, and she wished she could withdraw it.

Charles, however, could not discern what she was truly feeling. He was looking at a thoroughly aroused, contemptuous woman, whose glare indicated a total lack of regard for him and his feelings.

His common sense told him that if he wanted to heal the rift with Ruth—and he knew he very much wanted to heal it—he should lie. It would be so easy to deny his liaison in Djakarta with the Fat Dutchman's attractive slave girl, but a sense of bravado, prodded by his deep feelings of guilt, impelled him to say, "I prefer not to lie to you. Yes, I did engage in an affair."

He wanted to add that the girl had meant nothing to him, that he had not been emotionally involved with her in any way, and that his relationship with her had no real significance. He had bedded her when he felt erotic urges, just as he enjoyed eating a beefsteak and fried potatoes when he was hungry.

Ruth, however, failed to grasp this, and would have had difficulty understanding it even with help. All she knew was that her guess had been right, and she attributed his indifference to an interest in another woman.

No wonder he had not made love to her! No wonder he ignored her, behaving as though she were a total stranger!

Crushed by his candid admission, Ruth turned away quickly and, clutching her negligee around her, fled to her own bedchamber. There she securely locked the door behind her, and only then did she dissolve in a flood of helpless tears.

# II

Relations between Ruth and Charles Boynton degenerated swiftly, and only the proprieties and a mutual sense of responsibility for little David's welfare kept the couple together. In private they had nothing to say to each other and consequently avoided being alone. In the presence of other members of the family, their pride took hold of them, and they went through the motions of maintaining a relationship, with neither in any way revealing that they were merely keeping up a façade.

One evening, like so many others that had preceded it, the Boyntons adjourned to the informal sitting room for after-dinner coffee. There Sir Alan and his son discussed business matters, while Jessica divided her time between their conversation and the lighter chatter of the younger women. The routine was broken, however, when Sir Ronald Weybright came calling on Elizabeth. She had grown tired of the flirtatious games she had been playing with Ronnie, and she found that rather than forgetting Jonathan Rakehell, he was more on her mind than ever. Thus, she had no desire to be alone with her suitor, although he would have vastly preferred it, and she simply asked him to join the group. So he did.

Lady Boynton saw an opportunity to leave gracefully, and soon she and Sir Alan took their departure, leaving the younger people to their own devices.

Charles poured himself a stiff drink and offered a round to

the others, but only Erika was interested. The talk that followed was general, with Sir Ronald asking Charles innumerable questions about the Far East, in which all upper-class Englishmen were very interested. Charles had covered the same ground many times previously, but tried conscientiously to reply honestly and at length to each question.

Elizabeth and Ruth had heard the same recital many times, and both were bored, scarcely able to conceal their feelings. At least, Ruth thought, she was spared the necessity of smiling brightly at Charles and replying to his statements.

Erika was equally bored but did not show it. She intended to learn about the Orient in due time, but she would do it by paying a personal visit to the cities of the Middle Kingdom and Indonesia. While pretending to be listening with rapt attention to what Charles was saying, she amused herself by flirting with Ronnie Weybright, who sat adjacent to her. She leaned against him so delicately that no one else was aware of what she was doing, and she pressed her shapely leg against his.

Ronnie, however, was interested exclusively in Elizabeth, and wanted no part of the flame-haired baroness from the free-port city of Hamburg. He inched away from her, thinking that her close proximity to him was accidental.

As Charles spoke, he gradually became conscious of Erika, however. In fact, he had discussed the Far East so many times that he was somewhat bored by his own recital, and his ennui was relieved largely by the presence of the very alluring German woman, who was listening to him with such seemingly rapt attention.

After Charles had held forth for about an hour on the subject of the Far East, Elizabeth's boredom got the better of her, and she suggested to Sir Ronald that they go out for a walk. He readily agreed, and the young couple took their leave.

Ruth took advantage of the breakup of the little party to announce that she was tired and intended to retire. David had a head cold, which she insisted on attending herself, and that meant that she would be awakened during the night. So she withdrew, too, leaving her husband alone with Erika.

Erika was restless, and although she had reconciled herself to the need to be on good behavior for a protracted period of time, she nevertheless wanted relief from the orderly existence that the Boynton family led. What was more, she was eager to forge ahead in her campaign to snare Jonathan Rakehell.

She deliberately held her glass in her hand after she had finished her drink, and at last Charles took the hint. "Will you have another?" he asked politely.

Erika pretended to hesitate. "If you will," she said demurely, "I'll gladly keep you company." She watched with approval as Charles prepared a moderate drink for her and gave himself a very stiff one. They chatted aimlessly for a time, and ultimately Erika asked, "Are you planning on making a visit to America one of these days?"

"As a matter of fact, I am," Charles replied. "We're all going because we have some urgent business matters to discuss with our partners in the American end of our family."

"I envy you," Erika replied, deliberately drinking quickly.

Charles matched her swallow for swallow without realizing that was what he was doing. "How could you possible envy me?" he wanted to know.

"I've always wanted to see the New World for myself," the baroness replied. "I've been curious about it all my life." Charles smiled as he rose to his feet and again refilled their glasses.

"That's an easy ambition to fill," Charles replied. "If you can spare the time, come with us to New London. I'm sure the Rakehells will have ample room to put you up and will be delighted to have you."

This was almost too good to be true, but she played her role perfectly. "You don't think I'd be imposing on total strangers?"

"They're not strangers," Charles said as he dropped to the divan beside her. "You're a friend of ours, and anyone who is close to the Boyntons is automatically close to the Rakehells."

145

"You make it sound so attractive, Charles," she said breathlessly, "that I don't think I can resist the temptation. If I may, I'll accept the invitation now, before you change your mind."

"I won't change my mind, I assure you," he said. She raised her glass to him and drank.

He did the same. Erika's caution, already dulled by liquor, deserted her. She had an opportunity now to create some excitement, and she couldn't resist taking a chance. She leaned slightly toward him, artfully exposing her breasts beneath her low-cut gown, and her full lips parted as she gazed soulfully at him.

Even if Charles had been completely sober, it was doubtful that he could have resisted the German woman's advances. As it was, the liquor had heightened his sexual urges, and all he knew was that the baroness was exceptionally attractive and that she was available.

She sat now, looking at Charles and not moving. She made herself a wager that he would reach for her within ten seconds, and she did not even have to wait that long. He drew her into his arms, and his mouth sought hers hungrily. Erika knew beyond any doubt that if she wished it, they would have intercourse here and now on the sitting room divan.

Charles's grip tightened, and he could not prevent his hands from roaming. The front door opened and shut in the distance, and Erika heard the sounds of the voices of Elizabeth and Sir Ronald. That interruption brought her abruptly to her senses. An affair with Charles would serve no practical purpose. She would be sure to earn the enmity of his wife, with whom she had an armed truce, and she would jeopardize her chances of attracting his cousin and partner, Jonathan Rakehell. She would be very wise if she left well enough alone.

Even this move required finesse, but she was equal to the gesture. She extricated herself from his grasp, then stood and smoothed her skirt. "I know we're attracted to each other, my dear," she murmured, "but we must stop this before we go too far. We can't afford to forget that you're a married man."

The reminder of his wife had the precise effect on Charles that Erika had intended, and his hands dropped to his sides. He behaved in a typically British manner thereafter, retiring into a shell, apologizing to her rather cryptically, and withdrawing after a curt good-night bow. Erika had good cause to be satisfied with herself: she had halted her affair with Charles before it had started, and had in no way placed her potential relationship with Jonathan Rakehell in any jeopardy.

On Sunday, when the whole family dined together at noon, a custom that Jessica Rakehell Boynton had brought to England with her from America, Charles tried to make amends to his wife. They happened to leave their bedchambers at the same moment, with David accompanying Ruth.

"You're the very people I wanted to see," Charles said, trying to hide his discomfort. "You haven't been home to America in a very long time, Ruth, and as for you, David, I know that you'd rather be with your Cousin Julian than anything else in the world. So I propose that you both come with me when I sail to New London next week."

David crowed with glee. Ruth was pleased, but didn't want her husband to know it. "That's very kind of you, Charles," she said demurely. "We will go with you, and thank you very much." She went ahead of him down the stairs to the dining room.

As they took their places at the dinner table, Charles addressed his parents. "I assume," he said, "that you'll be coming to New London with me when I go to America next week."

"By all means," Sir Alan answered. "We have to decide what to do next after we've exhausted the funds that you so cleverly raised with your sale of pepper."

Erika felt it appropriate to renew her claim. "I hope you have not forgotten, Charles, that you've offered me the opportunity also of fulfilling a lifelong dream of going to America."

"I haven't forgotten," Charles told her as he salted the soup made from tomato essence that he had brought with him from Canton. The Boyntons were virtually the only family in England privileged to be eating tomato soup.

Elizabeth had become alert. Here was her opportunity to see Jonathan Rakehell again, and she didn't intend to miss the chance. "I hope that you're planning to take me, too," she said.

Charles couldn't resist the opportunity to tease her. "I couldn't imagine any reason you'd want to go to America," he said.

Elizabeth promptly demonstrated that she was becoming an adult and that it did not pay to taunt her. "As it happens," she said, "I have a block of stock in the Rakehell and Boynton Company in my own right that my natural father left me. Papa has always voted that stock on my behalf, but I'm old enough now to attend to my own affairs."

Sir Alan chuckled appreciatively.

Lady Boynton laughed aloud. "Good for you, dear," she said. "I daresay that puts you in your place, Charles."

Charles raised his wineglass to his sister. "Remind me," he said, "not to play a game of chess with you. I don't think I'd stand very much chance of winning."

The dinner hour was borrowed from America, but the menu was typically English. The tomato soup, a novelty that created considerable discussion, was followed by a roast of beef served with Yorkshire pudding, roasted potatoes, and onions and carrots that had been done in the beef pan. A salad of several kinds of lettuce and cucumbers, still known in England as Italian greens, followed, and in the last course Jessica revealed her American antecedents by serving American-style apple pie with a slice of mild cheese on each piece. David immediately asked for a second helping.

"If I were you," Ruth said, gently rebuking, "I'd eat what is on my plate first, and then we'll see if there's enough for you to have more."

The little boy nodded somberly. Sir Alan, sitting at the head of the table, caught his grandson's eye and winked.

148

David, assured now of a second piece of pie, could not resist grinning but had the good sense to lower his head so no one would see his triumphant expression.

As it was an extraordinarily fine day, Charles suggested to Ruth after they adjourned from the dinner table that they take a carriage ride to Hyde Park with David. There the boy could sail his handsome new sailboat, an exact replica of a Rakehell and Boynton clipper, which one of the ship carpenters had made as a gift.

It was a short ride to Hyde Park from the house in Belgravia, and when the carriage let them off, they strolled down the tree-lined paths to the lake known as the Serpentine. Charles bought some ice cream from one of the numerous vendors in the park, and he and Ruth sat quietly on a bench, eating their ice cream while David sailed his boat.

The sun was warm, and Ruth became lost in her thoughts as she watched the bright white sails of the children's boats floating on the sparkling water. She didn't even notice when Charles rose from the bench and went to the assistance of a young nursemaid who had gotten stuck with her perambulator on one of the gravel paths. Charles helped the woman push the carriage to the broad, paved walk, then struck up a conversation with her, his eyes taking in the full figure of the woman in the tight-fitting nursemaid's uniform.

Ruth had almost begun to doze off, when she was wakened by the shouts of children at play. David was sailing his boat along with those of some other boys, and Ruth began to look around for Charles, finally seeing him off to the distance with the nursemaid. She watched as he talked to her, and she noticed the way he looked at her, and suddenly all the months of anger and frustration came to a head. She simply could not take any more of Charles and his flirtations and philandering.

Rising quickly, she went to David and told him they were going home. The little boy had no idea what was wrong, but he saw that his mother was very upset, and he complied silently, collecting his sailboat and walking beside her as she headed out of the park.

"What about Papa?" he asked, running to catch up with her.

"Your father will find his own way," she said, trying hard to control her emotions.

The pair walked hastily along the path. Tears were threatening to come to Ruth's eyes, but she vowed not to cry. She had made up her mind once and for all: she was going to leave Charles. She didn't know exactly where she would go, and she had no idea what she would do, but she did know she could no longer live with him and pretend to be happily married, despite her earlier resolve.

Meanwhile, Charles had said good day to the governess and was returning to Ruth, when he noticed that his wife and son were missing. He scanned the park in every direction, and then he saw them in the distance. They were heading out of the park, and he ran after them, calling Ruth's name.

Ruth clasped David's hand and began walking even faster, fighting the tears.

Charles, breathless, finally caught up with them. "Ruth," he said, "what are you doing? Where are you going?"

Ruth did not stop walking. Charles caught her by the shoulder and spun her around. The tears were already streaming down her face.

"Ruth," Charles exclaimed, "what's come over you?"

"I'm—I'm leaving you, Charles. I saw you with—with that woman, and I—I simply cannot take any more."

David, still holding Ruth's hand, did not understand what was taking place, and he looked quizzically first at his mother, then at his father.

"Ruth, Ruth," Charles said helplessly. "What did I do wrong? I helped a young woman; I talked to a young woman. What's the harm?"

Ruth had no answer for him. All she knew was that she was miserable, and she wanted nothing more to do with Charles.

Large, dark clouds had been gathering overhead, and finally they broke loose, drenching the ground with a torrential rain shower.

Charles took off his coat and draped it over Ruth and

David. "Come," he said, reaching for Ruth's hand. "Let's get to the carriage."

Ruth pulled her hand away. "No! I'm not going anywhere with you."

"This is ridiculous," Charles said loudly, in order to be heard over the sound of the beating rain. "Come to the carriage."

"No!" Ruth cried, and began to run.

Charles dashed after her and caught her in his arms. "You are not leaving me, now or ever. I could never live without you." He held her tightly as tears streamed down her face and the rain drenched them. "I love you, Ruth," he said, kissing her face, her hair. "I love you. Don't you understand that?"

David saw his parents embracing, and suddenly he knew that whatever had been wrong before, the world was all right again now. He ran up to them and squeezed between them.

"Let's get the three of us home, and quickly, before we catch our deaths," Charles said, and he hurriedly led Ruth and David to the waiting carriage.

When they were seated inside, they covered themselves up with blankets, and at least they were warm, if not dry. Ruth looked at her husband and son, their hair dripping wet and their faces streaming with water, and she tried to run a hand through her own sopping wet hair. "Look at us," she said helplessly. "Just look at us."

Suddenly Charles began to laugh. David joined in the laughter, and Ruth, looking first at her husband, then at her son, didn't know whether to laugh or cry. Then, despite herself, she broke into peals of laughter, too, and the family continued to laugh all the way back to their house in Belgravia.

There they went directly to their rooms to change clothes. Ruth was in her robe, sitting in front of the fireplace of her dressing room, when Charles, also wearing a robe, entered. He came to her from behind and put his arms around her.

"You gave me a good fright back there in the park," he said softly. "If you had left me, I don't know what I would have done."

They looked at each other, and miraculously, the wall that had separated them seemed to have disappeared. Ruth's eyes were open and frank, and Charles met her gaze in the same spirit. Then, slowly and deliberately, he reached out and covered her hand with his.

She made no attempt to withdraw from him.

"My father," Charles said, "is at his club, and I know my mother, along with Elizabeth and her guest, is attending a social function this afternoon. David is being looked after by his governess."

She nodded, her gaze fixed on him.

"That leaves us free," he went on, "to do what we please, in our own way." He returned her gaze, then suddenly leaned toward her and kissed her.

Ruth returned the kiss with a fervor that matched his.

When they drew apart, she managed to say, "Really, Charles, we must be more circumspect. What would the servants say if they walked in on us just now?"

"I imagine they would have observed that it was high time we started acting like a husband and wife, and I must say I agree with them thoroughly. What about you?"

Ruth rose slowly to her feet and held out her hand to him. He took it and led her out of the dressing room toward the bedchamber.

There was no further need for conversation between them. The misunderstandings that had multiplied over the months had seemingly vanished, and when they made love, Ruth was fervently kissing her husband, Charles, not some fantasy image of Jonathan Rakehell.

Charles subsequently demonstrated in actions rather than words the understanding they had reached. Still saying nothing, he moved his personal belongings from his own bedchamber into Ruth's.

The monsoon season came to an abrupt end, and the Portuguese, as well as the British and the other Europeans in Macao, breathed more easily. The heat was still intense, to be sure, particularly under the midday sun, but at least the rains stopped and the enervating humidity was much lessened.

Dom Manuel Sebastian, Marquês de Braga, seemed more active, as did his subjects. He busied himself with international trade, interviewing the captains of Portuguese vessels, insisting that his customs officials collect appropriate fees from ships flying foreign flags, and stepping up the tempo of activities in the port. Not until late one evening, after the sun had set, did a disreputable character, known along the Macao waterfront only as Weng, appear at the Marquês de Braga's large palace.

Weng was cautious, as was his custom, and showed up at a small side door used by servants. Had anyone been observing his arrival, it would have been noted that he was expected. He was admitted without delay and was taken through a labyrinth of corridors to a chamber on the second floor, where he was served with both food and drink by one of the Chinese girls in what the old-timers in Macao jocularly, but privately, referred to as the governor-general's harem. Eventually, after he had consumed the food and drink provided for him, he was led down another corridor and from a distance could see uniformed Portuguese soldiers armed with muskets guarding the entrances to a large suite. This, as anyone familiar with the palace well knew, was the governor's personal domain. Weng was led by the girl through a private door into the suite, and there, after depositing him in an anteroom, she vanished.

The visitor did not have long to wait. Soon the double doors opened and Dom Manuel, resplendent in a brocaded coat, cloth-of-gold waistcoat, and satin trousers, stood in the entrance and imperiously beckoned to him. "Come in," he said. "We haven't met for quite a long time."

"It has been a little more than a year since I last served Your Excellency," Weng replied carefully.

The man's fastidiousness and precision were qualities that appealed to the Marquês de Braga. The three most recent imperial viceroys in Canton had put a price on Weng's head, as they had on several of his subordinates, but he had found a permanent refuge in Macao, where he made his headquarters and was safe from the authorities of the Middle Kingdom. Anyone acquainted with him well knew that he was a criminal who could be hired for any task, ranging from smuggling opium to murder; he was reliable and punctual, and those who had need for his services were pleasantly surprised that he did not overcharge them.

Dom Manuel waved him to a chair, and they sat facing each other warily, like two fencers, both of whom were ready to start a duel on an instant's notice.

Weng broke the silence, as was expected of him in the august presence of the governor-general. "Do I gather correctly that Your Excellency has a task that you want performed?"

The marquês studied the large ruby ring that graced his little finger. "You might say that I'd find it convenient if you had time to spare on my behalf," he said. "As usual, I am prepared to make the venture worth your time and effort."

"There's no need to pay me, Your Excellency," the Chinese man said in his most servile manner. "No matter what service you want performed, I'm at your beck and call, always."

Dom Manuel grinned without humor. As he and his visitor knew all too well, he insisted on paying for any odd jobs that he required of Weng. It was his theory never to be beholden to inferiors, and he made a point of paying well for any tasks that he wanted performed.

"You are familiar, no doubt, with the new British colony of Hong Kong?" Dom Manuel inquired conversationally.

Weng nodded cautiously.

"In your visits there," the governor-general continued, "perhaps you encountered a Balinese woman named Molinda. She resembles the beautiful girls whom I have assembled here, but it happens that she is a woman of business and is the permanent representative in the Orient for the Anglo-American firm of shippers known as Rakehell and Boynton."

Weng nodded slowly. "I have seen the lady, but I have not

154

had the honor of meeting her," he replied. "She is truly unique, as Your Excellency has indicated."

"If Rakehell and Boynton loses business in this part of the world, there is more money in my pockets," Dom Manuel said speaking calmly, conversationally. "It would be a great convenience to me if the woman called Molinda should disappear from Hong Kong."

The task was no more difficult than many others that Weng had been called upon to perform. "I think that can be arranged, Your Excellency," he said with a half-smile.

The marquês held up a pudgy hand and indicated that he was not yet finished with his request. "It would be too great a waste," he said, "if a woman as beautiful as Molinda should end her days at the bottom of Hong Kong harbor, let us say. I am opposed to such waste. How much better it would be for all concerned if she were brought to Macao, and could enjoy the privilege of becoming a concubine here in my palace."

If Weng was surprised, he did not show it. "That, too, can be arranged, Your Excellency, although the details would be more complex and hence somewhat more difficult to work out. But I think you can rest assured that you will be having a new, succulent concubine attending your needs in the very near future."

The marquês was all business now. "How soon can this arrangement be consummated?" he wanted to know.

Weng thought rapidly. "I shall require a maximum of forty-eight hours," he said.

Dom Manuel reached into the pocket of his coat, brought out a small heavy bag that clinked as it moved, and placed it on the table beside him. "This," he said, "is by way of an advance payment, as you may have certain expenses to bear, and I see no reason why you should be out of pocket yourself for them. There will be an equal sum when the bargain is completed."

The Chinese criminal knew he was being dismissed, and sweeping up the bag of gold, he kowtowed, jumped to his

155

feet, and then backed out of the room. There was nothing more that needed to be said on either side.

Sitting on his thronelike chair, the Marquês de Braga waited for the man to leave the room, then clapped his hands twice. In an instant a long-haired girl wearing a flowing robe entered the room and kowtowed.

"Dance for me," Dom Manuel commanded to his concubine.

The girl knew just what her master wanted, and she rose gracefully, doffed her robe, and began to gyrate seductively in front of the governor-general.

But even the sensuous motions of the naked girl in front of him failed to distract Dom Manuel, whose mind had been in a state of great agitation for the last few months. He had been infuriated at the failure of the plan to waylay Jonathan Rakehell's ship, and he had executed the pirate Ling Ch'i. He had also learned from his spies how Bruce's plans to steal the silk had failed, and this, too, had disgusted him. No, if he wanted anything done he would have to do it himself; he would have to take matters into his own hands; and as he thought of the prize he had just assigned Weng to get him, he chuckled with delight. He had been promised Molinda as a gift once before, and that, too, had not come to pass, but now it could not help but succeed. Just the anticipation of such a prize—not to mention the blow that Molinda's abduction would cause Rakehell and Boynton, and Jonathan Rakehell in particular—made the blood in Dom Manuel's veins stir. He now studied the nude girl dancing in front of him, and with a wicked smile of delight, he summoned her to him.

Returning without delay to his own comfortable house, Weng immediately became busy. With only forty-eight hours in which to operate, he had no time to lose. His principal concern was to instruct a half-dozen subordinates in the method of carrying out Molinda's abduction, which would involve gagging and binding her and bringing her to the waterfront concealed in a sedan chair. Then she was to be lodged in the interior of the junk that Weng owned and that was, at present, tied up at a Macao dock. The junk would sail on the morning tide to Hong Kong, where the plan would immediately be put into effect. Making sure that all was in order, Weng finally retired for the night, bedding down with a half-Chinese, half-Portuguese girl who happened to be his mistress of the moment.

He had set the wheels in motion and had so perfected his organization that he had no doubt that all would be done precisely as he wished. He was right, to be sure, but he was not as well informed as he might have been. One of his principal lieutenants was active in the Society of Oxen, and having learned the purpose of the journey that Weng planned to make to Hong Kong the following day, the lieutenant acted at once. He went to an all-night food stall for an order of noodles and Chinese cabbage, and there he fell into a low-voiced conversation with the humble owner of the food stall, who was also a member of the Oxen. The lieutenant was no sooner on his way back to Weng's house when the food-stall owner closed his establishment for the night and promptly left Macao in a small junk himself. It would have struck an outsider as odd that a man in such a humble vocational position could afford to command the services of a swift-moving junk.

The nondescript man reached Hong Kong sometime after midnight, and tying up at a public dock open to all ships, he immediately went ashore and hurried to the offices of Rakehell and Boynton. There the chief of night security gave him Molinda's address on the Peak, and he made his way without delay to her house.

There, as he anticipated, Lo Fang came to the door and, recognizing him, joined him without delay in the yard. They conversed at length, and the humble food-stall operator from Macao returned to his junk. His mission in the British Crown Colony accomplished, he returned to his home, arriving there well before breakfast, and no one was any the wiser.

Lo Fang, in the meantime, rested, though he stayed wide

157

awake, and in the morning he came into the dining room as Molinda was having a simple breakfast of boiled fish, rice, and tea.

His interruption of her meal was so unusual that she stopped eating and looked up at him in surprise. "What's wrong?" she demanded.

"Everything and nothing," the head of the Society of Oxen replied cryptically. "I apologize for interrupting you, but it is necessary that I speak with you at once."

Molinda promptly invited him to sit, and ordered a serving maid to bring him a cup of tea. Lo Fang waited for the tea to be served, then spoke quietly. "Does Molinda happen to be acquainted with a Chinese from Macao named Weng?" he asked.

She shook her head. "I'm not familiar with the man by name. Should I know him?"

"He is the lowest of scum in all the Middle Kingdom," Lo Fang replied contemptuously. "He is worse than the swill that is fed to pigs, and that is nothing."

"In that case," Molinda replied, "perhaps it is just as well that I am not acquainted with him." She smiled.

Lo Fang remained stone-faced. "Before this day ends," Lo Fang declared, "Molinda will know this man. He will come to her on some pretense and will insist on seeing her in private. When he is alone with her, he and his men plan to gag her, bind her hands and feet, and make her his prisoner." He spoke calmly, as though discussing the prospects for the day's weather.

"Why?"

"He is being paid a large sum by Dom Manuel Sebastian, the Marquês de Braga, to take you to Macao, where it is his wish to make you a slave girl in his palace."

She shook her head in disbelief. "But why, Lo Fang? Surely the governor-general knows by now, after his earlier failure to abduct me, that I am well protected, that I have bodyguards, and that I will not let myself be trapped again."

Lo Fang's voice dropped and sounded like a deep growl. "Molinda," he said, "is in the employ of Rakehell and

158

Boynton, and as Jonathan warned in his letter to us, the Marquês de Braga and his partner Owen Bruce want to see Rakehell and Boynton in ruins. If the company loses the services of Molinda, it will be a great and terrible loss, and they well could lose all of their business in the Middle Kingdom for many months to come. Not until Jonathan would return to Whampoa and Hong Kong could he find ways to compensate for the loss of Molinda.''

She gnawed at her lower lip. ''How do you know this?''

Lo Fang's eyes resembled narrow slits. ''It is enough for Molinda to know,'' he said, ''that I am informed of the comings and goings of her enemies.''

She realized now that he would reveal nothing more regarding his sources of information.

''If it is the wish of Molinda to be spared the sight of this vermin, she need only say so,'' Lo Fang declared, gulping his tea. ''I will attend to him, and you need have no more concerns.''

She thought for a moment, and then took the sort of stand that had won her the affection of Lo Fang and his subordinates. ''I think I prefer to see the man and to speak with him,'' she said. ''Then you will be free to dispose of him as you wish.''

Lo Fang nodded and grinned as he hauled himself to his feet. His immediate employer was half-Balinese and half-French, but he had to admit that she had a mind that functioned like those of members of the Society of Oxen.

Early that afternoon, after she had spent a busy morning at her office, Lo Fang appeared at the entrance to her private sanctum to announce, ''Weng is here.''

''Show him in,'' she demanded.

''Very well,'' he said, ''but I will not leave you alone with him.''

Molinda was astonished at the appearance of the tall, handsome Chinese man in Western garb who came into her office. He looked like a highly successful international trader who had had long experience with the West, and in no way did he resemble a criminal. His smile was ingratiating, and he bowed in the Western manner as he stood in front of the

159

woman. "I thank you, Madame Molinda, for your graciousness in receiving me," he said. "I bring you the prospects of a business deal that will make you pleased that you did not turn away this stranger to you."

Lo Fang stood just inside the doorway, which he filled with his bulk. His feet were planted far apart, his massive arms were folded, and his right hand rested only inches from the long, curved double-bladed knife with the pronglike attachment protruding from its sharp end. This was a modern version of one of the most ancient of Chinese weapons, and it was said that there were no more than one hundred persons in all of the Middle Kingdom who were proficient in its use. The mere fact that Lo Fang carried such a weapon spoke volumes for his prowess.

Weng was surprised that the majordomo remained in the room, but he was in no position to protest. However, apparently he reasoned that it could do no harm for him to try to get rid of the unwanted protector of the young woman whom he intended to kidnap. "If you please, Madame Molinda," he said, "my business with you is private—very private indeed. I will be grateful for an opportunity to speak with you alone, please."

Molinda smiled at him blandly. "There's no one here, Mr. Weng, except you and me."

"And—and this person," Weng said, nodding in the direction of Lo Fang.

"He is my majordomo," Molinda declared. "Where he goes, I go, and what I hear, he hears. I assure you, he is totally reliable in all things." Her flat statement indicated that under no circumstances would she dismiss Lo Fang, and this created a problem for Weng. He had built his kidnapping scheme on the supposition that he would have some time alone with the woman. Now, if he were forced to grapple with this ferocious giant, it would be a far different matter, and he would need the help of the subordinates who awaited him outside the building.

His most immediate need was to summon help in order to subdue the huge majordomo. He sidled toward the door. Lo

Fang didn't budge. "Before I begin to explain my mission, Madame Molinda," he said, "I would like to summon my associates who await me outside."

Molinda decided the moment had come for her to take charge. "That will be unnecessary, Mr. Weng," she said. "Your associates are no longer awaiting you."

He was startled, confused by her meaning.

Lo Fang clarified his thinking for him. "Your gang," he said, "has been captured and awaits the arrival of the Hong Kong constabulary, who will be delighted to place them under arrest. It isn't every day that members of such a notorious group can be captured and subdued without difficulty."

Weng was alarmed but tried to put as good a face on the situation as he could muster. "I don't know what you're talking about," he said loudly.

"I think you well know," Molinda replied. "Be good enough to sit down."

He continued to stand. She nodded to Lo Fang, who, taking several steps that brought him into the room, placed his hands on Weng's shoulders and then pushed down without seeming to exert himself. Weng dropped onto the nearest three-cornered stool as though he had been struck across the head by a heavy club.

"You made a mistake, Mr. Weng," Molinda said sweetly.

Weng began to stammer a response.

Lo Fang cut him short. "You arrived in Hong Kong from Macao this very day," he said. "You intended to kidnap Molinda and to transport her to Macao in the hold of your junk. You planned to take her to the palace of your employer and friend, the Marquês de Braga. How he disposed of her, you neither knew nor cared. That was not your concern. Your only care was for the gold you would receive when you had completed your mission."

Weng had no idea how this giant had gleaned so much accurate information about his business. That, however, was beside the point. One did not achieve a highly successful criminal record by evasions, lies, and above all, words. There was a time when action—violent and direct—was necessary, and Weng was prepared to do what the situation demanded. He reached under his Western-style coat for a long nickel-plated Scottish pistol.

As he drew it, however, Lo Fang saw the gleam of the metal and was too quick for him. Reaching out, the giant majordomo struck him sharply across the wrist with the edge of his hand in a move familiar to all who practiced the martial arts. The pistol clattered to the floor.

Then Lo Fang sprang forward and delivered a stunning chop to the side of the other man's head. This was followed by a series of moves so rapid that Molinda, even though her attention was riveted to the scene, could scarcely follow what was happening. All she knew was that Weng slumped on the stool and seemed to be resting with his eyes closed.

"This worthless scum has lost consciousness now," Lo Fang announced. "I shall remove him from Molinda's presence, and she will not be troubled by him again."

Molinda, in spite of her ultrafeminine nature, had been a disciple of the Fat Dutchman for a long time and, hence, never wasted her substance on false sentiments. "What do you intend to do with him now?" she asked crisply.

Had Lo Fang been dealing with any other woman, he would have dissembled or procrastinated; under the circumstances, however, he felt compelled to tell the absolute, unvarnished truth. "First," he said, "he will be removed to the junk that sits at the waterfront. There his throat will be slit."

Molinda nodded thoughtfully. "That is all?" she asked quietly.

Lo Fang paid her the rare compliment of respecting her intelligence. "If Molinda has any ideas to suggest," he said, "I would be very pleased to hear them."

She tapped a high-heeled shoe on the tile floor. "It seems to me," she said, "that a notice of some kind—a gift—should be sent to the Marquês de Braga. I would like to thank him—in a manner of speaking—for his deep interest in me."

Lo Fang caught her meaning instantly, and a chuckle

rumbled up from deep within him. "It shall be done as you suggest."

"Splendid," she said, and her smile was cold and unfeeling. She, too, was an Easterner, and lived according to the harsh codes of the Orient. "It might be well," she said, "if a special box were made for the gift we wish to send to the Marquês de Braga."

"It shall be done," Lo Fang replied, and picking up the unconscious Weng with scarcely an effort, he slung the man over his shoulder and quietly left the office.

So it happened that late that same night, a large tea crate containing the corpse of the once-feared criminal, Weng, was delivered to the palace of the governor-general of Macao. Attached to it was a brief note written in Portuguese in a flowing female hand. It read: *With the compliments of Molinda.*

Dom Manuel Sebastian knew nothing about the delivery of the grisly gift until morning, when he eagerly opened the tea crate and saw the body of Weng. Only then did he read the note attached to the box.

Another scheme had backfired on him, and he was furious. Now his bitterness was also directed toward Molinda, and he swore to obtain vengeance against her, as well as against her employers, Rakehell and Boynton.

Dr. Matthew Melton arrived in Hong Kong on board a Rakehell and Boynton clipper that made the voyage from New London to the British Crown Colony in ninety-seven days, a good time but far from a record. In Hong Kong, Molinda took charge of the newcomer and saw to it that he had quarters in her own house while she arranged for his final journey to Tientsin by special junk, and then overland for the final ninety miles to Peking. Hong Kong was the gateway to the East, and the doctor was fascinated by the sights, sounds, and smells of the Orient. But Molinda explained to him that what he was seeing and hearing scarcely scratched the surface.

"You've entered a world unlike any you've ever known, Doctor," she said. "I don't know you well enough to have any idea whether you can tolerate the East and enjoy it, or

163

whether you will loathe it. Only time will tell. Jonathan Rakehell has written me a very frank letter about your circumstances, and I can only ask you to get in touch with me immediately if you find that you wish to leave Cathay.''

Matthew thanked her. Struck by Molinda's beauty, intelligence, and warmth, he was deeply impressed by her and realized that Jonathan Rakehell's representative in the Middle Kingdom was unique.

Still absorbing the culture so vastly different from his own, the young American physician remained in Hong Kong for seventy-two hours, then he embarked on a Rakehell and Boynton coastal junk for Tientsin. The voyage up the coast of China was uneventful, and he marveled at the comfort and speed of the strange craft, unlike any that he had ever before seen. His quarters were spacious, and though the sea was choppy, the junk rode smoothly, with a minimum of rolling and pitching. Apparently the Chinese had much to commend in their way of life.

The captain of the junk exchanged elaborate signals with the commander of the ancient fort that overlooked the Tientsin harbor, and ultimately was permitted to land. To Matthew's surprise, his arrival had been anticipated, and a company of forty yellow-uniformed troops waited for him to escort him from the seaport to the capital. He was provided with a spirited horse, and it was fortunate, he thought, that he knew how to ride. The troops expected it of him. He spent three days in the open on the ride to Peking, sharing the rough fare of the troops, which consisted mostly of rice, bean curds, and vegetables that were totally alien to the young American.

He was fascinated by the sights and sounds of Peking, a far larger city than any he had ever seen or imagined. His escorts penetrated to the heart of the metropolis, being passed formally through thick gates to each succeeding inner realm, and finally they came to the Forbidden City, the home of the Celestial Emperor. Here Wu-ling was on hand to greet him, and to his great pleasure, she addressed him in English, the first time since he had left Hong Kong that anyone had spoken to him in a tongue he could understand. Suddenly this new world didn't seem quite so strange.

"Welcome to Peking, Dr. Melton," she said, and led him to his quarters.

He was deeply impressed by the apartment he had been assigned in the royal palace. He had a living room and a bedchamber, both of them large and comfortably furnished with highly lacquered tables and chairs, and there was also a third chamber that actually boasted a sink with running water.

"This is your laboratory, should you desire one," Wu-ling said. "Princess An Mien insisted that you should have it."

"That was very thoughtful of her," he murmured. "I suppose I can store my medical supplies in here?"

"Of course," Wu-ling replied, "wherever you wish." She hesitated for a moment and then said, "You've arrived at a very opportune time, or perhaps it is a very bad time."

He looked at her blankly, not understanding.

"I am permitted to say nothing more," the girl declared in a lowered voice. "Her Highness will explain to you. She's been notified of your arrival, so she should be here at any time."

He nodded and decided that the mystery, whatever it was, could wait until the emperor's sister saw fit to explain it to him. He was curious about Wu-ling, and studied her surreptitiously but thoroughly. He hadn't known what to expect, but it hadn't occurred to him that she would be young, pretty, and vivacious, with a rounded, slender figure under a silk cheongsam that left little to the imagination.

Wu-ling was aware of his scrutiny and returned it with interest. She had expected him to be much older and far more somber, like the physicians she had met in London and New England who had treated the members of the Rakehell and Boynton families. She was surprised to find that he was as young as he was, and if she did admit it to herself, quite attractive.

The door opened, and the Princess An Mien, severe in a high-necked, long gown of watered silk, swept into the room.

"I am happier to see you than you could possibly know, Dr. Melton," she said, and extended her hand to him in a Western-style greeting, proud of her ability to communicate in the English language.

Matthew was struck, as were virtually all of the few foreigners who met An Mien, by her direct, forthright manner. She seemed far more European or American, in spite of her appearance and dress.

"I must thank you," he said, "for the magnificent suite you've made available to me. I'm quite overwhelmed by it."

"Never fear, you shall earn it," she replied dryly, and then turning to Wu-ling she asked, "Does he know?"

"No, Your Highness," the young woman replied.

The princess nodded, waved the young physician to a seat, and lowered herself to a cushioned three-legged stool opposite him. "I regret to inform you," she said, "that my brother is ill, quite ill."

"I'm sorry to hear it," Matthew replied. "What seems to be wrong with him?"

The princess tried to maintain a brave façade but revealed her true feelings when she wearily passed a hand across her forehead. "We have no idea, Doctor," she replied. "There are certain traditions that govern the treatment of the Celestial Emperor when he is ailing, and that may hamper obtaining a diagnosis. Perhaps you would care to see him for yourself."

Apparently he was going to begin his practice in China sooner than he had anticipated. "Of course," he said, and going to his luggage, he took out the small black leather bag containing various instruments and medicines that he always carried when making house calls.

The princess and Wu-ling flanked him as they made their way down one marble-lined corridor, then turned into another and then yet another. The walk seemed endless, but their goal was eventually within sight, as was evidenced by the appearance of a large number of uniformed guards in the corridor. They clustered in front of each doorway, and all of them looked appropriately ferocious in spite of the chrysanthemum-yellow uniforms and headgear they wore. Each of them carried a huge, double-edged sword and a long musket. The swords undoubtedly were sharp and could do considerable damage, but the muskets, Matthew noted, were useless. They were made according to an ancient model, and it was doubtful that they could be fired, much less successfully aimed at a target.

At last they approached a doorway where guards stood three deep, and the princess pushed her way through them, with the soldiers falling back at her approach. Her abrupt gesture clearly included her companions, and they were allowed to accompany her. The door closed behind them, and Matthew found himself in the largest bedchamber that he had ever seen.

A pagodalike roof actually covered a portion of the chamber inside the windows, and directly beneath the pagoda was a huge divan, large enough for at least a dozen sleepers. There, with pillows and bolsters of pure silk surrounding him, lay the Tao Kuang Emperor, his face waxen, his eyes closed, and his hands motionless above the bedclothes. On the other side of the room stood several elderly white-bearded men with long black silk robes of Chinese scholars, and as Matthew looked at them, he could scarcely believe his eyes. They surrounded a metal statue of a heroic figure and were delicately probing various parts of it with gloved hands.

Wu-ling murmured softly into his ear. "Those are the royal physicians," she whispered, "and they are examining a statue of the emperor."

The young physician shook his head. "Why do they examine a statue rather than the patient himself?"

"The emperor is far too august a personage to have the hands of human beings touch him," Wu-ling replied. "He would order the miscreant who showed him such disrespect beheaded instantly."

He shook his head and couldn't help saying, "With all due respect to these gentlemen and their methods, I don't see how it's possible for them to obtain an accurate diagnosis unless they examine the patient."

Princess An Mien stared at him. "Is that what you would do, Doctor?"

"If the emperor were my patient, I would," he replied. "I don't mean to mock the customs of the Middle Kingdom, Your Highness, but how is it possible to tell what ails him by poking at a statue made of brass?"

The concept was new to An Mien, but she caught on swiftly and nodded.

Wu-ling was alarmed. "Dr. Melton does not understand, Your Highness," she said, addressing the princess in English for his sake. "If he uses the techniques of the West in his examination of the Celestial Emperor and the emperor dies, he will be considered the murderer of him and will be put to death himself in a horrible manner."

Matthew could only stare incredulously.

The princess made up her mind swiftly. "I shall guarantee your safety, no matter what may transpire, Doctor," she said.

Matthew breathed more easily and privately wondered whether he had gone from civilization to a mad world. "I shall begin my examination of the patient at once, then," he said.

"Do you want the room cleared for you?" Wu-ling asked, having some idea of the techniques of Western medicine.

"Not at all," he replied. "Let the local physicians accompany me, and I can report my findings to them."

The elderly men looked duly shocked when Wu-ling translated Dr. Melton's intentions, but they immediately followed him to the side of the Tao Kuang Emperor's bed, and all of them were so apprehensive that they edged behind one another as he went to the patient, pulled down the bedclothes, and began his examination. He ran his hands over the neck and chest of the patient beneath the ornate pajamas of silk that he was wearing, and he tried to ignore the gasps of the audience. Then, when he was fingering the emperor's face he found a pair of eyes staring at him steadily from the bed.

The Tao Kuang Emperor spoke in a hoarse whisper.

An Mien bent low over her brother and replied earnestly in Mandarin.

Wu-ling translated for the benefit of the young physician. "The Tao Kuang Emperor wanted to know the identity of the foreign devil who dared to touch him," she said, "and the princess has identified you."

Matthew suddenly straightened above his patient. "Your Highness," he said, "I cannot possibly conduct an examination under these circumstances. Either the patient submits willingly, or I shall be forced to withdraw from the case."

Wu-ling looked dubious, and the elderly Chinese physicians were badly frightened.

An Mien, however, demonstrated her mettle by calmly translating his remarks for her brother. He responded with an effort, and Matthew felt certain that he saw a gleam of humor appear in the sick man's eyes.

He now spoke briefly in a low tone of voice, and his words seemed to satisfy everyone. An Mien smiled in relief, as did Wu-ling, and the bearded physicians nodded sagely.

"The Tao Kuang Emperor," Princess An Mien said in English to Matthew, "is no longer present with us, Dr. Melton."

Matthew glanced first at the patient and then at the princess again. "May I ask what has become of him?" he inquired.

Wu-ling came to the assistance of the princess. "The Tao Kuang Emperor is not like other, ordinary, people," she declared. "He is divine. This quality enables him to be present with us or to withdraw as he pleases, when he pleases. He has chosen now to withdraw, and he is no longer present in the chamber with us."

She actually seemed to be believing the gibberish she was spouting, Matthew concluded.

"Therefore," she said, prodding him, "you are free to examine your patient at will and do what you think necessary for his benefit."

At least that much was accomplished, and Matthew returned to his examination, giving the emperor all the attention he could muster and studying him thoroughly. The results seemed conclusive to him.

"Be good enough to inform the royal physicians, if you will, that the emperor has all the symptoms of the ague."

"You mean the patient who lies there on the bed," Wu-ling declared.

"This man, whoever he may be, has the ague," he replied curtly. "It's a rather severe case, but I've seen many that were far worse." He proceeded to rummage in his black bag while the young woman translated his words.

It was obvious from the reactions of the elderly Chinese physicians that they had no idea what illness he meant, nor did they have any notion as to how to treat it.

"What are your intentions now, Doctor?" An Mien wanted to know.

He found what he was seeking. "Ah, here we are. This is a rather pungent medication intended for just this illness. It contains both sulphur and laudanum, so I'm afraid that it has a very bitter taste, but that can't be helped. May I have a spoon, please?"

Wu-ling hurried to the door, and a few moments later a manservant in silk livery appeared with a velvet cushion on which a golden spoon rested. He kowtowed, abasing himself on the floor as he offered the utensil for the sick emperor.

Matthew began to understand that nothing in the royal household was simple. He took the spoon, poured medicine into it, and held it close to the emperor's face. "Here," he directed, "drink this."

The emperor struggled in an attempt to sit up. Matthew placed a hand behind his head and hoisted him to a sitting position, then forced him to drink the medicine. The taste apparently was loathsome. The Tao Kuang Emperor gagged, but recovered and, breathing deeply, managed to hold the medicine down.

Matthew took his pocket watch from his waistcoat pocket and glanced at it. "The next dose is in four hours," he said, "and I'll give it to him myself. I urge everyone to leave now because the laudanum in the medication will make the patient sleepy, and he'll want to take a nap." He turned to An Mien with a reassuring smile. "You need have no further worries," he said. "I assure you, the emperor will recover completely."

She looked at him with a new respect. "If you say he will recover, Doctor, then I'm sure he will," she replied.

The emperor sank back onto his pillows, and when he spoke, he, too, used English for the benefit of the physician from the United States. "It is good," he said, "that the Tao Kuang Emperor absented himself from this room. He has a very delicate body, and it is unlikely that he would have been able to tolerate the horrible taste of that strange medicine. But he is curious, Dr. Melton, because had he remained with us, it would have been the first time in his long life that he would have received medication of any kind from any physician. I shall have to tell him of my experience, so he will understand what he has missed."

Matthew glanced at him sharply, and suddenly he understood completely. The Tao Kuang Emperor was resorting to a ruse in order to circumvent the superstitions that surrounded the throne and inhibited him and those who served him. His confidence restored, the doctor grinned as he bowed to the sick man, and he couldn't help smiling broadly as he said, "I shall return myself in four hours."

"Good," the Tao Kuang Emperor responded. "Perhaps by that time, I shall feel strong enough to have a chat with you. I am pleased that you have elected to come to the Middle Kingdom and serve us and our people."

Somewhat to Matthew's surprise, he discovered that he, too, was pleased with the choice of careers that he had made.

# III

Matthew Melton had no idea what he was eating and realized only that the bite-sized food was delicious. He identified the taste of ginger, a hint of citrus fruit, and several other tastes that seemed familiar but whose identity eluded him. The meal was served in the living quarters of his suite at the palace by a pajama-clad waiter, who came in and out of the room repeatedly with one lacquer bowl after another, in endless profusion.

Wu-ling, sitting at the polished table opposite him and handling her bowl and ivory chopsticks with consummate ease, seemed completely at home with these strange foods, as well she might, having lived for quite a time at the imperial palace in the Forbidden City.

"You see the behavior of the Tao Kuang Emperor yesterday as a way of saving face," she said. "You see it as a way of circumventing tradition and ancient customs by giving in to a subterfuge, a pretense."

"Of course," Matthew replied as he helped himself to more of the dish that, he suspected, was duck with a rich lobster and oyster sauce.

"It was my observation while I was in America," Wu-ling went on, "that there all is new. Traditions are less important than accomplishments. If one achieves what one aims to do, that is far more important than observing traditions while doing it. In the Middle Kingdom, the very opposite is true.

173

Our customs mean everything to us, and the results of one's endeavors are relatively unimportant.''

"Is that why there is so little progress here? Is that why the Middle Kingdom is so far behind the other civilized nations of the world?''

Wu-ling nodded slowly. "It is hard for foreigners to believe," she said, "that in this land was invented gunpowder. Here the printing press was conceived, and here the first books were printed. Inventions that the West claims, hundreds of them, actually originated here. But the people have been so hidebound by customs that they stand in the way of their own progress. What you fail to understand is that you—by defying tradition—place yourself in great jeopardy. The Tao Kuang Emperor, who is perhaps the most civilized man in the entire realm, was the first to realize this. Had he not intervened when he did and permitted you to treat him yourself, you would have been beheaded for your temerity.''

"This," Matthew said forcefully, "is what I find so difficult to accept. Do you honestly mean to tell me that I could have lost my head because I dared to practice my profession by examining a patient and giving him medication?''

"There's no question about it," Wu-ling declared equally firmly. "Princess An Mien was there to protect you, of course, but if the royal physicians had become excited, it might not have been possible to control the troops of the imperial guard. You surely would have been beheaded. But the Tao Kuang Emperor is a wise man, so he spared you that pain and humiliation by supporting that which you did. Even had he failed to recover from his ailment—and it certainly looks as if he will recover fully—you would have remained unmolested.''

"But how is it possible," he demanded, "for any nation to be this backward? We're living in 1845, after all, not the Dark Ages.''

"In the Middle Kingdom," Wu-ling replied, "there is no recognition of the Dark Ages, just as the calendar of the West is unknown here. Time has an odd way of standing still in this land. Here men and women are beasts of burden, and pull plows through the fields. Life is less precious, and everyone is acquainted with death.''

He sighed, trying to acclimate his thoughts to this strange country, when a tap sounded at the door and a servingwoman came into the room, bearing a large package, which she placed before her on the floor as she kowtowed.

Not only did her obeisance make Matthew nervous, but he was conscious of the fact that she was a member of the imperial entourage. He had learned that much about the meaning of chrysanthemum-yellow clothes.

The woman remained stretched on the floor, and Wu-ling addressed her quietly. She rose, then took her leave.

Matthew realized he had been rebuked, that it had been his place to acknowledge the servingwoman's presence and allow her to rise to her feet. Apparently he still had a good deal to learn.

Wu-ling smiled at him. ''The contents of the box appear to be for you,'' she said.

He shrugged, opened the box, and gasped when he saw the contents. Nestling in cotton batting was a bowl about thirty-six inches in diameter and about twelve inches deep, the most exquisite Matthew had ever seen. It appeared to have been carved out of a single piece of jade, and was so thin that it was almost transparent. On the outside were various stylized scenes, and looking at them quickly, the young American physician realized they were representations of a Chinese doctor practicing his profession with various patients, among them a scholar, a child, and a peasant woman. The artist who had created the bowl had been extraordinary, and the gift was worth a king's ransom.

Wu-ling read his thoughts and grinned at him. ''Yes,'' she said, ''there's no card telling you the donor, and the servingwoman mentioned no names. That means the Tao Kuang Emperor chose to make you this gift personally.''

Matthew was dazed. ''But why?''

''Because he is recovering from the ailment that threatened his life as recently as yesterday. It is his way of expressing his thanks to you.''

"I'm overwhelmed," he replied. "I've never seen anything this lovely."

She smiled demurely. "Perhaps," she said, "it is the Tao Kuang Emperor's way of telling you that we are a superstitious people, but we are not barbarians. Only the inheritors of an ancient civilization could have made such a beautiful bowl."

He could feel color rising to his face. "I begin to see the point," he said, "and I'm afraid I stand corrected."

"There is only one other thing that I feel I must mention in connection with this gift. Had the emperor wished to acknowledge that he was the donor, he would have identified himself. As he did not, it would be the worst of very bad manners to mention the subject to him."

"You mean I mustn't thank him?" Matthew was incredulous.

"Exactly so," Wu-ling replied. "If the emperor were to thank you for treating him, he would ruin the myth that he had taken himself elsewhere and that you had treated some other person in his stead. I urge you to place the bowl on display here in your living room, and when the emperor visits you, which he certainly will do, he will see that you have given his gift a place of honor, and that will more than satisfy him."

"It must take years," Matthew said, "to learn the dos and don'ts of living in Cathay."

Wu-ling giggled slightly. "I am afraid that is so," she said. "I have lived here the better part of my life, and I find I am still learning much."

They were interrupted by a loud, sharp tap at the outer door of the suite, which then opened, and the Tao Kuang Emperor came in, dressed in his usual seedy black, his pearl cap, the badge of his high office, riding on the crown of his head. He was far livelier than he had been the previous day, and his coloring was less sallow, but he nevertheless used an ivory cane to help support him when he walked.

The instant that Matthew saw him, he started to rise, but Wu-ling whispered to him urgently. "No," she said, "pay no attention. The Celestial Emperor is invisible."

The Tao Kuang Emperor heard her remark and nodded

equitably. "That is so," he said. "The emperor has chosen today to render himself unseen by human eyes." He dropped onto the stool between them and reached for a bowl of fruit on the table.

"I must remember," Matthew said, speaking to no one in particular, "to drop into the imperial suite sometime today and warn the person I treated to eat no fresh fruit for at least another twenty-four hours. It doesn't mix well with the medication that he's been given, and is likely to cause him considerable stomach distress."

The emperor hastily pushed the bowl away from him, and after glancing longingly at some peaches, he removed his gaze from the fruit and did not look at it again.

"I suppose," he said, speaking casually in English for the sake of his visitor, "that Wu-ling has not yet learned the interesting news of the day. That's not surprising, to be sure, because the latest royal proclamation hasn't yet been published."

The young woman gave no direct reply but nodded vaguely.

Matthew had already gleaned that when the emperor rendered himself "invisible," one did not reply directly to any statements he made.

"The royal physicians will be in a wild fury tonight," the emperor said, and astonished Matthew by chuckling and rubbing his hands together. "They were greatly perturbed yesterday when the foreign devil who practices medicine cured a certain personage of his distress and restored him to good health within a remarkably short time. How much angrier they will be when they find that a royal proclamation has been issued that grants Dr. Melton the right to practice medicine at the imperial court in the Forbidden City and anywhere he chooses within our realm. He may practice according to his own knowledge and his own ways, and is not obliged to observe the customs of the Middle Kingdom."

Matthew was both relieved and pleased, and it did not occur to him until he saw the expression on Wu-ling's face that he was being accorded a rare honor. To be granted the privilege of serving in his own way, as he saw fit, was unique, something new in the modern history of the Middle

Kingdom. By granting him this right, the Tao Kuang Emperor had defied the traditions that had guided his Manchu predecessors for hundreds of years, and had inaugurated a new era. Progress might be slow, at times invisible, but there would be no turning back the clock now.

The emperor rose to his feet. "I thought," the emperor said pleasantly, as though talking to himself, "that Wu-ling and Dr. Melton would be glad to hear about the proclamation that will be issued at the end of the day."

Matthew could not allow the Tao Kuang Emperor to depart without expressing his thanks. But he took care to adopt the same technique that the ruler of the Middle Kingdom used. "I must pay a visit to the imperial suite this afternoon," he declared, addressing no one in particular, "because I wish to administer another dose of ague medicine to the patient. I also want to warn him not to move around too freely just yet. He'd be very wise to rest in bed for another few days before he tries wandering around in the long corridors of this palace."

The emperor nodded, obviously taking the advice to heart.

"And I must find some way to thank him," Matthew continued boldly, "not only for the beautiful gift that he made to me, but, most of all, for his confidence in my talents as a medical practitioner."

Wu-ling shook her head slightly, to tell him that this was not a wise tactic. But the pleased expression on the emperor's face indicated that he took no exception to the remarks.

"I promised Jonathan Rakehell that I would spend one month in Peking," Matthew said, "and then would decide whether to return to America without delay, or whether I would stay on in the Middle Kingdom and accept the post that he outlined for me. I don't need that much time. I've already decided that I shall stay here and do my best to serve the emperor."

The Tao Kuang Emperor beamed at him. Even Wu-ling was so pleased that she forgot to warn him to desist.

Still smiling, the emperor limped off, leaning on his ivory cane.

Wu-ling remained silent until the door closed behind him. "You must remember to exercise great caution when the Tao Kuang Emperor chooses to become invisible. He's very touchy about such matters."

"He appears to be a gentleman of great sensitivity," Matthew replied. "I like him."

Wu-ling shook her head in wonder. "For a total stranger to forbid him to eat a peach, and for the emperor to obey that stranger's command, is unique, and I have never seen anything like that scene. I shall remember it always."

Matthew was satisfied that he was making his own mark, in his own way, at the Chinese court.

Wu-ling sighed and looked at the ornate sundial that stood just outside the nearest window. "I must return now to my own quarters where I have much translation awaiting me," she said. "I thank you for your invitation to dine with you, and as I part with you, I can only give you a word of quiet warning. Do not go too far in your desire to reform the Middle Kingdom and bring it forcibly into the modern world. Time here is not measured as it is in other parts of the earth, and patience is necessary always in dealing with the people of the Middle Kingdom. Including," she added pointedly, "the Tao Kuang Emperor."

Matthew nodded, and a totally different thought passed through his mind, that Wu-ling was an exceptionally attractive, appealing girl. Jonathan Rakehell hadn't mentioned those aspects of her nature when he'd been describing the life that awaited the young doctor in Peking.

The parchment envelope was heavy and was addressed to Jonathan Rakehell, Esquire, in a flowing hand. Delivered by a special messenger who had been on board the coastal brig that had sailed from Baltimore to New London, the note inside was brief and to the point: President James K. Polk requested the presence of Mr. Jonathan Rakehell at the Executive Mansion in Washington City at his earliest convenience.

Jonathan was busy, but a request from the White House

was the equivalent of a command, so he dropped everything and traveled to Baltimore on one of his clippers. From there he made his way to the nation's capital on horseback, and obtaining quarters for himself at O'Neal's Tavern, he deposited his luggage and immediately went to the White House. There he was received by a courteous staff member, who was surprised at the promptness of his response. He was told that the President would see him shortly.

James Polk of Tennessee was a man who always kept his word, and within a very few minutes Jonathan was ushered into his private office. Unlike his predecessor, John Tyler, who was a tall, imposing-looking man, Polk was short, slightly pudgy, and balding. Anyone who had been unfamiliar with his background as a leader of Congress and a confidante of Andrew Jackson's for many years would have underestimated his talents. Even though he had served only a short time in office so far, he had a quiet air of confidence in himself and in the destiny of his country. During his single term the United States would expand more explosively than ever before in her history.

The President's desk, as always, was remarkably neat. In one corner was a basket containing outgoing documents, and mail in it was piled high. Beside it, in another basket, were incoming dispatches, and it was not accidental that it was empty. As staff members were learning about President Polk, his efficiency was prodigious.

Concealing the pain that gnawed at his stomach, an ailment that would limit him to a single term as his nation's Chief Executive, Polk smiled broadly and extended his hand. "I'm delighted to see you, Mr. Rakehell. I've been looking forward to this occasion."

"Your servant, Mr. President," Jonathan replied crisply, and accepted the chair that was offered to him.

"The Congress," the President said, "has seen fit to pass special trade legislation that enables us to take full advantage of the treaty that Caleb Cushing signed with the Tao Kuang Emperor. I might add that the Senate has ratified that treaty. None of these facts are public knowledge as yet, but you and the members of your family have contributed so much to this day that I felt it was only fitting that you be the first to know."

"I'm grateful to you for that, sir," Jonathan replied, "but I don't think that I deserve any special commendations for it. Any man in my place would have done the same thing."

"I beg to disagree with you, but I won't press the point. What I really want to know, Mr. Rakehell, is what can I do to show you that this administration is grateful to you for opening the gates of Cathay to American trade?"

"You say that none of what you've told me is generally known yet, Mr. President?"

Polk nodded genially.

"I recommended to Mr. Cushing," Jonathan said, "that any American shipper who wanted to trade with Cathay should obtain a special license from the United States government, preferably signed by the secretary of state. That would enable the State Department to keep track of the legitimate organizations that will engage in business in Cathay, and it should keep out the riffraff who want only to enrich themselves in the opium trade."

"I've taken your advice to Cushing to heart, Mr. Rakehell," President Polk told him. "Like President Tyler before me, I've been very deeply concerned that Americans not become involved in the opium trade, and I think your system is by far the best." He opened a drawer, removed a manila folder, and took several sheets of paper from it. "You might look at these, if you will."

Jonathan took the documents from him, and was stunned. He found himself looking at three separate licenses, granting Rakehell and Boynton ships the right to engage in commercial trade with the shipping companies of the Middle Kingdom under the terms of the treaty negotiated by Caleb Cushing. One license was for clipper ships, a second was for schooners, and a third—obviously looking forward to the future—was for steam-propelled vessels. The single most impressive fact about the documents was that they bore the signature of James K. Polk, rather than his secretary of state. These were

181

papers worth preserving for his children and for their children after them.

"I—I'm overwhelmed, sir," Jonathan declared.

The President rose and again extended his hand. "It strikes me that this is the very least I can do for you, Mr. Rakehell," he said. Then, as he sat again, a glint of humor appeared in his deceptively mild eyes. "I understand there's considerable competition in your business these days, Mr. Rakehell," he said. "And from the records that your clipper ships establish on their runs to the Orient, I gather that every day cut off a voyage is very important to you."

"Indeed it is, sir," Jonathan replied.

"In that case," Polk said, breaking into a broad grin, "I think I can oblige you in a more practical way by telling you that the information regarding these permits won't be made public for several weeks. If your competitors don't know that they can obtain permits as yet, they won't apply for them, and you'll have the field to yourself for a period of several weeks, perhaps several months."

This was truly a great boon, and Jonathan was overwhelmed. "This is good news indeed, Mr. President," he said. "This comes at a time when my company can use all the help it can get, and I'm delighted to gain a head start, so to speak, on my opposition."

"It's your friendship with the rulers of China that has made our treaty possible, Mr. Rakehell," he said. Then, a somewhat plaintive note creeping into his voice, he added, "If I have a little time to spare someday, which appears to be a luxury that someone in my position can ill afford, I wonder if perhaps you would be good enough to arrange for me to make a brief voyage on board one of your clipper ships."

"I'd like nothing better, sir," Jonathan replied.

"I'll let you know," Polk told him, and added with a sigh, "It won't be within the foreseeable future, I fear. My calendar is filled for months to come, and there is no respite in sight."

Jonathan vowed that he would never again feel sorry for himself. What he couldn't quite understand was what motivated any man to become President of the United States. The first Chief Executive whom he had ever met was Andrew Jackson, who had the same hollow-eyed look that distinguished President Polk. The position, combining the duties of an actual head of state with those of a ceremonial leader, had to be utterly exhausting.

"When you next have a ship that is sailing to the Orient, I'll appreciate it if you'd give me a few days' advance notice," President Polk said. "I am in the process of writing and having translated into Chinese a letter that I'm sending to the emperor, informing him of my intentions to honor our agreement and expressing the hope that both of our peoples will prosper as a result of it."

That news remained in Jonathan's mind all the way back to New London. It was typical of Polk to think in human terms, of the feelings of the Tao Kuang Emperor. The young shipping executive was heartened. Not only was the Rakehell and Boynton firm gaining a significant head start on all of the potential American competition in the China trade, but the President's letter to the emperor certainly should help smooth the way to far more harmonious relations. It appeared that a new era was opening in the hitherto sketchy relations between the United States and the Middle Kingdom, and Jonathan was pleased that he was playing a major role in opening doors wide. His only regret was that Lai-tse lu was not beside him to share his feeling of accomplishment.

On the orders of Princess An Mien, Dr. Matthew Melton was given free access to the emperor's private suite at any time he wished. This was a rare privilege, as Matthew soon learned from Wu-ling.

"Of all the millions of people in the Middle Kingdom," the young woman said, "those who may come and go as they please from the quarters of the Celestial Emperor may be counted on the fingers of one hand. Not even his wives or his favorite concubines are so honored, nor are any of his government ministers."

The position that Matthew had achieved through his successful care of the Tao Kuang Emperor began to dawn on him. "Who are the others?" he wanted to know.

"I know of only two," Wu-ling said. "One is the Princess An Mien herself, and the other is the emperor's eldest son and heir. It may be that the commander of the imperial bodyguard may come and go as he pleases, but I've heard nothing definite about that."

"Is nothing private here?" he asked, teasing.

She shook her head. "Every move the emperor makes, every word he speaks, every sound, is considered significant. You of the Western world have no idea how powerful our emperor is, or how he is revered by his people. That is why the imperial physicians are so upset by your deeds."

"I don't see why they should be disturbed," he said. "The emperor is recovering nicely, and as I see it, that's what all of us have been trying to accomplish."

His continued ignorance of the customs and thoughts of China caused her to smile and shake her head. "You of the West," she said, "lack subtlety. Can't you see that the royal physicians feel disgraced because their powders and nostrums had no effect, but you, a total foreigner and a white devil, as you are called, cured him with medicines that are unknown here? Therefore you have caused the royal physicians to lose face."

"I'll gladly go to them," Matthew said, "and tell them that I certainly wasn't trying to usurp their places or cause them any embarrassment."

Wu-ling shook her head. "It is best, I believe, if you leave well enough alone. In time they will become accustomed to your presence here, and will accept you. If you ignore the way they feel, they can change more easily. If you formally express an opinion concerning it, they will feel obliged to cling to the stand they have taken, regardless of the consequences."

Matthew marveled privately at the complexity of existence at the royal court in the Forbidden City, and he couldn't help wondering if all relations in the Middle Kingdom were this complicated.

He would not learn the answer to that question for a long time to come, but in the meantime he continued to learn rapidly. He called daily on his distinguished patient, and soon grew accustomed to the pretext that the emperor was "not present," even while he was being examined.

The young American doctor developed the habit of discussing each step before he took it during an examination, and then announcing the results of that phase of his examination at once. Ordinarily he and the emperor were alone in the huge bedchamber at such times, and his patient nodded gratefully as he absorbed knowledge himself of the medical practices of the West.

Soon there came the day for which Matthew Melton had been waiting, and he felt a surge of relief as he said to the all-powerful ruler of the Middle Kingdom, "Perhaps you will be good enough to pass along a message from me to the Celestial Emperor."

Tao Kuang nodded slowly. "I think something of the sort could possibly be arranged," he said solemnly.

"Inform him, then, that he may leave his bed at any time that he wishes. He is not to overdo himself or exert undue efforts, however. I would say he is permitted to see his government ministers and conduct the business of state during the morning hours, but promptly at noon he must stop and then devote the rest of the day to his rehabilitation. He was much weakened by his illness, and he will require large quantities of healthy food and extended but gentle exercise to recover his full buoyancy."

"Does the American physician know of any special exercises that he cares to recommend?" the emperor inquired politely.

Matthew thought that no doctor could ever have a more cooperative patient. "Indeed I do, and I'll be delighted to teach them to you so that you can pass them along to the emperor, sir."

Tao Kuang clapped his hands and rubbed them together gleefully. "That will be splendid," he said. "I'm prepared to learn at any time."

Taking him at his word, the emperor climbed out of his bed, and within minutes they were stretched out side by side on the floor, raising their arms, then their legs in vigorous exercise patterns.

Both were so engrossed that they failed to see or hear An Mien come into the emperor's sickroom, followed by Wu-ling. Both women stopped short, and Wu-ling would have fled had not the princess firmly detained her.

All at once Matthew became conscious of his audience and sprang to his feet.

"Don't stop now," the Tao Kuang Emperor complained, "I'm just beginning to feel comfortable in these movements."

"If the emperor learns to do all that I have taught you so far with ease and speed and grace," Matthew said, "then I will teach you more."

The emperor nodded, then turned to his sister and grinned at her. "I am permitted to dress and spend my mornings at work," he told his sister. "This young man is a healer, unique in all the history of the Middle Kingdom."

Matthew could not allow such an extravagant statement to go unchallenged. "It may be that there are no others in this part of the world," he said, "but in America, in England, and in Europe there are many physicians of great competence, experience, and wisdom."

Wu-ling looked stricken. She would have to warn the doctor to mind his manners with greater care hereafter, and never to contradict anything the emperor said, no matter how inaccurate or outrageous the comment might be.

An Mien intervened and managed to avert a crisis. "We are fortunate to have such an able practitioner of medicine in our midst," she said.

Her brother nodded emphatically. "It is not accidental," he declared, "and we cannot claim that luck was responsible, either. Wu-ling, perhaps you will be good enough to write a special letter. I know the emperor will be very grateful if you perform this mission on his behalf."

The young woman nodded, long accustomed to such back-handed commands.

"Write," the Tao Kuang Emperor said, "to her that represents the business interests of Rakehell Jonathan in the Middle Kingdom, and invite her to visit Peking at her earliest opportunity. If the letter is sent to her on board a royal junk, that ship will then be available to transport her to Tientsin as soon as it is convenient for her to come."

"What do you suppose the emperor has in mind?" An Mien asked.

Tao Kuang grinned at her. "He who sits on the Chrysanthemum Throne," he said, "knows that those who serve him best deserve to be rewarded. So it is with Rakehell Jonathan. If he were here now, the emperor would want to thank him and make him a gift for having sent Dr. Melton halfway around the world just to serve us. Since he is not here, however, but is at his own home beyond our reach, the emperor must content himself with granting an informal audience to her who acts as his representative."

Wu-ling duly wrote a letter to Molinda in accordance with the emperor's wishes, and the communication was sent via his private junk.

When Molinda read the invitation to come to the Forbidden City at "her convenience" she had the good sense to drop everything and leave Hong Kong immediately. There was no indication in the letter as to why she was being summoned to the imperial palace, but that did not matter. All she knew was that the sooner she made the journey, the better it would be for Rakehell and Boynton, as well as for her.

Lo Fang and several of his subordinates quietly accompanied her and remained unobtrusively in the background, both on board ship and during the escorted march to Tientsin. She arrived without fanfare at the imperial palace, and there Wu-ling greeted her, taking pains to reintroduce her to Dr. Melton.

The young American physician, again struck by Molinda's beauty, intelligence, and warmth, chatted with her for two hours or more, and she conversed easily in English with him. Wu-ling was present throughout the talk, but seemed to retreat into her shell in the presence of the infinitely more glamorous Molinda. The Chinese girl, ordinarily effervescent and bubbling, remained silent and withdrawn, seldom entering into the conversation unless directly questioned.

The get-together was interrupted, suddenly and unexpectedly, when the door opened and a middle-aged man with a pearl cap jammed onto the back of his head shuffled unobtrusively into the room.

Everyone present realized instantly that the Tao Kuang Emperor was rendering himself "invisible" once again, so they pretended to pay no attention to him.

He saw a bowl of salted sunflower seeds, which he relished, and taking a handful, he slid unobtrusively into a cushioned stone chair, shaped like the head of a tiger. Seemingly unconcerned, he munched contentedly on the salted seeds.

The others had no choice, and continued their discussion, although his presence made all of them self-conscious.

At last he saw fit to interrupt. "She who represents Rakehell Jonathan in Cathay," he said, making a general statement without directly addressing Molinda, "will be interested to learn of a new development. She will wish to write to Rakehell that the association of merchants who deal with foreigners in all five of the treaty ports will be partial to him and to his wares and will give their first preference to the goods that he wishes to sell and to buy."

Molinda could scarcely believe that Rakehell and Boynton was enjoying such an extraordinary stroke of good fortune. Copying the emperor's manner, she spoke to no one in particular as she said, "Rakehell Jonathan will want to know how these developments came to pass."

The emperor grinned and shoved his pearl-studded cap farther toward the crown of his head. "It may be," he said, a mischievous expression appearing in his eyes, "that the associations of merchants in the five treaty ports received instructions from one whom they hastened to obey. It is difficult to ascertain precisely what happened, to be sure. Other shippers would be very angry and upset and would issue protests that the imperial viceroys in the ports would be compelled to deal with, and that would be both difficult and embarrassing for them. Let it suffice that no one knows exactly how this development transpired, but let Rakehell Jonathan rest assured that it is authentic."

Molinda was more than satisfied with his revelation.

The emperor rose to his feet, smiled vaguely at Dr. Melton, and helping himself to a handful of salted sunflower seeds, started toward the door. Then he had second thoughts, paused, and turning back, poured about half the contents of the bowl into a pocket. He actually looked guilty as he scurried out of the room.

Matthew Melton couldn't help laughing aloud, but Wu-ling remained sober-faced, as did Molinda. Either they found nothing strange in the Celestial Emperor's conduct, or else they were being diplomatic and refraining from expressing their true feelings about him.

Molinda shook her head in wonder. "I shall send the good news to Jonathan and Charles at once," she said. "Fortunately, there's a company clipper tied up at Hong Kong right now, and I shall order it to return to New London with all possible speed." As she well knew, the partiality toward Rakehell and Boynton shown by the merchants of China would go far to alleviate the financial crisis that the company was suffering.

The *Lai-tse lu* was one of the clipper ships with enough cabins to accommodate the entire Boynton family and their guest, Erika von Klausner, on a long voyage. The great clipper, flagship of the fleet, was making a round-trip run between her home port in New England and London prior to returning to the Far Eastern route, and Charles hastened to book all the available cabins for himself and his family.

Although none of the Boyntons knew it, there was something of a crisis when Erika broke the news to her associate, Reinhardt Braun. She had been horseback riding with Elizabeth and returned to the Boynton house to find Braun, whom she had summoned, waiting for her. Not bothering to change from her riding attire, she went into the family sitting room where he awaited her, and there she greeted him.

He was bored and consequently was in a sullen mood.

"Your message," he said, "indicated you had some information of importance to impart to me."

"Correct," she replied pleasantly, tapping her riding crop lightly against the side of one boot. "We are going to America on Thursday of this week, sailing on board the largest and most luxurious of Rakehell and Boynton clipper ships." She made the plan sound like an exciting adventure.

Braun continued to regard her sourly. "I fail to see what is so wonderful about this plan," he said.

A note of steel entered her voice. "Regardless of what you see," she told him, "I find the prospects highly encouraging. I'm further ingratiating myself with the British branch of the family, and I'll be introduced to the American branch under the best auspices. I'm not able to ask for much more than that."

He grimaced, shifted his weight from one foot to the other, and slid his hands under his broad belt. "I suppose," he said sullenly, "that I will have to travel as your manservant."

Erika realized now what was troubling him and smiled sweetly. "Precisely so," she said. "You've already been presented to the Boyntons as my servant, so it's impossible to change your status now. I can think of many things worse for you."

"I cannot," he replied, his anger beginning to get the better of him. "When I accepted this post, I had no intention of spending many months masquerading as a servant, and I demand better treatment."

Erika's smile faded, and her eyes became cold as she stared at him. Suddenly she raised her riding crop and struck him with all her might across the face.

The assault was so unexpected that he fell back instinctively, raising his hand to the broad, livid welt on his cheek. Even now, however, he did not lose his aplomb; very much aware that he was in the Boynton house and that it would be dangerous to create a scene, he remained silent, only the hatred seething in his eyes expressing his feelings.

"You deserve that," Erika said in a quiet matter-of-fact tone. "You seem to forget who is in charge and who is the subordinate on this assignment. I give the orders, and you follow them. That was clearly understood from the beginning, and that's the way we shall function until we return to Hamburg and I am rid of you. I trust I make myself understood."

"The Fräulein Baroness makes her position very clear," he said, clicking his heels and bowing ironically.

"Good," Erika replied. "Then there's no need for any additional unpleasantness between us. In due time we shall travel to the Far East in order to complete our assignment there. When there are no Rakehells and no Boyntons present, we will change your status and you will become my equal, let us say. Perhaps I will even honor you by calling you my cousin."

Braun knew that she was deliberately taunting him, but he continued to keep his temper under tight rein. "When does the baroness require that I present myself for boarding on this ship that will take us to America?" he wanted to know.

"I'll send a message to your lodgings in the next day or two," she replied. "Keep watch for it!"

The welt on the side of Braun's face was fading by the time the *Lai-tse lu* set sail. A River Thames pilot was in command on the quarterdeck as the sleek vessel made her way down the great river toward the English Channel and the open sea.

Erika enjoyed herself immensely on the voyage, although the same could not be said for Braun, who was given a hammock in the crew quarters and ate with the ordinary seamen. He was accustomed to fancier accommodations and better food, and he seethed on the entire journey.

Charles spent several hours each day on the quarterdeck, although he left the handling of the ship to her captain and officers. He took full advantage of the opportunity that presented itself, however, to keep David fully occupied as a cabin boy, in order to acquire sea time and experience. The child had no regular duties, but learned the routines of shipboard life from the officers as he familiarized himself with every phase of the sailing operation.

Ruth's heart stood still while she watched little David

climbing barefoot into the rigging. But the boy had the surefooted agility of a natural-born sailor and acquitted himself well.

Jessica could scarcely conceal her delight. "Every man in the family," she said, "has learned seamanship from the time that he was a small child. I'm so glad that David is continuing in the tradition!"

Charles nodded gravely. "He'll have his master's papers by the time he reaches his majority," he said. "That's part of the family tradition, too."

Erika was curious. "Why is it," she wanted to know, "that the men of your family must learn to sail vessels? They are first and foremost businessmen and traders, is it not so?"

"Indeed they are," Charles replied, "but in order to be a successful merchant and trader, one must know all that he can about the winds and the seas and the carrying of cargo. In no other way can he expect to prosper."

The German woman began to understand the "formula" that made the Rakehell-Boynton dynasty so successful.

The westerly winds were fair but strong, and combined with high seas, slowed the clipper somewhat on her journey to North America. But as Charles remarked, speed was relative, especially when one dealt with clippers. A slow voyage on a clipper ship was the equivalent of making superb time on an ordinary brig.

At last the vessel sighted Block Island, and a short time later the coast of Long Island came into view. Rounding the tip past the Montauk Point lighthouse, the *Lai-tse lu* headed for the estuary of the Thames in New London and her home berth. A cannon sounded three times, the signal that the clipper was entering the port. Missy Sarah Rakehell and Judith Rakehell Ellison did not stir from their Pequot Avenue homes on the waterfront, however, as they had no idea that the English branch of the family was on board the vessel. When they were seen standing at the rail, however, Jeremiah immediately dispatched a messenger to alert his wife and his daughter, and they were on hand in the throng when the

*Lai-tse lu* was maneuvered into her berth. The greeting was warm, and Missy Sarah immediately agreed that she would have ample room to take care of Erika von Klausner and her servant.

Elizabeth's heart stopped beating when she first caught sight of Jonathan standing at the base of the pier. He looked older than when she had last seen him, there were fresh lines in his tanned face, and his hair was flecked with gray. His suffering had aged him, but in no way did it detract from his great attractiveness. He was still the most handsome, debonair man she had ever seen, and she caught her breath as he came to her, put his hands on her shoulders, and gave her a light, cousinly kiss on the cheek. That had to satisfy her for the moment, but she vowed that the day would come when he would no longer think of her as a relative.

Erika von Klausner was pleasantly surprised by Jonathan Rakehell's appearance. She had heard Elizabeth rave about him but had attributed the better part of the girl's enthusiasm to her avowed love for him. He was every bit as distinguished and masculine as Elizabeth had said.

Braun, inconspicuous in his servant's livery, studied Jonathan with equal interest. This was the man responsible for his degradation, he thought, and he conceived an immediate deep hatred for him.

The ladies immediately went off to the Rakehell mansion, with David, ecstatically reunited with Julian and Jade, cavorting wildly. Harmony celebrated the reunion, too, by barking so loudly that Sarah and Jessica had to raise their voices when they conversed. Sir Alan and Charles stayed behind and adjourned to the boardroom in the headquarters building for an emergency meeting with Jeremiah, his son, and his new son-in-law.

"You've arrived just in time," Homer Ellison told the Boyntons. "Just yesterday, Jonnie had a letter from Molinda, together with a fuller explanation from a young physician whom he sent off to the Middle Kingdom."

Jonathan nodded. "It seems we're in great luck," he said.

"The Tao Kuang Emperor has ordered that our captains be shown preferential treatment. I assume that it will be openly demonstrated in the Chinese dealings with Americans, and necessarily somewhat more subtle in their dealings with the British."

Charles grinned. "Yes, that makes sense," he said. "The British East India Company would be inclined to start a new war if they felt there was discrimination against them in any Chinese port. To what do we attribute this preferential treatment?"

Jonathan explained that he had sent Dr. Matthew Melton to Cathay at his own expense and that the young physician had been instrumental in curing the emperor of an illness.

"That isn't our only good news," Jeremiah said, sitting back in his chair at the head of the polished oak table. "Tell them about your meeting in Washington City with President Polk, Jonnie."

Jonathan told them about how he had been summoned to the nation's capital the preceding week and had been informed by the President himself that, in return for services rendered in connection with Caleb Cushing's mission that had opened Cathay to American trade, Rakehell and Boynton had been granted the first licenses issued by the United States government to engage in such business. "Other companies will be given similar licenses, naturally," Jonathan said, "but it will be some time before they're issued. I couldn't pin the President down, of course, because that would have been too rude, but I think we can count on being the only American firm authorized to trade with the Chinese for several months."

Sir Alan whistled under his breath in admiration. "The speed of clippers being what it is," he said, "this head start can be of tremendous financial advantage to us."

"Precisely," Homer Ellison said. "I've been busy rerouting clippers and rearranging schedules in order to make every last ship available for the China trade, but I need to know where the vessels that operate out of London stand. You couldn't have come here at a better time."

Charles reached into an inner pocket and produced his own

194

schedules. He and Homer immediately went to work with a vengeance to set as many of them free as they could.

"I've already written to Molinda to expect a positive inundation of clippers," Jonathan said, "and I've requested her to buy or rent additional dock space in Hong Kong."

"What this amounts to," Jeremiah Rakehell said slowly, "is that, thanks to the fortuitous circumstances of President Polk's favor and the extreme kindness of the Tao Kuang Emperor, we've been granted an additional respite. I quite agreed with your estimate, Alan, that the funds from Charles's brilliant pepper deal would take care of our financial problems for six months. Now, if we're sufficiently alert, we'll be able to get by for an additional six to twelve months."

"Twelve is closer to the mark, I believe," Jonathan interjected, and his father nodded.

Sir Alan leaned forward in his chair. "Can you show me in black and white why that should be?"

"Certainly, Uncle Alan," Jonathan replied, and began to jot down figures. As always, he had a phenomenal memory for facts, and knew almost to the penny what any individual clipper ship could earn on a voyage, depending on the cargo that she carried.

They worked steadily until it was time to go to the Rakehell house for supper. What they were working out was basically simple. They were replacing clippers on various European runs with the company's older, conventional ships, which was just what they had done in the New World coastal trade as well as in the Caribbean and South American runs. They spent a long time discussing the new vessels being turned out of the New London yard, and Jonathan, who was in exclusive charge of such projects, was emphatic.

"We have only our yard here," he said, "for the production of new ships. I stress this because the Boynton shipyard in Southwark is now being used exclusively for purposes of repairs and overhauls. This means we are producing four clippers per year. That's our absolute capacity, and we have shipwrights and carpenters working seven days and seven nights a week to keep up a blistering pace."

"Is there any way," Sir Alan wanted to know, "that you could build new facilities and add another clipper or two to your annual output?"

"I'm afraid not, Uncle Alan," Jonathan said. "I've investigated the possibilities thoroughly. We need experienced men to do the job, and we're using veteran crews that are already perilously thin. I can't spare a single veteran shipwright or carpenter for any additional new ships."

Charles, as always, accepted his cousin's word as final. "We'll assume that what Jonnie says is so," he said. "It always is. That means of the four new ships a year that are turned out by the yard here, we are required to sell two to outside interests and that leaves us with two to add to our own fleet."

"Actually," Sir Alan said, fingering the watch fob that dangled from a waistcoat pocket, "it doesn't disturb me overly much that we can add only two ships per year to our fleet. Our present financial problems have been caused by the rapidity of our expansion. If we'd been satisfied on our previous level of trade, we'd have been making vast sums of money now. But the cost of new ships, plus the crews, plus the cost of new shore facilities in so many ports, has taken its toll, and the cash demands on us are frightful, far worse than anything you and I ever envisioned when we were younger, Jerry, and were taking over the business from our fathers."

Jeremiah sighed gently. "The price of success is very strange," he said. "We're the envy of everyone in the business, and yet we're having a dreadful time scraping together enough cash to keep going."

"What I'd like to know," Jeremiah said, "is when this crisis is going to end, or if it's going to end. Perhaps we'll keep expanding for years and years to come, and will always be short of cash."

Jonathan and Charles grinned at each other, and the young Englishman acted as their spokesman. "Jonnie and I worked separately on this problem," he said, "and I'm glad to say that we came up with almost identical answers. Both of us feel that this isn't a permanent, insoluble problem. It will end

196

one day. The pepper deal brought us a windfall, and now it appears we can expect another as a result of our being the only American company to engage in the China trade for a time—with the enthusiastic support of the Chinese government. So the situation is constantly improving.''

"Correct,'' Jonathan said. "Beyond all else, we must not allow ourselves to be hampered or tied down by a fear of bankruptcy. Right now is the time for us to be expanding, just as we've been doing. The company that stands still is actually moving backward on the treadmill and will lose what standing it already possesses.''

Homer broke the tension by laughing. "I must confess something,'' he said. "As all of you no doubt know, I've been quite conservative all my life. I haven't believed in taking unnecessary risks, and I've been cautious in all things. Then, as it happens, I became associated with Jonnie and Charles. They taught me a new way of looking at business and life. The shipping industry belongs to the bold, just as the world itself belongs to the bold, so I changed accordingly. There was a time when I would have been worried sick knowing that we've been leaping from crisis to crisis. But I'm no longer in the least concerned that a day of reckoning will ultimately come. Let it come, I say, and we'll find ways to deal with it when it does.''

"Hear, hear!'' Charles cried enthusiastically. Jonathan nodded in agreement, too.

Jeremiah and Sir Alan exchanged a long look, and each knew the other's mind. Their way of doing business was not the younger generation's, but these younger men were the inheritors of the Rakehell and Boynton company and had to be allowed to proceed as they saw fit. Their elders were prepared to give them a free hand and to trust in them implicitly.

The rearrangement of the schedules was a task that could not be completed in a single day, and ultimately they adjourned their efforts and walked the short distance to the Rakehell home. The barking of Harmony and the ecstatic shrieks of the children told them, as they approached the house, all they needed to know. The visit of the English side of the family was already a huge success.

They joined the ladies in Jeremiah's study for aperitifs before dinner, and Elizabeth, clad in a new gown of sophisticated black, with a white silk collar and cuffs, did her best to arouse the interest of Jonathan. To her dismay, although he replied politely, it was obvious that he continued to regard her as a relative and an adolescent.

Missy Sarah felt sorry for the young woman, and so did Jessica. It was painfully evident that Elizabeth was hopelessly in love with Jonathan and was doomed to be frustrated. He was incapable of returning her interest, or so it seemed.

Ruth Boynton was secretly relieved that she herself had overcome her lifelong infatuation with Jonathan. She had loved him since the time when she had been much younger than Elizabeth now was, and she had twice taken second place when he had given his heart to someone else. Now, however, her relationship with Charles had improved so greatly that there was no room in her heart or in her mind for any man other than her husband.

Ruth could not help noting that Erika von Klausner was doing her very best to attract Jonathan. The baroness was wearing a gown of lightweight pale green silk that set off her red hair to its best advantage, and she had even dared to daub some green shadow on her eyelids, but it was the daring cut of her gown that set her apart from the women of the Rakehell-Boynton family. They habitually showed good taste in their clothes and were inclined to be conservative. Erika, however, had cast all caution to the wind, and even Jeremiah and Sir Alan found their gaze inadvertently returning again and again to her prominent cleavage. Jonathan, too, was aware of her presence, much to Elizabeth's private consternation, but the German woman was too experienced to create enemies by behaving with blatant overtness. Her flirtation with Jonathan was very subtle, very quiet, very refined—and equally insistent.

Erika sat directly opposite him at the dinner table, and Missy Sarah noted that he paid far more attention to her than he did to Elizabeth, whom she had taken care to seat at his right.

Although none of the men were aware of these subtleties, the women noted all of them, and as Judith Ellison later confided to Ruth, "I can't help feeling sorry for Elizabeth, who has a wildly exaggerated puppy love for Jonnie."

"Perhaps not puppy love," Ruth replied. "She's getting a bit old for that."

"Call it what you will, you know what I mean," Judith replied. "In any event, I'm glad that the baroness appears to have made an impression on him. It shows that—whether he realizes it or not—he's finally getting over the blow that he suffered when Lai-tse lu died."

"Do you think that he'll ever marry again?" Ruth asked.

Judith shrugged. "That's anyone's guess," she said. "Jonnie is always very closemouthed about his feelings, and he confides in no one except Missy Sarah. I have no idea what he tells her, because she'd rather be boiled in oil than break his confidence."

Ruth considered the situation for a time. "Well," she said at last, "if he should ever marry again, I can't help hoping that he'd pick someone like Elizabeth, simply because she has loved him so hard for such a long time."

"This is premature, of course," Judith said, "but I find myself wondering about the baroness. She's flamboyantly attractive, to be sure, but what sort of person is she beyond that?"

"I can't honestly say," Ruth replied. "She's been visiting with us for some time now, but she keeps her emotions under very strict control and keeps her innermost thoughts very much to herself."

Judith's smile was tight. "Then perhaps she and Jonnie will get together," she said. "They sound just like birds of a feather to me."

# IV

Displaying great caution, Erika von Klausner worked steadily to improve her relationship with Jonathan Rakehell. She took care, however, not to overplay her hand at any time. She won the friendship of his two motherless children slowly and carefully, without seeming to fawn over them. In the same way, she gradually moved to a far easier, more relaxed relationship with Jonathan himself, and somewhat to the surprise of his sister and Ruth, she eventually was exchanging good-natured raillery with him. This was something that he had never done with any other woman. In the meantime, he, along with the other male members of the family, was immersed in the reorganization that would mean so much to the long-range future of the company. While they were in the midst of rescheduling and planning on trade with Cathay, they were so busy that they instituted a new procedure and took sandwiches and cold meats to the office with them so they could save time and not return home for noon dinner.

Hence, the ladies were alone all day, and each day was like so many others. Early one afternoon, Missy Sarah and Jessica were sitting together on the back porch of the house crocheting, when a serving maid interrupted them. "Excuse me, Mrs. Rakehell," she said, "but there's a young man here to see you."

Sarah was surprised. "A young man here to see me?" she asked. "Land sakes!"

"He says that he's related to you. His name is Josiah Dowling."

Sarah had to think for a moment, and finally she said, "It could be that he's the son of my first husband's sister. She married a Dowling. Well, I'll soon find out. Send him in, May."

The maid retreated, and soon returned with a ruggedly handsome young man in tow. He was in his late twenties, and his expression, as well as his walk, indicated that he was self-confident without being brash. He went straight to Sarah and bowed to her. "Cousin Sarah," he said, "I'd know you anywhere. My parents had a painting of you the day you married Captain Applegate, and you look the same as you did then—"

"Except that I'm a great deal older now," Sarah said pointedly.

"Well, a mite older," the young man conceded, and a laughing Sarah presented him to Lady Boynton.

"I'd know you too, ma'am," the young man said. "You look like all the Rakehells in the picture gallery where I stood waiting to be received."

Sarah decided that, whoever he was, he was very bright and very observant. She soon satisfied herself as to his identity. He was indeed the nephew of her late first husband, for whom he had been named. He had grown up, it appeared, in Providence, and still made his home there. "What brings you to New London, Josiah?" Missy Sarah asked.

His reply was blunt. "If you really want to know, Cousin Sarah," he said, "I'm a ship's captain by trade, and I've held my master's papers for five years now. I first went to sea as a youngster. I heard it said that a Sarah Applegate, who'd been living in Cathay, was married to the head of the Rakehell-Boynton Company, so I felt sure we were related."

"I do wish you'd sit down and stop pacing," Sarah told him. "You make me nervous."

"That's because I am kind of nervous, ma'am," he said. "I had to force myself to get up my nerve enough to come down here to New London to see you."

Missy Sarah bristled. "Why?" she demanded. "Do I have a reputation for being an ogre?"

"No, ma'am," he replied politely, "but my purpose in coming to see you wasn't just to pay a visit to a relative I've never before known. To be honest about it, I'm hoping you will use your influence to get me a job."

She was immediately on her guard, and stiffened.

"I've sailed only conventional ships," Josiah Dowling said, "but I've had a hankering, as every master has, to stand on the quarterdeck of a clipper ship. You're married to the head of the biggest fleet of such ships in the business, so I finally got up my nerve. I think my records will speak for themselves, and I carry enough credentials and letters of recommendation with me to satisfy blame near anybody."

Missy Sarah looked him up and down and decided she liked him. He could have pretended he was getting in touch with her because they were related, and then, after getting acquainted, he could have revealed his real motive. Instead, he had elected to be honest.

Without further ado, she sent him off to see Homer Ellison. Neither Sarah nor Jessica was surprised when Josiah came home at the end of the day with the male members of the family. He had been hired as a ship's captain, Homer having been more than satisfied with his credentials and his letters of recommendation. He would go into immediate training as master of a clipper ship. It was not difficult for an experienced merchant marine officer to learn how to handle a clipper, but Jonathan insisted that all in his fleet be thoroughly familiar with the type of vessel they were commanding. In the meantime, Jeremiah had invited the new employee home for supper.

Dowling proved to be a valuable addition to the family group. Erika, who was learning to know and understand Jonathan far better than he realized, was secretly amused to notice that he was relieved because Josiah eased his own burden. The newcomer was a bachelor and consequently was attentive to Elizabeth and to Erika, thus allowing Jonathan to dispense with having to make conversation with the ladies.

Erika was indifferent to his reaction. She was determined to pursue him relentlessly, no matter what might happen, and would allow nothing to stand between her and her goal. Elizabeth, less experienced and certainly less strong-willed, gave in to the course of least resistance, and in the vain hope of trying to arouse Jonathan's jealousy, she began to pay far more attention to Josiah than she otherwise would have done. The young man was flattered by the attentions of the lovely young heiress.

Ruth and Judith, concerned because the male members of the family were working so hard, had connived and arranged a picnic to be held on Sunday noon. They reasoned, quite rightly, that the plan would thwart any attempt on the part of Jonathan and Homer to spend the Sabbath at the shipyard. Josiah Dowling was also invited to the picnic, and accepted with alacrity.

The scheme of the women succeeded, and on Sunday Jonathan and Homer accompanied the entire group as they set out in carriages for a picnic site located farther upstream on the Thames. The women and children occupied carriages, which were also laden with provisions, and the men accompanied them on horseback. Erika stole a march on Elizabeth by also riding a mount, and instead of using a sidesaddle, she wore a pair of snug, neatly tailored trousers, enabling her to use a man's saddle, which was highly unusual.

Erika saw to it that she rode beside Jonathan on the journey upstream, and she pretended not to notice that Elizabeth was definitely displeased.

At the picnic itself the children played catch with a large rubber ball, and when Julian and David tried to keep the ball away from Jade, the little girl got the better of them by whispering instructions to Harmony. The dog, understanding her perfectly, leaped high in the air as Julian threw the ball to David and managed to deflect it sufficiently so that it traveled directly to Jade.

Some of the adults who were aware of the contest looked at the little girl admiringly. Jonathan grinned proudly. "My daughter," he said to Erika, who sat on a blanket beside him at the river's edge, "is a rather extraordinary child. She always manages to get her own way, and when she wants something, she allows nothing to stand between her and it."

"We are kindred spirits then, I believe," Erika told him. "I, too, set goals for myself, and I achieve them no matter what the consequences."

"Good for you!" Jonathan said, and chuckled aloud as he watched Jade throw the ball to Harmony, who somehow blocked and halted it, then stood guard over it, growling and holding David and Julian at bay until his daughter retrieved it.

"I hope you aren't as ruthless as Jade," he said. "As you can see, she's giving her brother and her cousin a very rough time that they're not likely to forget."

"I approve heartily of her conduct," Erika said bluntly. "She is a woman in a man's world, surrounded by men, so she uses every stratagem, every trick at her command to get what she wants."

Something in her tone caught Jonathan's attention, and he studied her more intently. He became convinced that she was not joking in the least. The only women he had ever known with a similar approach to life were his wife, the Princess An Mien, and Molinda, and consequently Erika von Klausner impressed him. She was no ordinary young woman.

Seated on a blanket a short distance from the couple was Elizabeth, with an attentive Josiah close behind her. She watched Erika creating an impression on Jonathan, capturing and holding his full attention as she herself had never yet been able to do, and she found herself growing desperate.

In her frustration, she began to flirt with Josiah Dowling far more baldly than she realized. She laughed at everything he said and inched closer and closer to him, so that their faces were almost touching.

Ruth, who was keeping an eye on the children, noted the byplay between Elizabeth and Josiah and, looking up, caught the eye of Charles, who was engrossed in a business conversation with Homer.

He became aware of his wife's summons, however, and responded to it promptly, excusing himself and hurrying to her side.

Words were unnecessary; Ruth drew her husband's attention to Elizabeth and Josiah with a brief nod. He watched them for a time, frowning. "What in the devil does Elizabeth think she's doing?" he demanded, deliberately keeping his voice low. "She's practically asking to be seduced."

"Unfortunately," Ruth said, "she doesn't realize it. In fact, she'd be startled and shocked if you were to accuse her of it."

"I don't understand," Charles muttered.

This was not the time or the place to explain. "I'll fill you in on the background later, my dear," Ruth said. "I simply thought I should call your attention to her right now so that you can intervene."

"How very awkward," he replied. In spite of his bold, inventive nature, Charles could be a traditional, hidebound Englishman on occasion, Ruth decided. She, however, was still an American in spite of the years she had spent in London, and acted accordingly, taking her husband's arm and approaching the young couple.

Elizabeth looked up in surprise and moved several inches away from the young sea captain. Josiah, who had been enjoying himself thoroughly, sobered instantly, aware of the proximity of a senior partner of Rakehell and Boynton.

Ruth began to chat about inconsequentials, and though Elizabeth wanted to be rid of her and of her brother, she didn't know quite how to proceed.

Charles quietly admired his wife's cleverness, and took advantage of the opportunity to ask Josiah to join him for a brief discussion.

They left Ruth with Elizabeth, and the two men walked parallel to the river as they strolled on the bank. "I note," Charles said, "that you're somewhat taken with my sister."

Josiah did not believe in dissembling. "Indeed I am, sir," he said. "She's not only as lovely a girl as ever I've seen, but she has great wit and charm as well."

"True, she has all those qualities," Charles replied, and weighed his words carefully. "She's also endowed with others that are less fortunate."

Josiah was startled by the sudden turn of the conversation.

"She isn't a natural flirt," Charles went on, "although I certainly couldn't blame you for thinking of her as one."

"I was enjoying her company so much that my mind wasn't turned in such a direction, sir," Josiah said.

"So much the better," Charles told him. "Better for you, and better for Elizabeth."

The young sea captain became confused.

"All I know," Charles said, "is that at the moment, Elizabeth is somewhat troubled about something. This has apparently made her both restless and reckless, and she isn't behaving as she usually does."

"I'm sorry to hear it," Josiah murmured.

"Naturally, I'm very fond of my sister," Charles went on.

The young sea captain nodded.

"I would hate to see her getting herself into trouble or placing herself in a compromising situation." For all of his vagueness, Charles could be brutally candid when the occasion demanded it. "She's old enough to know her own mind, to be sure, and I have no intention of trying to intervene like a nanny to protect her. On the other hand, I think it only fair to make you privy to the facts as I see and know them."

"I understand, Mr. Boynton," Josiah said, and he, too, spoke with great candor. "I'm not the type who takes advantage of a lady in distress."

"I'm very pleased to hear it," Charles said, smiling and extending his hand.

Josiah shook it firmly, looking him squarely in the eyes.

Charles knew they had reached a meeting of the minds, and the sea captain's manner was virtually a guarantee that he could be trusted. Under no circumstances, now, would he take advantage of Elizabeth's seeming vulnerability, under no conditions would he misinterpret her flirtatiousness and make advances to her. They returned to the group, and Elizabeth Boynton became aware of a distinct change in Josiah Dowling's

207

attitude toward her. He was still friendly, to be sure, but he was definitely remote and saw to it that he kept his distance from her. She had no idea what was responsible for this abrupt change, but she assumed that it had something to do with her own personality, and consequently she became withdrawn and increasingly silent.

Josiah felt sorry for her, but he knew there was nothing he could do to help her. The warning he had received from Charles Boynton had been clear and explicit. An enterprising and ambitious young man who wanted a long-range future with the company would be wise to heed the advice of an active partner.

Elizabeth's withdrawal left Jonathan free for Erika von Klausner, and the baroness was quick to take full advantage of her opportunity. She waited until after he had assured himself that his children were engrossed in their game, and then she approached him. "I'm surprised to find so many hills here," she said. "This reminds me, on a smaller scale, of the terrain in Bavaria. Are there any places nearby from which I could obtain an overall view?"

He thought for a moment. "If you don't mind a rather rugged walk," he said, "I think I can take you to such a place."

Erika nodded eagerly.

They set out side by side and followed the Thames as it wound toward the north. They began to climb to higher ground, and when the steep incline, combined with the underbrush, made progress difficult for the baroness, she extended a hand with seeming impulsiveness. Jonathan grasped it as he guided her, and somehow her hand continued to nestle in his. It seemed like a natural and normal development, and he had no idea that she had calculated this closely. At last they reached the crest of a high hill, and Jonathan indicated the vista with a sweep of his hand. It was not accidental that Erika stood so close to him that their shoulders touched.

Then, as they enjoyed the view together, Erika subtly leaned against him, making it necessary for him to put an arm around her in order to support her weight.

"I had no idea that there was so much lovely scenery in America," Erika said. "One hears about your great cities like New York and Boston and Philadelphia, but one is quite unprepared for the natural beauty of your country."

She had not struck him as the type of woman who appreciated the beauties of nature, and he began to describe some of his favorite scenery in the United States, his enthusiasm mounting as he told her about the rugged coast of Maine, the vast solitude of the beaches in the Floridas, and the grandeur of the Mississippi River.

Erika listened with seeming intensity, her gaze fixed on his, her lips slightly parted, her eyes limpid as she gazed silently up at him. It was irrelevant that she actually heard very little of what he was telling her; she was concentrating on the strength of his grasp as he held her, and she willed him to kiss her.

Somehow that message communicated itself to Jonathan. He had not thought in intimate terms of Erika, to be sure, but the circumstances seemed to be bringing them much closer together than he had anticipated.

Before he quite realized what was happening, he turned her toward him and, his hands grasping her shoulders, kissed her soundly.

Erika responded to his advance delicately, her timing perfect. Her lips were soft and yielding, and ultimately they parted in an unspoken invitation for him to proceed still further.

The forces of nature took charge. Many months had passed since Jonathan had made love to Molinda, and his masculine desires came alive, asserting themselves beyond his ability to curb or control them.

He was reacting precisely as Erika had hoped. Seemingly crushed and helpless in his embrace, she was actually very much in charge, very much in command.

She allowed him to do what he pleased, and was delighted when his grip grew tighter. Then, when his hands could no longer remain still, she decided the time had come to change tactics.

209

She managed to disengage herself from him, gently but swiftly, and in such a way that he would not take offense.

A warning bell rang in Jonathan's mind, and he realized that the German woman was calling a halt before it was too late. He released her and took a half-step backward.

Both of them breathing hard, struggling for composure, they stared at each other.

Jonathan wanted to apologize, but a sixth sense warned him to say nothing. He had made it very clear by his actions that he wanted Erika—somewhat to his own surprise—and he knew that she well might misinterpret an apology and feel insulted, so he followed his instinct and said nothing.

Erika privately congratulated herself: her timing had been perfect. Jonathan had become aroused, but she had called a halt in time to thwart his desires, and consequently he would want her more than ever now. She had made an indelible impression on him while, at the same time, leaving him to believe that she was chaste and ladylike. If she knew men, and she was quite certain that she did, she had taken a long step forward in her campaign to conquer Jonathan Rakehell.

They took their time wandering down the hill to the picnic site, and Erika was uncertain whether Elizabeth had caught a glimpse of the hand-holding, but finally convinced herself that she had not, because her friend remained pleasant and calm for the rest of the day.

The picnic itself was a triumph. It was a New England clambake, in which the men prepared a huge fire and did as much of the cooking as the ladies. The meal began with steamer clams that were dipped into hot, melted butter, and this dish was followed by clam chowder, which Jessica had prepared earlier in the day from an old Rakehell family recipe. The main course was lobsters, which had been steamed in seaweed, accompanied by steamed potatoes and ears of fresh corn. For those who were able to eat dessert there was a choice between watermelon and apple pie. Only Julian and David elected to eat both.

The sun was sinking as the party returned home, and Sarah

suggested that they meet in the dining room for cold meats and a pot of baked beans, which had been simmering on her stove all day.

Elizabeth, rather than going directly down to the dining room, headed instead for Erika's bedchamber, and there she found the baroness, who had changed into a red silk gown, patching her makeup before a dressing-table mirror.

Erika looked at her friend's reflection in her mirror, smiled, and said something innocuous about how much she enjoyed American picnics.

Elizabeth, however, had not come to make idle chatter. Her face was set, and in her features one could catch a glimpse of the mature woman she would become. While losing none of her beauty, she had an unexpected, hidden strength.

"Erika," she said calmly, almost conversationally, "I think the time is at hand for you to move on."

The startled Erika could only gape at her.

"When I learned you were coming to England and asked you to pay me a visit," Elizabeth went on, "I didn't envisage a stay that would go on and on for many months. I realize that it may be inconvenient for you to part company here in America, so far from your own home, but I'm sure that transportation can be provided for you and your manservant, all the way to Hamburg, in fact, if that's what you would like."

Erika could be blunt when the occasion required it. "Have I offended you in some way?" she demanded.

"You have," Elizabeth replied quietly but firmly. "I've made no secret to you of my feelings for Jonathan Rakehell, yet you've gone out of your way to flirt with him and attract him. Seeing you holding hands with him this afternoon when you returned from a stroll was the last straw. I'm sorry, but I can't help but regard your conduct as deliberate and vicious toward me."

"If Jonathan were drawn to you," Erika replied, "rest assured that I would have avoided him. I have no need to steal other women's men. But he has made it very clear by

211

his own attitude that his relationship with you is quite casual. Therefore, as he is exceptionally handsome and interesting, I have felt free to pursue my own interests with him.''

"That's your privilege, to be sure," Elizabeth told her, "but I prefer that you conduct your pursuit from some position other than as my guest."

Before Erika could reply, a servingwoman tapped at the door. "Forgive the interruption, baroness," she said, "but your manservant is downstairs and is quite insistent on having immediate words with you."

Without further ado, Erika gathered her skirts and hurried down to an auxiliary parlor, where Reinhardt Braun stood with his back toward her, staring out toward the beach and the saltwater estuary of the Thames beyond it. He turned as he heard her footsteps, and she was shocked to see that his face was badly battered. One eye was swollen and closed, his cheeks were puffy, and there were several gashes and bruises elsewhere on his face.

"What happened to you?" she demanded curtly.

"As you can see," Braun told her, "I've been in a fight."

"That appears obvious," Erika said contemptuously. "I just hope it wasn't so obvious to everyone in the household."

"No one saw me but the housemaid, I assure you," Braun said.

Erika tapped her foot impatiently. "I thought you had better sense than to become involved in a row."

"While you have been cavorting with the wealthy British and American shipowners," he said spitefully, "I have been left to my own devices. The servants in this household, with whom it appears to have been assumed that I would consort, are stupid, ignorant, and shortsighted. So I have been left to my own devices, and I have been forced to seek my own entertainment where I could find it. Unfortunately, the opportunities in this town are limited, to say the least. There are a number of taverns on a thoroughfare called Bank Street, and these are low places that cater to merchant seamen. However, their schnapps and beer are first-rate, and their

212

prices are very reasonable. Unfortunately, I became involved in an altercation.''

Erika did not know whether to be annoyed or to laugh. ''What sort of an altercation?'' she wanted to know.

The short, swarthy man drew himself up to his full height. ''I took a fancy to a barmaid,'' he said, ''who gave promise of providing me a distraction from the perpetual boredom of my present existence. Unfortunately, however, she appears to have far too many blood relations in this community. Two brothers and a cousin, who are merchant seamen, attacked me, and although I defended myself ably, they managed to inflict the damage that is all too visible. Then another cousin of hers, who is a member of the local constabulary, warned me that if I ever set foot in the establishment again or attempt to get in touch with the barmaid in any way I shall be—in his words—deposited in jail and the key will be thrown away.''

It was all that Erika could do to keep from laughing aloud.

''So I beseech you, Fräulein Baroness,'' Braun said, ''let us put this benighted community behind us, and allow me to give up this absurd disguise of a servant.''

''As it happens,'' Erika told him thoughtfully, ''I'd reached the same conclusion independently.'' It was true, she thought, that the time had come for her to move on. She had created an indelible impression on Jonathan Rakehell, and he needed time now to become acclimated to the thought of a long-term, intimate association with her. If Braun was in trouble with the local authorities, that was all the more reason to leave New London. She had accomplished all that she had set out to do, and was well satisfied with the results.

''When will we leave?'' Braun asked eagerly.

''I hope I will be able to tell you in the very near future,'' Erika told him.

Never one to dawdle when time for action was at hand, Erika promptly sought out Jonathan, and waited patiently until she had the chance to speak a few words with him in private. ''I wonder,'' she asked, her green eyes enormous as she touched his sleeve lightly, ''if I could ask a great favor of you?''

"Of course," he replied, not realizing that he already felt obligated to her.

"My visit with the Boyntons was merely the first step in a unique journey around the world," she said. "I'm enjoying the opportunity of a lifetime, and I was permitted to make the journey provided I'm escorted by the manservant you've seen with me. He acts more or less as a bodyguard for me."

"I see." He was more impressed than he let on. Never before had he heard of any woman traveling alone around the world.

"I'm wondering," Erika said, "whether you have a clipper ship traveling to the Orient in the fairly near future? If so, I should like to book a passage on it—if that is possible."

"Well," Jonathan replied, "it so happens that we have a clipper leaving for Djakarta the day after tomorrow, if that isn't too short notice for you."

She rejoiced inwardly. How stunned Elizabeth would be when she discovered the woman whose friendship she had rejected was losing no time in clearing out.

"You'll require various fresh fruits and vegetables for the initial stages of your voyage," Jonathan told her, "but there'll be ample time to buy what you need tomorrow. As for engaging passage, I hope you'll allow me to present you and your servant with quarters on board our clipper as my guests."

Her hand rested on his arm. "I wouldn't dream of imposing on you, Jonathan," she said softly.

"It's no imposition, I assure you. The passenger cabin would go empty if you weren't going to use it, and I promise you that the small profit that we'd make from your fare will neither make nor break Rakehell and Boynton."

"In that case," she replied gracefully, "I'm much beholden to you, and I accept. You say that the ship sails to a place called Djakarta?"

"It's the largest town on the island of Java," he said, "and is the capital of the Dutch East Indies. As a matter of fact, I have a close friend and business associate there, and I'll gladly give you a letter to him. He enjoys nothing more than entertaining a lovely lady, so your visit will be mutually beneficial."

Erika rejoiced inwardly and told herself that her luck was all to the good. Not only was she being given free transportation by the fastest possible means to distant Djakarta, but she would actually travel with a letter of introduction to the Fat Dutchman, whose business relationship she sought on behalf of her Hamburg employers. Everything was working out for the best, and she knew from the way that Jonathan Rakehell looked at her, he would not forget her. They would meet again in the East.

Elizabeth Boynton suffered a convenient "headache" and consequently did not go to the Rakehell and Boynton shipyard to say farewell to Erika von Klausner, who set sail to Djakarta.

Elizabeth remained cloistered in her room, and she appeared much subdued as Ruth Boynton, who had attended the sailing, returned immediately thereafter to the Rakehell mansion. "It's too bad you couldn't see Erika go," Ruth told the younger woman.

Elizabeth shook her head. "I know she's gone, and that's what counts." Her curiosity got the better of her. "I suppose Jonathan was there?"

Ruth nodded.

"I might have guessed it," Elizabeth said bitterly.

"Don't give too much significance to his appearance," Ruth told her. "He always goes to the docks when one of his clippers sails off on a long voyage. As you know, Charles does the exact same thing in London. It's part of the family tradition."

Elizabeth smiled and shrugged.

"Your competition is gone, and that's what matters," Ruth said gently.

"The reason she is gone," Elizabeth replied, "is because I made it very plain to her that she was no longer welcome.

That was petty and cowardly of me, I suppose, but I just couldn't tolerate watching her making eyes at Jonnie and pawing him."

Ruth could easily sympathize with her sister-in-law, having herself spent too many years loving Jonathan in vain. She could only pray that never again would she fall under his spell.

"Anyway, she's not gone for good," Elizabeth continued. "The mere fact that Erika has sailed off to the Orient convinces me more than ever that she's set her cap for Jonnie."

"How does that follow?" Ruth asked.

"She knows that he goes to the Orient fairly regularly. He's been home for a long time now, at least a long time for him, and it won't surprise me in the least if he goes dashing off to Djakarta and Canton and Hong Kong one of these days. When he gets there, you can bet your last ha'penny that Erika will be there as a welcoming committee of one to greet him."

Ruth started to laugh.

"I'm in earnest," Elizabeth said. "That woman will go to any lengths to snare him, I know it!"

"The principal difference between you and Erika von Klausner," Ruth said softly, "is that you're a lady and she merely pretends to be one."

"Perhaps I should be bolder, then," Elizabeth said. "Don't you agree, Ruth? I could throw myself at Jonnie, too."

Ruth shook her head. "Don't, Elizabeth," she cautioned. "I know of no more certain way of losing him."

"You mean Erika is making a mistake by chasing after him?"

Ruth pondered for a time and then shrugged. "Maybe and maybe not," she said. "Erika von Klausner has her own techniques, and I must say they're very effective with men. But you can only be what you are. If you pretend, if you try to adopt another personality, you'll make yourself look foolish. You're too honest and forthright a person for that. Just be yourself and hope for the best."

Elizabeth let out a long sigh. "Oh, you're right as usual,

Ruth. The only thing is, I don't know any longer how to be myself, and I don't even know what the 'best' is anymore." She paused, then went on. "Perhaps one of my problems is that for my whole life, I've never really been denied anything I've wanted, and that's why I'm so angry about not being able to make Jonathan Rakehell notice me."

Hong Kong continued to grow so rapidly that Molinda considered herself fortunate to have obtained enough waterfront space for six double docks. This meant that twelve ships could be berthed and serviced simultaneously, and if Rakehell and Boynton didn't have that many vessels in the Orient, the unused space could be rented out to shippers who were desperate for a place to dock. The opening of Cathay to foreign trade was transforming not only burgeoning Hong Kong but the great, hitherto closed cities of the Middle Kingdom as well. Since earliest times Cathay had barred foreigners from her midst, and only now were Europeans and Americans appearing in substantial numbers.

The British sea captains who had been coming to Whampoa, the harbor just outside Canton, for twenty years and longer had their own private predictions, of course. They were agreed that the foreigners would be influenced far more than the people of China. "Cathay," said an English merchant who had grown old in service, "is unique. It absorbs people, ideas, and innovations. It's like a gigantic sponge that eats and drinks everything in sight, but doesn't seem to lose its original shape. I tell you flatly that the rest of the world will be far more influenced than will China. Generations well may pass before the Chinese show the effect of the tremendous revolution that's now taking place in the treaty ports."

Molinda was inclined to agree with this analysis, though she thought it was a bit oversimplified. The development of the Middle Kingdom, she felt, depended on the nature and the thrust of the guidance given the people of Cathay by the Tao Kuang Emperor and the Princess An Mien, the primary modernizing forces in the ancient country.

In Hong Kong, of course, far different circumstances

prevailed. Here the tempo of life was set by the British, who imposed their own culture, their own laws, and even, to an extent, their own food, on a community that continued to spread with lightninglike rapidity. But even here, or so it seemed to Molinda, the Chinese who flocked to the Royal Crown Colony to find work as porters and dockhands, as day laborers and servants, as shop owners and shop employees, managed to cling to their traditional values. The clothes they wore were the clothes to which they had become accustomed in Canton and the countryside. They prepared their food in the manner of their ancestors, and they shunned British dishes. When necessary, they reluctantly learned to speak and even to read and write English, but among themselves they continued to speak in the tongues of their ancestors.

Understanding all this, Molinda thought herself fortunate because she enjoyed the best of several worlds. She could be as Chinese as any native, and could think like one. When it suited her purposes, she could become a Westerner, or when she chose, she could revert to a combination of the ways of the Dutch and her native Bali.

So she moved freely and was accepted by people on every level—including most of those in the ruling circle of the English. Her relations with the deputy director of the Hong Kong constabulary, Sir Cedric Poole, had developed to the point where she gave herself freely to him for the simple reason that she liked his company and found him attractive, just as he was drawn to her. She noted, however, that despite her acceptance by the governor-general and his wife, there were still some company executives who came to Hong Kong from Great Britain who treated her quite differently. They accepted her as a business associate because they had no choice: Rakehell and Boynton was too large and powerful a firm for them to snub its Oriental head. At no time, however, did this clique invite her to their homes or to the new social club that they were forming in Hong Kong.

Sir Cedric fumed at these fellow countrymen, calling them narrowminded bigots. But Molinda merely laughed and shrugged them off. She had no need for them socially, and she cared

218

nothing about their wives, the tightly corseted ladies who gathered for tea every afternoon in each other's houses and exchanged gossip about anyone in their circle who happened to be absent that day.

Certainly Molinda regarded herself as fortunate. She selected her own lover regardless of color or caste, she selected her own friends, and she did business with anyone except Owen Bruce, who went out of his way to make it plain that he felt unyielding hatred for Rakehell and Boynton and would do anything in his power to assure their failure. She decided the best way to handle Bruce was to ignore him, to pretend that he didn't exist.

Her majordomo, Lo Fang, did not agree, and raised the subject of him one night as he escorted her from her waterfront office to her home, partway up the Peak, a curved, double-edged sword in a massive hand discouraging any passerby who might be tempted to rob or molest the stunningly beautiful woman. They passed the burly Bruce near the docks shortly after leaving Molinda's office, and he glowered at them but did not speak, even though he was well aware of their identities.

Molinda shrugged off the Scotsman's rudeness; she literally did not care whether he acknowledged her presence or not.

Lo Fang, however, had ideas of his own. "That man is very dangerous," he said, "and I think he has probably already forgotten the warning I sent him after he was involved in stealing our silks. It may be wise that he is paid a visit by men whose identities are kept secret."

Molinda became alarmed. "No, Lo Fang," she said, "that wouldn't do at all. The justice of Britain rules here, and I can assure you they don't look very kindly on members of a secret society who threaten citizens who mind their own business."

Lo Fang's smile was tight. "I was not thinking in terms of threats," he said. "I was thinking in terms of direct action. There is an old fable in the Middle Kingdom that concerns a serpent that descended from the mountains and devoured travelers who were passing through the mountains. The people of the area made many attempts to pacify the serpent. They offered him food and other gifts and made sacrifices to him, but nothing satisfied him. Then one day a ferocious warrior decided he had had enough, so he went alone into the mountains with his battle-ax and sought out the serpent in his lair. The serpent was asleep, and awakened just in time to see the battle-ax descend. Then he knew no more because the ax severed his head from his body. From that time forward, travelers were safe and could proceed unmolested through the mountains. All were safe and no payments of tribute, no gifts, were required.''

"Are you suggesting,'' Molinda asked with a trace of asperity in her voice, "that the Society of Oxen might do away with Owen Bruce?''

Lo Fang shrugged casually. "It has been known for a man to disappear without a trace. This happens in Cathay, and it can happen also in Hong Kong.''

"No, Lo Fang,'' Molinda said. "Sir Cedric is expending every effort to stamp out just that kind of terror, and I'd be an awful hypocrite if I encouraged it.''

"Bruce is a bad, bad man,'' Lo Fang said, making a final pronouncement. "It would be better for all, for Jonnie and Charles and Molinda, too, if he were to vanish.''

She shook her head firmly. "We can't live according to the laws of the jungle,'' she said. "The British wouldn't stand for it, and we'd be severely punished.''

Lo Fang took a practical approach. "The British Fan Kuei—the foreign devils—would not know what became of him,'' he said. "He would be gone.''

"I admit that I am sometimes tempted to be rid of him that way,'' Molinda said, "but it must not be. I shall hold you responsible for his continuing safety, Lo Fang.''

The majordomo nodded grudgingly, accepting the responsibility because she gave him no choice.

When they reached the house Molinda paused in the garden to inspect her favorite view, that of the magnificent harbor spread out below her. Suddenly, however, she froze. Two plumes of heavy black smoke were rising from the near shore, and she pointed in horror. Lo Fang turned quickly, and his eyes narrowed as he inspected the fire raging below them. "The flames," he said, "come from our docks. It is one of our ships that burns!"

Molinda's hand crept to her throat. In these days when every vessel was a precious asset, Rakehell and Boynton could not afford to lose one of their priceless clippers.

Summoning two guards who had remained hidden behind the heavy foliage of the garden, Lo Fang made them responsible for Molinda's welfare. "Do not leave this property until I myself come for you," Lo Fang told her. "We don't know what is happening, and I wish to take no needless risks." He darted off down the steep hill before she could reply.

Molinda went into the house, where a serving maid tried to soothe her by giving her a cup of steaming mint tea, but she was incapable of enjoying the fragrant beverage right now. Hurrying to a window on the second floor of the house from which she could obtain a better view of the harbor, she watched the smoke continuing to billow skyward. Occasionally she caught a glimpse of yellow flames that looked pale, almost harmless, in the daylight, and she hoped against hope that the fire was not serious. She knew, however, that it was far worse than she had dreamed possible.

Time passed, and an hour later the plumes of smoke narrowed, though they continued to rise. Seeing Lo Fang racing up the hill on foot, she hurried downstairs and out the front door to meet him at the entrance gate. The two members of the Society of Oxen materialized silently out of nowhere, obviously intending to halt her if she intended to leave the property.

Lo Fang's pajamalike tunic and trousers of black cotton were soot-covered and charred, and there were black smears on his hands and face. His explanation of what was happening was both simple and direct. "The fire refuses to go out," he said. "We have tried pouring water on it, and we have tried to smother it with sand, but it burns as fiercely as the breath of a dragon. It is like a dragon, too, in its stubborn refusal to be extinguished."

Molinda braced herself. "How bad is the damage?" she wanted to know.

There was nothing to be gained by dissembling. "The clipper has been reduced to a hulk, and is unfit for further use," Lo Fang told her. "It is already burned to the waterline, and the interior below decks is also damaged beyond repair. When the harbor water finally puts out the flames, there will be nothing of the clipper left that is worth salvaging."

The news was jarring; the blow to Rakehell and Boynton was serious. Molinda did her best to speak calmly as she asked, "How did it happen that the fire could not be extinguished?"

The majordomo was grim. "Large amounts of pitch," he said, "were spread on the decks and on the interior of the ship as well."

She was stunned. "Pitch?" she asked incredulously. "Who was responsible?"

Lo Fang looked at her, his eyes narrowed. "I intend to find out for sure. The Oxen have many resources, and before the sun rises tomorrow morning, I hope to have the answer to Molinda's question."

"Take me to the clipper," she said. "I want to see her and assess the damage for myself."

The firmness of her tone convinced the majordomo that it was useless to argue with her, so he fell in beside her as she started toward the waterfront from the Peak. They walked rapidly, and Molinda was oblivious to the steep decline of the path or the broken ground underfoot. When she reached the docks, she saw several dozen men, who had formed a bucket brigade, pouring water on the remains of the fire, but a single glance at the stricken clipper told her that their efforts were a waste of time. The only good they could accomplish now was to prevent the fire from spreading to other Rakehell and Boynton vessels nearby.

The once proud clipper was in ruins. What was left of her timbers was charred and twisted, her entire superstructure had vanished, and she had literally burned to the waterline, where flames continued to lick at the last vestiges of her hull. The damage, Molinda knew, was virtually incalculable. The loss of a precious clipper meant that the entire schedule of ships would have to be altered, and that the flourishing trade with the United States and Great Britain would necessarily be reduced.

What she found it impossible to calculate was the loss in actual income, but she knew that the total sum had to be staggering. She felt ill, because the blow was one that the company, struggling to regain its feet after its swift expansion, would find very difficult to sustain.

Sir Cedric Poole arrived at the scene, and Molinda repeated to him what Lo Fang had told her about finding large quantities of pitch smeared on the clipper to make certain that it would burn.

"I know," Sir Cedric replied. "We've found the same thing, and we're trying to follow up on possible clues, but I must warn you it could prove very difficult to trace."

"I'm well aware of that," Molinda said.

"Do you know of anyone who is an enemy of your employers or perhaps a personal enemy of your own?" He was already thoroughly familiar with the bad feeling that existed between Owen Bruce and the Rakehells, but he was acting now in an official capacity, so she answered accordingly.

"The Scotsman Bruce, whose docks lay adjacent to ours, and whose warehouse lies across an alleyway from our warehouses."

Sir Cedric nodded. "It will come as no surprise to you," he said, "to learn that I anticipated that answer, and I assigned two of my best operatives to check on Bruce. They say they can find nothing whatever to connect him with this crime."

Molinda was both surprised and disappointed. "I know of no one else who would do this."

Sir Cedric grasped her shoulder lightly. "Suppose you put the problem out of your mind as best you're able, and leave it up to me," he said. "That's what I'm paid to handle. And to make good and certain your mind doesn't wander into depressing channels, I propose that you dine with me this evening."

She glanced involuntarily at her Balinese gown, a simple, single garment that she had donned when she had arisen that morning. "I'll have to go home again to change," she said.

He shook his head and smiled at her. "You're far more attractive than any other lady in all Hong Kong," he said. "Besides, I don't want you to have an opportunity to brood."

They dined at a new inn owned by an enterprising citizen of Canton who was determined to teach the British and other foreigners in Hong Kong the great cuisine of the Middle Kingdom. He was succeeding brilliantly in this aim, and the place was so crowded that only Sir Cedric's position in the colonial government won them a table.

The meal was ordered by Molinda because of her greater familiarity with Chinese food. They started with *dim sum*, which in this case consisted of small dumplings with a variety of stuffings, ranging from freshly caught shrimp to vegetables and smoked meats. The principal dish was a variation on the Peking duck specialty so popular in the north. Its base was baby duckling, steamed until done and then lightly and quickly roasted in peanut oil in order to crisp the skin. The duckling rested on a bed of mung bean noodles, which were light and transparent, resembling the spaghetti which Marco Polo had taken back to Europe with him from his venture into the then unknown Cathay. Over the duckling were sprinkled chopped scallions and water chestnuts, and the whole was blended together with a rich sauce of cream, in which chunks of fresh lobster had been simmered.

The duckling was delicious, as Sir Cedric quickly discovered, but Molinda merely toyed with her food.

Her companion became increasingly concerned for her. "I wish," he said, "you wouldn't take the fire so much to heart."

"I wish I could shrug it off, too," she said, "but I can't."

"Let me give you something else to occupy your mind,"

he said with a faint smile. "Molinda, I have the honor of asking you to become my wife."

She was deeply touched and impulsively reached across the table and put a hand on his arm. "You're very sweet, Cedric," she said, "and I shall remember this for a very long time to come. However, I must refuse your proposal—with great regret, I might add."

"Why must you refuse it?" he demanded.

"It would be all wrong—for both of us," she said. "You're a man of great ambition, and your assignment here in Hong Kong is just another step up the ladder. What would your superiors think if they knew you were married to someone other than a white Englishwoman?"

"If they were that narrowminded and bigoted," he replied forcibly, "I really wouldn't give a hang what they thought."

She shook her head. "You say that now and undoubtedly you believe it's true," she said, "but when the time came and you lost an important post, perhaps the governorship of a colony, for example, because you were married to the wrong wife, I'm not sure that our marriage could survive."

He started to protest, but she gave him no chance to intervene. "What's more," she said, "you deserve a wife who will look after you, take care of you, and rear your children. You don't want a wife who is devoted to her career. Specifically, in my case, a woman who is devoted to her employers and who wouldn't dream of letting them down by walking out on them."

Cedric put down the ivory chopsticks that he was learning to handle with great dexterity. "Why," he demanded, "should it be that you show such devotion to Rakehell and Boynton?"

"For one thing," she replied discreetly, avoiding any reference to the company's precarious financial situation, "they rely on me to handle their very complex operations in the East. They trust me, and I couldn't possibly desert them."

"Presumably," Sir Cedric said, "someone else could take charge one day. Am I correct?"

"Presumably, someone could," she replied modestly.

"Well, then"—he spread his hands in a firm gesture—"their need for you will obviously be less great when that day comes."

"I've learned better than to predict how great their needs may or may not be. Right now I'm in charge, and I am unable to foresee what will take place tomorrow or the next day. But I have another, far more valid reason for my loyalty. You recall that I told you that I was sold into slavery by pirates who captured me in Bali?"

He nodded.

"As I understand it, this was not a unique event. There are bands who prey on young girls throughout the islands, because the demand for attractive females is so great. I was fortunate to be sold to the Fat Dutchman, who recognized my talent for business and gave me an opportunity to work for him. I was even more fortunate that Charles Boynton and Jonathan Rakehell were doing business with the Dutchman. I owe my freedom exclusively to them, and consequently I'm in their debt forever."

Sir Cedric saw the fervent expression on her face, and he nodded silently.

"I'll tell you the details some other time if you like," she went on, "but it was Jonnie and Charles who won my freedom for me, the most precious gift that anyone could have given me and something that I never could have achieved without their help. It was through Jonathan that I had the privilege of meeting the Tao Kuang Emperor and his sister, and becoming a member of their family when they married me to their cousin. So I owe all that I am or hope to become to Rakehell and Boynton—my social position and freedom itself. That's why I could never let them down by leaving their employment. I could marry again only on the very clear understanding that I shall continue to work for many years to come, and that would be very unfair to you, dear Cedric. No, I believe we are fated to stay together for a brief time only. I would like to continue seeing you, but sooner or later we will have to go our separate ways. Perhaps it will be for the best."

She knew her own mind so well that there was nothing he could say to change her views. They finished their meal, drinking a small bottle of brown rice wine with it, and then they walked slowly back to Molinda's house. She was more tired than she had realized, and she clung to Sir Cedric's arm for support. He was gentle with her and deliberately slowed his pace as he conducted her to her house. She invited him to spend the night, but he demurred. "We'll wait until another night when you're less tired," he told her.

The events of the day indeed had drained Molinda, and she slept heavily.

The booming of cannons in the harbor as the Union Jack was raised on British warships there awakened her in the morning, and she rose refreshed, bathed, and made up her face for her customary day at the office. She would have to write to Jonathan and Charles this morning to tell them of the loss of a clipper, and she was not looking forward to the chore, but nevertheless knew it had to be faced. While she was finishing her breakfast of mushrooms, peppers, and Chinese cabbage in rice, Lo Fang came to the door of the dining room.

Molinda saw the hollows beneath his eyes and suspected he had not slept. She knew better than to ask him a personal question, however, because she knew he would only tell her what he wished.

"The authorities of Hong Kong," he told her, "will find nothing that points them toward the criminal who was responsible for burning your ship. They will go to Sir Cedric this morning and notify him of their failure."

She was familiar with the majordomo's techniques, saw the loophole that he had left, and she responded deliberately. "But the members of your society enjoyed better fortune than did the constabulary," she said.

He nodded gravely and then surprised her by sighing. "It is sad," he said. "Our investigation was successful, yet the British would not accept the results as legal proof. But I have found out enough to satisfy myself."

She responded in the Chinese manner, folding her hands in front of her and lowering her head, then sitting motionless while she waited for him to continue.

"It is as I suspected from the beginning," Lo Fang said. "The man who is responsible for burning your ship is Owen Bruce."

"Are you quite certain of that?" Molinda demanded.

He nodded. "I would stake my life on it," he replied, "although the British judges who sit in the law courts here would say that my evidence is not sufficient."

"What is that evidence?"

"In his warehouse, Bruce occupies a large office," Lo Fang said. "Behind that office is an empty chamber, and only he has a key to it. It is not a difficult matter for certain of my friends to open locks that stubbornly remain closed, so I visited that chamber myself last night, and there I found two barrels of pitch. On the floor beside them were marks that indicated there had been four other barrels there until recently. So I say to you that the four barrels were emptied onto the decks and the interior of the clipper ship, and the other two barrels which are still full remain in Bruce's warehouse. I do not say he spread the pitch himself with his own hands, or that he lighted the fire with his own hands. That would not be necessary. He has much gold, and there are Chinese so impoverished they will sell their souls for a coin or two."

Molinda was grateful to Lo Fang and thanked him. His face did not change, but his eyes glittered, and a metallic note crept into his voice as he said, "If Molinda speaks the word, Bruce will disappear from his office or his home and will never be seen again, his body will not be found, and no trace of him will be discovered. This I swear to you."

She shook her head slowly. "I'm tempted, Lo Fang," she replied, "but I must abide by the laws of the civilization that I serve."

He didn't understand and stared at her. "Molinda is a woman of the East," he said.

"My heart is in the East," she replied, 'but my mind lies in the West, where it was trained and where I now serve.

228

I won't forget your offer, though, and someday, if Bruce goes too far, I shall accept your proposition.''

Lo Fang's expression told her that he wished devoutly that she would order the death of Owen Bruce without delay.

She spent an even busier morning than usual, reassigning schedules and transferring cargo from one hold to another in order to take full advantage of the necessary changes that she was making. Even as she worked, however, her conversation with Lo Fang simmered in the back of her mind, and as noon approached, she decided to take action of her own. She leaped to her feet and left the Rakehell and Boynton warehouse-office, two of the bodyguards assigned to her by Lo Fang automatically falling in beside her. She went only a short distance to Owen Bruce's headquarters, and her protectors insisted on going inside with her.

A secretary-clerk took the surprising news to his master that the head of the Rakehell and Boynton office was calling on him.

Owen Bruce could be urbane when he wished, just as he could be ruthless. Registering no surprise, he hurried to the anteroom himself and greeted Molinda jovially. "Well," he said, "this *is* a surprise! To what do I owe the honor of this visit?"

"I want a word with you in private," Molinda replied, and immediately headed for his office, giving him no chance to refuse. He was obliged to follow her, but if he was in the least uneasy, he did not show it.

"Accept my condolences on the loss of a fine clipper ship," he told her as he waved her to a seat opposite his desk. He might despise her employers, Molinda knew, but his expression was openly lecherous as he studied her.

"Of course," he went on, "you have so many clippers in your fleet that the loss of a single ship undoubtedly means little to you."

"The contrary is true, as you well know," Molinda said. "The loss of a ship always is hurtful, and this fire has come at a very bad time for us. You could have been more considerate, you know, when you planned to burn it. ''

Owen Bruce was caught completely off guard by the woman's candor, but he recovered swiftly, and only the burning look in his dark eyes revealed his inner rage. "I'm afraid I don't know quite what you mean," he murmured.

"I think you do," she said. "The fire was set deliberately, and quantities of pitch were spread on the decks and in the interior. Two additional barrels of pitch have been found in the room that adjoins this office." She pointed dramatically to a closed door.

Bruce's lips parted slowly, and a caricature of a smile formed. "I admit freely that I have two barrels of pitch, which I'm going to use to have the roof repaired before the new monsoon season begins. I refuse to believe that their presence constitutes evidence that I set the fire."

"It is sufficient to satisfy me," Molinda replied.

"Surely you know," Bruce replied with a shrug, "that if you bring charges against me on such flimsy grounds, no judge in Hong Kong will even deign to hear your case. It would be thrown out of court."

"That is the precise reason that I have no intention of going to court, Mr. Bruce," she replied. "I chose instead to come here in order to give you a solemn warning."

He laughed unpleasantly. "So now you're going to warn me, are you?" he demanded. "I've heard rumors about you and Sir Cedric Poole for some little time now. But don't think that because you've ingratiated yourself with him you can act as you please. I'm a British subject, and this is a Royal Crown Colony. We have our own ways of dealing with underhanded threats."

"I haven't threatened you—yet," Molinda replied succinctly, "but I shall do so right now. Hong Kong should be big enough for both your company and mine, Mr. Bruce, and God knows the Middle Kingdom is large enough and has enough goods to trade to support Rakehell and Boynton and your company as well. See to it hereafter that you deal in legitimate ways with my employers. See to it that there are no more tricks, and that you'll be honest and straightforward in your dealings."

"You tell me what I will and won't do, what I must and mustn't do," he declared, his voice becoming strident. "But what if I dared to disobey you, ma'am? Suppose I were to tell you to go straight to hell and take your threats there with you?"

Molinda rose slowly to her feet, and although he towered above her, his weight almost double her own, she was totally unafraid of him. Returning his hostile stare calmly and quietly, she spoke in a soft but clear voice. "If you knew me better, Mr. Bruce," she said, "you would realize automatically that I never make threats that I am incapable of keeping. So hear me and listen well. You have spent many years in the Orient and you have dealt for a long time with the people of the Middle Kingdom. No doubt you have heard of the secret societies here?"

"Of course," he replied impatiently, "what of them?"

Her expression and tone of voice remained unchanged. "My employers and I have friends in high places in one of these societies. If there should be any mysterious destruction of our property ever again in the future I shall not be responsible for your personal safety, Mr. Bruce."

"If you were a man," he declared angrily, "I'd challenge you to a duel for that."

"And if you were a man, sir, it would be unnecessary for me to speak to you so bluntly. For better or worse, we're neighbors here, Mr. Bruce, but for the sake of your safety, your property, and your personal health, I urge you not to cross the line onto my employers' property again. That is all I have to say to you, and I do not issue this warning lightly."

She turned on her high heels and stalked out of his office, wishing that her wraparound Javanese gown of silk were less clinging. She hoped with all her heart that she had frightened Owen Bruce sufficiently.

# V

No two days in the great palace in the Forbidden City were alike, but Dr. Matthew Melton discovered that paradoxically the weeks, at least in retrospect, seemed identical.

Each morning he went to his newly furnished office, and there he waited for patients to appear. As a general rule, he had two or three individuals who came to him each morning, and a few more appeared in the afternoons. These were, by and large, younger people, including junior officers and civil servants of the middle ranks. The reluctance of people to come to him with their ailments puzzled him, and he asked Wu-ling why they continued to absent themselves.

"The people of the Middle Kingdom," she said, "believe in tradition. The ways of our fathers are always better to us than new ways. I have lived in the West, so I know and appreciate what your medicine can do. Others here are afraid. Those who have come to you are the very bold who have heard that you have treated the Tao Kuang Emperor and the Princess An Mien, and therefore they hope to ingratiate themselves in imperial favor by visiting you."

"But that's ridiculous," Matthew protested. "I have no influence on the emperor or his sister."

"Those who come to you with their ailments do not know this," Wu-ling replied. "How you will persuade large numbers of the emperor's subjects to adopt the ways of Western medicine, I do not know."

"It's a shame, really," Matthew said. "Western medicine is so superior to the Chinese."

Wu-ling looked at him and grinned impudently. "Are you so certain of that, Doctor?"

"Well—uh—of course," he replied.

"You have learned little or nothing about our herbal remedies and about the practice of what we call acupuncture."

"That is no fault of mine!" he retorted. "I've tried again and again to persuade the royal physicians to teach me the rudiments of their profession, but my pleas fall on deaf ears."

"Of course, because they fear you," Wu-ling said. "But each time you are successful in treating someone ill, there is greater confidence in you. If you are patient, in time all the people will trust you."

"I'm afraid," he said, "I'll have to be a very old man before that happens."

"The gods are mysterious, and it is not our place to question them," she replied.

He was uncertain whether she was serious or joking, so he dropped the subject. He supposed he deserved her rebuke; it was true that he knew nothing about either acupuncture or Chinese herbal medicine, and he despaired of finding out until he perfected his growing command of the language.

He spent the better part of his free time daily studying Chinese, and he made a point of not asking Wu-ling to interpret for him when a patient came to visit him. Gradually his proficiency in the tongue improved, and although his accent remained alien, at least he could make himself understood now, just as he could make out what was said to him, at least in Mandarin. When a speaker reverted to one of the many dialects of the country, he had to give up.

The summer ended abruptly, and the weather became chillier as autumn came, but there still was virtually no rain. The ground was dry and parched, almost desertlike, and as Matthew stared out his windows at the fields that lay beyond the inhabited portion of the city, it occurred to him that Peking was set in a virtual desert.

The dust he inhaled irritated his nose and throat, and

ultimately he caught a severe head cold, running a fever with it and feeling miserable.

Twenty-four hours after he contracted the ailment, he felt even worse, but drinking only tea for his breakfast he dragged himself to his office to await the arrival of potential patients. To his surprise, Wu-ling appeared a few moments after he arrived, and she further confused him when she announced that she had not come for treatment and had never in her life felt better. "I'm here," she said quietly, "because there are no secrets in this place. I heard it said on every side this morning that the physician from the West is ill."

"It's just a nasty head cold," Matthew told her, "nothing serious."

She looked at him intently. "You look awful," she told him in English. "Your eyes are glazed, your nose is very red, and you appear to be positively miserable."

"Well, if you want to know the truth, that's exactly how I feel."

She raised a hand to pat a stray lock of her long, blue black hair into place. "You have an opportunity now, if you will use it, to prove the great worth of your Western medicine. If you cure yourself quickly, you will find many more converts in the palace."

Matthew's smile was forced. "Unfortunately," he said, "Western medicine knows of no cure for my present ailment. Research has been done at Edinburgh and at Harvard, but at neither school have the doctors in charge met with success. I'm sure a cure will be found someday, but that day hasn't yet come."

Wu-ling nodded sympathetically. "I know," she said. "When I was in London, I had what the doctors there called a head cold, and I was so miserable that I had to go to bed for two or three days. That's where you belong right now."

He shook his head stubbornly. "Patients may come here in search of me," he said, "and it's my duty to be on hand to treat them if they do appear. Since a great deal of courage apparently is required before any native will dare trust himself with a Western physician, I've got to be present and ready to help when they do come." He was attacked by a violent sneezing fit, and Wu-ling remained silent until it subsided.

"You really do need help," she said.

He tried without success to grin at her. "I have medical supplies I've brought with me for fifty to one hundred different ailments," he said, "but I know of nothing that will cure a cold."

Wu-ling looked at him thoughtfully. "Have you ever heard of the *gen-ging* plant?" she asked.

He shook his head.

"It's a common plant that grows in the highlands that approach the mountains in our western provinces," she said. "I know of no comparable plant in Great Britain or in America."

"What about it?" he demanded, not realizing he sounded irritable.

"When I was a small child in Canton," Wu-ling said, "I heard my grandmother, who was a very wise and wonderful woman, speak often of the miraculous medicinal properties of the *gen-ging* plant. We were very poor in those days—in fact, we were poverty-stricken. So whenever I caught what you in the West call a head cold, my grandmother lamented that we could not afford to buy a piece of the root of the *gen-ging* because it was very dear. She always swore that if she could only acquire enough of it, I would be cured immediately."

He didn't wish to appear to be scoffing. "You never actually were administered this plant, then?"

"Unfortunately, no," she said.

He tried to be polite. "Perhaps your grandmother just imagined that it had curative qualities."

"If she said it cured one of a head cold, that is what it did," Wu-ling said stubbornly. "I'll look in on you later in the day, and if you aren't feeling any better, I wish—for your own sake—that you'd go to bed!"

Matthew became busy soon after she departed. An administrator in the ministry of fisheries came to him with a broken bone that required setting, and he was followed by the second-ranking officer on board a war junk, who had an eye infection. Then an army officer appeared with his wife, who required medical attention, and the husband, not trusting the Fan Kuei doctor, remained in the room while Matthew examined and treated the woman. And so the morning passed fairly rapidly, but when he was alone again he began to wonder if he should perhaps take Wu-ling's advice. He couldn't remember a time when he felt worse. Then the outer door opened, and a smiling Wu-ling entered without bothering to knock. "I found some," she said.

Matthew sneezed repeatedly before he could ask, "Found what?"

"I located a quantity of the root of the *gen-ging* plant," she said. "One of the advantages of my position here," she said, "is knowing just about everybody of consequence. So I was able to obtain this from one of the royal physicians. He had no idea, of course, that I was getting it for you. After all, I wouldn't want to embarrass you in front of your Chinese colleagues."

Matthew knew that his illness was making him irritable, and he couldn't force himself to sound pleasant as he asked, "What makes you think I'm going to take this stuff?"

Wu-ling looked at him calmly. "Oh, you'll take it," she said. "I've gone to a great deal of bother to get it, and I've had to neglect my work almost all morning, so you'll take a good, big dose immediately." She rummaged in his instruments, and he was outraged.

"Leave those alone," he shouted.

Wu-ling continued to rummage. "I'm just looking for something I can use to grate some root."

"For goodness' sake, here." In his impatience, he handed her a small scalpel.

She reached into the pocket of her cheongsam and produced a gnarled length of plant root about six inches long. It was dark gray and vaguely resembled the celery root that Matthew recalled having seen in his mother's kitchen when he was young. Working swiftly and deftly, the girl removed wafer-thin slices from the root.

Matthew admired her dexterity but had no intention of taking the remedy that he regarded as useless. Wu-ling made a small mound out of the root and piled it onto an exquisite porcelain plate, which she handed to him. "Here," she said, "eat it all."

Matthew stared down at the plate but made no move.

"I've gone to a great deal of bother. I think the least you can do is to cooperate with me."

She had succeeded in shaming him, and although he didn't realize it, that had been her intention. Slowly he picked up the plate and sniffed it gingerly, realizing, to be sure, that he was wasting his time because his nose was so stuffy that he could smell nothing.

"For goodness' sake!" Wu-ling exclaimed, stamping a foot. "You wouldn't think that a little harmless *gen-ging* root was going to kill you."

Picking up a number of the wafer-thin slices from the plate, he popped them into his mouth and began to chew them. Slightly to his surprise, the root had no taste, but eventually his tongue and the interior of his mouth began to tingle.

"Finish it," Wu-ling commanded sternly.

Rather than argue with her, Matthew ate the rest of the root that she had sliced. By the time that he was done, the tingling sensation had increased, but it caused him no discomfort.

"There, that wasn't so bad, was it?"

He made an effort to be pleasant. "I've survived so far," he said, "and in any event, I'm grateful to you for your concern and for going to so much bother on my account."

She waved aside his thanks. "You must eat only thin soup, with nothing more substantial in it than mung bean noodles," she said, "and then you must repeat the dose. Do you want me to cut more of the root for you?"

"I think I can manage it myself," he said, and tried to smile.

"Be sure you do," she said. "The appropriate dosage is very important."

He nodded, not daring to laugh, and told himself that she

238

sounded precisely like a physician. He ordered some clear broth with mung bean noodles in it for his noon meal, and after he'd eaten it, he copied Wu-ling and prepared himself another dose of the *gen-ging* root. Again he felt a tingling sensation, but the so-called medicine had no other effect on him.

Matthew knew that, barring an emergency, he would have no patients for the next hour or more, so he sat down with a book of Mandarin Chinese characters which he was committing to memory. There was no other way, he discovered, to learn the language, and he could understand why a scholar, who necessarily had to possess an extensive vocabulary, had to study for many years in order to be able to read the works of authorities.

The sun streamed in through the windows, blazing in a sky of pale blue, and although the day was chilly out-of-doors it was warm inside. So warm, in fact, that Matthew felt drowsy. Moving from a three-legged stool to a divan, he doggedly continued his studies, but the desire for sleep was so overpowering that he was unable to resist it, and at last he dropped off.

When he awakened, his watch told him that he had slept for about an hour and a half. He regained command of his faculties gradually, and not until he was wide awake did it occur to him that his head cold had vanished miraculously. His nose and chest were clear, his stuffiness was gone, and the aches in his bones also had vanished. He found it difficult to believe what had happened, and he tested himself repeatedly before he could accept the fact that his cold was gone.

Ordinarily, as he well knew, a head cold lasted for many days, so the root of the *gen-ging* plant had to be responsible for this astonishingly swift cure. Unwilling to wait until the end of the day to confront Wu-ling, he hurried off to her quarters immediately, making his way through the labyrinths of the palace with the speed of one who has become familiar with the unknown.

Wu-ling was immersed in a translation of an article on railroads in a magazine that Jonathan had sent to the emperor and his sister, and she barely glanced up from her labors. Then, recognizing her guest, she rose slowly to her feet, not knowing what to expect.

Matthew Melton bowed to her from the waist. "Dr. Wu-ling," he said, "I salute you. I'm blamed if I know how that celery root—or whatever it was—got rid of my head cold so quickly, but all I can say is that it really did work."

She grinned at him. "I knew it would," she said. "My grandmother was never mistaken in anything."

"I am not only cured," Matthew told her, "but I learned a very great lesson as well. I was arrogant in my assumption that Western medicine is the final answer to the ailments of mankind. I forgot, I'm sorry to say, that in this civilization of yours, which has existed for thousands of years, there have been bound to be developments about which we in the West know nothing. I'm now changing my objectives. I'm here not only to teach, but also to learn."

She was impressed by his ardor.

"I'll be grateful if you'll get me several books on herbal medicine and on acupuncture, and I'll see if I can't get the Princess An Mien to persuade the royal physicians to allow me to watch them practicing acupuncture."

Wu-ling giggled. "It will not be necessary for her to use persuasion," she said. "All the princess needs to do is to express a wish that something be done and it is done."

"So much the better then," he said. "I'm able to envisage opportunities here that I've never even contemplated before."

All the Westerners whom Wu-ling had ever known, with the exception of Jonathan Rakehell, had adopted a superior attitude toward the culture of China, taking it for granted that what had been developed in the West was superior to that found in the Orient. So Matthew Melton's reaction to the medicines of Cathay was rather stunning. He now knew from his own experience that medical practice here was based on more than superstitious tradition, and his desire to learn what he could about the practices of the Middle Kingdom was unique.

Scarcely realizing what she was doing, Wu-ling walked up to him and kissed him on the cheek.

Matthew had no idea why she kissed him, but he did not dwell on the matter. All he knew at the moment was that Wu-ling was an unusually gifted, very attractive young lady.

# Book III

Book II

# I

Sir Alan and Charles Boynton concluded their necessary meetings with the Rakehells, and the time had come for them to think of returning to London. No clipper ships were available to convey them, all available vessels of the class having been transferred to the Orient run. It was relatively easy, however, for Homer Ellison to juggle the schedules of the various ships on the Atlantic crossing, and he arranged for the party to be comfortably ensconced on one of the larger Rakehell and Boynton brigs.

The voyage was routine, but the Rakehells nevertheless accompanied the Boyntons to the dock and saw their relatives off. The sailing threatened to be delayed when Julian and Jade hid themselves on board the brig with David's assistance and refused to come when called, somehow hoping they would be able to sail off to England, too. But Harmony gave them away by barking outside the forward hold, where they had secreted themselves, and they were unceremoniously hauled ashore. Jonathan could not be angry with his children for their pranks, and they were not punished for it.

At least the incident alleviated the usual gloom of parting, and members of both the American and British sides of the family smiled broadly as the brig made her way down the Thames estuary into Long Island Sound, en route to the open Atlantic.

Only Elizabeth did not remain on deck, and Ruth mentioned

her absence to her mother-in-law. "I do hope she's all right," she said.

"I know of no cure for her ailment," Jessica replied wryly. "Unfortunately the only cure for her is time, a dash of common sense, and the appearance in her life of some other man."

"I think I'll look in on her," Ruth replied, and went off to her sister-in-law's cabin.

Elizabeth was stretched out on her bed, her face buried in pillows, and she made no move when Ruth came in.

"I'm afraid that moping will get you nowhere," Ruth said sympathetically.

"I know." Elizabeth's voice was muffled by the bed-clothes. "I've got to give up, Ruth. I swore to myself that I'd will him to notice me, to pay attention to me as an eligible woman and stop treating me like a little cousin, but it's no use. He's wearing blinders, and he simply won't remove them."

"You expect too much, I think," Ruth said, trying a new tactic. "I don't think he's ready to notice anyone."

"That isn't true!" Elizabeth cried, clenching her fists. "He was quick enough to appreciate Erika."

Ruth had no reply because she knew her sister-in-law was right.

"I don't know how I'm going to achieve it," Elizabeth said, sitting up and speaking through clenched teeth. "I tried once before and was unsuccessful, but this time I intend to put Jonathan out of my mind once and for all."

"Good for you," Ruth told her.

"There are a great many women who pine away for their lost loves and ruin their entire lives," Elizabeth said, "but I'm damned if I'm going to be one of them. Somehow, in one way or another, I'm going to give up my dream of Jonnie, and I'm going to act as though he never lived." She promptly demonstrated that she was fully prepared to keep her word to the best of her ability. With no prompting she left her cabin and joined the rest of the family in the saloon.

Thereafter, for the remainder of the voyage, she was very

much in evidence and was always cheerful, always good-natured. If the effort required supreme concentration and playacting on her part, she did not show it. She frequently engaged in banter with her father and her brother, and she treated the two unmarried mates on board the brig with consideration, but to the family's relief remembered her place and refrained from flirting with them. When the voyage came to an end, Sir Ronald was waiting for them at the dock, and Elizabeth, apparently delighted to see him, went off with him to some social event. Thereafter he called at the house daily and became her constant escort.

"I think Ronnie Weybright is good for her," Jessica said. "I don't believe she's really serious about him, but he's very attentive. If she isn't forgetting her grand passion for Jonathan, at least Ronnie is helping her to restore her sense of balance."

"He's good for her," Ruth replied thoughtfully, "provided he knows what he's doing. He appears to be badly smitten, and that worries me somewhat because they are both like blindfolded horses galloping on a great meadow. They both lack a sense of direction."

Elizabeth and Sir Ronald became inseparable. Sir Alan ultimately noted that they were always together and said to his wife, "I think I'd best inquire regarding the young man's intentions, don't you think?"

"I emphatically do not," Jessica replied. "I happen to know that he's eager to marry her and proposes to her almost daily. But Elizabeth puts him off."

He was surprised. "She isn't serious about him, then?"

"I honestly don't believe she knows how she feels," Jessica said, "and this is no time to back her into a corner. Give her air—an opportunity to find herself—and she'll know fast enough whether or not she really wants Ronnie Weybright."

Sir Ronald maintained his dogged pursuit, heartened by Elizabeth's willingness to keep seeing him so frequently. He was further encouraged by the increasing liberties that she permitted him. They kissed and embraced regularly in the carriage that brought Elizabeth home every night, and she seemed to enjoy the intimacies as much as he did.

Ultimately his family invited Elizabeth to visit them at their estate in Cornwall, with Sir Ronald escorting her there. Lord and Lady Weybright were pleased to see her and offered her every hospitality, but they had an active social life of their own, and the young couple often were left to their own devices. One afternoon Ronald took her to see the gatehouse, a small stone building that stood high on a cliff overlooking the sea.

"I loved this place as a boy," he said. "In fact, I spent so much of my time here that my father actually gave me the house."

"Whatever do you do with it?" she wanted to know.

"When I come down to the country, I stay in the gatehouse, as a rule," he said. "It feels more like home to me than the manor house."

She was inclined to agree with him. The building was a solid edifice of gray stone, the furnishings were plain but very comfortable, and the view overlooking waves that pounded at the base of the cliff below them was spectacular.

"I can see the attraction," Elizabeth said as she gazed out the living room windows. "I think I'd prefer to live here, too."

"You can very easily, my dear," he told her quietly, placing his hands on her shoulders. "Accept my proposal, and this place shall be yours. I'll give it to you as a wedding present."

"Please, Ronnie," she said, "don't make things more difficult for me than they already are."

"You mean," he said, "that you're stalling me again."

She started to deny the charge but cut herself short. "I suppose I am," she said, "and I'm terribly sorry. Please, may I have a drink?"

He had only Scotch whiskey in the little house, so he poured quantities into two tumblers to which he then added water.

Elizabeth perched on a window seat overlooking the view and sipped her drink. "I know I'm not being fair to you, Ronnie," she said, "and I wish I could explain. But it's too difficult, so all I ask instead is that you be patient with me—very patient."

"I'll try," he promised.

She reached for his hand and squeezed it in gratitude.

He chose not to relinquish his grasp but continued to cling to her fingers, and she made no attempt to withdraw.

Gradually the atmosphere in the little tower sitting room changed. A new tension filled the air, a sexual tension that had been lacking previously. They were two extremely attractive young people who had been spending a great deal of time together, and now they faced a long afternoon with no specific plans for keeping busy.

Their growing intimacy was spontaneous, with neither aware that they were becoming far more deeply involved than they intended. Before they quite knew what was happening, they were kissing passionately, locked in a fervent embrace, and both were becoming thoroughly aroused. Ultimately, they knew they were going beyond the bounds of propriety, but by then it was too late to halt. Only someone older, wiser, and far more self-disciplined could have stopped. These two young people were too inexperienced to be able to call a halt to their lovemaking.

Neither then nor later did either recall undressing, but their clothes were heaped on the rug as the young couple grappled on the divan, with the pounding surf booming dully in their ears.

Ronald Weybright fought hard for Elizabeth's honor, but he was waging a battle he could not win. Eventually he took her.

Her eyes closed, she pulled him more closely to her. Then, as her desire mounted, her breathing quickened and she gasped.

He, too, fought for breath.

As Elizabeth found release, her voice broke the silence. "Oh, Jonnie! Jonnie, my love—Jonnie, my darling!"

Ronnie was too far gone to stop, but what he heard caused his blood to freeze. It was all too apparent to him that Elizabeth, in the throes of passion, was imagining that he was someone else.

He neither knew nor cared about the identity of "Jonnie." A great deal that had mystified him was suddenly clear. The reason that Elizabeth so regularly rejected his proposals was because she was secretly in love with another man.

After she had found release, the world began to right itself for her, and she had no idea that she had cried out, much less that she had called Jonathan's name.

Ronald remained the perfect gentleman. At no time, neither then nor later, did he refer to the incident. At no time, neither then nor later, did Elizabeth Boynton become aware of her indiscretion.

Afterward, as she and Sir Ronald strolled along the beach, she finally spoke. "I think it will be best," she said, "if you and I stop seeing each other for a time. We've become far more involved than we intended—certainly far more than I've intended—and I think we need to put some distance between us for a time."

Earlier that same day, Sir Ronald would have protested vehemently and would have resisted such a suggestion, but now everything was changed. The knowledge that Elizabeth carried the image of someone else locked away in her heart was enough to discourage him, to make him realize that her suggestion was sound.

It would not be easy for him to put her out of his mind or to forget her, especially now that they had become intimate, but he realized that he had no real choice in the matter. He would never be able to win her no matter how long and arduously he wooed her.

They spent another two days and nights in Cornwall and by common consent kept very busy, never allowing themselves to be alone and tempted to repeat their experience again. Then they returned to London, and when Elizabeth lightly kissed Sir Ronald good-bye at the door to her family's Belgravia house, she knew she would not see him again. She felt no regrets, no sense of loss. An interlude in her life had come to an end and had left her untouched. She supposed that, in the deepest sense, her relationship with Ronnie Weybright had been a miserable failure. Even though she had

250

actually indulged in an affair with him—somewhat to her own amazement—she found that her yearning for Jonathan Rakehell was in no way lessened. Despite her resolve, her unrequited love for Jonathan was still so strong that it swept aside all other emotions.

She supposed that she would have to reconcile herself to the inevitability of spending the rest of her days yearning for what would never be. She could call herself adolescent and foolish and romantic and any other names that she pleased; her feelings were in no way alleviated, and she loved Jonathan as much as, if not more than, ever before.

Sir Alan Boynton long had boasted that he had never taken a real holiday in the true meaning of the word, that he had worked all of his adult life and that he intended to die in harness. Therefore he was as shocked as were the members of his family when he fell seriously ill.

He was hospitalized, and a team of London's finest physicians examined him at length. After consultation, they broke the bad news to him and to Lady Boynton. "I'm afraid, Sir Alan," the senior physician said solemnly, "that it's my painful duty to notify you that you have an infection of the lungs."

Sir Alan was stunned. "How very strange," he murmured. "I've never had trouble with my lungs in my life."

The doctor shrugged. "Ultimately, I'm sure, medicine will develop a quick, positive cure for such an ailment," the physician said. "But until then only one cure is known. We urgently recommend that you leave the city because the autumn climate here leaves a great deal to be desired. We recommend that you take up residence on one of the Channel Islands—either Jersey or Guernsey—and that you stay there for at least six months."

Alan was alarmed. "Six months!"

The physician addressed himself to Lady Boynton. "We realize we're asking a great deal of a man who's been as active as Sir Alan has been. However, if he fails to take care of himself and to get rid of the infection in the only way known, by doing nothing and by spending much of his time in the sun in a salubrious environment, the infection will surely kill him. He has a clear choice.''

Jessica made up her mind instantly. "The choice has been made. By me. Alan and I will go to the Isle of Jersey, and we'll remain there until spring. At that time we'll return to London, where you can examine him again, and if he's not cured of the infection, we'll go straight back to Jersey until he is.''

Sir Alan opened his mouth to protest but could say nothing. Not only was he shocked by the news of his sickness and of the drastic cure involved, but he knew his wife was right. For the first time in his life, he was compelled to rest, to do absolutely nothing if he wanted to live.

The decision having been made, Jessica wasted no time, and writing ahead for quarters, she supervised the packing of clothes. Within seventy-two hours, she and her husband left London.

The full weight of responsibility fell suddenly on the shoulders of Charles and Ruth. Charles discovered that with his father's duties added to his own, he was busier than he had ever been before. He left the house an hour and a half earlier in the morning than had been his custom, and instead of adjourning to one of his clubs in the West End for lunch, he ate a light meal at his desk. He fully intended to get home at a reasonable hour at the end of the day, but there were so many inevitable crises they caused countless delays. Consequently, he found himself arriving home at all hours of the evening, and on occasion very late at night. "I realize it's asking too much of you, Ruth, and far too much of the servants to accommodate your schedules to me. I suggest that you and Elizabeth eat dinner at the regular hour, and if I can't join you, which it appears I can't, you might keep something hot for me for when I eventually show up."

The suggestion was thoroughly unsatisfactory, but Ruth knew of no alternative, and she followed it. She and Elizabeth dined at the family's usual hour, and she made a point of staying up, waiting for her husband and sitting with him while he ate. Often it was midnight or later when he finally came home, and he was so tired that he found it impossible to go through more than the motions of eating. Ruth became increasingly concerned, and finally one Sunday morning as he sat gulping his breakfast, she could remain silent no longer. "Surely you aren't going to the shipyard today?" she asked. "It's Sunday!"

Charles shrugged wearily. "The day of the week doesn't seem to matter much," he said. "The work keeps piling up, and I've got to get it done."

"Can't you get someone to help you?"

He shook his head. "An assistant like Homer Ellison would be perfect, but there's no one on this side of the Atlantic who fills the bill. Papa ran a one-man operation for many years, and when I joined him I gradually expanded it to a two-man operation. But I lacked the foresight to train competent assistants, and I'm afraid that I'm paying for my lack of vision now."

"How long will it be necessary for you to keep up this insane schedule?" Ruth demanded.

Charles shrugged and smiled wanly. "I hope—with all my heart—that it continues at this pace indefinitely. If business slackens and begins to fall off, Rakehell and Boynton will be in far more serious trouble and there won't be any cure for it." He reached across the table and patted her hand. "I'm sorry, Ruth," he said. "I know it's rough on you, but there's very little I can do about it." Then, as though ashamed of his display of emotion, he seemed to be concentrating on his kippers and fried eggs.

"It's far more difficult for you than it is for me, Charles," she said, "and I don't want you to follow your father's example and fall ill."

"There's not a chance of that," he replied forcefully. "I'm needed at the yard, and I intend to fulfill my obligations."

"Of course you will," she said.

He hesitated before he spoke again. "You and I," he said,

"were finally hitting it off together after a great many misunderstandings. I hope this mad schedule of mine won't cause new misunderstandings."

"Indeed it won't," she said firmly.

He wanted to explain that their lack of sex was caused exclusively by his exhaustion, not by a lack of love for her, but he hadn't been trained to discuss such delicate matters. He could only hope that she truly understood.

"David and I will get along just fine," she told him, "and we'll be right here whenever you want and need us."

"That's all I can ask," he said. "By the way, we have a Channel trader sailing today to St. Helier in Jersey, so you might want to send a letter to my mother."

"Indeed I do," Ruth said. "What time must it be at the yard?"

"Have the coachman bring it no later than noon," he said, "and I'll see that it goes into the captain's personal pouch."

She nodded, and as he rose from the table, she stood, too.

"Sit down," he told her. "There's no need for you to rush. Finish your coffee."

She continued to stand, and put her arms around his neck. They embraced briefly, hungrily, but were interrupted by some lewd observations made by Dieter, the parrot the Fat Dutchman had given Charles. The bird, which was multicolored, with blues and purples, reds and oranges predominating, had been brought on its perch into the dining room, where there was bright early morning sunshine, and now the parrot let loose with a stream of vulgar expressions and curses. In spite of herself, Ruth giggled, and Charles couldn't help bursting into loud laughter, too.

Little David hurried into the dining room, afraid that he had missed his father, and was rewarded by the sight of his parents laughing aloud. He had no idea what amused them, but didn't care and joined in their merriment. Charles picked him up, hugged him, and ruffled his hair. "Son," he said, "if you were a dozen years older, I'd have you down at the office with me every day and every night."

"I'll go, Papa. I'll go," David said eagerly.

Ruth smiled. "Not just yet," she said, then added to her husband, "as this is Sunday, perhaps you can get away a little earlier this evening."

"I will if I can," he replied, but it was obvious from his tone that he considered it unlikely.

He kissed them good-bye, then parted, and Ruth sat down and poured herself a fresh cup of coffee as a serving maid brought David his usual cereal and fruit. The child began to babble about an invitation he'd received to drive out to the country that afternoon, and Dieter elected to turn the air blue with some of his usual scatological observations, fortunately expressing himself in Dutch. Ruth paid scant attention to either the child or the parrot, and was actually relieved when Elizabeth came into the room, clad in a dressing gown. It would be good to have some adult conversation.

Ruth summoned the serving maid and Elizabeth rejected offers of French toast, eggs and kippers, and kidneys and bacon. Ruth noted that her sister-in-law looked pale and listless, and without meaning to sound harsh, she snapped, "You've got to eat something, you know."

Elizabeth meekly agreed to accept a portion of poached Channel sole and a soft-boiled egg. She also wanted a pot of strong tea. The serving maid ultimately brought her order, and she toyed with her food. David finished his breakfast and asked, "May I be excused?"

"Yes, but don't go outdoors to play," his mother said. "We're going to church this morning."

"We are?" the boy sounded dismayed.

"We are," Ruth said firmly. "This is Sunday. Are you coming with us, Elizabeth?"

The younger woman hesitated, then nodded. David wandered off, and Ruth waited until he was out of earshot before she said, "Whatever is wrong, Elizabeth? You've been moping like this for the past week. If you're concerned for your father, please don't be. I assure you that he's going to recover."

"I'm not in the least worried about him," Elizabeth replied. "He'll do what Mama tells him, and so I know he's going to be all right." She put some sole on a fork but couldn't be bothered lifting it to her mouth.

"You're the one who behaves as though you're ill," Ruth said. "You haven't eaten a meal in days, and you mope constantly."

Elizabeth nodded and made no reply. The silence in the room was broken by her long, tremulous sigh.

"I've had very little experience being mistress of a family," Ruth said. "Particularly acting as a surrogate mother to someone who's not all that much younger than I am. However, I'm willing to try. Obviously you're either ill or something is troubling you."

"I'm troubled, all right," Elizabeth said. "I'm in a nasty fix, and I don't know quite what to do about it."

Ruth assumed she was exaggerating and looked at her, nodding calmly.

"I went to see a physician a week ago yesterday," Elizabeth said in a small but distinct voice. "He's no one we know, but he's quite reliable and quite reputable, I made sure of that. I went to him under an assumed name."

"Whatever for?"

"Because of the nature of the examination that I requested. Ruth, I don't know how to tell you this—but—I'm pregnant."

The secure world of Ruth Boynton was shattered. Ultimately she found her voice. "Who is the man?"

"His identity doesn't matter," Elizabeth said defiantly.

Ruth tried to appear tranquil. "Does he know?"

"Certainly not," Elizabeth replied. "And I have no intention of telling him, now or ever."

"But don't you think he has a right—"

"No, I do not!" Elizabeth interjected. "I made a mistake, that's all. I have no intention of marrying him. If he had any inkling of my condition, he'd insist that we marry, and I'd have an even harder task of putting him off than I had."

The room whirled, and Ruth needed several moments to get her bearings. "What do you intend to do about it?"

"I don't really know," Elizabeth said. "That's why I decided to confide in you. With Papa ill, it would be wrong to burden him and Mama with this problem. As for Charles, he has quite enough on his mind."

"More than enough," Ruth said.

It was not difficult for Ruth to ascertain the identity of the unborn infant's father. Necessarily the finger of suspicion pointed at Sir Ronald Weybright, the only man who had been seeing Elizabeth socially since they had returned to London from America. Knowing Ronnie Weybright and his family, she felt certain he would want to do the right and honorable thing if he learned of the true situation. But obviously the matter had to be handled with great care. "Rather than lose your honor, cause a scandal, and rock the entire West End of London," she said, "you may want to reconsider your position in due time, and perhaps you'll agree to be married after all."

"I will not," Elizabeth said with quiet emphasis. "My affair, if you can call it that, was a mistake. I learned that, more than ever, I love and want only one man, and if I can't have him, I'll be satisfied with no one."

"Then we'll have to make plans to send you out of England for a time," Ruth said. "I don't know offhand where you'll go, but we'll have to work that out. You simply cannot remain here. Papa would have a relapse if he learned of your condition, and Mama would become quite ill, too."

"They will never know about it," Elizabeth said firmly.

Ruth wanted to reply that Elizabeth's news could not be kept secret indefinitely, especially from members of her own immediate family, but there was a hard gleam in the younger woman's blue eyes that she didn't quite fathom, so she kept her thoughts to herself. "I can see," she said, "that you have some sort of plan."

Elizabeth nodded slowly. "It isn't what I choose, but as John Heywood wrote in his famous sixteenth-century book of proverbs, beggars are in no position to be choosers. Are they?" She was picking a bad time to show off her knowledge, and Ruth couldn't help being annoyed. She compressed her lips to a severe line and waited silently.

Elizabeth braced herself. "The pressure on me to marry

will become worse and worse as each month succeeds another. I don't think I could tolerate that, just as I certainly wouldn't relish the gossip that will rock so-called London society. I've never considered myself a femme fatale, and I certainly don't feel like one, so I'm damned if I'm going to be tarred as one, and be so identified for the rest of my days. Since I won't consider marriage to the child's father, I'm left with only one alternative."

Ruth drew in her breath sharply and, without realizing it, held it.

"I must have an abortion," Elizabeth announced flatly.

The dining room spun, and Ruth gripped the edge of the table. "You're mad," she said. "It's dangerous and degrading and loathsome and—"

"Call it what you will," Elizabeth told her, "and I'll agree with you. If there were any way to avoid it, I would. But there isn't, so I am going to solve my problem by having an abortion. All I ask of you is that you stand by me in this, because I'm not quite as strong as I think I am, and I badly need some support."

Sir Alan was gradually shaking off his lung infection in the sunny warmth of the English Channel Isle of Jersey, and Ruth, like her sister-in-law, wanted nothing to interfere with his recovery. She agreed not to say anything to her mother-in-law, either, because there was nothing that Jessica could do about the situation, and there was no need to cause her worry.

But Ruth was adamant in her demand that Charles be told. For all practical purposes, he was the head of the family now, and she felt it was his place to be informed of the truth. Elizabeth demurred, but Ruth held firm, and finally the young woman agreed.

The immediate problem was to find a time when he would not be too exhausted to absorb the information. They finally decided to wait until the following Sunday morning, when they had their customary breakfast with him, prior to his departure for the shipyard.

Charles took the information in his stride, and Ruth was

proud of the way that he handled himself in the crisis. He continued to eat his kippers and eggs with seeming calm, and nodded from time to time as he listened, apparently feeling nothing. When Elizabeth finished her recital, he asked calmly, "Who is the man?"

Elizabeth clenched her fists, and color burned in her cheeks. "It doesn't matter, Charles," she said. "I have nothing to do with him anymore, and we've stopped seeing each other."

He brushed aside her protests. "It's Ronnie Weybright, of course," he said.

"I forbid you to tell him," Elizabeth cried. "This is strictly my own business, not his."

"Ronnie is an honorable man," he said, "and I'm quite positive he would regard the news as his business, too. In fact, he would be quite insistent that you marry him at once."

She faced her brother defiantly across the breakfast table. "That, my dear Charles, is precisely the reason I don't want Ronnie told. I have no intention of marrying him, and I see no need to complicate a nasty situation."

Charles raised an eyebrow. "Be sensible, Elizabeth," he said. "Our society isn't yet so advanced that a single woman may raise a child herself."

"I have no intention of having the baby, much less raising it," she said. "I'm determined to have an abortion."

Abortions were common enough, Charles supposed, but very little was known about them. They were illegal, so that no reputable physician or surgeon performed them, and the whole subject was shrouded in mystery.

"How do you propose to go about doing that?" Charles demanded.

"I've been making inquiries," she replied, "discreet inquiries to be sure, and I've obtained the name of a practitioner who performs the operation. He's safe and reliable, and I'll be in no danger. I'll go to him, and that will be the end of the matter."

Charles was stunned, and glanced at his wife for help.

"I knew this was what she has been planning," Ruth said, "but I thought she should tell you herself."

"I don't quite know what to say," Charles murmured, badly shaken.

"Say nothing and do nothing," Elizabeth told him succinctly. "The problem is mine, and the solution is mine. I'll take the consequences, if any."

Charles was genuinely puzzled, not knowing how to react, uncertain what to say. He tried in vain to figure out how his father would have reacted under similar circumstances, but he was soon forced to give up the attempt.

"I didn't want to burden you unnecessarily, Charles," Ruth said, "but I insisted that you be told because you're the acting head of the family."

"Quite right," he said, and nodded, controlling a desire to bite his lower lip.

"I've had far more time than you to consider this matter," she said, "and it strikes me that we're obliged to let Elizabeth form her own judgments and make her own decisions. I don't approve of abortion as a solution, and I know you don't either—"

"I certainly don't," he interjected forcefully. "I think it's all wrong."

"Nevertheless," Ruth went on, "the fundamental problem is Elizabeth's, and we have no right, really, to interfere."

He frowned, tapping on the table with the fingers of one hand as he pondered. "I'm reluctant to say so," he declared, "but I suppose you're right."

"Thank you," Elizabeth said with great sincerity.

Charles looked hard at her. "I could ask you how you could have allowed yourself to get into this unpleasant position," he said, "but I have no intention of lecturing you. I've made enough mistakes in my own time to realize how very easy it is to slip from the straight and narrow path."

"I'm grateful to you for not lecturing me," Elizabeth told him. "In fact, a sermon is about the very last thing on earth that I could tolerate at this point."

"Never fear," he said, "you shall have no sermons. The question now is how to proceed from here."

"I have the name and address of the man who performs abortions," Elizabeth said, "and I intend to visit him in the next few days."

Charles hesitated and took the plunge. "Do me a favor, if you will. I've heard some very unsavory stories about these chaps, and for your own protection, I urge you not to go to him alone. Let Ruth come with you."

"Is that really necessary?" Elizabeth demanded.

"If it weren't essential," Charles told her, "I wouldn't ask it of you." He had taken her shocking news with such good grace that Elizabeth could not in good conscience refuse his request.

They went the following Tuesday morning, on sudden impulse. Charles had left the house early. David was in the care of his governess, and Ruth was busy organizing her household routines when her sister-in-law came to her. "I'm going to see Mr. Winkler now, if you wish to come along," she said.

Ruth was blank. "Who?"

"Roscoe Winkler," Elizabeth replied. "He's the man who performs certain operations."

Ruth could see by the younger woman's face that her mind was made up. She fully intended to visit the abortionist this morning, and would go alone if Ruth demurred. So, dropping everything, Ruth accompanied her. They drove in the carriage to the neighborhood of the food stalls in the Covent Garden area, and the coachman finally called down, "I'm afraid I can't come no closer than this, ladies. You'll have to complete your journey on foot."

They left the carriage and instinctively drew closer together as they walked down the narrow, cobbled walk past stalls filled with fruit and vegetables, and bins laden with fish. They came at last to a dilapidated two-story building of stone and clapboard, and Elizabeth hesitated.

"Surely this isn't the place," Ruth said.

Elizabeth shrugged. "It's the address I was given, all right," she replied. "Mr. Winkler occupies the second floor, I believe."

They entered the building, the door creaking open, and lifting their skirts, they climbed a grimy staircase to the second floor. Elizabeth drew a deep breath and then tapped tentatively on the closed door.

There was a considerable wait, and then they heard a man's voice demand gruffly, "What do you want?"

"I—I'm looking for Mr. Winkler."

They could hear bolts being slid, and suddenly the door burst open. "You found him," the man inside declared.

Ruth was revolted. The man was pudgy, clad in a soiled shirt and rumpled trousers, and she noted that his hands were unwashed, with quantities of grime showing beneath his fingernails.

He revealed a gold tooth in the front of his mouth when he smiled. "I know why you ladies are here, so there's no need to cool your heels out there. Come in, ladies, come in." He ushered them into a living room with old, battered furniture resting on a worn rug that had seen better days, and insisted on taking their coats. They could hear dishes rattling and clanking in an adjacent chamber, apparently a kitchen, and a slatternly, middle-aged woman wearing a dust cap and a dirty apron came in, carrying a tray on which a steaming pot of tea and two chipped, empty mugs rested. She placed the tray on a table and filled the mugs without a look at either of the young women. Ruth hesitated, but her mug looked clean enough, so she drew a deep breath, picked it up, and sipped. The tea was unusually strong, and had a bitter taste.

Roscoe Winkler bustled back into the room, rubbing his hands. "Are both of you here for treatment?"

Unable to speak, Elizabeth shook her head.

"Ah, let me guess which of you is here to avail yourself of my professional services," he said.

Elizabeth found his coyness revolting. "I'm the patient," she announced. "I'm told that you perform a certain operation for a fee, and that the whole thing can be accomplished rather quickly and neatly."

"Indeed it can, ma'am," he boomed. "Satisfaction is guaranteed. If you wish, we'll get to it right now."

The prospect of immediate action was stunning, and Ruth swallowed hard.

Elizabeth took a deep breath. "How long a process is involved?"

"The operation is over and done with quicker than two shakes of a lamb's tail," Winkler declared. "I advise my patients to rest for about an hour, and then you go on your way."

"It's that simple?" the wide-eyed Elizabeth wanted to know.

He nodded briskly. "There's a great fuss made about the whole business," he said, "but it's far simpler than most of my colleagues in the medical profession will admit."

Ruth conceived a strong dislike for the grubby man who spoke so confidently about his "medical colleagues."

"My fee," he said briskly, "is three guineas, payable in advance."

Aware that she was committing herself now, Elizabeth opened her purse and handed him several coins. He bit them one by one to assure himself that they weren't counterfeit, and when he was satisfied, he dropped them into his pocket. "Come with me," he demanded, and then added as an afterthought, "Your friend is welcome to come, too, if she wishes."

They followed him down the corridor to a large chamber located in a corner of the building, which, thanks to the double exposure, was lighter than the other rooms. It was dominated by a large wooden table, obviously built as a kitchen table, on which a contraption that looked like stirrups rested. In one corner of the room were piled mounds and mounds of rags and cloths.

Winkler went to a cabinet, removed a tumbler from which he blew dust, and then filled it with a colorless liquid that he

263

poured from a bottle. "Here," he directed, "drink this."

Elizabeth sniffed the substance, and the raw, pungent odor made her feel faintly ill. "What is it?"

"Gin," he said. "Believe me, you'll soon be glad you had it. Now do as I tell you and drink up."

She steeled herself, then held her breath and downed the contents of the tumbler in a swallow. Color drained from her face, and for a few moments she looked faint; then, gradually, the color returned, and her cheeks became a bright pink.

The man went to the door and bellowed. "We're ready for you, Mrs. Ryder," he called.

The slatternly woman who had served the tea bustled in, wiping her hands on her soiled apron.

Roscoe Winkler patted the table. "Up you go," he said. "Lie down, if you please, and put your feet in these. You'll want to be comfortable, so I suggest you take off your hat, your gloves, and your shoes."

Elizabeth was frightened but tried hard not to show it, and obediently did as he directed. Ruth was forgotten and stood on the far side of the room, feeling queasy. She had no idea who had recommended this man to her sister-in-law, but his callousness, combined with the lack of sanitation, revolted her.

Elizabeth was directed to haul up her skirts, which she did. "Give her a tooth clamp, Mrs. Ryder," the man said.

The woman handed Elizabeth a block of wood. "If you clamp your teeth on this good and hard," Winkler said, "I guarantee you won't scream." He returned to a cabinet and removed something that he proceeded to wipe absently on his shirt front.

Ruth's blood ran cold when she saw that he was holding a long, metal button hook.

Moments later an anguished scream of pain and terror was torn from Elizabeth, and her gushing blood spread on the top of the table. The woman hastily gathered up armloads of rags and deposited them on the table, where they soaked up the blood.

Ruth felt faint but was determined not to lose consciousness. "She—she's hemorrhaging badly," she cried. "Can't you do something to stop the flow of blood?"

Winkler eyed her coldly. "Some of them are heavy bleeders, and some ain't," he said. "She'll stop in her own good time when she's good and ready."

Ruth was somewhat relieved to see that Elizabeth had lost consciousness. At least she was no longer aware of her suffering.

She continued to bleed heavily, and Ruth's alarm increased, but neither Roscoe Winkler nor his silent assistant appeared to think that anything was amiss. They threw soaked rags into a garbage pail and piled others onto the table occasionally, but otherwise they paid no further attention to the patient. Winkler wiped off the button hook on a bit of cloth, and replaced it in the cabinet. Then he turned and peered intently at Elizabeth. "She'll be coming round soon," he said to Ruth. "If you're smart, you'll wait about an hour before you venture out onto the street with her. She'll be a trifle wobbly for a time." He hastened out of the room, leaving the door open behind him, and the woman who had assisted him soon followed him.

To Ruth's infinite relief, Elizabeth stopped bleeding. Then the girl stirred, moaned, and opened her eyes.

"The worst is over," Ruth told her. "The operation is finished."

A long, slow shudder seemed to pass slowly up Elizabeth's slender body. "If I had known," she said, "if I had had any idea of what was in store for me, I—I don't think I could have done it." She tried to struggle to a sitting position.

"Stay where you are," Ruth told her. "You must rest for a time before you try to walk."

"I—I can't bear the thought of spending a moment longer here than is absolutely necessary," Elizabeth told her. Her color was pasty and resembled uncooked dough.

"I know what you mean," Ruth replied, "but you will have to be sensible. You've lost a considerable quantity of blood." She didn't want to reveal that her sister-in-law had lost an alarming quantity of blood.

Elizabeth sighed. "I suppose you're right," she said. "Thank you for being so helpful."

"Nonsense," Ruth replied briskly, and glanced at her watch. Somehow the time would pass until it would be safe for Elizabeth to stand and walk again.

Neither later remembered what they discussed in their desultory conversations during the next hour. Ruth glanced at her watch frequently and at last said, "If you're strong enough, we'll try to leave now, but let's clean you up a bit first." She went to the corner and then returned to the table with a mound of rags.

Elizabeth discovered that she could scarcely stand and that it was torture for her to walk, but she was determined to leave this loathsome place behind her, and gritting her teeth to keep from screaming aloud, she leaned on Ruth and somehow managed to leave the second-floor flat and to descend the flight of rickety stairs.

Elizabeth's ordeal was far from ended when they reached the street. She still had to walk the better part of two city blocks to the waiting carriage, and Ruth half supported, half dragged her as they virtually crawled down the cobbled walk.

The coachman saw them coming and, jumping down from his box, helped to lift the half-conscious Elizabeth into the carriage. Like all aristocrats' servants, he was superbly trained, so his face revealed no surprise, and he asked no questions.

Later Elizabeth remembered nothing about the drive back to the house in Belgravia and didn't recall being put to bed. She fell asleep at once and was still sleeping soundly late that evening when Charles returned home.

Color drained from his face as he listened to his wife's account of the nightmare experience that Elizabeth had undergone. "I wonder if we shouldn't send for the doctor?" he said at last.

Ruth nodded. "I don't think there's much question about it," she said, "but Elizabeth is running no fever, and she's sleeping soundly. Obviously she needs the rest. I thought we might wait until morning and then send for the doctor. She should be that much stronger by then, too.''

Charles agreed, and the following morning he refrained from going off to the shipyard; it was the first time he had taken off since his father had been stricken.

Elizabeth awakened early and, although weak, seemed somewhat improved. Charles immediately wrote to Dr. Featherstone, long the family physician, and sent a groom hurrying to the doctor's Harley Street residence with the communication. Elizabeth was hungry, which was also a good sign, and Ruth allowed her to have a cup of broth before the physician appeared. Dr. Featherstone showed up in a remarkably short time, and Charles conducted him to the family sitting room. There the gray-haired doctor sat silently while Charles and Ruth filled him in on the nature of Elizabeth's ailment. He listened carefully but made no comment.

Ruth was suffused with feelings of guilt. ''I suppose we should have stopped her, Dr. Featherstone,'' she said. ''We should have found some way to persuade her not to run the risk of having an abortion, but frankly I had no idea that the experience could be so terrible.''

''Very few people know it, you may be sure, Mrs. Boynton,'' he murmured as he stood and picked up his little black bag containing instruments and medicines. ''Will you show me to her sickroom now, if you please?''

They conducted him to Elizabeth's room and remained outside while he went in. Having known the girl since she'd been a small child, he was successful in putting her at her ease before he examined her. Then, when he finally emerged, he looked grave.

Ruth led the way back to the study.

''Well, Doctor?'' Charles asked.

Dr. Featherstone ran a hand through his silvery hair. ''If I had my way,'' he said, ''men like this fellow Winkler would be subjected to the most severe penalties the law is capable of devising. There is no excuse for the brutality and the lack of medical precautions that characterize the practice of such men.''

Ruth's heart sank. "What is Elizabeth's condition?" she ventured.

The physician drew a deep breath. "Fortunately, she's young and has a strong constitution," he said, "so she'll not only survive the experience, but it appears she'll escape without infection. The loss of blood has temporarily weakened her, but given sufficient rest for a week or two, she should show no ill results."

Charles looked relieved.

"Thank God for that," Ruth murmured.

"However," the physician went on, "there is one very grave consequence of the abortion. Elizabeth is still too sore and tender to tolerate a full examination, but based on my preliminary findings, I'd be inclined to say that my diagnosis is definitive."

They leaned forward in their chairs, waiting anxiously.

"I'm afraid that Elizabeth will pay a heavy price for her careless behavior," Dr. Featherstone said. "She is sterile, and will remain so for the rest of her days."

Ruth involuntarily gasped, and Charles clenched his fists.

"I preferred not to discuss this bad news with her when she's in her present weakened state. In another week, when she's recovered her strength and resilience, either I'll return and will break the news to her, or you two may do it, as you please. But nothing is to be said for at least a week."

The following week passed slowly and was far more difficult for Ruth than for Charles, who was able to escape to his office for long periods. Ruth saw Elizabeth all through the day and, unable to share the bad news with her, had to maintain a cheerful façade. It was almost more than she could bear.

The following week, Dr. Featherstone called on the patient again, and Charles again deliberately stayed home from work to give his wife all the assistance and support that he could.

The physician spoke briefly to the couple as they conducted him to the front door after he had completed his examination of his patient. "She continues to improve physically and should suffer no setbacks," he said. "In addition, I've broken the bad news to her."

"How did she take it, Doctor?" Charles asked.

The physician sighed and shrugged. "One seldom knows what goes on in the mind of a lady at such a time," he said. "I can only tell you that she received the news calmly and didn't grow in the least panicky. What she may have been suffering inside herself is something that you would know far better than I." He promised to return at any time that he was wanted and needed, and shook hands with them at the front door.

They went directly to Elizabeth's bedchamber, and their footsteps slowed as they approached the room. Elizabeth was sitting up in bed, her back and head supported by pillows. "Yes, I know," she said as they came into the room. "As Dr. Featherstone probably told you, he broke the news to me."

They continued to smile, desperately seeking the right thing to say.

"There's no question about it, he tells me," Elizabeth went on. "If I wish, he'll call in a colleague for a corroborating opinion, but I'm sure I've heard quite enough. There's little doubt that I will never be able to bear children."

Several responses occurred to Ruth, but she was afraid that she would sound sententious. Charles had no idea of how to handle the situation and wished he were at the shipyard. He could face a thousand angry yardworkers without flinching and could sail a clipper ship through a raging gale at sea without suffering a qualm, but in this situation, he felt completely helpless.

"I've been reminded," Elizabeth said lightly—a trifle too lightly—"of the sermons we had to hear when we were children, subjects like the wages of sin. I always thought that such matters were theological rubbish, but I'm no longer so certain. Strange, isn't it, but I'm paying a terribly high price for what seemed at the time like a very minor and unimportant breaking of moral law."

Ruth approached the bed and kissed her sister-in-law.

Charles took Elizabeth's hand in his and gripped it hard. "We're sorry," he said. "But there's no use in crying over spilled milk."

Charles, wracking his brain for some way to convey his sympathy, gave up. He couldn't help glancing at his pocket watch. He had just received Molinda's letter—a copy of the one she had also sent Jonathan—explaining about the sabotage of the clipper, and he was anxious to get back to his office to see what he could do to help make up for the loss of the valuable ship.

Elizabeth noticed Charles looking at his watch. "Please don't stay home on my account," she said. "You're inundated with work at the office, so don't make me feel even guiltier than I otherwise would."

Charles hesitated and glanced at his wife.

"Elizabeth is right, dear," she said cheerfully. "Off you go to the shipyard. We'll be just fine here."

He was reluctant to leave, but at the same time a sense of relief flooded him. The situation made him very uncomfortable, and he could only think that women were better able to handle it.

When the sisters-in-law were alone, Elizabeth smiled painfully and shook her head. "It's strange and rather terrifying, isn't it?" she mused. "All I ever wanted in life was to love Jonnie and to be loved by him, and now I find myself in this nasty bind. Life plays odd tricks on one."

"It does indeed," Ruth said. "I'll tell you something that no one else has ever known. I imagined myself in love with Jonathan Rakehell for a long time, a very long time. I was convinced I loved him at the time I married your brother, and consequently I had a horrible hurdle to overcome in my marriage."

Elizabeth stared at her in fascination. "I—I had no idea," she murmured. "Did you—will yourself to stop feeling as you had?" she asked breathlessly.

Ruth shook her head. "I was able to do nothing consciously that helped. I don't know how it happened, but one day I knew I was free of my infatuation with Jonnie. I realized that

I loved Charles, and I've loved him without reservation from that day to this."

"If there were someone else in my life to whom I could really transfer my affections, then I'd do it," Elizabeth said. "As a matter of fact, that's what I tried to do with Ronnie, and we all know how I botched that up. I'd give anything to get over this feeling I have for Jonnie, but hope is a strong emotion, so strong that it refuses to die. It stayed alive through Jonathan's first marriage and through his second. I don't suppose it would survive a third, but I'm not sure, and as long as he remains a bachelor, I keep telling myself there's always a chance that he'll turn to me."

Ruth realized she had to be brutally honest. "You've made enough of a shambles of your life," she said. "I'll grant you that there's always a possibility that Jonathan will turn to you and find that he loves you, but as I told you once before, the odds are against it. When we last saw him, he was much taken with your friend, Erika von Klausner, and I'd be willing to wager that he'll develop a romance with her far more rapidly and far more readily than he would ever do with you."

"That is what I fear most," Elizabeth said. "Isn't there anything I can do to prevent it?"

"From this sickbed, you can do literally nothing," Ruth told her. "You can provide competition for Erika and for any other woman he might fancy only if you're alive and vibrant and healthy. You have two choices, my dear. Either you can go into retirement, whimpering and feeling very sorry for yourself, or you can fight for what you believe. You happen to believe that you love Jonnie. Find ways to prove it—and don't ask me for guidance. Do what you think must be done, and he'll come to you. It's strictly up to you."

# II

The sights and sounds and smells of the East that greeted the visitor to Djakarta quickly convinced any newcomer that he had indeed arrived in the Orient. Even the waterfront was different, and the only resemblance it bore the great harbor of Hamburg was in the number of foreign vessels that rode at anchor there. But here the resemblance ended. There were clippers, most of them built by Rakehell and Boynton, from Great Britain and the United States. There were windjammers from Holland and France and Portugal, Spain and Sweden. There were large numbers of seagoing junks, together with scores of tiny sampans and the awkward-looking dhows that carried the goods of trade from the states of the Arab peninsula to the Orient. The smells of cooking lingered in the hot tropical air and mingled with the perfume of flowers and the decaying odor of vegetation that was prevalent in all tropical lands where there were jungles. The odor of peanut oil was strong, but overcoming it were the more pungent scents of exotic herbs and spices. The Dutch East Indies were the point of origin of most of the spices currently in demand in Europe and North America, and the economy of the islands, particularly of Java, the capital, revolved around these rare, exotic plants.

Erika von Klausner was fascinated by everything that she saw and heard, and committed to memory scenes unlike any she had ever witnessed before. Only a short distance from the

Djakarta waterfront, her carriage slowed to ford a shallow river, and there she saw a half-dozen native women, all with black hair streaming down their backs, all of them naked to the waist and clad in a single wraparound garment, washing clothes in the most primitive of manners by rubbing them between two stones. Beyond, in the crowded streets where small huts were jumbled together in vast profusion, small boys and girls were entirely nude, playing without self-consciousness. Most adult males, all of them armed with what appeared to be throwing knives, wore loincloths of cotton and were small, wiry, and self-sufficient in appearance.

Erika had assumed that, as Djakarta was the heart and soul of the Dutch East Indies, there would be a great many Hollanders here, but that did not appear to be true. Only occasionally did she catch a glimpse of blond hair and pale skin.

Reinhardt Braun, who rode beside her in the carriage, was in a happy mood. Attired like a proper German gentleman in a high, stiff collar, cutaway coat, and waistcoat, he strained in his seat, peering at the half-naked women whom he saw everywhere. Erika felt only contempt for him and ignored the man.

After they had driven a short distance, they came to a broad, palm-lined avenue, at the end of which was a vast estate, guarded by brown-skinned, knife-throwing men. A magnificent sprawling house stood in the middle of an impeccably manicured green lawn, and on the grounds behind the dwelling, placid in the midst of a cacophony of parrot calls and cries, were a dozen or more exquisitely beautiful young women. In their midst, seated in a huge wicker chair, was the strangest-looking man Erika had ever encountered. His head was totally bald, though his gray eyebrows were thick and bushy. What made him so extraordinary, however, was his size. His weight was at least double that of two ordinary men, and though he was perspiring, he seemed at ease in his suit of white silk pongee. His collar was open, as befitted tropical dwelling, and around his neck was a chain from which a perfect, square-cut emerald was suspended. A matching emerald graced a ring that he wore on one pudgy finger. The Fat Dutchman read Jonathan Rakehell's letter of introduction and extended his hand. "I bid you and your associate welcome to Djakarta," he declared. "Heh-heh. Anyone who is a friend of Jonathan Rakehell and Charles Boynton is welcome here."

One of the handsome slave girls conducted Erika to the quarters she would occupy, and another, to Reinhardt Braun's delight, led him toward another cottage.

The pulchritude of the girls aroused a competitive spirit in Erika, and she primped at length before a dressing-table mirror in her bedchamber before she was satisfied with the results and returned to the tropical garden. As she well knew, her appearance was unique. Her flaming red hair contrasted with the brunette tresses of the slave girls, and her gown of delicately fragile pale green silk set off her superb figure to its best advantage. The Dutchman, she told herself, wouldn't bother to glance at the women of his harem while she was present.

One of the girls brought her a strange but delicious concoction which she later discovered was Dutch gin mixed with passion fruit juices and the milk of a coconut. She fully intended to dazzle the Dutchman, but to her surprise, he took charge of the proceedings at once.

"As you're from Hamburg," he said, "you must be acquainted with Herr von Bolligen."

"I know him very well. He's a director of the company with which I happen to be associated," she said.

He nodded, his round overweight face bland. "Then you undoubtedly also know Herr Schneider and Herr Weiboldt," he said.

She nodded, silently marveling at his familiarity with the directors of the shipping conglomerate who had been responsible for her employment.

"I have competed with their company many times in Europe," he said, "but, of course, they don't do business in this part of the world."

"Perhaps," she suggested lightly, "they're hoping to change all that."

"Really. Heh-heh-heh." He chuckled, then fell silent. "How do they hope to gain a foothold?"

She sipped her drink and then reflected that it would be wise to reveal at least part of the truth to him. He was not the type of man who could be fooled, and knowing she was dependent on him for favors so far from home, she decided to take the frank approach. "They're relying on me to obtain the initial contracts for them," she said. "Then, after that, I suppose they'll send some shipping men to the Orient to strengthen any deals I may make."

He raised an eyebrow. "You must have rare talents. Heh-heh. I've never heard of a responsible shipping firm placing such trust in a woman."

"Surely you're mistaken," Erika replied firmly. "Apparently you've forgotten a woman named Molinda, who was once employed by you, and as I understand it, is chief of operations in this part of the world for Rakehell and Boynton."

He chuckled again and scrutinized her even more carefully. It was clear to him that here was a woman whose beauty might be ornamental, but whose mind obviously was sharp. She had made it her business to become familiar with the world into which she'd been thrust. "Your associate, Braun," he said, "heh-heh-heh. What part does he play?"

"He has come with me to act as my bodyguard and protector," Erika said. "As I understand it, in this part of the world it is more unusual than it is in Europe for a woman alone, on her own, to function in business."

"Your Hamburg employers obviously have great faith in you," he said.

"I think their faith is justified," she replied calmly. "I'd prefer that we come to know each other somewhat better before we begin talking business, but I'm quite certain that when we do, you will find the terms I offer you for contracts are both lucrative and attractive." She proceeded to flirt with him expertly.

The Dutchman was both amused and fascinated. The redheaded young woman from Hamburg had great nerve and great self-confidence which, no doubt, were sparked by her beauty. She was sufficiently attractive that she would feel at ease anywhere.

It was obvious to the Dutchman, however, that in spite of her preparations for her assault on his stronghold, she was less well informed than she realized. Rarely had any woman flirted with him so consistently and so blatantly. In Djakarta, it was common knowledge that he was impotent and, consequently, was impervious to female blandishments. This was something that Erika von Klausner had yet to learn, and the Dutchman could scarcely control his urge to laugh aloud.

As soon as Reinhardt Braun joined them, they adjourned to the dining room, and there the German couple were treated to their initial meal of *rijsttafel*. This consisted of literally scores of dishes, perhaps as many as one hundred and fifty separate, individual dishes ranging from seafoods to local fruits and vegetables. They were served with curries and other exotic sauces that ran the full gamut of the local spices, and the variety of tastes was bewildering.

It was polite, Erika quickly learned, to take only a token portion of each dish on her plate, and to sip from a cool glass of wine between bites. Braun, however, was enjoying himself too much to pay much attention to local customs, and piling his plate high, he ogled the semiclad girls who waited on them. Erika was annoyed with her companion, afraid that he was creating complications for her, but the Dutchman seemed impervious to his manners, and gradually she became calmer. She concentrated her full attention on her host, and was her most charming and effervescent self. Knowing her sex appeal was her principal weapon, she used it to the best of her advantage.

The Dutchman, leaving most of the *rijsttafel* foods untouched, ate a small portion of boiled chicken and another of plain, steamed fish.

"Do you always eat so lightly?" Erika questioned.

"Not always, heh-heh," he answered her. "In the past, I ate enough for five men, and that is how I came to achieve my grossly overweight condition. But my physicians have instructed me to be more spartan in my eating habits, and so I follow their advice, even though I still remain obese. No one knows why that is, but I am reconciled to my fate."

She had succeeded in personalizing the conversation, but the Dutchman soon slipped away from her again and began to discuss specifics of the shipping industry.

He required only a quarter of an hour to assure himself that Erika, although the official representative of the Hamburg shipping conglomerate, knew virtually nothing about the business, nor for that matter did Braun, who continued to ogle the girls as he ate steadily.

The Dutchman could have rejected Erika von Klausner instantly, but that was not his way. Her employers had a purpose in mind in assigning her to represent them, and he wanted to delve into the matter further. He had accumulated much of his vast fortune by employing just such tactics and relying on his instincts rather than common sense. He wanted to know more, a great deal more, about the Hamburg operations, and he saw an opportunity to benefit accordingly if he was shrewd enough. Certainly this young woman and her doltish companion were no match for him.

Erika's attempts to arouse his sexual interest in her ultimately bored him, particularly after they had finished their meal and Braun left the table to be conducted back to his quarters by one of the slave girls. Erika saw an opportunity to endear herself to the Dutchman while they were alone, and she became so cloying, so obvious, that he deliberately dangled a potential contract under her nose in order to turn her attention away from himself.

She responded promptly, astonished and delighted by her good fortune. Granted that the offer of a contract whereby he would send a shipload of Indonesian cloves and other spices to Hamburg in return for a shipload of manufactured goods was minor, and involved the exchange of only small sums of money, but it was a beginning, and would convince the directors in Hamburg that she was doing her job. So she discussed the deal with him in detail and readily agreed to the terms he suggested. "I'll have a contract drawn accordingly.

Heh-heh," the Dutchman told her, "and it will be ready for you to sign after you've had your *siesta*."

"*Siesta?*" She looked blank.

"A word borrowed from the Spanish," the Dutchman told her. "In the heat of the afternoon, especially after one has eaten a hearty meal, one can do little but sleep."

"Well," she said, "I don't in the least mind going to bed, but I don't know that I'll sleep."

He deliberately ignored the opportunity to explore that subject with her further, and she was led off to her own quarters.

Alone again, the Dutchman slowly made his way back to his oversized wicker chair and sank into it. A slave girl brought him a glass of fruit juice, mildly flavored with Dutch *genever,* and two others began to cool him with long-handled ostrich feather fans. He was aware of something unsettling in the air, something that had disturbed his ordinarily unruffled female companions, and their ministrations left him untouched. He stared at a half-Chinese, half-Indonesian girl who was one of his current favorites.

"What is troubling you and your companions, Wang-sha?" he asked politely.

The girl averted her face and made no reply.

"I trust someone will tell me, heh-heh," the Dutchman said in a low, pleasant tone.

A total silence greeted his remark, and even the chattering parrots stopped squawking.

The Dutchman sighed and reached into a leather saddlebag attached to one side of his chair. He slowly withdrew a riding crop and swished it experimentally. "I hate to see beauty marred, as all of you know," he said conversationally, "but sometimes it becomes necessary to take a firm stand for the good of us all. Perhaps one of you will be good enough to summon Deru for me."

Deru was a chief of his bodyguards and often performed services that the Dutchman preferred to let others do for him. Among them was the task of chastising a girl who became

279

rebellious or disobedient. It was Deru's duty to whip her until she repented of her rebellious ways.

As he had anticipated, the young women raised their voices in protest and were so upset that the sound of their voices quickly drowned the noise from the parrots, which were squawking once again. The Dutchman sighed and put a long, thin cheroot in one corner of his mouth. One of the girls hastily lit it for him with a tinderbox and flint. He puffed thoughtfully on the cheroot, keeping it in one corner of his hamlike hand. "I'm waiting," he said to no one in particular. "I believe I'm showing great patience."

They assured him that he was a model of patience. Then, all at once, the reason for their upset came tumbling out.

The white-skinned man who had accompanied the redhaired lady to the Dutchman's house was responsible. He had threatened the girl who had first shown him to his quarters, swearing he would shoot her with a pistol he carried unless she gave in to him. The girl, her companions assured the Dutchman earnestly, well knew the rules of the establishment. Sexual intercourse was forbidden, except when ordered by the master, in which case it was obligatory.

The Dutchman shook his head. Braun, the idiot, had failed to understand that in the normal course of events he would have been presented with one of the young women as a gift to be used as he saw fit during his stay here. His impetuous, bad-mannered approach, however, put a far different light on the matter.

"Where is the girl now?" the Dutchman asked casually.

He was told that she had gone off to her own quarters in despair and bewilderment. He sent for her at once. The delicate-featured girl was terror-stricken as she approached the oversized bamboo chair. She knew she had broken one of the Dutchman's inviolable rules by acceding to the visitor's threats and going to bed with him, and at the very least, she expected to be severely thrashed. The Dutchman, however, often surprised his subordinates. "Tell me in your own words what happened," he said gently.

The girl's story was simple and direct. Braun had made

remarks to her in a language that she hadn't understood, but his meaning had been very clear. She had demurred, making it evident that she would not go to bed with him, and he had thrown her to the floor, drawn his pistol, cocked it, and held it to her temple. She had seen a seaman killed in a fight in a waterfront saloon in the days before the Dutchman had purchased her from her previous masters, and she knew how lethal the firearms of the Westerner could be. Therefore, in terror, she had given herself to the man.

The Dutchman reached out, stroked her hair, and then gently drew a hand across her bare breasts. The gesture was intended to be soothing, and it had precisely that effect. His touch could be astonishingly light in spite of the size of his hands. He was lost in thought for a moment, and then he smiled. The girls, who saw the bloodless grimace and who were aware of the iciness in his eyes, shuddered. "Be good enough," he said to one of them, "to fetch the foreign gentleman now. I wish two of you to go," he said, "because if I send only one, then she, too, might be threatened." The two girls he chose for the errand departed somewhat reluctantly. Soon they returned and joined their comrades, who were relaxing on the ground, eating fruit, and both looked relieved that they had accomplished their mission without complications. The girl whom Braun had intimidated stood close beside the Dutchman at his request.

Reinhardt Braun soon appeared, his eyes still puffy from sleep. He had no idea why his host wanted to see him, but he was in high spirits. The food here was wonderful, and nowhere on earth had he seen so many attractive half-nude women, all of whom could be his on demand.

Braun sauntered toward the Dutchman and sat down, unbidden, in a chair opposite the oversized bamboo chair that continued to dominate the scene.

The Dutchman chuckled without humor and snapped his fingers twice. A pair of lean, brown-skinned men, wearing only loincloths with belts studded with throwing knives around their waists, appeared out of nowhere, and taking hold of Braun's arms, they lifted him to his feet.

"I wasn't aware that I had invited you to sit. Heh-heh," the Dutchman said quietly.

Unaccustomed to such outrageous treatment, Braun began to sputter. The Dutchman held up a hand for silence.

Ordinarily Reinhardt Braun would have paid no attention to the admonition, but it occurred to him that he was in no position to exhibit his prowess. He was thousands of miles from home on a small, heavily populated island of whose existence he had been totally unaware until Jonathan Rakehell's clipper ship had deposited him and Erika in Java. The Dutchman was a huge mountain of fat flesh who could be easily handled in a fight, but the two bodyguards who continued to grip the German's arms were another matter altogether. They were wiry, remarkably strong, and the gleam in their eyes indicated they would like nothing better than to have an excuse to use Braun as a target for their thin, sharp throwing knives.

He promptly subsided and instead said with surprising meekness, "I would appreciate knowing the reason that I am being treated in this fashion."

The Dutchman chuckled, then nodded in the direction of the girl whom Braun had threatened and then abused. "Is this girl familiar to you?"

"Of course," Braun replied quickly. "She escorted me to my room."

"And in the sequence of events that followed, you drew your pistol, threatening to kill her with it unless she gave in to you, which she did in order to save her life."

Braun laughed aloud and shook his head. "That, my dear sir, is the most absurd story I have heard in a very long time. Do you think I would be so foolish as to incur your enmity that way?"

"Obviously, you were that foolish, and you have indeed become my enemy." The Dutchman laughed as though he had just been told a very funny story.

Braun's blood froze, and he instinctively reached for the pistol that he carried in a holster at his side. But the two Indonesian bodyguards were too fast for him, and he found his arms again held in a grip of steel. He was unable to move and began to sputter again.

"He makes more noise than a parrot," the Dutchman said. "Perhaps someone will silence him." The bodyguards stuffed a cloth into his mouth to gag him. Braun continued to protest, but the sounds he was able to make were not words.

The Dutchman laughed more heartily and said something in a native tongue that the German did not understand. The young woman Braun had abused stepped forward hesitantly, shyly, and drew a throwing knife from the belt of one of the grinning bodyguards. Then, her shyness fading, she slashed suddenly with it, and Braun's belt was cut neatly in two. His trousers began to slide over his hips, and the girl helped the movement by jerking on the cloth and then deliberately lowering his underclothes. He was naked from the waist down, and all the girls began to laugh and titter. The Dutchman, chuckling indulgently, addressed the young woman again. She reached out with the blade and placed the sharp edge tentatively but firmly against Braun's testicles.

"You are not in Hamburg now, my friend," the Fat Dutchman told him. "You are in Djakarta, the capital of the Dutch East Indies. Here life is simple, and honor is easier to protect than in Europe. You are new here, so you do not yet know our ways, therefore we have decided to take pity on you. Ordinarily, in return for your behavior today, the girl you mistreated would have had the right to cut off your testicles and parade you on a leash for all to see. That, however, will not happen to you. She has decided to show you compassion, and you will be paraded, but otherwise you will be left unharmed."

Two of the girls cut a length of supple vine growing up a tree and fashioned a loop out of it, then dropped the loop around Braun's neck. The bodyguards meantime fastened his hands securely behind his back. The girl said something to him in a tongue that he did not understand.

She emphasized her words by prodding him in the buttocks with the sharp point of the knife. He jumped and squirmed, but there was no escaping the probing blade. "You will be paraded around the property for all to see, and for the amusement of all who are in my employ," the Dutchman told him. "In this way, the members of my staff learn that I am not partial to those whose skins are white, and I do not grant them favors that are denied to others. Heh-heh. Let this be a warning to you. If you should ever again molest a young lady on my property, I promise that you will be emasculated, and that the whole world will know of your shame." He picked up his glass, sipped his drink, and, chuckling, turned to engage several of the girls in conversation. That was the signal to the young woman Braun had dishonored, and she again prodded her captive with the knife.

Braun found it difficult to walk because his trousers and underclothes were clinging to his ankles, but rather than be jabbed with the knife again, he began to shuffle. The young woman moved ahead of him and, picking up the loose end of the vine, led him like a captive animal.

Her face showed no pleasure, nor any other emotion, as she deliberately led him around the entire property. She was true to the Dutchman's word, and Braun was being shown to all who worked for the Dutchman as an example.

Shamed and furious, Reinhardt Braun could do nothing to escape the cruel punishment being inflicted on him.

The Fat Dutchman was well satisfied with his day's efforts. He had succeeded in taming Braun, who would be far more malleable, far easier to handle henceforth, and by promising a contract to Erika, he had won her support, too. Now he was much better able to weigh the potentialities of doing business with the proprietors of the Hamburg shipping conglomerate, and to deal with them accordingly.


The entire court of the Tao Kuang Emperor was startled when word was received that a major revolt had broken out in the city of Tsinan, a major metropolis on the Yellow River. What made the insurrection so unusual was not the fact that it was taking place—there were dissidents everywhere in the Middle Kingdom and the outbreak of insurrections was common. But Tsinan was the capital of Shantung Province, which lay due south of Hopeh Province, where Peking was located. The mere fact that rebels dared to defy the authority of the Celestial Emperor within a striking distance of his capital indicated that they were either very confident or very foolhardy.

The Tao Kuang Emperor ordinarily was a gentle, mild-mannered man who abhorred violence, but he quickly reverted to the ways of his Manchu ancestors when his authority was questioned. He sent at once for his most esteemed generals, Wing Po and Wu Tsung, and ordered them to stamp out the revolt by all possible means. The generals promptly announced that they would form an army ten-thousand strong to march against Tsinan.

The atmosphere in the Forbidden City was changed in an instant, and a martial spirit prevailed. Even clerks who did nothing more warlike than copy military documents began showing up for work with battle-axes and other ancient weapons. The insurrection was the major topic of discussion at the court, and little else was discussed.

Matthew Melton was unaffected, however. He continued to receive patients at the same steady pace, and his life seemed unchanged. Then, forty-eight hours after it had been announced that Wing Po and Wu Tsung were being dispatched with an elite force to teach the rebels a lesson, the Tao Kuang Emperor made one of his rare, unexpected appearances in Matthew's office suite. He showed up unobtrusively and entered so quietly that Matthew, who was making notes to himself on the condition of a patient he had just treated, scarcely heard him come in. He looked up from his writing, recognized the emperor, and almost jumped to his feet, but he managed to control himself just in time. Tao Kuang was unaccompanied, which meant that he was choosing to appear here incognito, and Matthew knew the rules well enough to pretend that no one had come in.

The emperor looked around for a tray of the salted sunflower seeds that he always enjoyed here, and he munched contentedly. "No doubt," he said quietly, "it has come to the attention of the learned physician of the West that there are those in Shantung Province who have dared to question the might and majesty of the emperor."

Matthew nodded. "I've heard of the insurrection," he admitted.

"When there is bad that sours the tea in a pot," the emperor declared vaguely, "it often happens that sugar finds its way into the pot and makes the tea more palatable."

Unsure of his meaning, Matthew remained silent.

"The learned physician from the West," the emperor said, "has not had an easy time in the Middle Kingdom. He has encountered much jealousy from his colleagues here, and they have not only hampered his practice, but they have refrained from showing him the techniques of their own practice."

Matthew had heard that the emperor was aware of everything that happened in the Forbidden City, and he could only assume that, in this instance, Wu-ling had revealed details of his situation.

"The coming of war changes all that," the emperor announced with a smile. "When men are wounded in battle, those who treat them must work swiftly, and they gladly accept help from all who offer it. If the physician from the West cares to accompany the punitive expedition that is being sent to Shantung Province, he will not only have an opportunity to demonstrate his own methods of caring for the sick, but he will have ample opportunities to learn the methods used by his colleagues in the Middle Kingdom."

The emperor's observation was remarkably shrewd, Matthew decided, and he marveled that the Tao Kuang Emperor could be bothered with his welfare at such a time. Recognizing the generous, unexpected offer that had been made to him, he knew that he had to respond to it instantly.

"I am very grateful," he said slowly, "for the opportunity to teach my colleagues here more of the medicine that I practice, and I am equally grateful for the chance to learn more about the methods and techniques of medical practitioners in the Middle Kingdom."

That was all that the emperor wanted to hear. He had many things on his mind, and as far as he was concerned, here was a problem that had been settled. He nodded cheerfully and, jumping to his feet, reached for another handful of salted sunflower seeds as he departed.

Less than an hour later, Wu-ling came to Matthew's suite and was very excited. "I suppose you know," she said, "that we are going into Shantung Province tomorrow with Generals Wing Po and Wu Tsung."

Matthew was duly astonished. "I'm not surprised that I'm being sent," he said, "but I'm amazed that you're going, too."

"I'm being relieved of my other duties to spend the entire time acting as your interpreter," she said proudly. "The emperor himself has ordered it, and none, not even his generals, dare to disobey him."

Matthew was surprised. "Your regular translating work is going to be allowed to wait while this campaign is waged?" he demanded.

She nodded. "It has been decided by the Celestial Emperor that the knowledge of the Western physician must be enlarged, and that which he already knows must be disseminated to his colleagues here. You now speak Chinese well enough to communicate your basic needs and desires, but it would be impossible for you to carry on a conversation in depth with learned physicians. So, as I am the only individual in the entire land who is capable of acting as an interpreter, I have been relieved of my other duties."

"But won't you be in danger going into a combat zone?" he demanded.

"I think not," she said. "The medical practitioners will work near the headquarters of General Wing Po, and Wing is a cautious soldier, so there will be no fighting in the vicinity of his pavilion."

He smiled and then sobered again. "I hope it won't seem too strange to you to be the only woman accompanying the expedition."

"It is obvious, Dr. Melton, that you know nothing about

armies in the Middle Kingdom. The cooks and personal servants and concubines of the officers will ride in a separate body, and with so large an army on the march, there will be many harlots who will be traveling to Shantung also, to prevent the troops from becoming too lonely. There will be many, many women on this expedition.''

He was relieved to hear it, and although he made no analysis of his own feelings, he was privately pleased that Wu-ling would be spending so much time in his company.

Late that same day imperial servants brought Matthew a number of gifts, including several pairs of footgear, ranging from felt boots to heavy leather boots that had been treated in some way to make them water-repellent. He received several pairs of heavy cotton trousers, and shirts and two ponchos, one to ward off the cold and the other to wear when it rained. The following morning, Wu-ling appeared, apparently dressed for travel in a dark cheongsam, and she told him that he was being provided with two horses, one for his person and the other for such medical equipment as he cared to take with him. He saw to it that he would carry what he regarded as an adequate number of splints and bandages.

The army that assembled in the courtyard of the imperial palace was, to put it mildly, an extraordinary force. The officers, who wore ornamental armor, rode small but spirited horses that were sturdy enough to carry great weight. All of them were armed with vicious-looking weapons, known as *ku ming*, that dated back to the thirteenth century. They were spears, with a second shorter blade, resembling a sword, projecting from the same shaft, and they had the added advantage of a hooked, pronglike extension that was similar to possessing yet another weapon. The common soldiers, in their cotton uniforms of imperial chrysanthemum-yellow, carried shorter versions of the same weapons, in addition to strange-looking muskets with barrels easily as long as the famous long rifles of the early American frontier. But here, any resemblance in weapons ended abruptly. The Chinese muskets were museum pieces rather than active, usable weapons, and many of them had been gathering dust in imperial arsenals for several hundred years. Each man carried his own supplies of gunpowder and ammunition, which were ample.

The entourage that would follow the troops was also extraordinary, in the opinion of the dazed young doctor from the United States. There were several hundred middle-aged women who would cook the meals and gather the firewood for the troops, and as Matthew would ultimately learn, some of these women also attended to the chore of washing the clothes of the officers. By far the single largest contingent was comprised of heavily painted harlots who wore skintight cheongsams with slits in their skirts that extended high onto their shapely thighs. They would travel in carts pulled by larger horses than those used by the military, and each night when the army called a halt, a contingent of servants who traveled with the harlots would erect their gaudily colored pavilions for them.

The royal physicians who would march with the expedition were civilians, all of them mounted, and they made it plain that they were a breed apart. They were going to travel separately, neither mingling with the troops nor the many women. As Matthew was to learn, much to his amusement, they would set up their tents in a separate enclave, too.

Generals Wing Po and Wu Tsung, as well as the many staff officers gathered in the huge inner courtyard in the Forbidden City, kept looking up at a curtained window on the third floor of the palace, which led Matthew to believe that the Tao Kuang Emperor was watching the departure of his expedition from there. Wu-ling confirmed his guess.

The expedition began with a flourish, a corps of drummers led the procession, and to the surprise of Matthew, no two drummers beat their instruments in unison. They appeared to be competing with one another rather than playing in unison, and the result was a confusing medley of sounds. Since no attempt was being made to march together, however, the lack of cooperation between drummers was irrelevant.

The expedition strung out over several miles on the road, with the food carts, pulled by donkeys, bringing up the rear. Matthew knew relatively little of military matters, but he marveled at the lack of cohesion in the expeditionary force. No guards of any kind were provided for the supply wagons, so it would have been an easy matter for an enemy to cut them off from the main body of troops, confiscate them, and render the attacking force impotent. The army became strung out even farther on the dusty road after Peking was left behind. Most of the soldiers elected to ride together, but those who didn't often fell far behind the main column, and no attempt was made to urge them to rejoin their units. Every man, it appeared, was more or less on his own. Never had Matthew seen such a complete lack of organization.

His comments to that effect were shrugged off by Wu-ling, however. She knew virtually nothing about military affairs, and it was apparent that she had no interest in them.

No halt was made for a noon meal, so the strange ensemble made fairly good time, and by the end of the day, Matthew was surprised to discover that the column had covered the respectable distance of twenty-three miles. The stamina of the Chinese soldier was as surprising as it was rugged.

The young American was pleased when a silk pavilion was erected for his use only a short distance from the tents of General Wing Po and his principal aides. The bivouac of the Chinese physicians was located elsewhere, and as Matthew ultimately learned, it was known that he was a favorite of the Tao Kuang Emperor and the Princess An Mien, and, consequently, the commander of the expedition gave him a place of honor. His pavilion swarmed with servants.

Apparently the organization of the camp was less chaotic than Matthew had assumed. As soon as his pavilion was erected, he was served with a gourmet meal that included such delicacies as marinated lotus root sprinkled with sesame seeds, "long-knife" thin, fresh egg noodles, served with minced green onions and ground pork butt, and a curry of beef, peppers, and onion root. The noodles, he knew, were a delicacy ordinarily served on birthdays and other personal holidays. According to tradition, they represented long life and consequently were never cut. They were to be eaten by wrapping them around one's chopsticks, an art which the

American was now mastering. He dined in lonely splendor in his pavilion, and although he wondered what had become of Wu-ling, there was no sign of her. Then, suddenly the flap entrance to his tent was flung aside, and Wu-ling entered, her eyes blazing with anger and her step firm and deliberate.

"Have you eaten as yet?" he asked politely.

She shook her head. "No, I have no appetite just now, thank you. I'm too annoyed."

"What's happened?" he wanted to know.

Her voice shook with rage as she said, "I've been grossly insulted! My pavilion has been placed in the midst of the harlots' tents. I've been assigned to their encampment."

Matthew stared at her. "Who assigned you?" he wanted to know.

"I don't know, and I don't care," she said tossing her head defiantly. "I tried just now to speak to General Wing Po, but his sentries won't let me near him."

"Perhaps I can help you." Matthew rose, his own meal quickly forgotten. "Come along." He went to the door of the tent, and Wu-ling fell in beside him.

They walked a short distance to the headquarters of the expeditionary force, and a team of sentries armed with curved double-edged swords tried to bar their way, but Matthew impatiently pushed past them. One of the officers, sitting at the commander-in-chief's table, eating dinner from exquisite porcelain bowls, said something in a low tone, and the sentries stood aside to let the couple approach.

The individual least interested in them was Wing Po, the senior officer of the expedition. The general, it was said, had achieved his high rank after spending his entire life as a civilian. He was fortunate because his younger sister had attracted the Tao Kuang Emperor's persistent attention, she had agreed to become his mistress, and her brother had been awarded his high rank. Seated beside the general was the veteran officer who was the true military commander of the expedition. General Wu Tsung had distinguished himself in the Opium War against the British, had fought with distinction against the Portuguese in Macao, and had been personally responsible for quelling several uprisings in the interior. It was he, rather than his superior, who demanded severely, "What is the meaning of this interruption?"

Wu-ling wanted to reply in her own words but knew that far more attention would be paid to anything that Matthew said. He had learned enough of the Chinese language to speak effectively, if somewhat awkwardly, and he thus obliged her with a blistering comment. "The favorite of Tao Kuang Emperor and Princess An Mien has been subject to gross insult," he declared, striving to find the correct words. "Her tent has been placed with tents of courtesans."

General Wing Po absently wrapped several strands of long-knife noodles around his chopsticks. General Wu Tsung, however, remained alert and replied, "I take full responsibility for that assignment."

"Must be changed at once," Matthew said emphatically. "She who translates for emperor is lady and must be treated as lady."

The general did not back down. "The authority of the deputy commander of this expedition has been questioned. I would lose face if I were to amend my orders now. The tent of the young woman must remain where it is."

Matthew had not yet lived long enough in the East to understand the importance that Orientals attached to the maintenance of what they called "face." This was a difficult subject to grasp for anyone lacking long experience in the area. So, to his surprise, he proceeded to lose his temper and spoke far more stridently than he realized. "I demand this situation be corrected."

General Wu Tsung drew himself up proudly. "You demand, Fan Kuei?" he asked venomously. "Who are you to demand anything of one who serves the emperor in a high military place?"

The officer's opposition seemed senseless to Matthew, who became even angrier. "I will go to any length—repeat, any length—to obtain justice. If necessary I shall appeal direct to Princess An Mien." He well knew, or at least strongly suspected, that the emperor's sister would support the position he had taken. Wu-ling, he was pleased to see, was delighted that he was acting as her champion, and the sheen of gratitude he saw in her eyes made him all the more determined to fight to the end on her behalf.

The deadlock was complete; Wu Tsung stubbornly refused to budge. His superior, however, was as wise in political matters as he was inexperienced in war. Wing Po well knew that no one in the Middle Kingdom was more influential than the Princess An Mien. In fact, if she chose to do so, the emperor would almost certainly heed her advice and discard a concubine.

Not wanting to make an enemy of someone so closely associated with the princess, especially in a matter that had no significance, Wing Po decided the time had come for him to intervene. "We are engaged in a campaign together," he said, "for the purpose of putting down an uprising of rebels. Let us stand united in all things. Since the foreigner insists that the pavilion of the translator be moved, let it be moved to a place adjacent to his own tent and let him henceforth assume full responsibility for the young woman."

Having taken care of the matter, at least to his own satisfaction, the general once again directed his full attention to the food on his plate.

Wu Tsung had received a direct slap and glared malevolently, first at Matthew and then at Wu-ling.

Matthew was somewhat jarred by the senior general's ruling. He hadn't expected to be given responsibility for Wu-ling, but he had no real choice in the matter, and therefore he accepted. Besides, she was so pleased at the outcome of the battle he had waged on her behalf that his own spirits were raised.

Thereafter, Matthew and Wu-ling were always together, not only riding side by side on each day's march, but eating their meals in each other's company and spending their leisure time together. It was through Wu-ling that Matthew learned of the implacable opposition to him on the part of the physicians assigned to accompany the expedition.

"The physicians who march with us are young," she told

293

him at dinner one night, "and therefore you would expect them to be more malleable and open-minded than those who are older, but that is not the case."

He raised an eyebrow.

"They are the sons and nephews of imperial physicians," she said. "They have won their places in this expedition through family influence because it will look good in their records to have taken part in a military enterprise. But they are ignorant of even the medicine of their forebears. They know little about the herbs to prescribe for various ailments, and they have not practiced acupuncture. They are young, and their families are wealthy, and they are what the Americans and English call spoiled."

"That's too bad," Matthew said, and hoped that casualties would be light when the force went into combat.

"Unfortunately," she went on, "they realize that your knowledge is vast—much greater than their own—so they are very jealous of you, and are afraid that when the time comes you will steal much glory from them."

He was annoyed. "Maybe it would help," he said, "if I speak to them and make it very clear that my only interest lies in healing the sick. I have no desire to deprive them or anyone else of glory."

Wu-ling shook her head. "It is best that nothing be said and that you pretend to be unaware of their attitude. If you know of it, there is certain to be trouble, and they have the support of General Wu Tsung, who has not forgotten that you caused him to lose face. It is best that the entire matter be allowed to rest."

One day was like another, and as they crossed through open countryside they passed walled villages and isolated farmhouses, wooded areas and small towns. The entire province was devoted, it seemed, to the raising of silkworms, from which a unique, lightweight silk was woven. Shantung silk was in great demand in Great Britain and France, and Americans, who were just learning of it, were clamoring for it, too. So thousands of Shantung residents were trying to meet the insatiable demand.

At last the high walls of the city of Tsinan came in view, and the expedition halted just out of range of the catapults of the defenders. There were numerous cannons inside the city walls, too, but apparently they had become rusty with disuse and were ineffective.

General Wing Po sent an officer with a mellifluous voice to the enemy, and he read a long proclamation. The gist of the message was that the people of Tsinan were covering themselves with shame by rebelling, and if they surrendered at once, only a half-dozen ringleaders, who were mentioned by name, would lose their lives as punishment. General Wing Po, acting on the authority of the ever-merciful Tao Kuang Emperor, would grant full, complete pardons to everyone else associated with the rebellion.

The rebels replied by throwing a bucket of boiling pitch from the walls on General Wing Po's emissary, and he lost his life as a consequence.

The entire army was incensed by this cavalier treatment, and General Wu Tsung ordered that no more alcohol be consumed with the harlots for seventy-two hours. It was clear that as a result of these commands, an assault on the city of Tsinan would be made in three days' time. From reports received by their scouts stationed outside the city walls, the defenders learned of the enemy's war preparations, and they fortified themselves accordingly.

The morning of the attack came, and Matthew watched the assault from a vantage point near his pavilion. The defenders opened the battle by firing several salvos with their ancient cannons. Most of the guns refused to fire, and the shots of the others went wild, but honor had been satisfied and that was what mattered.

Then the attackers replied in kind, and they were less fortunate. Three of their decrepit guns exploded, immediately killing their entire crews. Only two shots cleared the high stone wall surrounding Tsinan, the other iron balls bouncing harmlessly across the thick stones. In any event, the combat was now joined. The rebels poured boiling oil and hurled projectiles from the tops of the wall, but these did no harm, as the attackers were keeping clear. Then General Wu Tsung personally led a sortie, and the fight was beginning in earnest. Yellow-clad troops advanced in phalanxes of one hundred men each, wielding their ferocious sword-spears and forgetting their muskets, which were of little value. They were able to climb the wall, in spite of the efforts of the defenders to dislodge them, and once the breach had been made, the imperial troops poured into the city relentlessly. They fanned out in Tsinan and used their sword-spears ruthlessly, cutting down anyone in their path. The defenders soon had enough.

Panic spread rapidly, and the commander in chief of the defending force had been so disgraced that he fell on his own sword, committing suicide before he could be captured. Three of his immediate subordinates, who were also on the proscribed list, followed his example, preferring a quick, relatively painless death to the hours of torture that awaited them if they should be returned in chains to Peking.

Casualties were light, particularly in the attacking force. The troops were veterans and knew how to handle themselves, with the result that no more than one man in twenty suffered even minor injuries.

Matthew was kept busy bandaging wounds and performing minor surgery. Wu-ling, promoted through necessity to a role far greater than that of his translator, helped him, and once she learned what was expected of her, it was no longer necessary to instruct her.

Significantly, none of the Chinese physicians came near Matthew's pavilion.

At last he and Wu-ling had a breathing spell, and the young woman vanished briefly, returning with grave news.

"General Wu Tsung was badly wounded," she informed him. "He led the final attack, you know, and the defenders concentrated their attack on him."

"Where is he now?" Matthew wanted to know, his personal feud with the officer forgotten.

"The physicians are exorcising the devils from his body."

Matthew was stunned. "They're doing what?" he asked. She repeated her statement.

"That's absurd," he said, and picking up his instrument bag, he called to her, "take me to him right away."

She hesitated briefly, and then complied. They hurried across the bivouac area and, at the far side of the encampment, came to a large tent. Wu-ling, afraid to enter herself, merely pointed.

Matthew raised the flap, coughed, and almost gagged. Clouds of perfumed incense smoke filled the interior, and he heard several people chanting a senseless refrain. He needed no one to interpret for him, however. It was obvious that the Chinese physicians were calling on the "devils" who had invaded the body of Wu Tsung to depart. The primitive, senseless nature of the so-called cure annoyed him, and he ripped away the flap at the entrance of the pavilion and then stamped out a fire burning near the head of a divan. Stretched on the divan was the pale, motionless body of Wu Tsung, who had been wounded in the head and, judging from the bloodstains on his clothes, in the abdomen.

Matthew buckled down to work. He cleaned the blood from the patient's face and body with a cloth that he dipped in brandywine, and then he rummaged in his kit for some medicine. "Get a glass of water," he told Wu-ling, who had summoned the courage to follow him into the tent, "and pour this into it." He handed her a packet of laudanum, an opiate long used to dull pain. "Then feed this to him as fast as you can. He's barely conscious, but I think he's able to drink. I'm going to cauterize these wounds as soon as the opiate takes effect, and then we'll see what has to be done next. The poor devil is in a bad way."

Wu-ling managed to feed Wu Tsung the dose of laudanum, and Matthew went to work swiftly and deftly, cauterizing the ugly wounds that the general had sustained.

His efforts were in vain, however. Too much time had been spent by the Chinese physicians on the exorcism of the supposed devils, and the patient had lost so much blood and so much strength that he was no longer able to sustain life. Even as Matthew worked, his patient slumped on the divan, shuddered slightly, and died.

Always sad and disturbed when he lost a patient, Matthew was angry, too. "This needn't have happened," he said to Wu-ling as he started back to his own pavilion. "That primitive nonsense of getting rid of devils weakened the poor fellow, and by the time that we got to him, I'm afraid that nothing could have saved him."

The victory of the imperial forces was complete, and Tsinan capitulated unconditionally to General Wing Po. He hastily wrote a celebratory poem, commemorating the occasion, and a messenger was dispatched to Peking with the good news. The victorious troops returned slowly to the bivouac area where the cooks had prepared a larger than usual dinner for them, and Matthew, with nothing else to occupy him, decided that he and Wu-ling might as well eat, too. He was astonished when a junior officer approached him, spoke so rapidly that he was unable to understand, and then proceeded to seize and bind his wrists behind his back. Before Matthew realized what was happening, there were chains attached to his ankles and wrists, and they in turn were fastened to a heavy iron collar that was closed around his neck.

Wu-ling was on the verge of tears. "This is horrible," she said. "The physicians have charged you with the murder of General Wu Tsung. They recalled the argument you had with him and say that he was your bitter enemy and you chose to kill him after he was wounded in battle."

"That's utter rubbish," Matthew said hotly.

"Of course it is," she replied, unable to stem the tears streaming down her face now. "But they've obtained the ear of the general, and he's personally signed the order for your arrest. There's nothing now that can be done."

"I demand to see the general," he said.

She shook her head. "You don't understand. He will neither see you nor listen to you. You will be returned to Peking as a common criminal." Before she could say more,

298

two armed sentries intervened and pushed her away, not allowing her to come near the prisoner again.

The chains were never removed from his wrists and neck, and when the army and its retainers started back to Peking, Matthew was forced to make the long march on foot. Whenever he faltered, a sentry armed with a horsewhip lashed out at him and forced him to continue.

Days and nights blended and became a long torment. He was given little food, and he soon found that his guards beat him for the sheer pleasure they derived from the act. He was helpless, and there seemed to be no recourse. He was forbidden to go to the general or any member of his staff, and it was obvious from Wu-ling's continuing absence that she was not being permitted to visit him. Indeed, the physicians, realizing Wu-ling was a favorite of the court and would no doubt go to the princess to speak in behalf of the Western physician, kept the young Chinese woman under close watch and even imposed a quarantine upon her, forbidding her to see or speak to anyone.

At last the long column came to Peking, and thousands of citizens filled the streets to greet the victors. The spectacle of the white man in chains was an added fillip, and Matthew was a constant center of attention and abuse.

"Fan Kuei! Foreign Devil!" People shouted at him, and pelted him with rocks and garbage.

Matthew was hauled to an underground dungeon in a prison complex located somewhere in the sprawling palace, and he heard a door of metal and wood clang shut. The walls of his cell were of damp stone and there was no outside air, no daylight. The dampness was all-permeating, and he shivered.

Matthew lost all count of time, and had no idea how many days might have passed. He slept fitfully because there was literally nothing else to keep him occupied, and although he tried to engage in physical exercises in the dark, the atmosphere discouraged any such activity.

Suddenly, however, the door of the cell was opened wide and an official in a long gown of imperial yellow bowed low to him. "The Celestial Emperor," the official declared, "extends his deepest regrets and apologies for the treatment that the physician from the West has received."

Two underlings who stood behind the man came forward and, taking Matthew's arms, helped him into the corridor and up a steep flight of stone stairs. He blinked at the bright sunlight that streamed in through windows, and scarcely recognized the scrawny, ragged scarecrow who stared at him in a full-length mirror.

Hot water had been poured into a marble tub, Matthew's filthy clothes were cut from his body, and then he was invited to soak luxuriously in the tub. An imperial barber appeared to shave him, but he preferred to wield the razor himself, and the man quickly yielded the blade to him. Then he was dressed in Chinese clothes, including a tunic and trousers of yellow silk with a long mandarin's robe of matching yellow silk to be worn as an outer garment. Even the shoes he was given, which fitted him surprisingly well, were of soft, yellow-dyed leather.

He was taken into another chamber, and there he was ceremoniously served with a huge, steaming bowl containing seafood, meat, and a bewildering variety of vegetables. The pungent odors emanating from the bowl were delicious, but he ate slowly and sparingly, since his system would have difficulty adjusting to a hearty meal after the long days of near-starvation. Feeling like himself for the first time in many days, he grinned at his reflection in the mirror, amused by the Chinese costume in which he was clad.

Then the door opened, and Wu-ling came unannounced into the room. There was an expression of deep concern on her face, but when she saw him, she was relieved and smiled. "You look thinner, but well," she said, scrutinizing him carefully.

"I've been on what you might call a starvation diet," he said. "To what do I owe this sudden change in my fortunes?"

"I—I related the incident of your arrest and treatment to the Princess An Mien," she said. "The imperial physicians tried to prevent me from gaining her ear and almost succeeded by putting me under a quarantine, but I managed to outwit them by sending her a message saying it was urgent that I speak to her as soon as possible. She is very angry at the treatment you received, and so is the Celestial Emperor. The jealous physicians who connived against you have been sentenced to death by torture, and they will be executed this very day. You will be glad to hear that justice has prevailed.''

"Justice?'' he demanded bitterly. "I don't think anyone in this benighted land knows the meaning of the word.''

"You're mistaken,'' Wu-ling assured him earnestly. "The Princess An Mien has been mortified by the way you were treated, and even the Celestial Emperor was covered with shame. They are not seeing you themselves immediately because they feel they cannot face you until wrong has been righted and those who were responsible for your treatment have been punished.''

"I think there has been more than enough punishment,'' Matthew declared. "I don't see what possible good it can do to torture and murder physicians who were acting on what they considered were their own best interests and those of their country. I say—enough!''

He was so worked up that she didn't quite know how to reply. Matthew made a supreme effort to calm himself. "I am more grateful to you than I can tell you, more appreciative than you'll ever know that you persisted in your efforts to have me set free. I owe you a great debt, and I hope that someday I'll be able to repay it. Perhaps there's something you particularly want that I might send you from the United States.''

Wu-ling looked at him blankly. "From America?''

"I've pondered for endless hours, because I've had nothing better to do with my time,'' he said, "and I've come to the conclusion that I must notify Jonathan Rakehell that my mission has failed, and that I want to return to New England as rapidly as possible.''

"Oh, no!'' The girl looked stricken.

"I'll grant you that I probably came to Cathay filled with false ideas and ideals that couldn't be realized in the real

301

world," Matthew said. "Be that as it may, I see no opportunity to practice medicine here—as I know and believe it should be practiced."

Wu-ling began to shake her head in violent disagreement.

"I became a physician because, as far back as I can remember, I've wanted to heal the sick," he said. "Here I've been surrounded by superstition and have become involved against my will in senseless political struggles. I've had enough, and I intend to go home. In fact, I shall write to Molinda in Hong Kong, and perhaps she'll be good enough to arrange passage for me on the first Rakehell and Boynton clipper ship sailing to New England."

Wu-ling looked very pale and subdued, but she managed to rally sufficiently to say, "You do not intend to practice medicine again in the Middle Kingdom?"

"Not if I can help it," he retorted.

"Perhaps, then, you will spend the afternoon with me," she said.

He was puzzled by her request.

"You have thanked me for intervening with the emperor and his sister on your behalf, and for winning your freedom for you. All I ask in return is a few hours of your time. I would like you to come with me this afternoon."

He shrugged and nodded.

Wasting no time, Wu-ling led him down a long corridor, and she paused at a large, imposing office to hold an earnest, private conversation with the high official who occupied it.

Matthew could not hear what was being said, but apparently the official was in agreement with her, and began to give orders to several subordinates.

Wu-ling was satisfied but remained grim as she rejoined Matthew. They continued on their way and ultimately came to an inner courtyard, where several horses with chrysanthemum-yellow trappings awaited them. They mounted and were immediately surrounded by a small cordon of young officers in the uniform of the imperial guard regiment. Then, without further ado, they started to ride, rapidly increasing their pace to a canter.

"Where are we going?" Matthew wanted to know.

Wu-ling apparently failed to hear him; in any event, she did not reply.

They rode through the open gate that separated the Forbidden City from the Imperial City and ultimately left the Imperial City behind, too. Now they had come to that section of the community where ordinary citizens lived and worked. For block after block there stretched an endless morass of single-story huts, some made of stone, some fashioned of wood, others pieced together with discarded refuse.

The initial impression was one of teeming humanity. Men and women were everywhere, the women cooking in open pits in front of their huts, their men painstakingly foraging for bits of firewood. Naked children played and squabbled and fought outside the simple buildings, and Matthew noted that many of them had the distended stomachs that starvation causes.

Wu-ling seemed to be in charge of the expedition. She said something in a low tone to one of the officers, and they formed a wedge, then started to penetrate the maze of buildings. Wu-ling, looking out of place in her silk cheongsam and delicately fashioned high-heeled slippers, nevertheless acted as though she were completely at home in the neighborhood, and after they had proceeded several hundred feet, she suddenly called a halt. Then she went to the entrance of a hut and beckoned to Matthew. He looked in and saw, to his surprise, that several people were crowded into the tiny interior. Light came in through an open window that, when the weather became too cold, could be closed by letting down a ragged cloth over the opening. A couple sat on the dirt floor, their back supported by the wall of simple stone. Both were gray-haired and elderly. A younger man, perhaps their son, was pounding grain with an old-fashioned wooden mortar and pestle. A single glance at his work was enough to show Matthew that he had started the project with very little grain. Outside the hut, a woman of about the same age was boiling rice in a pot over an open fire that burned in a hole in the ground, and two small, naked boys wrestled with each other.

Wu-ling spoke rapidly in the dialect of Hopeh Province, and the man and woman replied briefly. She turned to Matthew and said earnestly, "These people have granted us permission to inspect their home. As you can see, the couple live here with their elderly parents and their four children. Two of the children are now at work. One is ten, and the other is twelve. These two boys will also go to work in another year, or less. I have chosen this house for you to see because it is typical of the homes of the citizens of China who live in the cities. The woman is cooking rice. If she were fortunate, her sons would have caught a rat or a mouse, and there would have been meat in the dish as well. Otherwise they have nothing to eat but rice. That is what they ate yesterday, that is what they are eating today, that is what they will eat tomorrow."

"But surely," the aghast physician said, "with several members of the family working they can afford—"

"They can afford only what they put on their table, nothing more," Wu-ling assured him. "The boys work long hours for a handful of coppers. The man is a construction worker, and his pay is low." She addressed a question to the head of the household, and he grunted a reply. "He rises before dawn and works twelve hours each day, seven days a week," Wu-ling said, "and for this he is paid five yuan."

Matthew was stunned. "Five yuan!" he exclaimed. "Those are starvation wages."

"Unless he works for the pay that is offered to him," Wu-ling said, "he will surely starve, and there are many others who are happy to take his place."

They went outdoors again and wandered down the lane, and Matthew saw that a crowd of curious passersby had gathered and were following them. The throng grew thicker by the moment.

At last Wu-ling paused in another hut, where she also took care to ask permission to enter. An even larger group was assembled here, including a man who was crippled and appeared to have suffered a stroke. There were two women, one middle-aged, one somewhat younger, who were racked by consumptive coughs, and all three of the children present had the bloated stomachs of the undernourished. Wu-ling made no comment and resumed her march. Matthew began to understand the point of her peregrinations. On every side he saw the grinding poverty, the misery, and the ailments of the ordinary people of Cathay.

But Wu-ling was far from finished. She paused briefly in hut after hut, and some of the sights that Matthew saw remained indelibly etched in his mind. He would never forget the girl in a tight-fitting cheongsam, heavily made-up and looking like a child attending a masquerade party. But she was not, and it developed that although she was only eleven years of age, she had already spent two years as a professional prostitute. There were families that subsisted exclusively on noodles or on rice. There were families where a single bed served as many as eight people who took turns, in pairs, sleeping in it. There was even a family in which three brothers, all of them grown men, could leave the hut only one at a time because among them they owned only a single shirt and one pair of trousers.

The inspection of dwelling after dwelling lasted for only an hour and a half. As a physician, Matthew had seen more than his share of human suffering, but never had he encountered such widespread misery.

The tour came to an abrupt end, and they rode in silence back to the Forbidden City. There Wu-ling led the way to her own quarters, and when they reached her book-littered living room, she turned toward the young physician and addressed him in an impassioned voice.

"You may think that what you have seen today is unusual. It is not. Those slums are everywhere in the Middle Kingdom. Those homes are among the best to be shown. I could have shown you many worse. I know what I am talking about, because I myself come from just such a home. Until Charles Boynton hired me to go with him to America and to England to take care of his son, David, who is my sister's baby, I knew no other life."

Matthew started to speak, but Wu-ling gave him no chance to interrupt. "You have seen the emperor's subjects," she said, "the people of the Middle Kingdom. They wallow in ignorance and filth and superstition. They have too little food to eat, and they are inadequately clothed. They fight in vain against colossal ignorance more dreadful than the most ferocious dragons in our mythology." The spirit seemed to drain out of her, her arms hung limply at her sides, and she looked at and through him, her dark eyes unseeing. "This," she murmured, "is the Middle Kingdom you intend to desert. It is true you have a right to be aggrieved. You were treated poorly, but those responsible for your treatment are paying for their malice with their lives."

She seemed so helpless, so defenseless that Matthew couldn't help asking, "What would you have me do, Wu-ling?"

"It is not what I would have you do," she replied. "It is what you yourself came to Cathay from America to do. The sick here cry out for your help. You have waited patiently, and now you are in a position to help them. The cabal of imperial physicians that blocked you at every turn has been destroyed. The Celestial Emperor and his sister are aware at last of the difficulties and dangers that you have faced, and are prepared to render every assistance. Without you, there will be no progress in our time. The clock will move very slowly. If you are here, the health of the entire nation can be improved. You can accomplish what no other physician in the long history of Cathay has been able to do."

He saw that she was sincere, and he knew she was not exaggerating. The question was whether he could forget the insults and damage that he had suffered in order to achieve the goals that had brought him halfway around the world. He took a deep breath as he pondered.

"I have had fear in my heart," Wu-ling continued, "that it would be your wish to leave. I expressed my fear to the Princess An Mien, and she has authorized me to offer you half my time to assist you in your efforts if you will stay. I have done all in my power to persuade you that your mission here is a noble one and that you are needed. I can do no more; the choice is yours alone." Utterly drained, she sank onto a three-cornered stool, and her head drooping, her hands folded in her lap, she waited listlessly for his decision.

Matthew's confidence as a physician and a man would not allow him to leave Cathay with his work undone. Somehow he had to put the mistreatment he had received behind him, forget it, and pitch in for the sake of the health of the millions whom he was in the position to save.

"As I'm sure you realize," he said, "I can't possibly leave. I'm staying."

She raised her head, and her smile was radiant as she gazed at him.

Their eyes met and held. All at once Matthew's feeling of oppression lifted, and he felt pleased with himself, happy over the difficult decision he had just made. The thought occurred to him that more had gone into the making of that decision than the desire to be of help to China's poor. Somehow, Wu-ling was personally involved. He was unsure of how or to what extent, but he knew beyond all doubt that he was elated because they would be spending so much of their time working together toward the same goal.

# III

A sensation was created in London when a ship, just arrived from India with her cargo of tea, was seized by Her Majesty's Customs Service. Rather than carrying tea, it was revealed that the ship had brought a large quantity of opium into England.

This was the first time a ship carrying opium had been seized by the British government, so the case received great attention in the press. Everyone in England seemed to be following the story.

Charles Boynton was still cruelly overworked, his father not yet having returned from the Channel Isle of Jersey, where he was convalescing. Nevertheless, he felt it was his duty to testify in court. "I find myself in the curious position of being something of an expert on opium," he told Ruth, as he ate a late supper after he arrived home one night. "I shouldn't spare the time, but Jonnie and I worked so hard to stop the opium trade that I'd be neglecting a principle unless I appeared for the prosecution and made my views known."

He volunteered his services as an expert witness, and the crown prosecutor eagerly accepted. The testimony that Charles gave was blunt and forthright. "Opium," he said, "is an exceptionally powerful drug that affects the mind of man. It's addictive, and in time will kill the user. It destroys one's appetite as well as one's will, and the addict literally wastes away."

The defense attorney tried valiantly to build up a case for the owners of the ship. "It's true, is it not, Mr. Boynton, that you base these conclusions on your personal observations of the Chinese you have seen in the Orient who are addicted to the use of opium?"

"In part, yes," Charles told him. "I've seen many Chinese who take the drug, and they react in the manner I just described."

"I respectfully draw the court's attention to the fact that these persons were Orientals," the barrister for the defense said. "The court will note that they were not white and certainly not English."

Charles was quick to cut in. "With all due respect to the defense counsel," he said, "he's trying to create the impression that opium has no effect on white men, particularly on Englishmen. That, if I may say so, is utter nonsense."

There was a buzz in the courtroom, and the bewigged judge hearing the case rapped his gavel for order.

"Opium," Charles declared, "is no respecter of race or nationality. I assure you it will reduce the most vital and intelligent of Englishmen to a gibbering wreck as rapidly and as effectively as it will a Chinese coolie. The opium that has been confiscated is a dangerous drug, and the English government was quite right to seize the ship. You wouldn't want your wife and your children to play with a ball of fire. By that same token, no sane man would permit them to use opium in any form."

His testimony so impressed the court that opium was declared a lethal substance, and the maximum penalty permitted under the law was imposed on the captain and the owners of the cargo.

Ruth was justly proud of her husband, who had done his duty, although it had been inconvenient for him to give testimony, and he had to work even longer hours during the next couple of weeks because of it.

He soon had an unexpected reward, however, when he received a note on embossed parchment, inviting him and his wife to tea on Sunday afternoon at Windsor Castle with

Queen Victoria and the prince consort. The invitation was a royal command, and Charles and Ruth appeared privately at the appointment hour at the living quarters of Victoria and Albert.

Queen Victoria had lost the slenderness of youth, and was now a comfortably plump matron. Her husband, still slender and ramrod-tall, towered over her, and it was obvious at a glance to Charles, who had known the monarch and her husband for years, that they were still very much in love with each other.

Amenities were exchanged while the queen poured tea in the modestly furnished sitting room in the royal suite, and Victoria was shocked when she learned that Lai-tse lu Rakehell had died the previous year in China. "What a pity," she murmured. "She was an extraordinary woman."

Ruth and Charles heartily agreed.

Prince Albert brought up recent events. "We wanted the opportunity, Mr. Boynton," he said in his slightly German-accented English, "to thank you ourselves for the effective blow you struck at the opium trade."

"Indeed," the queen added, "you and Mr. and Mrs. Rakehell first opened our eyes to the dangers of opium, and we've exerted our own efforts constantly in behalf of stamping out the trade. Your court testimony was exceptionally effective, and I think our subjects will be on their guard against the drug henceforth."

"If they're not," the prince consort added emphatically, "it will be because they've ignored your very clear warning. The nation is in your debt, Mr. Boynton."

"You're very kind to say so, Your Royal Highness," Charles replied, "but I don't see it that way. I have a young son who will one day inherit my place in the family business, and it strikes me that I owe it to him as well as to his unborn children to make the perils of opium very clear and very plain. It's my duty as a father that is paramount here, rather than my duty as a patriotic Englishman."

"Call it what you will," the queen said, "you've still done yeoman's service. We hope that you and Mrs. Boynton will avail yourselves of the right to visit us at any time without having received a formal invitation."

"That's very kind," Ruth murmured, aware that she and Charles had received an unusual honor, rarely conferred.

"And when Mrs. Rakehell's little daughter grows older— what is the child's name—I hope you will remind her that the same privilege is extended to her, just as it was to her mother."

"Her name is Jade, Your Majesty, and we shall be certain to give her the understanding that she is welcome at all times under your roof. She won't be insensitive to the honor, just as we appreciate it."

Sir Alan Boynton, accompanied by his wife, returned to London after spending more than a year on the Channel Isle of Jersey. He went directly to Dr. Featherstone's office, and was subjected to a thorough examination that revealed he was clear of the lung infection that had so debilitated him.

But the doctor also told him it would be wise to take no chances, and his convalescence should be prolonged for another month, during which time he and Lady Boynton would go to their country home in Sussex.

That night the entire Boynton family was reunited at dinner. Charles came home early from the shipyard for the first time in many months to be present, and Ruth ordered the cook to prepare a rib roast of beef for the occasion.

Sir Alan looked around the table and smiled. "You have no idea how good it is to be with all of you again."

Jessica added, "Speaking on behalf of us all, this is a very happy occasion."

Sir Alan went on to explain what he had learned from the doctor that afternoon. "I was eager to get back to the office to give you a hand at once, Charles," he said, "but I'm afraid I must delay again."

"I must say, I'm not surprised," Charles told him. "Dr. Featherstone hinted to me that you wouldn't be coming back to work quite as soon as you'd anticipated."

"So you might say we've been prepared for this news," Ruth added.

"When will you go on to Sussex, Papa?" Elizabeth wanted to know.

"In two or three days, I expect. It will take a little time for the servants to air the house and prepare it for our visit."

Charles seemed lost in thought for some moments. "I've been holding some plans of my own in abeyance, pending your return, Papa, and I've been putting off visiting Jonnie and sitting down with the American board. But I can delay no longer, and despite your trip to Sussex for the next month or six weeks, I must go to America. One of our clippers is due to arrive in port at any time, and I'll sail to New England on her when she returns next week."

David, eating with the adults because it was a special occasion, couldn't resist asking, "Can I go, too, Papa? I'll work on the ship, and then I can see Julian. Jade, too," he added.

"Of course, David," his father said. "I wouldn't think of going to America without taking you and Mama with me."

Elizabeth, sitting directly opposite him, paused with a spoon of raspberry trifle uneaten. "I hope," she said quietly but firmly, "that there will be space on board for me to make the voyage, too."

Charles and Ruth exchanged a swift glance, and both knew that, once again, Elizabeth would use every means at her disposal to encourage a romance with Jonathan. She had recovered her physical strength, after suffering the nightmare of her operation, and although Dr. Featherstone continued to insist that the surgery had made her barren, it had no harmful effect on her beauty and had not altered her disposition. She was as determined now as she'd been all through her childhood and adolescence to win Jonathan's affection.

Charles was inclined to respond flippantly, but a single glance at his sister warned him to speak carefully. Elizabeth was staring at him, her blue eyes boring into him, and he knew that she was in dead earnest. "It will give me great pleasure," he said, "to have you come with us."

Jessica was aware of the nuances in the byplay she had just heard, and she asked casually, "By the way, Elizabeth, how is Ronnie Weybright?"

"To the best of my knowledge, he is well," she replied evenly. "We no longer see each other."

"Oh, dear, you had no falling out, I hope."

"Oh, no, nothing like that," Elizabeth replied. "You might just say we drifted apart."

Sir Alan entered the conversation because he thought it was his duty. "Who are you seeing these days, my dear?"

"No one, Papa," Elizabeth answered with a steady smile. "Charles works until all hours every night, and I've been keeping Ruth company at dinner."

Jessica Rakehell Boynton was troubled but kept her thoughts to herself. It was obvious to her that her daughter was, after all this time, still in love with Jonathan Rakehell. Unaware of Elizabeth's abortion, Lady Boynton nevertheless realized that her daughter had matured, and she wished devoutly that some proper, eligible man would appear and sweep her off her feet. It just wasn't healthy for her to cling so hard to the portrait she had drawn for herself of Jonathan as her future husband.

Sir Alan and Lady Boynton left two days later for the country house in Sussex, and the rest of the family began to prepare frantically for a voyage across the Atlantic. A clipper commanded by Josiah Dowling had just arrived, and Charles had announced to his wife and sister that they had to be ready to sail in no more than five days' time.

"But there won't be a chance of having any new clothes made in five days," Elizabeth wailed. "Be reasonable, Charles."

"We're operating on the tightest of tight schedules these days," Charles replied. "Every day that we save is vital to our financial security. So I'm afraid your wardrobe will have to suffer accordingly."

Elizabeth knew better than to protest anew and fell silent. As a member of a shipping family, she understood that schedules were vital and took precedence over everything else.

Captain Dowling came to the Boynton house for dinner two

nights prior to the ship's sailing. Elizabeth hadn't thought about him since their brief acquaintance in New London, but his presence now relieved the monotony of her existence. She had isolated herself since her operation, seeing few of her friends; and going out seldom, she was more bored, more restless than she realized. Dowling, who was alert and vital, as handsome as any leading man currently appearing in the London theater, was as strongly drawn to Elizabeth as he had been the last time he had seen her; and completely forgetting the warning Charles had given him in America, he made no attempt to hide his feelings.

Charles was reflective about the renewed relationship between Elizabeth and the ship's captain. "Do you suppose," he asked Ruth, "that Dowling might be the chap after all to make her forget her hopeless infatuation for Jonnie? I know we discounted such a possibility when we were in America the last time, but surely the situation is changed."

Ruth shook her head slowly. "I don't think so."

Charles's face fell. "Why ever not?"

"She's bored because she's been staying at home, talking to no one but me. At her age she needs a great deal of male companionship, and she hasn't had it. So Dowling, like before, is someone new and exciting, and he offers a challenge to her. She's meeting that challenge. Once she realizes he's smitten with her, I'm afraid she'll lose interest in him."

"You sound rather positive," her husband said.

"Don't forget," Ruth told him, "although I don't know young Captain Dowling very well, I do know Jonathan, and there's no comparison between them. That, unfortunately, is Elizabeth's greatest trouble. She's going to search very long and very hard to find a man with Jonathan's qualities. It doesn't look very promising."

When the Boyntons sailed to America, Elizabeth maintained her lively interest in Josiah Dowling. For his part, he was delighted, and continued to pay court to her in whatever spare time was available to him. Her motive for flirting with him and attaching him to her, she told herself, was that she was going to take a new, fresh approach to Jonathan Rakehell. If

315

she had an obvious suitor who was interested in her, she convinced herself, perhaps she could spark Jonathan into awakening to her presence as a woman.

What she failed to take into consideration, because she was not conscious of it herself, was her fundamental frame of mind. As Ruth had realized, she was bored and restless after absenting herself from London society for months. In addition, the knowledge that the frightening abortion had rendered her barren was a constant source of depression. She didn't know it, but she was in need of relief from unseen and unrecognized pressures.

Therefore, to the private dismay of Charles and Ruth, she openly conducted her campaign for Josiah Dowling's attention on board his ship. He responded to her with a vengeance, and whenever he could spare time from his duties, they were inseparable.

"I don't like the looks of this," Ruth said to Charles. "I'm afraid no good can come of it. Do you want to speak to Elizabeth, or would you prefer that I have a few words with her?"

"Neither, I think," Charles replied. "She's in a strange, stubborn mood, and she's as likely as not to dig in her heels just to defy us if we suggest that she's getting too close to Dowling for her own good. I suppose I could have a few words with Dowling, as I did once before, but I think the really sensible thing to do this time is to let nature take its course and hope that they'll soon drift apart and go their separate ways."

Ruth agreed.

"But we're still taking somewhat of a risk," Charles added. "For one thing, Elizabeth is so very pretty that any man is sure to be flattered by her attention and wouldn't voluntarily give her up. For another, she and Dowling are both hot-blooded, and I hope they can exercise real self-control. Do you think there's any danger of—"

"There's always the danger," she interjected. "How serious it is, I honestly am in no position to judge. We'll just have to be patient ourselves and hope for the best."

As Elizabeth and Josiah drifted closer and closer together, their intimacy increasing each day, they were watched surreptitiously by his officers and crew. The single men envied him, and those who were married had to admit to themselves that he was accomplishing a great deal. Not only was the young lady of his choice very beautiful, but she was an heiress in her own right as a prominent member of the Rakehell-Boynton family.

Elizabeth relearned some of the fundamentals of seamanship and navigation, and as something of a lark, she took command of the clipper from time to time while Josiah stood close beside her, ready to countermand any error that she might make. Here again, she was motivated by a desire to impress Jonathan with her knowledge, and it was a source of considerable satisfaction to her to know that she was proficient in the handling of a ship.

One night, when the seas were somewhat choppy, she took the quarterdeck for an hour and acquitted herself well. Then, flushed with triumph, she accepted Josiah's invitation to drink a glass of brandywine.

They repaired to the master's cabin, by far the largest of the private quarters on board the ship, and there they laughed and chatted as they drank their brandywine. There was something electric in the air, and although Elizabeth didn't realize it, her radiant beauty made her more desirable than ever. For her part, she was flattered that a young man as alive and as masculine as Josiah found her irresistibly attractive. What was more—and she admitted it to herself—his rugged good looks and his familiarity with the sea reminded her of Jonathan.

One thing led to another, and before either of them quite realized it, they were making love in earnest. Their passions mastered them, sweeping away all sense of restraint. Elizabeth pulled Josiah on top of her on the divan, and he took her then and there, both of them moaning softly as they reached their climax.

Josiah was dazed by the experience and was unable to think clearly. Elizabeth, however, was filled with a loathing

317

and self-contempt. This was the second time she had lost control of herself, the second man with whom she had gone to bed, and she was afraid that she was using her yearning for Jonathan as an excuse for her unseemly behavior.

She stunned Josiah by withdrawing into a shell and informing him that they would be wise to terminate their relationship at once. He was bewildered by her conduct, but he had no choice and felt compelled to accept her suggestion.

Charles and Ruth were aware of the seeming rift that sprang up between the young couple, and although they didn't know the reasons for it, they assumed that, as Ruth had said, nature was taking its course.

The damage, however, was done. It was impossible for anyone, including the master of the vessel, to lead a strictly private existence in the confined quarters of the clipper ship. Consequently the officers and the crew well knew that Elizabeth and Josiah had slept together, and inevitably the seamen gossiped among themselves. Then they reached New London, and the story spread.

But Elizabeth saw Jonathan again, and all else was driven from her mind. He was lean and looked a little more tired, a little older, perhaps, but otherwise he was the same as he had always been. He, like Charles, worked incessantly, leaving the house immediately after breakfast with his children, and he rarely returned at the normal dinner hour in the evening. In fact, frequently Julian and Jade went to sleep at night before he came home from work.

His recreation and pleasures were virtually nonexistent. He seemed delighted at dinner one night when he explained that Julian and Jade were making remarkable progress in the martial arts under Kai's guidance, but he admitted in the same breath that he was so busy now that he no longer had time to watch them in exhibits.

Charles's appearance in New London sparked new meetings of the Rakehell and Boynton high command, and for several days Jonathan was rarely seen at home. Missy Sarah did her best to counteract his tendency to overwork, and scheduled a family picnic on Sunday, reasoning that he would be compelled to attend and not be chained to his desk.

Homer Ellison, in charge of seagoing personnel for the company, kept his eyes and ears open, so it was no accident that he heard the rumors about the affair that had taken place between Elizabeth and Josiah Dowling. He immediately sought Charles's private company and repeated what he had heard.

Charles grimaced and shook his head. "Ruth and I were very much concerned throughout the entire voyage from England," he said. "Apparently we should have been still more concerned."

"You don't think this is a genuine romance?" Homer demanded.

Charles shook his head. "In no way," he said. "I'm quite sure of it now."

"Then, if you don't mind," Homer told him, "I'll take care of the matter myself, in my own way. You understand that if Jonathan or his father got wind of it, young Dowling would be discharged instantly, even though competent clipper ship captains are hard to find these days."

Charles nodded. "Do whatever you think best," he said. "I've had little control over Elizabeth for quite some time."

Homer immediately called the young shipmaster to his office, and minced no words with him. "I've heard some disturbing rumors about you and Elizabeth Boynton," he said. "Are they true?"

Josiah flushed but refused to take refuge in lies. "I don't know what you've heard, Mr. Ellison," he said, "but I can imagine, and I'll not evade the issue. Yes, sir, I'm sure that what you've been told is quite accurate."

Homer tilted back in his chair, put his feet on his desk, and stared up at the ceiling. "If either of the Rakehells heard this story," he said, "you'd be on the beach instantly, and you'd have hell's own time getting another ship for yourself. You were taking a horrible risk."

Dowling stared at him and swallowed hard. "I reckon I've been a bit stupid, Mr. Ellison," he said, "so maybe you'll tell it to me straight. Have I made a damn fool of myself over Elizabeth Boynton?''

Homer nodded somberly. "Indeed you have, but there's no permanent damage done. Just keep your distance from her from now on. That's all.''

Red spots burned in Josiah Dowling's cheeks beneath his heavy tan. "I'm much obliged to you, sir, and you don't need to worry about me after this. The point is, there's nothing between me and Elizabeth Boynton anymore.'' He rose to his feet, and as he left the office, he shook his head slowly from side to side. Clearly he was a badly disillusioned young man.

Homer felt sympathy for Dowling, but he was also vastly relieved. The potentially serious scandal that had threatened to emerge had been averted.

On Sunday, precisely as Missy Sarah had anticipated, the holding of a family picnic gave Jonathan little opportunity to spend the day at work. He went to his office in the morning, but even then Missy Sarah was one step ahead of him and asked him to return in time to prepare the fire for the cooking of the picnic meal. So he came home well before noon, and aided by an enthusiastic if somewhat less than efficient Julian and David, he dug a hole in the sand and built a substantial fire, then covered it with a layer of thick, damp seaweed.

Elizabeth insisted on helping him prepare the meal, and although Judy Ellison and Ruth Boynton were far more experienced, they recognized her motives and deferred to her. She placed the potatoes and corn in the seaweed and readied the buckets of steamer clams; Missy Sarah had cooked the clam chowder in advance, however, and it required only heating. The main course consisted of freshly caught lobsters, and steaks, and Elizabeth, assisted by little Jade, put them on the fire, too.

To Elizabeth's amazement, she was able to go about her tasks naturally, with not the slightest trace of self-consciousness that Jonathan was nearby and might be watching her. She was enjoying the work for its own sake, not for the fact that she was in the proximity of Jonathan, and as she felt the wind blowing in her hair and inhaled the salt air and the smell of cooking food, she was totally at peace and at ease.

Jonathan could not help being aware of Elizabeth's presence today. She was working very hard and was showing a truly marvelous rapport with Jade. They whispered together frequently as they prepared the meal, and they often burst into prolonged giggles.

It was strange, Jonathan thought, but he had never before noticed how lovely Elizabeth was, and it surprised him to note that she was an adult in every sense of the word. Somehow she had managed to grow up without his knowledge.

It seemed only natural for him to sit beside her as they ate the substantial meal, and further surprises were in store for him. Not only had she become adult, but she was charming, witty, and remarkably well informed on economic matters, as well as on American and British politics. He found himself truly interested in her.

Elizabeth's poise did not desert her as it became increasingly obvious to her that, for the first time in her life, Jonathan was indeed sparking to her, but her self-confidence ultimately drained away, and she felt hollow and nervous. She didn't show it, however, and Ruth and Judy, who suspected her true feelings, exchanged an occasional, quick smile.

Jonathan interrupted their conversation every now and then to speak a word or two to the children, or else to romp on the beach with them and their chow dog. "I think it's wonderful," Elizabeth said a trifle wistfully, when Jonathan returned to her side after engaging in a footrace with the children, "that youngsters can grow up in such an uninhibited atmosphere. You're a very different father from Sir Alan, I don't mind telling you, and if Lai-tse lu were here, I'm sure she would approve."

Jonathan, catching his breath from his exertions, peered at her closely. "What makes you say that?"

Elizabeth became flustered. "I don't know, really," she said. "I can't pretend that I knew her all that well, but from what I saw of her, she was a very determined woman who knew her own mind, and I'm sure that she wanted her children to grow up to be equally fearless."

Jonathan thought for a moment and then grinned. "I hadn't thought of her in relation to the children that way, but you're right."

Elizabeth had opened a floodgate, and he found that he could speak to her freely about Lai-tse lu. He talked about her at length, naturally and without self-consciousness.

Elizabeth was utterly astonished by her own reaction. Had anyone asked her in advance, she would have sworn that she would have felt only wild jealousy when he spoke with such obvious depth of love for his late wife. Instead, however, she discovered that she not only could listen carefully but that she was sympathetically receptive to what he was saying. In some strange way, she grasped an all-important essential of understanding Jonathan Rakehell: he had given himself wholeheartedly and unstintingly to Lai-tse lu, and a part of him always would belong to her and to her alone. If and when he married again, his wife would be forced to recognize his indissoluble bond with his late, Chinese wife. Any woman who could not share him with Lai-tse lu would be very wise not to marry him.

But the necessary sharing of his feelings was made far simpler, she was discovering, because she had herself known Lai-tse lu. She had been a remarkable, beautiful woman, and Elizabeth could empathize with Jonathan's deep regard for the wife he had loved, and she could join him in his quiet grief for her.

The thought did not occur to Elizabeth that she herself had matured emotionally far more than she knew. All she realized was that she recognized the validity of what he said, of what she knew he felt, and that she could agree with him wholeheartedly. This, in a sense, was a new Elizabeth Boynton. The arrogant, spoiled young heiress had undergone private suffering at length, and she understood now how others felt and could herself feel for them. Her warmth and humanity were vastly increased.

Jonathan, as she well knew, was an honorable man who

was capable of giving of himself unstintingly to a woman he loved. His memories of Lai-tse lu were potent and living, and somehow they seemed right in him. He was not morbid, nor was he dwelling on the past when he spoke of his wife. She was as strong an influence on him now as she had been while still alive.

Jonathan found himself increasingly absorbed in Elizabeth, and not until much later, when he thought of the outing in retrospect, did he realize how much he had enjoyed himself in her company. All he knew now was that she was very lovely, and that he felt completely at home with her.

"By the way," he asked casually, "have you heard from Erika von Klausner since she went off to the Orient?"

The jealousies that had been totally absent when he spoke of Lai-tse lu suddenly took shape and exploded within Elizabeth. She marveled that he had dared to mention Erika to her, and she had to restrain an impulse to slap him hard across the face. Instead she glared at him and, not deigning to reply, rose swiftly to her feet and suggested a game of tag to the children.

Soon she was thoroughly involved with the youngsters, running up and down the beach with them and laughing, and Jonathan watched her in bewilderment. He knew only that she had withdrawn from him and had been very annoyed, but he honestly didn't know what he had said or what he had done to suddenly cause such a change in her attitude.

It was certainly true that the children paid Elizabeth the supreme compliment of treating her as one of their own number. They withheld nothing from her, and were as free in their relationship with her as they were with one another.

Since autumn was coming and a new school term was about to start, young Brad Walker had recently returned from his latest tour of sea duty to return to school. Ultimately he would follow in the paths of his Rakehell ancestors and would go on to Yale College. He was a sturdy, self-reliant boy, who had learned to take care of himself, and as a result, the whole family made somewhat of a fuss over him at the picnic.

His younger sister, jealous of him and bewildered by the neglect of the adults, couldn't help sulking.

Elizabeth was the first to notice the girl's withdrawal, and instantly understood the reasons. Leaving the younger children to start a game by themselves, she sat on a flat rock on the beach beside Judy. "Mind if we have a little chat?" she asked.

Judy shrugged indifferently. "I suppose you're going to tell me how wonderful you think my brother is, too."

"No, as a matter of fact I'm not," Elizabeth replied. "Do you see my brother sitting over there, gorging on corn? It wasn't so long ago that he came back from sea and was treated by the whole family as a hero, too."

"Really?" Young Judy was interested in spite of herself.

"Oh, yes," Elizabeth answered airily. "It's an old family tradition, you know. A male learns how to navigate and how to sail a ship, and there's no one in the world quite like him. I sailed a clipper just for the fun of it across the Atlantic, just days ago, and you don't see anyone pinning any medals on me. Personally, I don't expect them to. We give all the credit to the men of the family."

Judy stared at her and took a deep breath. "Gee," she said. "I thought I was the only one who felt the way I do."

"Dear me, no," Elizabeth replied with a laugh. "I'm sure you'll find that Jessica Boynton and Sarah Rakehell feel the same way, although they'd never admit it, naturally. Your mother feels it, and so does Ruth, and so do I. Being a Rakehell-Boynton man is something very special in the world, and he's honored and praised for it. Being a Rakehell-Boynton woman is something quite different, and requires twice the stamina and twice the courage. The only difference is that we're the only ones who really recognize that fact."

Judy grinned at her. "I like you, Elizabeth," she said. "I really like you."

"Good," Elizabeth replied, "because I like you, too. And after all, we women must stand together, you know."

The girl impulsively hugged and kissed her. Neither Elizabeth nor young Judy realized it, but Homer and Judith Ellison overheard their conversation and grinned quietly.

Telling Jonathan the story later, his sister said, "I was impressed by the way Elizabeth handled herself. Judy is a sensitive girl, and she's very bright, so it's difficult to bamboozle her. Elizabeth said precisely the right things in the right way. It was quite an eye-opener."

Jonathan was also impressed. It was good to know that his opinion of Elizabeth was confirmed by someone whose judgment he valued.

Meantime, the dinner had been finished, and the children went to work collecting dishes. Missy Sarah went off to the kitchen to fetch coffee and lime pie for all, and asked Elizabeth to accompany and help her. As they strolled up the beach to the Rakehell house, she said quietly, "I noticed that you and Jonnie had quite a long chat today."

Elizabeth nodded self-consciously.

"It was obvious," Sarah said bluntly, "that you were having a good time. It was equally apparent that Jonnie was enjoying himself immensely. If I do say so, it's the first time since he lost Lai-tse lu that I've known him really to relax."

"You—you're not just saying that."

The older woman stared at her. "Land sake's alive, child!" she said severely. "I don't believe in flummididdling anybody. Truth is truth, no matter how you look at it."

Unaccustomed to the bluntness of the middle-aged American woman, Elizabeth remained silent.

"Your feelings for Jonnie," Sarah said gently, "have been no secret to me. I've been aware of them for a long time, ever since I first knew you, as a matter of fact."

Color rose to Elizabeth's face and burned in her cheeks.

"I've been wanting to talk with you," Sarah continued, "but until today, it would have been a rather futile exercise. Now, I think, it might do some good. I think I know Jonnie pretty well, so you'll pardon my bluntness."

Elizabeth nodded, uncertain what would be coming next.

"The first thing you need to know about him," Missy

Sarah went on, "is that he'll always love Lai-tse lu. There's a place in his heart that she'll fill as long as he lives, and no other woman can ever replace her there."

"Strangely," Elizabeth said, unperturbed by the statement, "I realized that very thing just today. Not in those words, perhaps, but certainly the idea behind them."

"And it doesn't bother you?" Missy Sarah peered sharply at her, her wise eyes probing intently.

Elizabeth shook her head. "I'm not sure why," she said quietly, "but it doesn't bother me in the least. It isn't like competing with a ghost, you know. It's just recognizing that Jonathan and Lai-tse lu had a special relationship, and their union, whatever it consisted of, will always be a part of him."

"Exactly." Sarah nodded in satisfaction. "At the same time," she said slowly, "he needs to love and be loved by a living woman. I hope you realized that, too."

"No, I didn't," Elizabeth said breathlessly. "It's a comforting thought, though."

"It's a fact of life," Missy Sarah said firmly. "He's a man who needs food and sleep and love. He's human, just like all the rest of us, and he has needs and hungers, just like all the rest of us."

Elizabeth nodded, aware that this was the most important conversation on the subject of Jonathan Rakehell that she had ever held.

They arrived in the pantry, and Missy Sarah opened the larder-box and removed two large lime pies, which she handed to Elizabeth. "We'll cut these outside," she said. "They'll be easier to manage. Can you handle both of them?"

Elizabeth nodded.

"Good," she said, "then we can bring everything in the one trip." Slowing her pace, Missy Sarah lowered her voice. "If you love Jonathan, and I assume you do—"

"I do," Elizabeth murmured, "with all my heart."

"Then you'll have to be patient with him—very patient," Missy Sarah said. "He's too much of a male to be able to see himself in relation to others, and all he'll know is that he sparks to you. I saw the beginnings of those sparks today.''

''Did you?'' Elizabeth asked eagerly.

The older woman nodded. ''Patience!'' she commanded. ''He'll develop an interest in you little by little, then he'll feel guilty. It'll occur to him that he's being unfaithful to Lai-tse lu's memory. That's sheer rubbish, but that's the way a man thinks.''

''Then I'll never be married to him.'' Elizabeth's heart sank.

Sarah grinned at her and shook her head. ''No, you're wrong,'' she said. ''You see, as he grows more and more interested in you, he'll want you, to put it bluntly, and that desire will overcome his guilt and his self-doubts. That, my dear child, is the way a man's mind works.''

''I see,'' Elizabeth murmured.

''But I tell you again, and I can't stress this enough, you must show extraordinary patience. Jonathan is struggling to save the business these days, and that takes precedence over everything else in life. It'll take him time to pause and recognize these other factors in his life before he deals with them.''

''I know,'' Elizabeth said, but was in no way depressed by the realization that she might have to wait for some time before Jonathan woke up to a true appreciation of her. What heartened her most and gave her the courage to believe that she was not dreaming in vain was the knowledge that she had won Sarah Rakehell's support. This was of primary importance to her because of the relationship Sarah had enjoyed with Lai-tse lu, her protégée. Elizabeth had heard many times that Missy Sarah was closer to Lai-tse lu than any other woman on earth, and this was the very woman who had approved of her as Lai-tse lu's successor. To have such potent support in such important quarters was heartening.

The following day, after noon dinner, at which neither Jonathan nor Charles appeared, Jeremiah Rakehell rose from his chair at the end of the meal with a smile. ''I'm not allowed to work at my son's pace,'' he said. ''My wife and my physician would horsewhip me, so I've got to dawdle here over a cup of coffee for a spell. You want to come into the study and keep me company, Elizabeth?"

His surprised niece readily agreed. She could not remember the last time that Uncle Jeremiah had singled her out for a private talk. She preceded him into his book-lined sanctuary, and lowered herself into a deep easy chair opposite him.

"My wife and I have had a little chat about you," he said, "and about your feelings. I'll admit, I was quite surprised, although I gather that your parents and Charles and Ruth have known about your feelings for quite some time."

She was too horrified to reply, and could only wish fervently that Missy Sarah had not confided in him.

He noted her expression and smiled soothingly. "Never fear," he said, "Rakehells are experts at keeping secrets. I sure wouldn't embarrass you by prematurely letting on what I know."

"Thank you," she said, and inclined her head.

He asked her permission to smoke, and when she freely granted it, he carefully lighted a long, black *cigarro* that he imported from the West Indies. "Jonathan," he said, "is my only son, so I worry about him quite a bit, more than I should, perhaps. Don't misunderstand me. No one is more devoted to duty than he is. In fact, he's too devoted to it, and he takes no time for his own pleasures. He's a splendid father, and I'm convinced that Julian will grow up in the family tradition and will be able to take his place in the family business when the time comes."

"Jade, too, I hope," Elizabeth said.

Jeremiah grinned and raised an eyebrow. "You remind me of your mother now," he said. "All right, I'll admit that women have a special place in our family these days, and that brings me to the point. I'm afraid that I'm every bit a Rakehell, as much as my son. That means that the business means everything to me. That's the way it is in our family, and there doesn't seem to be much I can do about it. I just want you to know that I think you'd be the best thing in the world for Jonnie. I can't imagine a woman anywhere who'd be a more suitable wife for him. After all, you're a major stockholder in the company yourself, and you're already familiar with the major problems that beset us.''

Elizabeth had to conquer a strong desire to laugh. Only a Rakehell or a Boynton would consider her to be the most eligible of brides because of the familiarity with the family shipping business. Uncle Jeremiah was every bit as narrow-minded and devoted to his business as were Papa and Charles, and for that matter, Jonathan.

''I don't rightly know,'' Jeremiah went on, ''that Jonnie will ever mention you to me. Frankly, I don't expect him to. He's too big a boy to be discussing his romantic life with his father, but there have got to be ways that I can influence him subtly, and I want you to know that I'm going to do it. I'll follow Missy Sarah's lead, naturally, because I'll need her guidance.''

The astonished and delighted Elizabeth stammered her thanks. Not only was Jonathan's stepmother in her corner, but his father was offering her support, too, and she was encouraged. Now let Mama and Ruth try to claim that she was wasting her time in daydreams!

On the day following the family picnic, Jonathan and Charles left the house at their usual early hour for the shipyard, when Homer Ellison stopped off to pick them up. They walked briskly along the waterfront, as was their custom, and arrived shortly before the yard opened for the day's business.

''If you lads have a few minutes to spare this morning, you might want to drop into my office,'' Jonathan said with a faint smile. ''I think I can promise it will be worth your time.''

Charles and Homer knew from his manner that something unusual was afoot, and they both responded to his challenge, coming to his office as soon as they had gone to their own quarters and leafed hastily through the mail. Jonathan awaited them, and his manner was strangely mysterious.

''I've devoted most of my time during the past year,'' he

said, "to thinking about our financial crisis and trying to find a permanent solution for it. I believe I've done just that. This company pioneered in the making of clipper ships, and we built our business accordingly. It isn't accidental that we are now at least four times larger than we were. That is why I've been looking beyond the clipper. Now don't misunderstand me; I love the clipper. There's never been anything like it on the high seas, and there never will be. Of all sailing ships, she's unique. But I haven't been able to keep from wondering about developing a brand-new type of ship—one that will be impervious to the wind and sea, and will be able to function and hold to her schedules, no matter what the weather."

Charles and Homer exchanged a quick glance. As experienced sailors they knew that weather at sea was the paramount consideration at all times. They could plan all they pleased, devising sailing schedules, only to see them destroyed by a spell of foul weather.

"Are you sure you're not daydreaming, Jonnie?" Homer asked.

Jonathan chuckled and shook his head. "As you know, I've spent the past year studying the subject of steamships in depth. Almost a half-century ago, Robert Fulton developed an idea that had started in England, and built the first steamship on this side of the Atlantic. It was small, of course, and suitable for travel on lakes and rivers. The steamship has been confined to such functions for almost a half-century now."

Homer pursed his lips and looked thoughtful. "The steamer isn't too ineffective for the coastal trade between states," he said, "but it's too blame small to carry any appreciable cargo or large numbers of passengers for considerable distances."

"I know," Jonathan replied. "That's been the primary handicap of ships propelled by steam. The early builders tried to get around this by using paddle wheels instead of propellers driven by steam power. But, as I'm sure you realize, paddle wheels soon proved dangerous and ineffective in the open seas of an ocean. Well, I've been experimenting privately.

330

That's what kept me chained to this yard on evenings and weekends." He opened a drawer and brought out several models of ships, which he placed on a row on his desk.

"The great weakness of the steam-propelled ship has been its size," Charles said. "Are you telling us you've licked this?"

"Not yet, perhaps, and not by myself," Jonathan said. "I've been following developments here and abroad, particularly in England and in Hamburg, where there are rather firm supporters of steam. The problem has been to generate sufficient power in large ships to accommodate numbers of passengers and cargoes of consequence. That problem appears to be on the verge of solution, if it isn't already solved. A half-dozen builders, and I admit that I've secretly been one of them, have been experimenting with propeller shafts built on the principle of the screw. The use of steam seems to lend itself to this type of propulsion, and results in considerably increased power. This, in turn, means that we'll be able to build much larger ships for freight and passengers."

"What are we talking about in terms of cargo and passengers?" Homer demanded.

Jonathan couldn't resist grinning at him. "Offhand," he said casually, "I predict that in the immediate future we'll be building steamships with the capacity for double the cargo currently being carried by our largest clipper ships. As for passengers, I'd say that the steamship will carry a minimum of fifty paying persons in comfort, and will become commonplace within a decade."

His calm announcement was electrifying. Charles was no longer able to keep his seat and, jumping to his feet, began to pace up and down the office. Homer revealed his excitement by gnawing anxiously on the stem of his pipe.

"We'll have to expand our plant and put up at least two or three new buildings," Jonathan explained.

Charles whistled softly under his breath.

"As I see the future," Jonathan went on, "we make no changes in our present production schedule of turning out sailing ships. There's going to be a market for clippers for many years to come, just as there will be a market for the older types of sailing vessels.''

"What you're proposing, then,'' Homer said, "is a major expansion.''

"Very major,'' Jonathan agreed.

"And that means,'' Charles declared, "that we'll require a very large capital outlay.''

Jonathan nodded. "And there's the crux of the problem. It'll cost the better part of a million dollars to produce the machinery and to hire the men who will build the steamships that will keep the name of Rakehell and Boynton afloat into the twentieth century.''

"Where in the devil are we going to come up with a million dollars in cash?'' Charles wanted to know. "We're having enough trouble just barely staying afloat and maintaining our present commitments.''

"I can't answer your question, Charles,'' Jonathan said. "I have no idea where we'll obtain our financing. All I can tell is that, from the very beginnings of my research, I've proceeded on the assumption that when the time comes, the money will somehow be available to us. I've got to go on that basis and remain optimistic. I can't allow myself to think that this company is going to fall behind in the most significant aspect of shipbuilding since the first clipper appeared. The very nature of man's travel by sea is going to be fundamentally altered by steamships, and we've got to be in on the building of such ships from the very beginning. It's mandatory.''

Charles nodded, in complete agreement with him. Homer Ellison looked at the two cousins, their eyes burning, their jaws set, and he had to marvel at them. It was no wonder that Rakehell and Boynton was at the forefront of the industry, or that the two men who were gradually taking over the reins from their fathers were as totally dedicated to the future as were Jonathan and Charles. Both were determined to succeed, no matter how insurmountable the odds against them.

"A great many technical problems are currently being solved, so there is no great rush about getting into production of the steamship just yet," Jonathan said. "For example, a suitable composition has been discovered for painting the outside surfaces of ships, and so far it seems to be sound and effective. Also, some trials carried out in Liverpool and at Deptford in England have appeared to solve the problem of how to persuade a compass to behave accurately on board a metal ship."

Steam machinery, all three knew, was not all that new in crossing the Atlantic. A ship called the *Savannah*, equipped with auxiliary steam power, crossed the Atlantic from Savannah, Georgia, to Ireland as early as 1819. The most renowned of ships on the transatlantic run was the *Great Western*, which crossed from Bristol to New York in fifteen days. It boasted a displacement of more than thirteen tons, and it was regarded as the equal to a clipper ship, although it could not compete in speed with a clipper when the winds were fair. A new transatlantic line founded by Samuel Cunard in 1840 was responsible for the building of so-called sister ships, identical vessels that could be built relatively inexpensively from a single set of blueprints.

The single most significant development, as Jonathan had explained, was the principle of the screw propeller, which was patented in 1836 by both an Englishman and a Swede. The first ships built under this principle were small, but they demonstrated the power and economy of the screw; Jonathan was correct when he indicated that this development more than any other was hurrying mankind into the age of steam propulsion.

"How much time do you reckon we have, Jonathan," Homer asked, "before we'll have to start producing steamships regularly?"

Jonathan shrugged. "There are so many new developments," he said, "that I really can't say. I'd be inclined offhand to suspect that we have perhaps five years, certainly not much more than that, before it will be too late for us to join the race."

The sense of excitement they felt that morning lingered through the day in their minds, and that night they continued

333

to discuss steamships at the Rakehell dinner table. Jeremiah, who had not been privy to the earlier discussion, joined in the talk, too, and the prospect of steam propulsion seemed to brighten.

Elizabeth quickly noticed that the Rakehell women were resigned to such talk. They found it dull, even boring, but they tolerated it with good humor. This was the inevitable fate of women, or so it seemed, in a family where ships took precedence over all else.

Elizabeth knew now what her mother and Sarah went through, and she could understand, too, why there had been so many tensions in the married life of Charles and Ruth. The young woman realized that marriage to a Rakehell involved far more than one's romantic concepts. A Rakehell wife knew that her place existed somewhere behind the ships that her husband created and sailed. She knew that if she ever became Jonathan's wife, she would seldom see him at noon and that he would often be detained at the shipyard until late at night. She would have social stature in the community and would be financially well off, but she already enjoyed those privileges.

But Elizabeth did not view these limitations as handicaps. To her they represented challenges. She, as a Rakehell-Boynton wife, rather than a mere daughter, would want to become an active partner in the development and growth of the ever-expanding business. She, like Charles and Jonathan, was caught up in the tensions of seeing a seagoing dream materialize.

She was well aware of the fact that the spirit of intimacy that had budded at the picnic in her relationship with Jonathan was totally lacking now. He was completely absorbed in the topic of steamships, and his whole being was devoted to that one subject. She was pleased by her ability to recognize the essential truths of the situation, and it comforted her to see that the other women of the family were literally in the same boat. While the men concentrated on the ship of the future, their wives ceased to exist.

So Elizabeth devoted herself to Julian and Jade and necessarily to David, too, because the three were inseparable. She discovered that Jade's birthday was pending, so she mentioned the fact to Missy Sarah.

"I do believe we'll have a party for her on Sunday," Sarah replied, a mischievous gleam in her eyes, "and it will just happen that the time will coincide with the usual Sunday dinner hour."

Elizabeth was puzzled for a moment, and then she laughed. "I see what you're doing, I believe," she said. "You know very well that Jonathan won't miss his daughter's birthday celebration, which means that he'll come home from the shipyard at noon on Sunday, and probably won't get back there again that day."

Missy Sarah nodded approvingly. "Now," she said, "you begin to think like a true Rakehell wife. The only way to get the minds of these men off business is to trick them, and I don't mind telling you that any trick at all is well worth the effort."

Jonathan reacted precisely as the ladies anticipated on Sunday, returning home from the shipyard promptly at noon and making no attempt to leave his daughter's festivities afterward. Jade opened her gifts before dinner, and Elizabeth's present struck a responsive chord in the child. Jade received a new dress made like a miniature version of a taffeta gown that Elizabeth herself wore, and the little girl was elated, so pleased that she wanted to change into it immediately.

"I don't think it's quite suitable for this time of day," Elizabeth told her. "It's the sort of dress that one wears in the evening."

"All right," Jade replied, "then I'll have to start staying awake after it gets dark at night."

The dinner was a preview of the Thanksgiving festivities to come, because the Boyntons wouldn't be there for the holiday, necessarily having to depart for England prior to it. They enjoyed roast turkey with sage, walnut, and oyster stuffing, mashed and candied sweet potatoes, cranberry sauce, and a half-dozen vegetables.

Jade, seated at her own request between Elizabeth and

Jonathan, did full justice to the meal, and Elizabeth called a halt only when she wanted her plate refilled for the third time. "If I were you, Jade, I'd save room for mince pie and birthday cake. If you eat any more turkey, you won't be able to touch your dessert."

The suggestion made sense to the child, who accepted it without further ado. Then she looked at Elizabeth quizzically, studying her intently with dark, solemn eyes.

Elizabeth became uncomfortable under the steady, unblinking scrutiny.

"You're going back to England this week when David leaves," she said, and sounded slightly accusing.

Elizabeth nodded. "Yes," she said, "Uncle Charles must go home to operate his own end of the business."

"But you could stay," Jade said.

Elizabeth shook her head and smiled. The suggestion was flattering, but under the circumstances it wasn't too practical. "I must go home, too," she said.

Jade thought about the matter briefly, frowning in concentration, and suddenly her face cleared. "I know!" she cried. "If you marry Papa, this will be your home and you won't have to go anywhere!"

Elizabeth was as startled as she was mortified, and color flamed in her cheeks.

Jade was too young to recognize her embarrassment or its cause. "Papa, Papa," she said, tugging at Jonathan's sleeve, "why don't you marry Elizabeth, and then she wouldn't have to go home to England this week?"

To Elizabeth's consternation, Jonathan did not reply immediately but pondered at length, apparently weighing the proposal.

"That's a splendid idea, Jade," Jonathan said with mock solemnity as he looked at Elizabeth over the child's small head.

Elizabeth froze and didn't know what to say or do. The little girl immediately compounded her problem. "Say you'll do it, Elizabeth, please," Jade begged.

Jonathan came to Elizabeth's rescue. "Grown-ups," he

said, "really can't decide such important matters on short notice, Jade. They need time to think and to weigh various aspects of the matter. So be a good girl, and give Elizabeth a chance to get her thoughts together."

The child was dissatisfied with his response. "What do you think your answer will be, Elizabeth?" she demanded anxiously.

Elizabeth took a deep breath. "I would rather be married to your father than anything else in the world," she said to Jade, her eyes somehow fixed on Jonathan. "I can think of nothing in the world that I'd like more."

"Then you'd be my mother," Jade said with great satisfaction.

"I would try very hard to be a mother to you," Elizabeth told her, "and I hope I'd succeed in taking the place of your own mother, at least to some extent. I could never replace her completely, of course; that would be asking too much."

"Then you'll do it?" the little girl asked anxiously.

Elizabeth knew she had to back down now. "I can't promise, Jade," she said. "It's as your father said, so many aspects of a matter like this must be weighed and taken into consideration when adults make up their minds. But I won't forget, and I give you my word that you'll be the very first to know my answer."

Jade was satisfied at last, and the arrival of dessert absorbed her total attention. The subject was not raised again, to the infinite relief of Elizabeth Boynton.

*Jade*, Missy Sarah later wrote to Jessica Boynton, *has a heap more common sense than her father. If he knew what was good for him, he'd listen to her and heed her advice!*

Less than a week later the Boyntons departed, via clipper, for London. The entire Rakehell clan saw them off, and Julian and David raced up and down the deck and climbed into the rigging, which ultimately made it necessary to retrieve them.

Jade, rather than accompanying her brother and cousin and behaving like a tomboy, elected to act like a lady and clung to Elizabeth's hand.

Her attention, which Elizabeth returned in full measure, was gratifying, and so were the reactions of Jeremiah and Sarah, who were sorry to see her leave.

Jonathan, as usual, was completely preoccupied and stood at the fantail with Charles discussing business matters in low tones until the last possible moment. At last the time for sailing came. Jonathan summoned his son from the rigging, bade farewell to Ruth, and then went to Elizabeth to retrieve his daughter. Jade hugged and kissed the young Englishwoman. "Don't forget your promise," she said.

"I certainly won't," Elizabeth told her emphatically. "A promise is a sacred vow, and it must be kept at all costs."

Jonathan looked at Elizabeth gratefully. "You're very sweet to indulge her this way."

"Not at all," Elizabeth assured him, "I enjoy her company as much as she appears to like mine. We shall see each other again, Jade." She extended a hand to Jonathan on sudden impulse. "We, too, shall meet again," she said, and emboldened by the imminence of their separation, did not release his hand.

Jonathan hesitated for a moment, then grinned and leaned toward her, his lips lightly brushing hers as he kissed her. As a kiss it was no more than a token, but later, in retrospect, Elizabeth could console herself with the thought that he had kissed her as an adult, not an adolescent to whom he happened to be related.

She could be pleased, too, that when the Rakehells went ashore to the dock and the clipper moved slowly out of her berth, Jonathan's gaze continued to be fixed on her. She couldn't interpret his expression from a distance, but she knew he was watching her, and that was all to the good. At the very least, he had become conscious of her existence as a woman.

# IV

The sun shone in a porcelain blue sky, the day was hot and muggy, with a humid breeze blowing in gently from the South China Sea, and the Portuguese flag fluttered from the flagpole in the inner courtyard of the palace of the governor-general of Macao.

The windows overlooking the courtyard were filled with spectators, and from the private quarters of the Marquês de Braga, Owen Bruce stood alone at a window and stared out of it miserably.

Bruce was present of necessity, not choice, as he had been directed by Dom Manuel Sebastian to observe what the governor called "the ceremony." Only the naturally ignorant and bloodthirsty could relish watching the disgusting show. A nondescript Chinese, unidentified to the observers but known to Bruce to be an opium smuggler of consequence, was about to lose his life because he had dared to cheat Dom Manuel and withhold a share of profits that the Marquês de Braga had demanded. Therefore, the smuggler's hands had been tied behind his back, and he had been compelled to kneel and place his head on a broad stool. A gate at the far end of the enclosure opened, and the awe-inspiring figure of Siroso, a trained bull elephant, lumbered slowly into the courtyard. The smuggler's head had been liberally annointed with a substance known to elephant handlers as certain to drive their charges into wild frenzies, and Siroso paused, lifted his trunk, and then moved forward with surprising speed.

Three Portuguese guards, armed with rifles, stood on a window ledge directly behind the victim and were prepared to shoot him in the legs if he tried to rise and flee from the scene. But Siroso was too quick, and the smuggler was too terrified to move.

The sickening scene lasted but a few moments. The elephant approached its victim, trumpeted loudly, and raising its foot, brought it down heavily on the head of its victim. The man's head was squashed like an eggshell, and his blood spread into a pool on the stone floor of the open area. Bruce closed his eyes and breathed heavily until the waves of nausea that assailed him subsided. The smuggler had endured the same grisly fate that Bradford Walker had met when he, too, had incurred the enmity of the Marquês de Braga.

Bruce knew that Dom Manuel was annoyed, and he couldn't really blame the Portuguese for his anger. So far all his plans to get revenge on Rakehell and Boynton had been thwarted, and the governor did not like being outwitted. Thus he took his frustrations out on his underlings, such as the insignificant Chinese bandit whom he had executed today in this garish public display.

There was also another, more immediate, reason for Dom Manuel's anger. Opium smuggling had become the primary business of the partnership that he and Owen Bruce enjoyed, and it accounted for virtually all the profits. The legitimate business that the Scotsman conducted was only a front for the smuggling of opium. But now it was becoming more difficult with each passing month to get any quantity of opium safely into China. The Chinese authorities could no longer be easily fooled, and the presence of an incorruptible imperial viceroy in Canton guaranteed that his underlings would be afraid to accept bribes. So Canton, long a port of entry for the drug, was now effectively sealed off. Alert customs officials now lined the border between Macao and China, and it was virtually impossible to pass any chests of opium into the Middle Kingdom by this time-honored route. Furthermore, as

Dom Manuel had explained, he could be recalled to Lisbon in disgrace if his part in the smuggling operation should be discovered. The efforts of Jonathan Rakehell and Charles Boynton in the Anglo-Saxon world were bearing fruit, and all European governments now frowned on illicit traffic of the drug.

The closing of these avenues of approach left only one still open. Opium was carried to the British Royal Crown Colony of Hong Kong in junks, and when it arrived there it disappeared. This was not too difficult to achieve, as Hong Kong, growing with astonishing rapidity, had already become one of the world's busiest ports.

But, even here the smugglers encountered serious difficulties.

Sir Cedric Poole was determined to crack down with all his might on smugglers, and he regularly confiscated large amounts of the drug. In addition, Molinda, with the assistance of her formidable bodyguard, was becoming more and more a force to reckon with in the Crown Colony.

Admittedly, Bruce reflected, he and the marquês had problems. The Scotsman opened his eyes, and although the ground was still bloody, the elephant was gone and the body of the Chinese man had vanished. He could breathe more easily.

The door opened, and Dom Manuel entered. He was in bubbling high spirits, as he always was after witnessing one of his bizarre executions. "I trust you enjoyed yourself, my dear Bruce," he said with a chuckle as he went to a sideboard and poured two large glasses of Portuguese brandywine.

Owen Bruce could only nod.

"What an edifying spectacle that was," the marquês declared, raising his glass and drinking a silent toast. "It should be a salutary lesson to all who would cheat me. Don't you agree?" he asked pointedly.

"By all means, Your Excellency," Bruce responded nervously.

The governor's smile was bloodless. "Have you given any additional thought to our problem and its possible solution?"

"I have thought of little else, Your Excellency."

"With what results?"

Bruce hated to admit failure, but was forced to shrug and spread out his hands in a gesture of defeat. "I regret to say that I've had no constructive thoughts whatever. This fellow Poole is one of those hard-bitten English civil servants who are so obnoxious, and I know of no way to get around him, nor does anybody else."

Dom Manuel was amused. "Try your drink," he said. "You'll find it has a splendid bouquet."

Bruce apprehensively gulped a quantity of his brandywine.

"I trust," the governor said caustically, "that you've made a study of the private life of Sir Cedric Poole and have gleaned some information of value."

Owen Bruce took a large swallow of his fiery drink. "Of course I've made a study of his background," he said, "and I've gleaned information of interest, if not of value."

Dom Manuel was poker-faced. "Oh?" he queried.

"He's been seen everywhere in the colony with Molinda, the Balinese-French woman, who is the Rakehell-Boynton manager for the Far East."

The marquês nodded. "So I've learned from my own sources," he said. "I've gone to some pains to establish as a fact that Poole spends a night or two at her house each week."

"I don't find that in the least surprising, as she's an extremely good-looking wench. What I do find out of the ordinary is his openhanded approach to her. The English ordinarily are far more secretive than the people of other European countries when they take mistresses in the Orient. Poole makes no secret of his admiration of Molinda, and he takes her everywhere, even escorting her to formal affairs at the new home of the governor-general of the colony."

Dom Manuel laughed aloud. "You've learned all this," he said, "but you still have no notion as to how this information can be useful?"

Bruce knew he was being mocked but didn't dare lose his temper, so he merely shook his head.

"I wonder why it should be," Dom Manuel asked with

rhetorical plaintiveness, "that I should be forced to solve all problems myself. Surely you can see where it is possible to use Poole's involvement with Molinda to kill two birds with one stone?"

Bruce thought hard and rapidly but could not solve the puzzle.

The Marquês de Braga deliberately adopted a condescending tone toward him. "You can not only make it far easier to neutralize Sir Cedric Poole, and smuggle opium in and out of Hong Kong," he said, "but at the same time you can deliver a severe blow to our enemies, Rakehell and Boynton."

Bruce immediately became absorbed and leaned forward, listening intently.

"Let us suppose," Dom Manuel said, again sipping his brandywine, "that a significant quantity of opium should find its way on board a coastal junk that flies the flag of Rakehell and Boynton. Let us then suppose that the authorities are notified of this unfortunate state of affairs. It goes without saying that the notification would necessarily be anonymous."

"Of course," Bruce murmured.

"Poole," the governor went on, "will necessarily be very tough in his handling of the guilty woman. Tougher, in fact, than he is on any ordinary smuggler."

Bruce was puzzled. "Why should that be?"

The governor sighed in exasperation. "Surely," he said, "Colonel Poole's romantic involvement with Molinda is no secret to any official in the British colony, from the governor to the lowest-ranking officer."

"I suppose they do know," Bruce said tentatively.

Dom Manuel pounded the arm of his chair for emphasis. "Can't you see, you fool," he demanded, "Sir Cedric's own reputation will be at stake. His mistress will be revealed as a smuggler. He will be absolutely compelled to treat her with the greatest of severity to protect his own good name. His entire future will depend on how he reacts. So I am sure— knowing British civil servants as I do—that he will exert every effort to bring total disgrace on her, and send her to prison for a long term."

Owen Bruce brightened. "One thing is very clear to me," he said. "I can see that Rakehell and Boynton will be badly crippled. The wench is efficient and knows the shipping business, I've got to hand that much to her. It will be virtually impossible for them to find someone of competence to replace her."

"Exactly so," Dom Manuel said in triumph. "And don't neglect the fact that while her trial is in progress, Poole will be badly shaken. He's the sort who will take a personal crisis of this kind very hard. So we must arrange during this period to send vast quantities of opium through Hong Kong into the Middle Kingdom. He will be too distracted, his mind too full, to conduct his usual diligent searches."

Bruce raised his glass to him. "Your Excellency," he said, "I salute your genius."

"I shall drink to that myself," Dom Manuel replied, and drained his brandywine.

The Scotsman happily followed his example.

"How much opium do you have stored in Hong Kong at the present time, Bruce?" Dom Manuel demanded.

"Six or eight tea casks, Your Excellency, no more than that."

"They're hidden in your usual place?"

Bruce trusted no one, not even his senior partner. "Let us say, sir, that they're securely hidden, but they're easily available to me."

"Good," Dom Manuel replied heartily. "Then you have all the materials already at hand to condemn Molinda of smuggling. Go to Hong Kong at once and see to it."

"With pleasure, sir." Bruce hauled himself to his feet.

The governor eyed him indolently. "If you succeed in this," he said, "you shall be wealthier than you ever imagined. If, on the other hand, you botch the attempt, may the Almighty have mercy on your soul, because I do not gladly tolerate fools."

Bruce could imagine nothing that could go amiss in such a simple operation. "Trust me, Your Excellency," he said. "The woman is as good as behind bars right now, and we'll

344

keep Sir Cedric so busy that he'll have no idea how much opium we're carrying into the Middle Kingdom under his nose.'' He laughed heartily, then bowed to the marquês and departed hastily.

Dom Manuel glanced at his gold pocket watch the moment that Bruce left the room. He had seen no reason to explain that he was expecting a visitor, whose presence he was looking forward to with anticipation. He had received a letter the previous day informing him that Erika von Klausner, the representative of the prominent von Eberling shipping interests of Hamburg, had arrived in Macao and wanted to see him on a matter of business.

Intrigued by her scented notepaper, Dom Manuel had made it his business to investigate, and had been pleased to learn that the envoy from von Eberling was young, shapely, and exceptionally good-looking. She was accompanied everywhere by a small, coarse-featured man who was her bodyguard, but Dom Manuel had already decided how to handle him, having ascertained that after she retired at night, the man who went by the name of Reinhardt Braun drifted to the port area, where he made the acquaintance of prostitutes in sailors' bars.

He chose to receive his visitors informally in his small audience chamber and, adjourning to it, seated himself on the leather armchair that resembled a throne. He deliberately sent for his Portuguese infantryman to act as his honor guard, and he sent instructions to his slave mistress that he and his guests would be served by the girls in his harem.

Erika von Klausner and her associate were announced by his chamberlain, and as the ravishingly beautiful woman came through the door, Dom Manuel was stunned. Her red hair cascaded in waves down her back; her extremely low-cut gown of pale green velvet—inappropriate in a climate as warm as Macao—was plastered to her body. He tried to appear casual but could not help reflecting the excitement that surged through him.

Erika, well aware of what she was doing, sank to the floor in a deep curtsy in front of the dais on which his armchair was located, and in the process, managed to treat him to a long, tantalizing glimpse of her incomparable breasts. Braun, who stood stiffly at attention several paces behind her, clicked his heels and bowed. The governor took an immediate, intense dislike to him. The man was obviously an arrogant German, and Dom Manuel long had despised the breed.

Dismissing the members of the court whom he had assembled so hastily, Dom Manuel offered his guests glasses of wine punch with chunks of fresh fruit in them. Erika, on her best behavior, was very much at home, and conducted herself with aplomb. Her charm was irresistible.

Braun, who was as much out of his element as he had been when disguised as a servant, sat glumly and silently. He could not conceal his interest, however, in the two young women who served the wine punch. Both were favorites among the governor's concubines, tiny, exquisitely formed Chinese girls, whom he was amused to dress in pseudo-Grecian abbreviated costumes of thin, semitransparent silk.

Braun stared surreptitiously first at one and then at the other, and a vein pounded in his temple.

The governor took note of his reaction and knew that he would encounter no problem in getting rid of the woman's bodyguard at the appropriate time. He chatted at length with Erika, listening with feigned interest to her account of her stay in Djakarta and her reactions to the Orient. He was pleased to note, too, that thanks to the almost insufferable heat and the high humidity, she soon had drained her glass. He promptly ordered another round. Then he boldly asked, "Is it needful that Senhor Braun remain with us while we converse?"

Erika appreciated the maneuver. "I think not," she said, "if he can amuse himself elsewhere."

"One is never at a loss for amusement in Macao," Dom Manuel said, clapping his hands together twice, sharply.

A third attractive Chinese girl, flimsily clad like the other two, entered and kowtowed to him. This was the slave mistress, and around her waist she carried a symbol of her rank, a whip that served as a belt.

"Perhaps, Senhor Braun," he said, "you will be interested

in accompanying the young lady, who will show you some of the more interesting sights in Macao."

"That will be my great pleasure, Your Excellency," Braun replied, and grinned. Then he caught the eye of the Chinese slave mistress, and when she returned his gaze boldly, he felt a surge of confidence. He swaggered out of the audience chamber after her, his mind racing. The whip she carried would add to the day's sport that he so accurately and eagerly anticipated. He didn't know how many girls would be provided for him, but their number didn't matter; he would take care of them all, and although he couldn't speak a word of Chinese, he was looking forward eagerly to an experiment. Armed with the leather whip, he felt confident of his ability to communicate his desires instantly and to the point. This was going to be the most pleasurable evening since he had left Hamburg so many months earlier.

Alone now with Erika, Dom Manuel left his leather "throne" and joined her on the divan at the base of the dais. There they enjoyed a second glass of wine punch and ultimately a third. By the time they had consumed their drinks, they had taken each other's measure. Erika knew that here was a man of gross, gargantuan sexual appetites, a man she could control. There was no question in her mind that she would obtain shipping contracts, similar to the few she had managed to obtain from the Fat Dutchman, that would give von Eberling shipping the base it needed to begin operations in the Orient.

For his part, Dom Manuel was equally satisfied. He recognized in Erika a true colleague, a sensualist who used her charms for the purpose and was always conscious of every nuance in her relations with those of consequence. He appreciated her gestures as she flirted with him, and he silently congratulated her on her techniques when her hand or an arm or a leg accidentally brushed against him for a moment. He still had not learned her purpose in seeking him out, but he was in no hurry. He would find out in good time, and meanwhile he was enjoying himself.

He invited Erika to dine with him, and she accepted warmly, after hesitating just long enough to remove the suspicion that she had been seeking just such a goal from the moment she had met him.

Ultimately, he realized that he would have to force her hand, and suggested that they go to the observation tower to see the view. This was his favorite seduction place, a fact that Erika recognized the moment she saw the huge divan with silk pillows scattered on it in a chamber on the very apex of the palace.

Quickly she took in the essentials of her surroundings. From a stone balcony encircling the suite that stood alone like a watchtower at the very top of the palace, she saw the harbor on one side and the hills of the Middle Kingdom beyond the Macao border on the other. There were several rooms to the suite, and when a slave girl brought them fresh glasses of wine punch, she knew that their dinner would be served here ultimately.

But, in the meantime, it was inevitable that she and her host would find their way into the chamber where the oversized divan was located. Erika allowed Dom Manuel to show her the view and explain it to her at length. She obligingly rewarded him by leaning against him and was gratified by the knowledge that his breathing quickened.

She suffered no illusions regarding this principal Portuguese official in the Orient. He was fat, self-indulgent, and in deplorable physical condition. But the excesses of pleasures with which he sated himself in no way compensated for his basic nature. He was cruel and harsh, and undoubtedly demanded full payment for that which he granted.

Well, that suited her. She also believed in obtaining payment in full for any favors she granted, and she was determined that Dom Manuel would not be given any lenient, special terms.

Letting her gestures and the way she held herself speak for her, Erika indicated her availability to him, then made certain that he grasped the full meaning of her message. That much accomplished, she made her own mission clear to him. She sought trade contracts for von Eberling shipping, and she was prepared to be generous with her gifts if he was equally generous with his contracts.

The Marquês de Braga was equally satisfied that he was striking a bargain. He loathed false sentiment, and here was a woman who spoke his language. She would pay with her body for every contract that he granted her, and the terms of the agreement suited him perfectly.

Jonathan was so busy that he failed to realize how much was missing from his life. He supervised every aspect of the operations at the Rakehell and Boynton yards, ranging from the building of new clipper ships to keeping watch on the far-flung trade operations that the company conducted in the Orient, Europe, and the Caribbean. In his alleged spare time, he corresponded with other shipping men who were interested in the development of steamships, and nothing in the field was too minor to capture his full attention.

Occasionally, his mind was wrenched away from business. Such an event occurred when he came home for dinner late one night and found a note awaiting him from the principal of the George Washington Grammar School, which Julian attended. The note itself was brief and revealed nothing:

*Dear Mr. Rakehell,*
   *Please see me at your earliest convenience on a matter of urgent, mutual interest.*
                              *Your Humble Servant,*
                              *C. W. Johnson*

The worried Jonathan tried to find out from Julian why the head of the school wanted to see him, but the child merely shrugged. So the next morning, instead of going to the shipyard, Jonathan accompanied his son to school. There he found out that "C. W. Johnson" was Mrs. Corinne Johnson, a sympathetic and attractive widow.

"I don't want to worry you, Mr. Rakehell," she said, "but you should know that your son was in a hectic fistfight the other day and, in fact, pounded his opponent to a pulp."

Jonathan frowned. "That doesn't sound like Julian," he said.

Corinne Johnson shrugged. "All I know is that the fight took place during recess. His teacher has tried to discuss it with him, and so have I, but neither of us has been able to persuade him to discuss it freely. Perhaps you'll have more luck."

"May we send for him right now?" Jonathan asked. "I'd like to question him in your presence, if you don't mind."

"By all means," she said, and sent a messenger to Julian's room.

A few minutes later the boy came into the principal's office, saw his father, and braced himself.

"I've just now learned that you were involved in a fight, Julian," his father said, deliberately sounding matter-of-fact. "Would you care to talk about it?"

The boy shook his head. "No, Papa."

"I'm afraid you'll have to discuss it all the same," Jonathan replied. "Fighting is a serious business, and from what I understand, you thrashed your opponent."

"Billy Watkins had it coming, the big bully," Julian said. "I warned him, but he wouldn't listen to me."

Jonathan turned to the principal. "Who is Billy Watkins?"

"He's an older boy," Corinne Johnson replied. "He's about twelve, and he's had a history of picking on younger and smaller children in the school yard."

Jonathan turned to his son for corroboration.

Julian thrust his jaw forward pugnaciously. "Most of the kids in my class have been scared of Billy ever since he beat up little Ted Graham," the boy said, "and he even threatened some of the girls. That's when I got good and mad."

Jonathan concealed his amusement. "You started the fight, then?"

"Not really, Papa," his son replied. "He came across the yard and began to pull Beth's pigtails. I told him to stop, but he didn't pay any attention to me. Then I said if he didn't pay

350

attention to me, he'd be sorry. He didn't stop"—Julian grinned up at his father—"so I made him sorry."

Jonathan reacted spontaneously and clapped his son on the shoulder. "Good for you, Julian," he said. "Unless there's something you're not telling me, you did exactly the right thing."

Suddenly he became aware of the principal's presence. "I hope you don't mind, Mrs. Johnson," he said, "but I had to tell Julian the way I honestly feel."

He was pleased when Corinne Johnson smiled and nodded.

"Under the circumstances," she said, "I can't help approving, too. Billy Watkins has been a troublemaker for the past two years, and he's desperately needed someone to put him in his place. Several boys his own age have tried it, but he's always managed to intimidate them. Your son, it appears, is a boy who doesn't frighten easily."

Jonathan chuckled. "Grandpa is going to be very proud of you for this, too. We'll have to discuss it at greater length with him, won't we?"

Julian was relieved that he was not going to be punished. "You bet, Papa," he said enthusiastically.

Soon thereafter, the child was dismissed and returned to his classroom, and Jonathan prepared to take his leave. He had no idea that Corinne Johnson was privately elated by his appearance at the school. She, like dozens of other widows and unmarried women in the New London area, was conscious of the eligibility of this wealthy widower. So by the time Jonathan left the school and started to walk to the shipyard, he found that he had accepted a supper engagement with Mrs. Johnson.

"I know Corinne Johnson from church, and she's undoubtedly set her cap for Jonnie," Missy Sarah told Jeremiah privately that night. "But she's too subtle for him, and he's so preoccupied that I doubt if he'll see her as anything but Julian's school principal."

Her prophecy proved to be remarkably accurate. Jonathan appeared at Mrs. Johnson's house, carrying a large bouquet

351

of flowers as a gift, and he had a pleasant if slightly dull evening. Julian was good for only a few minutes of conversation, and he found his mind reverting to business matters when she discussed other things. He thanked her for a pleasant evening when he departed, and it didn't cross his mind to seek out her company again.

Other women were far bolder than Corinne Johnson. One of the more blatant was Adele Snyder, an attractive single woman who had moved to New London from New Orleans when she had inherited a large interest in a ship's stores company. She took an active role in the operations of the business, and in that capacity she frequently had contact with Jonathan, who bought most of his supplies from her. Strictly as a matter of business, he invited Adele to dine with him at the Mohican Inn. She elected to regard the invitation as personally inspired, however, and she reacted accordingly throughout the evening, flirting with him incessantly.

Just that day, he had received a long communication on some experiments being made in Scotland on the thrust power of the newly developed screw propeller, and this news was so much on his mind that he was unaware that the young woman was making a rather desperate attempt to interest him in her. He escorted her to her home after dinner, and she insisted that he come into her parlor for a nightcap. He was tired, intending to rise early the following morning, but Adele made such an issue out of her invitation that he accepted it and went into her house for a final drink.

The woman thought that she was arousing his interest at last, but she soon learned better. She let him know as bluntly and as directly as she could that she would not be averse to his advances, but Jonathan's head was in the clouds, and he remained unaware of her attempts to enmesh him.

Leaving a bitterly disappointed Adele Snyder behind him, he could feel Lai-tse lu's jade medallion resting against his chest.

Never had he forgotten, nor would he forget, that it had given off intense heat at the moment of her death. This was something he could not explain, and he was sufficiently familiar with the ways of the Orient to know better than to try. There were aspects of human relationships that defied both logic and modern science, and remained inexplicable. He knew well enough to accept these phenomena and not probe into their causes.

Glancing at his pocket watch as he approached the dark Rakehell house, Jonathan was relieved to see that it wasn't too late for him to spend an hour culling newspapers and magazines for articles of interest to send on to the Tao Kuang Emperor and the Princess An Mien. He devoted at least three hours a week to this activity, and allowed nothing to interfere. To his delight, he found waiting for him in his study a letter from Wu-ling, thanking him for the most recent batch of books and articles that he had sent. In her typically chatty style, Wu-ling related to him that she was being kept busy translating for and also assisting Matthew Melton, who was making a secure place for himself in the Forbidden City. She went on at some length, too, about the health of the emperor and related some of the new projects in which An Mien was becoming involved.

All at once Jonathan felt homesick for the sights and sounds and smells of the Middle Kingdom. He had been driving himself mercilessly, without taking a break of any kind, and the strain was beginning to tell. So, on sudden impulse, he sent off a brief letter to Molinda, and another to Charles. He would plan a voyage to the Orient in about two months' time, he said, and would go first to visit the Fat Dutchman in Djakarta, and then would go on to see Molinda at the Hong Kong headquarters of Rakehell and Boynton; from there he would journey to Canton in order to visit his wife's grave, and finally he would journey to the Forbidden City to pay his respects to the Celestial Emperor.

Both of the letters would be dispatched within twenty-four hours. A brig was leaving for England in the morning, and a clipper was making the long voyage to the Far East on the afternoon tide. That night, Jonathan slept more soundly than he had in many weeks.

\*    \*    \*

Charles and Ruth Boynton were at the breakfast table in the spacious house in Belgravia when Jonathan's letter arrived. David, who was growing rapidly, already ate a larger meal than both of his parents, and Elizabeth, who drifted into the dining room and joined her brother and sister-in-law for a cup of coffee, shook her head in mock dismay at the child.

Charles was absorbed in Jonathan's letter, and when he was done with it, he passed it without comment to his wife. Ruth started to smile and nod, and after she had read no more than the opening paragraph she spoke enthusiastically. "Oh, good!" she said. "Jonnie's going to take the children with him."

"Of course he is," Charles replied, buttering another slice of toast. "We have so many interests there that he feels part of their heritage lies in the Orient, and he wants to familiarize them as much as possible with every aspect of living in the East."

"I think that's very wise," Ruth replied, glancing at David, who sat between them. "I think it's a principle that we might well follow."

"I'm all in favor of it," Charles replied. "As a matter of fact, I've been thinking myself lately that the time is right for another visit to the East."

Ruth's smile broadened. Whether Charles liked it or not he would be taking an enforced holiday of three months on board the ship that would carry him to the Orient.

"I'll not only take the boy," Charles said, "but you're invited too, my dear."

"I accept at once with great pleasure," Ruth said. This was the first time he had ever asked her to accompany him on a journey halfway around the world.

"What's all this?" a curious Elizabeth wanted to know.

Her sister-in-law glanced at Charles for approval, then reached for Jonathan's letter and handed it to her.

Elizabeth read it avidly, then she smiled at her brother. "I hope," she said, "that you're going to include me in your invitation, Charles."

"Sorry, old girl, but that can't be arranged this time."

Elizabeth became quietly belligerent. "Why in the world not?"

"The scheduling won't work out that way," he said. "The clipper that will be available to take us to Djakarta, so we arrive there at about the same time that Jonnie gets there, has only two passenger cabins, and one of them is quite small, barely large enough for David, so I'm afraid there will be no room for you on board. Sorry, Elizabeth."

She seemed unperturbed by the news and tugged at the belt of her dressing gown. "This sort of thing can't be helped," she said, apparently accepting his decision with the resignation of one who has spent her whole life in the shipping industry. "Do I gather that Jonathan and his children, and Kai no doubt, will be going from New London on board the *Lai-tse lu*?"

"I assume they will," Charles replied. "He always travels on her, you know." He pondered for a moment, figuring out the schedules of shipping between America and the Far East, and then he nodded vigorously. "Yes," he said, "he'll be using the *Lai-tse lu*. I'm quite certain that's why he'll be sailing when he is."

"In that case," Elizabeth said calmly, "I shall have no problem whatsoever. I'll simply go to America first, and then I'll sail with Jonathan and his children on board the clipper. It has more than enough passenger cabins to accommodate me."

Ruth blinked in astonishment, and Charles stared at his sister, who returned his gaze sweetly, her blue eyes tranquil.

"You're being rather forward, you know," he muttered.

Elizabeth nodded, and her long ash blond hair swayed back and forth. "I am rather cheeky, aren't I?" she replied.

"What will Jonathan think?" Ruth demanded.

Elizabeth remained very cool. "I assume that he'll accept the facts of the situation. As Charles has said, there will be no cabin for me on the ship sailing from London. There will be more than enough space for me on board Jonathan's ship. So I intend to avail myself of the privilege of family."

Charles sighed, and Ruth shook her head.

"The fact remains, dear," Ruth said, "that you'll be spending hours in Jonathan's company for three long months, with no passengers other than his children and no distractions but the operations of the ship—for which someone else will be responsible."

Elizabeth nodded brightly. "I daresay I'll have ample opportunities to consolidate my position, so to speak."

Her brother sighed in exasperation. "I hate to see our ships used for such conniving purposes," he sputtered.

Elizabeth regarded him steadily. "I won't implicate you in my scheme in the least, Charles. I shall write to Jonathan myself this very day and ask him if he'll be good enough to hold a cabin for me." She laughed mischievously. "At the same time, I shall communicate privately with Missy Sarah, just to make certain that I have an ally in the right place at the right time."

Charles gaped at her. "Don't tell me that Missy Sarah is a member of the conspiracy to end Jonathan's bachelor days!" he said.

Ruth picked up the silver teapot and poured him another cup of tea. "The carriage will be coming for you in ten minutes, Charles," she said, "so you'll have just enough time to drink your second cup of tea."

As a single woman, Molinda functioned at a distinct disadvantage in the busy social life of Hong Kong. There were those in the official hierarchy, among them the governor-general and his wife, Lord and Lady Williamson, who knew of her relationship with Sir Cedric Poole, and who consequently saw to it that she was invited to various social events. But in her business entertaining, which was far easier for her male colleagues and competitors, she was obliged to think in novel terms when she wanted to repay her social debts and entertain potential customers.

Such an idea occurred to her when a luxurious oceangoing junk she had recently purchased in Siam prepared to make its maiden voyage from Bangkok to Hong Kong. The ship had far larger than usual deck space, which gave Molinda the idea of holding a supper party on board. The galley below deck was spacious and well equipped, which meant that her cooks would be able to prepare the better part of the meal on board the junk while it rode at anchor in the harbor, making it unnecessary to prepare more than a minimum of dishes elsewhere. Thus she decided to hold a party in honor of Lord and Lady Williamson, and after obtaining their gracious consent, she set a date with them for the day after the new junk was scheduled to arrive in Hong Kong.

"Since I know they dislike having a fuss made over them," she told Sir Cedric Poole, "I'm going to hold the protocol and pomp to a minimum. The little monsoon season is ending, so we'll be able to entertain guests on deck, and I'll have supper served there. We'll decorate with paper lanterns, which will provide ample illumination, and I'll have the cooks concentrate on no more than a handful of main dishes. I really want to create a relaxed atmosphere for Their Excellencies."

Sir Cedric applauded her plans and could find no fault with them, so the preparations for the party gathered momentum.

Although Molinda didn't know it, she was playing directly into the hands of Owen Bruce, who had been awaiting just such an opportunity and saw his chance to destroy her reputation, ensure her arrest, and keep Colonel Poole thoroughly occupied.

It was almost absurdly simple for Bruce to make the arrangements that would cause her disgrace. The coming party for Lord and Lady Williamson was no secret, and it was common knowledge along the waterfront, too, that a crew would be hired locally and sent off to Bangkok to man the new ship. Wang Ning Po, long a junk captain and a veteran of the China coastal trade, whose service extended back into the era when the company had been owned by Soong Chao, was named by Molinda to be the master of the new vessel. While he was selecting his crew prior to going off to Bangkok, he received a mysterious visitor at his quarters near the waterfront one night. The man promised him considerable wealth if he were discreet and followed some safe, easy instructions. Wang hesitated but finally agreed to hear the whole story and was taken to Owen Bruce.

The request made of the captain was very simple. All he had to do, Bruce told him, was to include six lead-lined boxes of tea in the cargo that would be imported from Bangkok. Bruce even suggested to him that he could carry the six boxes with him on the junk that would carry him to Siam. In return for this favor, Bruce told him, he would be paid the glittering sum of one gold yuan for each tea box. Even though part of this sum would have to be used to pay men to load and unload the casks, this was a startling amount of money. A ship's captain could work for many years before he accumulated a fortune of that size.

Wang Ning Po agreed to the terms, and the bargain was struck. He was paid half of the gold in advance, and would receive the other half when he returned to Hong Kong from Bangkok.

He was slightly delayed by an unseasonable storm and arrived at the Rakehell and Boynton docks in Hong Kong on the morning of the party. The cooks and food handlers were already at the waterfront, awaiting the vessel's arrival, and a small army of cleaning personnel came on board to scrub the decks and interior, and put up the lanterns for the party that night.

Molinda soon appeared to supervise the operation, and the junk was scoured. Wang Ning Po was not needed at the ship and went to the office of Owen Bruce by a circuitous route. Admitted to the Scotman's presence without delay, he wasted no words. "It all is done as the Fan Kuei wished," he said in the Cantonese dialect. "The tea boxes are in the very top and center of the cargo that contains ivory and aromatic Siamese tea."

"You're quite certain that they're the boxes that I provided you with before you went off to Bangkok?"

The ship's captain nodded. The suspicions of white men galled him, but his face did not register his anger. "I have followed the instructions I received to the letter," he said.

"Now it is the turn of the Fan Kuei to keep his bargain with me."

Bruce would have preferred to wait until the authorities discovered the "tea" casks containing raw opium before he paid the rest of the Chinese master's fee, but this was no time to procrastinate. He well knew that Wang Ning Po would be very much on his own, and would be subjected to long, intense questioning by Sir Cedric Poole and his assistants. How the man fared would be his own problem, and if he received all his gold now, he would be far less inclined to reveal the agreement he had made.

So, hesitating only for a moment, Owen Bruce gave him the three gold yuan that completed the deal. The sum was outrageous, to be sure, but that was part of Bruce's technique for his own protection. If Wang Ning Po still decided to talk out of turn to the authorities, they would find it difficult to believe that a white man had paid such a fantastically high price for a limited quantity of opium.

The meal that Molinda's cooks were preparing was the replica in part of the so-called Great Chinese Banquet, which dated back several hundred years. Among the dishes were fresh turtle steak cooked with chives and ginger, a roast whole suckling pig, and deer heart garnished with plums. There were such delicacies as sautéed shark's fins and sparrows with chopped pine nuts and, as a final course, a squab and melon soup. Making certain that all was in readiness and that preparations were well under way, Molinda hurried off to her house and dressed for the evening in a spectacular single garment of shimmering white silk, trimmed in scarlet. With it she wore a scarlet hibiscus in her hair, and when Sir Cedric came to call for her, he was forced to admit that he had never seen her look lovelier.

The junk's gangplank had been festooned with flowers, and Molinda greeted her guests as they stepped on board the ship. Lord and Lady Williamson arrived promptly, and set the tone for the evening by being even more convivial than usual.

Sir Cedric was deeply troubled, although he went to great pains to conceal his upset. Shortly before leaving his own quarters, he had received a note delivered by a nondescript Chinese messenger, who had promptly vanished. The document was written in classical Chinese and was very much to the point. The note informed him that there were six cartons of raw opium on board the Rakehell and Boynton junk that had just arrived from Bangkok, and that they were disguised as tea containers.

Embarrassed and incredulous, Poole felt he had no choice in the matter and that he was obliged to handle the case precisely as he would direct an operation in which no one he knew was involved. The fact that he had been intimate with Molinda and that the long arm of suspicion pointed directly at her made the situation almost intolerable for him.

Nevertheless, as a public servant devoted to his duty, he did what was necessary. Most of his reliable, principal aides were fellow Englishmen, and he assigned them the task of coming to the dock after the party ended that night. He estimated it would be over by midnight, and he intended to conduct a raid on the junk then. His one concession to his relationship with Molinda was the fact that he ordered his subordinates to appear in civilian clothes rather than uniform.

The party was a great success, the guests eating and drinking heartily, and Lord and Lady Williamson enjoyed themselves thoroughly. Hovering unobtrusively in the background throughout the evening was Lo Fang, who observed everything, spoke to no one, and always remained within Molinda's easy reach. Certainly the British guests who saw this trained giant of a servant had no idea that he was, in actuality, the head of the Society of Oxen, one of the most powerful of the nation's patriotic secret societies. The Williamsons were having such a good time that, contrary to their custom, they did not depart at eleven o'clock or thereabouts. Instead, to the private consternation of Sir Cedric Poole, they lingered on board the junk.

The demands of protocol were strict and unvariable: the presence of the governor-general and his lady meant that no other guest could depart until they took their leave. So the party went on.

Molinda was delighted. The first social event of consequence that she had given was a total success, and she was
radiant, enjoying herself as much as the guests were relishing
her hospitality.

As midnight approached, Sir Cedric felt increasingly ill at
ease. He knew the arrival of his plainclothes subordinates
would create a sensation, but he could not call off the raid
now without laying himself open to the charge that he was
showing favoritism to Molinda because of their intimacy. No
matter what the consequences, the raid had to be conducted
on schedule, even though the Williamsons were still present.

Owen Bruce watched the proceedings from the nearby
vantage point of his own rooftop. Carefully refraining from
smoking so he wouldn't give away his presence, he had no
need for the ship's glass with which he had provided himself.
He could see everything plainly, and congratulated himself on
his good fortune. The presence of the personal representative
of Queen Victoria at the party was an important part of his
plan, and would bring increased notoriety to Molinda when
she was discredited.

Promptly at midnight the plainclothes constables moved up
the gangplank. Lo Fang immediately took up a position near
them on the deck. The officer in charge glanced apprehensively
at Sir Cedric, nervously saluted Lord Williamson, and then
addressed Molinda, who had approached him in perplexity.
"You'll forgive this interruption, ma'am," he said, "but I'm
acting under orders." He handed her a document bearing the
royal seal.

Molinda glanced at the paper and realized that the junk was
being raided on the personal orders of Colonel Sir Cedric
Poole, who had signed the communication himself. She
looked at him in utter bewilderment. "Is this a joke of some
sort, Cedric?" she wanted to know.

The embarrassed, perturbed officer shook his head. Lord
Williamson came hurrying forward, an imposing, portly figure in his dress uniform of gold-embroidered white, and
immediately asserted his own authority. "What's the meaning
of this, Poole?" he demanded brusquely.

"I have no desire to embarrass you, milord," the colonel replied. "When I gave the orders for this raid I assumed that you would have departed about an hour ago and that most of the guests would have gone home by now. I couldn't change the hour, however, to suit your personal convenience."

The governor-general made no attempt to hide his annoyance. "What are the reasons for the raid?"

Speaking clearly and slowly, Sir Cedric related that he had received an anonymous communication, in Chinese, telling him that six containers of opium had been brought on board in Bangkok and were being smuggled into Hong Kong.

The guests listened to the unexpected drama in an electric silence.

Molinda, however, proved equal to the occasion. "You actually believe such a story about me, Cedric?" she wanted to know. "You believed that I would stoop to smuggling opium?"

Perspiration ran down the colonel's face into the high collar of his tunic. "I neither believed nor disbelieved it, Molinda. It is my duty to determine the facts without fear or favor, and that is precisely what I am attempting to do. If I have caused you distress, then I'm sorry, but my duty comes ahead of any personal considerations."

Her face looked very Oriental as she listened to him, and her expression was inscrutable, her eyes veiled.

Sir Cedric turned to his principal subordinate.

"Very good, sir." The man saluted and went aft to the main hatch, followed by some of his men. The others went to the forward hatch, and all of them disappeared below the deck.

It was impossible for those remaining above to maintain a party atmosphere. Lord Williamson went to his wife when she beckoned to him, and he nodded vigorously when she whispered to him. "I quite agree with you my dear," he told her. "I'd feel the same way, as though we were deserting our hostess if we were to go home now. We shall await the outcome of this matter."

Molinda forced a smile as she looked at Lady Williamson

362

and then at her husband. So mortified that she could scarcely think straight, she stood immobile, statuelike, her head high, her chin thrust forward defiantly, her arms at her sides. Only her tightly clenched fists indicated the depth of her emotions.

The wait was awkward and seemed interminable while the constabulary team conducted their search of the cargo.

Molinda finally remembered her manners and ordered her waiters to start circulating again with trays laden with beverages. Many of the guests behaved as if all were well and resumed their light conversation. Such a pose was impossible for Sir Cedric Poole, however, and the governor-general, making no secret of his annoyance, glowered impatiently.

At long last the constables returned to the deck.

"Sir," the officer in charge said to Sir Cedric, "we found nothing. The message that you received told you the exact location of the supposed casks of opium in the cargo, but they weren't there. So we made good and sure, and we went through every chest of tea on the ship. I can state categorically, Colonel, that there is no opium on board this junk."

A wave of great relief swept over Colonel Poole.

The first to react was Lord Williamson, who immediately approached Molinda and extended his hand. "Accept my congratulations and at the same time, my apologies. The embarrassment you've been caused was inexcusable, and I assure you it won't be tolerated and certainly won't happen again."

She accepted her victory with good grace. "As long as my name has been cleared, Your Excellency, that's all that matters to me," she replied.

Sir Cedric was eager to make amends to her, and taking the message he had received from a waistcoat pocket, he unfolded the sheet of paper and silently handed it to her.

Molinda perused it carefully and then politely asked Lord Williamson if he would like to see it, too. He glanced at it, but obviously knew no Chinese, so Molinda translated it for him.

"It strikes me," he said, "that someone intended to cause this lady embarrassment."

"So it appears, sir," Sir Cedric replied, "I must take full blame for the discomfort that Molinda has been caused, and I will say in your presence, milord, what I would say to her privately—that my personal relationship with her, which has been no secret in this community, made it essential that I show no favoritism toward her. I did my duty as I conceived it."

The governor-general could not help feeling a tug of sympathy for the upright official whose duty had collided so violently with his own intimate, personal interests. Certainly he would take no punitive actions against the man.

The story having had a happy ending, the governor-general and Lady Williamson took their leave, followed by most of the guests.

Sir Cedric Poole lingered behind and approached Molinda after she had walked some of her other guests as far as the gangplank. The couple turned with one accord and walked to the railing at the opposite side of the deck overlooking the harbor. There they stood gazing out at a silver ribbon of light cast on the water by a three-quarters moon. "I hope that I shall be forgiven," Sir Cedric said earnestly. "I was in the devil's own position."

"You're forgiven," Molinda told him, but did not feel like elaborating.

He moved closer to her. Slowly, with great deliberation, she increased the space that separated them. "If you don't mind, Cedric," she said, "I feel very raw and abused tonight. I prefer not to discuss this matter any more."

He could appreciate her feelings, even though he knew she was dismissing him. He bowed stiffly, then took his leave and walked off down the dock without a backward glance. Watching him go, Molinda felt a twinge of regret, but it soon passed. She had just bidden farewell to Cedric Poole, she knew, and had terminated their affair. She was being unfair to him, perhaps, to use this unfortunate incident as an excuse to break off completely with him, but she knew it was just as well.

Their careers clashed, and she well realized that she would be a handicap to him if she continued to socialize with him—let alone marry him. By the same token, she was finding it increasingly difficult to do justice to her position at Rakehell and Boynton as Cedric Poole's lover.

The real reason she felt no regrets, she suspected, was that she didn't really love Cedric. She had drifted into an intimate relationship with him because she had been lonely, and she knew that her feelings for him, like his feelings for her, were no substitute for the love that would be necessary to see them over the rough spots of an interracial marriage in a part of the world where prejudices were still so strong.

While she continued to stand at the rail, musing silently, Lo Fang approached her and stood nearby waiting to be noticed.

At last Molinda became aware of his presence. "Ah, Lo Fang," she said. "You're just the person I wanted to see." She handed him the note and then said, "If you can, you might find out who is responsible for this crude attempt to implicate me in a drug-smuggling operation."

The giant majordomo took the paper, folded it carefully, and dropped it into a tunic pocket. A slow, crafty smile spread slowly across his face.

Molinda realized at once from his expression that he knew far more about the matter than he had revealed. "Tell me," she said, "I have a right to know."

"The lady Molinda has that right," the grinning Lo Fang agreed. "The letter was written by someone in the pay of Owen Bruce, although that is difficult to prove."

Molinda glanced at him sharply. "Don't be vague, please," she said. "I want to know everything."

"The Society of Oxen has members everywhere, so it happened that I learned of a scheme to plant six lead-lined tea cases of opium on board this junk. The drugs were carried to Bangkok on board the junk that carried the crew of this vessel to the place from which it sailed. The facts were reported to me, and it so happens that the opium did not reach its destination. I imagine it has killed many fish as it spread its poison through the waters of Bangkok harbor."

Molinda nodded thoughtfully as she listened to him.

"The rest was very simple," he said. "Siamese spices

were substituted for the opium in the six cases from which the drug had been removed. It is plain that an attempt was made to fool the British authorities of Hong Kong into thinking that Molinda was a drug smuggler. The Society of Oxen knows the identity of its friends, and we rejoice that we could be of help to you."

"I'm more grateful to you than I could tell you," she replied. "So Bruce continues to involve himself in schemes against us?"

"Yes," Lo Fang replied, "just as I am sure also that Wang Ning Po was involved."

The implication that her junk captain had plotted against her came as something of a shock.

"Wang Ning Po," Lo Fang went on, "is not a bad man. He was offered much money to place the opium in the cargo of his ship, and he gave in to temptation." He drew his curved, double-edged knife from his belt and thoughtfully tested the sharpness of a blade. "But Wang has seen the error of his ways. I have spoken to him myself, and he will not err again. The lady Molinda can be sure that he will be the most loyal of employees as long as Molinda wishes to keep him on her payroll. He knows that he is being watched by unseen eyes and that one more mistake will result in his immediate execution." He spoke in such casual terms that a shiver crept up Molinda's spine. The Society of Oxen meant business.

"What of the men who brought the casks of opium on board the other junk and transferred them to this ship," she said. "What has become of them?"

A harsh note crept into Lo Fang's voice. "Those men were Chinese," he said, "therefore they were subjects of the Celestial Emperor. They know that the people of China have been forbidden to use this drug. They know the reasons the emperor has commanded them to have nothing to do with opium. They were aware that it makes the user useless, and that it changes him from a healthy man to one who is very sick. They know also, that in time, opium kills. But they were greedy. They eagerly accepted the gold of the Scotsman Bruce and the Marquês de Braga." He folded his huge arms across his chest and said with finality, "Consequently, they deserved to die, and were duly executed."

It was readily apparent to Molinda that he did not shrink from his self-appointed tasks of acting as judge, jury, and principal executioner. "You're quite certain that the Marquês de Braga as well as Owen Bruce is involved in this scheme?"

"This was proved to the satisfaction of the Society of Oxen," he said. "The miserable creatures confessed before they died. The British would not accept their testimony because it was obtained under torture. The Oxen are satisfied, and the miscreants have paid with their lives for their errors."

Lo Fang gave Molinda a great deal to ponder and weigh. She well knew that Rakehell and Boynton—and she herself, as their Far Eastern representative—had powerful enemies in high places, and she promised herself that she would watch her step even more carefully. Obviously the Marquês de Braga and Bruce would stop at nothing to get rid of her and to cripple her employers.

# Book IV

Book IV

# I

Jonathan stood in his father's study, sipping a glass of mild sack as he addressed his father and Homer Ellison. "As I have written to Charles today," he said, "our financial problems have become urgent again. For a number of months, thanks to the kindness of President Polk, we enjoyed a virtual monopoly in the American trade with Cathay. However, other shipping companies have been anxious to share in the profits of this lucrative trade, and the State Department cannot deny them what is rightfully theirs. So our advantage has dwindled away to nothing. In the meantime, our expansion is well under way and is using every penny of the cash that we are able to accumulate. The next twelve to eighteen months will spell success or failure for us."

His father and brother-in-law were already familiar with the facts as he outlined them, and nodded soberly.

"If we can pay for our expansion," he said, "we'll be established as one of the world's leading, giant shipping companies. We'll be able to go on to greater glory and profits by going into the production and operation of steamships as well. If we should falter—well, I don't like to think of it, because I simply cannot bring myself to admit the possibility of defeat."

"Neither can I," Jeremiah said, "but we've got to face facts. We can do nothing more here, nothing more in London

371

to increase our income. We're working to our utmost capacity and we can't perform miracles.''

"I'm well aware of the situation," Jonathan said, "and so is Charles. We're meeting in Djakarta. He's going directly there from England, you know, and we're going to put our heads together and see if we can't pull the fat from the fire one last time.''

"I'd say the odds against you were rather strong," Homer said, "but when I recall how Charles carried out that magnificent pepper deal, and how President Polk told you that you'd have the exclusive right to trade with Cathay for an extended period of time—well, I'd say that between you you're capable of doing blame near anything.''

"If we're capable of it," Jonathan replied bleakly, "it's because we have no alternative. We have our backs to the wall, and we're fighting for our own futures and those of our children as well. All I can tell you, Homer, is that I have no idea how we're going to accomplish the impossible, but we're going to do it!'' He was still in the same mood, exuding grim determination, when he and his father went home from the office that night.

Missy Sarah, who was expert at gauging him, realized that this was not an appropriate time to add to his concerns, but knew it couldn't be helped. She waited until they had finished their vegetable soup, filled with fresh autumn vegetables from their own garden, and then she spoke casually. "I meant to mention to you," she said, "that I sent a letter off to London by the clipper that sailed to London this afternoon. I felt it necessary to write a note to Elizabeth Boynton.''

Her husband glanced down the table at her, and both were poker-faced. Jonathan made no comment, and concentrated on the last of his soup.

"We haven't really discussed Elizabeth's request to go to the Orient with you on the *Lai-tse lu*, Jonnie," she said. "What with one thing and another, we've been too busy to talk about it ever since we had our original letters from her.''

Jonathan nodded, unperturbed.

"In any event," Missy Sarah continued brightly, "I wrote

to her that you'd be delighted to provide the accommodations for her on the ship, and I asked her to come earlier so that she can spend a little time with us here before you sail."

Jonathan paused, his spoon partly raised to his mouth, then he slowly lowered it again and deposited the spoon in his bowl.

"I was quite sure," Sarah said hastily, "that I was expressing your wishes when I wrote to her, and that you're agreeable to providing her with a cabin."

Jonathan looked somewhat dubious as he slowly nodded. "Under the circumstances," he said, "I couldn't very well turn Elizabeth down, you know."

Jeremiah looked briefly at his wife and then said, "Well, it strikes me that she should be very useful in looking after Julian and Jade. Kai is very good at giving them Chinese food and culture and teaching them the martial arts, but he leaves something to be desired as a nursemaid." He chuckled at his own humor.

Jonathan's eyes remained somber. "There will be no one of Elizabeth's generation on board the ship, so I hope she doesn't become too bored. Three months is a very long time to spend at sea when time is hanging heavily on one's hands."

Jeremiah chuckled again. "If I were you, I wouldn't worry about that."

Missy Sarah knew she had to intervene, or Jonathan would guess that Elizabeth had set her cap for him. "Don't worry about her," she said emphatically, "Elizabeth is a most resourceful young lady, and you can be sure she'll keep herself gainfully occupied and amused. Consider yourself lucky, for the children's sake, that she's sailing with you, and do try to relax, Jonnie. You've been working far too hard, and you should take advantage of the opportunity to do nothing for the better part of three months."

"I'll try," he said dubiously, "but I can't promise."

"Very well, then," she replied. "When Elizabeth visits us prior to your sailing, I shall instruct her to see to it that you have nothing whatever on your mind."

373

"If she can keep me occupied," Jonathan said with a tired grin, "more power to her."

"I think you'll find," Sarah told him quietly, "that she's eminently capable of doing precisely that."

After an absence of many months, Sir Alan Boynton returned to his office without fanfare and, saying nothing to anyone about his return, quietly went back to work.

Charles, inundated with work prior to his departure to the Far East, learned of his father's return and was incredulous. Thanking the clerk who had brought him word, he hurried down the corridor of the London headquarters to his father's corner office.

Sir Alan sat behind great piles and stacks of documents on his desk and looked as though he had never been away.

"Well, Papa!" Charles exclaimed. "You're back!"

Sir Alan was enjoying the excitement of the moment. "So I am," he said quietly.

"Welcome!" Charles threw himself into a visitor's chair and grinned. "Just see to it now that you don't overdo things."

"I'll thank you to attend to your own affairs, young man," his father said austerely. "I've talked to the doctors, and I know precisely what I'm to do and what I'm not to do. Besides, I've come back for a specific purpose."

"May I know what it is?" Charles asked.

His father chuckled. "To let you sail off to the Orient with your wife and child. I'll be here to cover for you. The company has grown so large, and there are so many major decisions to be made every day, that someone in authority has got to be on the spot in order to say yes or no."

Charles was vastly relieved. "You've taken a heavy weight from my mind, Papa," he said.

Sir Alan's mood changed abruptly, and he frowned. "You've added a considerable burden to mine, my boy," he said. "I've just been reading your preliminary report to the stockholders, and I must say that our financial position is far more precarious than I knew or imagined."

374

Charles crossed and uncrossed his legs. "I admit that we've been in a far sounder position. I'll also agree that money is damnably tight these days."

"With no relief in sight, I take it," Sir Alan said flatly.

"Well," Charles temporized, "there's no solution in sight that's visible to the naked eye."

Sir Alan's sniff said more than he could have expressed in words.

"In our travels," Charles said, "Jonnie and I have acquired a liking for some unusual foods. There's 'shrimp bread,' *rijsttafel* in Indonesia, or there's a wonderful scallion and soy ginger sauce that Chinese cooks from Nanking make. Well, we've also acquired a taste for world leadership as a result of what we've done with Jonnie's clipper ships. Once we've tasted that leadership, it's hard to become accustomed to more ordinary fare once again."

"I applaud your ambition, Charles, and I hope that you and Jonathan achieve your ends. But at the same time, I hate to see you two bitterly disappointed. You've set yourselves some rather extraordinary goals, you know."

"I know," Charles replied cheerfully, "and the worst—or the best of it—is that Jonnie and I are both so supremely confident that we'll win out."

"I hope you're right," his father said. "You have any number of major competitors in this country, starting with the enormous British East India Company. The Dutch East India Company is also very powerful, and I've heard that von Eberling in Hamburg has his eye on Oriental markets, too."

"The more competition the merrier," Charles said. "I'll wager you a guinea to a sixpence that in one year's time, Jonnie and I will have Rakehell and Boynton on its feet and in good health!"

Erika von Klausner wore the single, loose-fitting garment of the East, and as she stood on the hilltop in Macao overlooking the harbor, the breeze flattened the lightweight cloth against her body, making it obvious that she wore nothing beneath it. She realized that Reinhardt Braun, who stood beside her, was staring at her, wondering if she had decided to emulate the women of the Orient, but she owed her subordinate no explanations.

As a matter of fact, she could not explain her situation to him; it was difficult enough to face the realities herself.

She had spent two weeks now as a guest at the palace of the governor-general of Macao, and she had had more than her fill of the Marquês de Braga. She had given in to his every whim, as she had never catered to any man previously, and she was heartily sick of him. She had spent countless hours allowing his Chinese slave girls to bathe, perfume, and anoint her with oil. She had sat through countless sessions while they had experimented with various exotic makeups, and she had worn every conceivable mode of dress and undress. All of these things, and a great deal more, she had done in order to gratify the insatiable appetites of Dom Sebastian. She had given in to his sexual demands, becoming first aggressive and then passive, yielding and demanding, soft and strident. Never had she gone to such lengths to please any man, and she was not only tired of the Marquês de Braga but was actually somewhat tired of herself.

At least she had achieved what she had set out to accomplish, and she had three shipping contracts to show for her herculean efforts. She had sent them off this very day on a von Eberling ship that had put into Macao, and she hoped her employers were satisfied. She had done literally everything she could for them.

She didn't know it, but Braun was tired, too. Two weeks of unrelieved dissolute living had taken their toll, and he had to admit to himself that he was totally exhausted. The slave girls, he suspected, had deliberately tried his strength and had kept him performing for hours on end while secretly laughing at him.

"How much longer must we stay in this place?" he asked petulantly.

Erika knew how he felt, and reflected that he could not be nearly as eager as she was to put Macao behind her. "Our mission here is almost completed," she said. "We'll go on to Hong Kong as soon as we're able."

"If your business here is done," he told her, "we can leave at once."

The matter was not quite as simple as he assumed it to be, and Erika saw no need to explain to him that the Marquês de Braga was a petty tyrant who would not hesitate to break his contracts if she displeased him. She knew that he was becoming satiated with her, but only when he agreed to release her freely would she be able to leave Macao and go on to the British Crown Colony of Hong Kong.

Her deep sigh told Braun more than she realized, and again he studied her out of the corner of his eye.

Aware of his scrutiny, she spoke impulsively. "I have disliked many men in my lifetime," she said, "but never have I hated anyone as I loathe the Marquês de Braga."

She did not elaborate because she couldn't bring herself to admit to the countless deliberate humiliations she had subjected herself to in recent weeks. She was certain that Dom Manuel had been amusing himself at her expense, that he actually enjoyed degrading her, and for that she could never forgive him. Ordinarily, in such circumstances, she would have yearned for revenge, but she was so exhausted physically that her one desire was to leave Macao and never return. She suspected, however, that the Marquês de Braga still had other, more subtle plans for her, and that before he let her go, he intended to make further use of her specialized talents for his own benefit. Very well, if he did so, she would not object if the pay was more than adequate.

Surely he had learned by now that she attached an exorbitant price tag to her favors.

Braun stared idly at the sparkling blue green waters of the South China Sea, and taking a small poniard from a holster at his waist, he absently cleaned his fingernails with it. "If you wish," he said, "I can take care of de Braga in such a way that he'll never annoy you again. After all, I've had no opportunity in the months that we've been together to practice my art in my own way."

If Erika had learned anything since she had been in Macao she knew that the spies in the employ of the Marquês de Braga were everywhere, and that he reacted ruthlessly to the slightest sign of disloyalty. Not that she cared what became of Braun, but for her own safety she had to remain loyal to Dom Manuel as long as she remained in Macao, and she had to yield to his slightest wish.

"I don't doubt your courage, Reinhardt, but this is neither the time nor the place to demonstrate it. I would rejoice if the throat of the Marquês de Braga were cut from one ear to the other, but he who kills him cannot possibly escape unscathed, and will himself die a violent and horrible death. Take my word for what I tell you. I know what I'm talking about."

Braun regarded her closely and realized that she meant every word that she said to him. For whatever reasons, she was afraid of Dom Manuel. That was unfortunate, but the pragmatic German accepted the facts of life at face value.

"I suggest you set a date for our departure and that we keep it," he said, "and that way I won't be tempted to do anything rash."

"Believe me," Erika told him, "there's nothing in the world I want more than to leave Macao. We shall go as soon as it's humanly possible for me to make arrangements!"

The dreaded Plague of the Two-Headed Dragon struck Peking suddenly, without warning. As was to be expected, the disaster first showed itself one day in a working-class district, where seven persons died. All had displayed similar symptoms. Their skin had turned a dark, purplish color, and in their last moments they had gasped, trying in vain to draw air into their lungs. No one paid any heed to this unfortunate occurrence, but forty-eight hours later civil servants and eunuchs in the Imperial City were stricken, and within a twenty-four-hour period eight of them died. Then the plague spread to the Forbidden City, and the Tao Kuang Emperor did not hesitate; ordering vehicles for his entire family, he fled to the imperial palace in the former capital city of Nanking.

Most of his court became panicky and followed him there without delay.

Wu-ling, deeply disturbed, went to the office of Dr. Matthew Melton to discuss the tragic phenomena with him. "I think," she said, "that the Two-Headed Dragon who watches over the affairs of men is very offended and must be propitiated."

Matthew stared at her. "Surely you don't believe such superstitious rubbish," he said.

"I will grant you it is a superstition," she said. "Whether it is rubbish, remains to be seen. There is much in the East that can't be explained in Western terms."

"I'll grant you that much," he replied, "but Western medicine has learned a few things about plagues. Some are infectious and are given from one human being to another. In the worst plagues of Europe's Middle Ages, the carriers were fleas and made their homes on the bodies of rats. You can be quite sure that the present outbreak here is due to such ordinary causes."

"Is it true," the girl demanded, "that as the Princess An Mien tells me, you intend to remain in this city during the illness?"

"I'd be a craven fool if I left," Matthew replied quietly. "I have an opportunity here, at last, to make a contribution of significance to the medical profession in the Middle Kingdom, and I have no intention of budging. As a matter of fact, the princess has informed me that my stand on this subject has influenced a number of the court's physicians, especially the younger ones, and that they've stated rather defiantly that they're going to stay here as long as I stay. So I'm going to organize some medical teams who will go out into the city to do what they can to alleviate the suffering of those who contract this strange disease."

Wu-ling drew in her breath and stood erect; she was too proud to reveal her deep fear. "If the princess is staying in Peking and if you are staying in Peking, I, too, shall stay here."

He shook his head. "That's very courageous of you, I'm

379

sure, but you'll accomplish nothing by sitting out the plague here. Go to Nanking with the emperor, and you'll know you'll be safe there."

"It is my wish," Wu-ling said stubbornly, "to be of help to you. I will assist you in forming the medical teams that will go out into the city, and I will accompany you myself whenever you go abroad."

It annoyed him that she chose to be so stubborn. "I know the princess assigned you to assist me, but there's no need for you to stay," he told her.

"But you will not be able to speak the language without me to translate for you," she said.

Matthew grimaced. "I have gained a fairly good knowledge of Mandarin, and also of the local dialect. I can understand what's said to me, and I can make myself understood. That's all that matters."

Wu-ling smiled politely, then spoke to him in a Chinese dialect.

The thought flickered through Matthew's mind that she was deliberately speaking with great rapidity in order to confuse him. Whatever her motive, he could not make out a single word of what she said. "I beg your pardon," he said politely.

She laughed aloud. "I merely observed in the dialect of Peking," she said, "that a smattering of knowledge is insufficient in times such as these. When people are sick and dying and others around them grow panicky, one needs to be clearly understood, and no one has this need more than a physician."

He knew her well enough to realize that she would not be swayed, and he spread his hands in a gesture of defeat. "Very well," he said, "have it your way. But take the same precautions that I take. I insist on it."

"What are they?" she demanded.

"You will wear a cloth of fine linen over your nose and mouth at all times when you are in the company of other people, regardless of whether you are in the palace or in the streets of Peking, and you will bathe in water with much soap every morning and every evening."

Wu-ling looked at him as though he had gone mad.

"Those are my terms," he said. "Agree to them, and I'll agree to let you stay and help me. Refuse, and I'll ask the princess as a personal favor to send you without delay to Nanking."

Wu-ling tried in vain to recapture her dignity. "Very well," she said, "I'll do as you request, although your orders make no sense to me."

The following day, with her very considerable assistance, he met with a motley group that consisted of a dozen imperial physicians, several eunuchs from government offices, and three concubines who had inadvertently been left behind in the great exodus of the emperor and his subordinates. Matthew first illustrated the use of a square of linen, which he tied around his own face, and insisted that they do likewise. Then he made plain to them that it was mandatory that they bathe morning and night. "We don't know the cause of this plague," he said, "but it is best to take no needless risks. Therefore it is essential that we stay clean at all times."

The groups formed into teams and promptly spread out into the Imperial City and beyond it into the workers' quarters, with each assigned to a roughly defined sector. Matthew, accompanied only by Wu-ling, went into one of the poorest sections of the city, and there he went from hut to hut, halting whenever he encountered an inhabitant who had been felled by the plague.

The symptoms, he soon discovered, showed up early in the disease. Those who were stricken seemed to feel normal and well one moment, and suddenly they were running a very high fever that caused them great discomfort. Then the disease progressed swiftly, and within twelve to twenty-four hours they died, gasping for breath, with their skins blotchy and purple as life left their bodies.

Matthew had no medications and knew of none that would cure the disease or prevent its spread. Ultimately, he decided, he would do what he could with the victims, and he developed a technique of wrapping them in cold, sopping wet sheets. This at least brought down their fever.

He and Wu-ling worked until late that night, and after they

had visited countless dwellings over a sixteen-hour period, they finally dragged themselves back to the palace, so tired that they had no appetite for the meal that awaited them.

"I realize that you're ready to drop, as I am," Matthew told Wu-ling as they parted, "but I beg you, don't forget to bathe before you go to sleep, and do the same in the morning."

The following day they returned to the neighborhood they visited previously, and there Matthew was astonished to find that six or eight of the plague's victims whom he had wrapped in sheets were not only relieved of the fever but were completely recovered. Although weakened by their ordeal, they showed no ill effects from it. He immediately began to wrap all who were ill in wet sheets, and that night at the palace, he gave orders to the other physicians and their helpers to do the same.

"It's just possible," he told the Princess An Mien, who joined him and Wu-ling for supper, "that I've stumbled onto a cure, of sorts. Why wrapping a patient in cold sheets is effective is beyond me, but if it works, that's good enough, and I'm satisfied."

The princess nodded gravely. "This will be good news for my brother," she said. "He will tell you himself in two days."

Wu-ling concealed her reaction, but Matthew was openly surprised. "The emperor is coming back to Peking?"

The princess nodded abruptly. "Yes," she said. "He was shamed into returning. Because I stayed, he believed he had lost face by fleeing to Nanking, so he will come back." She smiled. "He made the return of all who accompanied him voluntary, so only a small number of them will come back with him, but at least he will satisfy himself that he is doing his duty."

"Let us make certain," Matthew told her, "that he wears a mask of linen on his face at all times, and that he bathes in soap and water morning and night. It is vitally important that the Celestial Emperor be spared the ravages of the plague."

By the following day, the routines that Matthew established

were being observed by all the physicians and their helpers who were striving to combat the disease. The many victims were promptly wrapped in sheets soaked in cold water, and at Matthew's request they were visited again the next day. About fifty percent who were treated in this way had recovered, and Matthew was vastly encouraged.

"I realize that people are still dying by the hundreds, perhaps by the thousands," he said to the Princess An Mien that night. "So there is little cause for rejoicing, but the treatment works in approximately half of the cases, and that's blame near miraculous."

"You have no idea why this treatment should be effective?" An Mien asked him.

He shrugged. "Your guess is as good as mine, Your Highness," he said. "I'll look into the matter in greater detail once we have time for such niceties."

On the following day, the crashing of cymbals and the pounding of scores of drums heralded the return of the Celestial Emperor to his capital.

The streets through which he rode were deserted, and no crowds gathered in the Imperial City or the Forbidden City to greet him. People seemed to know instinctively that their chances of contracting the plague would be much greater if they gathered in large numbers.

Matthew, aided by Wu-ling, continued to go from one hut to the next in a never-ending attempt to combat the dreaded ailment. The young woman was fearless in the face of the disease and, to Matthew's surprise, remained cheerful hour after hour, no matter how tired she became. They neither rested nor paused for food after they left the Forbidden City in the morning, and not until they returned long after dark did they manage to relax for a short time.

They were both so tired at the end of the very long, grueling day that they stumbled, and Matthew finally called a halt. They mounted the spirited ponies they had been provided and at last started off in the direction of the Forbidden City.

But a curious spectacle caught their attention. People—entire families pushing carts and carrying household goods and packages of all sizes and descriptions—filled the main thoroughfare leaving from the Forbidden and Imperial Cities through the working-class district to the open countryside. The road was blocked by a large contingent of imperial troops who obviously meant business as they threatened any civilian who approached closer to them with the double-edged swords and the bayonets attached to their ancient muskets.

Matthew wondered what this was all about. Wu-ling promised to find out, and went off at a canter to speak with a young officer who was directing some of the troops. Her conversation with him was brief, and her face was grave as she returned to Matthew's side and they went on together toward the Forbidden City. "When the Celestial Emperor returned today," she said in a troubled voice, "he issued an edict. All residents of Peking were ordered to remain at their homes in the city and were forbidden to leave it for the open countryside or for visits to relatives elsewhere in the Middle Kingdom."

Matthew was shocked, and because he was so tired he overreacted. "And he's using armed troops to enforce his edict and prevent citizens from leaving the city. That's damnable! I've never heard of such vicious treatment of decent people."

It was impossible for Wu-ling to defend the emperor, and they returned in silence to the palace. There a meal awaited them, and an insignificant-looking man in a dusty black gown and pearl cap shuffled into the room. The Celestial Emperor looked somewhat sheepish and, no doubt, was feeling ashamed of his hasty departure from Peking. Wu-ling looked intently at Matthew, warning him with a gaze not to mention the incident they had witnessed on their return to the palace.

But Matthew was too indignant and too tired to exercise caution. His simple meal of pork fried-rice and cold eggs with mushrooms in ginger forgotten, he obeyed only the convention of pretending that the Tao Kuang Emperor was not present. "I have rarely been so shocked or disappointed in all my life," he said, addressing only Wu-ling, "to discover that the Celestial Emperor has himself ordered the residents of Peking to remain in this city. This is a cruel and cowardly act. Surely he must realize that husbands are trying to protect their wives and children and that whole families grow panicky."

Wu-ling caught her breath and barely dared to exhale. The young physician from the West had dared to criticize the Celestial Emperor harshly and in no uncertain terms. Men were known to have been executed instantly for demonstrating such temerity. To her astonishment, however, the emperor sighed plaintively.

"Let him who thinks he can rule the people of the Middle Kingdom wisely and well in the emperor's stead wear the hat that is the badge of his office, and sit in his place on the dragon throne of his ancestors," he said. "Is it true, as we have heard, that the doctor from the West has found a cure for about half of those who are stricken with the Plague of the Two-Headed Dragon?"

"Yes, that's true," Matthew admitted, not seeing the connection.

"All the same," the Tao Kuang Emperor went on, "thousands of our citizens are dying."

"Unfortunately they are," Matthew said.

The emperor stood, clasped his hands behind his back, and stared with unseeing eyes out the window that overlooked the courtyard of his mammoth palace. "What would the learned physician do if he were in the emperor's place?" he asked softly. "Would he let the citizens of Peking scatter to the far corners of the Middle Kingdom? No man yet knows the cause of the plague. If the people of the city are allowed to scatter, the plague will spread throughout the land. Then millions will die rather than thousands. Is it not a wise and beneficent thing to curb the rights of the people of this city in order that millions upon millions of our subjects who live elsewhere in this land be spared the ravages of this plague?"

Matthew wondered why he had not seen and understood the point of the emperor's order immediately. "I was wrong," he said to Wu-ling. "I am not fit to wear the emperor's pearl hat or to sit on his throne. I have experience in the practice of medicine, but I know nothing of the rule of great numbers of people. It is not easy to govern a land as vast and as complex as the Middle Kingdom. That which has seemed cruel at first glance is actually compassionate. Those who are prevented from fleeing the city will not save themselves from the illness because they run away, but by being forced to remain here they will indeed prevent the spread of the plague to other places.''

The emperor seemed pleased that he had made his point, and nodding pleasantly, he took his leave.

Wu-ling exhaled tremulously. Matthew looked at her in surprise.

"Each day," she said, "you risk your own health and life as you try to save those who have the plague. Tonight, however, by criticizing the emperor, you took the greatest risk of all.''

Matthew shrugged. "I now understand the point of his issuing the order confining residents of Peking to the city," he said, "and I'm very grateful to him for explaining it to me. I see no reason for anyone to be executed.''

She shook her head in amusement and exasperation. "You still do not understand the Middle Kingdom or its people," she said. "You are fortunate that you have won the friendship and esteem of the emperor and the Princess An Mien.''

"I need an additional touch of good fortune," he replied, "in combating the plague, and I'm not going to stay awake now worrying about hurting the emperor's feelings. There's work to be done again tomorrow!''

The following morning, he and Wu-ling resumed their travels through the city and continued to fight the plague with all the weapons at their command. The struggle seemed endless. For hour after hour, day after day, they visited the stricken and did what they could to help them.

The imperial physicians kept records at Matthew's request, and the results appeared to be definite. About half of the stricken patients who were wrapped in cold, wet sheets recovered. Matthew still had no idea why this was so.

Gradually word of the effectiveness of this primitive cure spread through the city, and when someone became ill of the plague, his family immediately wrapped him in a cold, wet cloth. It was known by all in Peking that those who were treated in this manner had a fifty-percent chance of recovery; those who were not subjected to such a treatment inevitably died.

Occasionally Wu-ling picked up a rumor, which she repeated to Matthew. She heard one day that officials who had returned to Peking with the emperor were being honored, and were being given their posts for life. Those who had continued to absent themselves from the capital, however, were dismissed from their posts and were exiled from Peking for life.

Until such time as he heard an explanation from the Tao Kuang Emperor himself, however, Matthew refused to sit in judgment on these matters. He had learned his lesson, and he well knew that the rule of the vast Middle Kingdom was extraordinarily complex, that no inexperienced outsider could judge what was right and what was wrong.

The needs of the people were so great that Matthew and Wu-ling—along with the young imperial physicians and the volunteers who were assisting them—worked longer and longer hours until they stretched themselves to the limit. They rode out of the Forbidden City shortly before dawn every morning and, more often than not, didn't return to snatch a bite to eat and fall into their beds until eighteen to twenty hours later. The grind was unceasing, never ending. Gradually, as the ordeal of the plague continued for the people of Peking, Matthew gained a new sympathy and appreciation for these uncomplaining citizens of Cathay who formed the backbone of the nation. They endured hardships without number, and added to these burdens was that of the frightful illness that snuffed out lives so rapidly. But they remained cheerful in the face of adversity, and accepting death with a resignation that few Westerners could emulate, they worked when they could and, without exception, looked forward to the future. A people with these attributes were remarkable, and Matthew formed bonds with them that would last as long as he lived.

Gradually, the young physician from the West came to

387

realize that those who recovered from the plague were marvelously immune to it thereafter. He saw to it that the victims themselves realized it, and to his delight they responded as he had hoped they would by volunteering their own services to assist those who were currently stricken. Little by little, an entire corps of volunteer workers came into being and was enlarged.

Matthew was at best only partly conscious of this development. He was so busy and working so hard that he had lost all of his perspective.

So had Wu-ling. The slightly built young woman threw herself into her work with a fearlessness and a zeal that inspired awe, and she worked ceaselessly at Matthew's side, never drooping, never showing her exhaustion.

Unexpectedly, one of the Chinese physicians was stricken with the plague. The bulk of the people had come to regard the doctors who aided them as being almost godlike, impervious to the ravages of the ailment, and the fact that a physician had fallen ill of the dreaded disease caused a near-panic in the city. People were positive now there was no escape, and the military regiments on sentry duty were forced to call out reserves in attempts to prevent masses of citizens from rushing off beyond the town boundaries into the open countryside.

Matthew relentlessly grilled the physicians, eunuchs, and other volunteers who had been closest to the physician who succumbed to the plague, and from them he finally gleaned that the Chinese doctor had been careless in his use of face masks and had been negligent in following the morning-and-night bathing routine. The opportunity to drive home a lesson to his colleagues was too great to be missed, and Matthew made a point of stressing that baths and face masks were obligatory for all who fought the plague.

He was developing several theories regarding the causes of the ailment and its spread, and finally, although he could not prove it, he was convinced that the plague was transmitted by body lice.

The members of the corps of eunuchs courageously kept

figures as accurately as they could on the status of the disease, and Matthew subsequently used these statistics to write a monograph on the subject that he sent to an organization just being formed in Philadelphia. The American Medical Association. Several years were destined to pass until he learned that his monograph had been printed by the association and that it had won him a considerable measure of renown. He was one of the first to determine the causes of the plague, and his findings, combined with those of others, would result in the elimination of the plague in the course of coming decades.

For the moment, however, renown was the furthest thing from Matthew's mind.

Beyond all else, he yearned for a luxury he could not afford: sleep. Very late one night, he and Wu-ling returned to the imperial palace in the Forbidden City so exhausted they could scarcely shuffle, and they went directly to Wu-ling's apartment, where a hot meal, including noodles, bean curds, and a fiery soup, awaited them. They forced themselves to eat and, conversing little, busied themselves with their chopsticks. To their surprise, an assistant chief of the corps of eunuchs, a smooth-faced, badly overweight man who wore heavy spectacles, interrupted them.

Matthew couldn't keep his surprise to himself. "What are you doing being awake at this hour?" he demanded.

The eunuch bowed first to Matthew, then to Wu-ling. "I've had the honor of awaiting Your Excellency's return," he said. "I have wonderful news for you. The plague is abating."

Wu-ling smiled a trifle tremulously. Matthew, however, merely shook his head. "I've seen no evidence of that in our visits to the sick tonight, any more than I've seen it any previous night," he said flatly.

The eunuch persisted, however. "Our figures do not lie, Your Excellency," he insisted, and thrust a sheet of parchment across the table.

Matthew could not yet read much Chinese, so Wu-ling had to translate the document for him. Assuming the figures were right, the statistics were heartening: in the past week the disease had claimed only half the number of victims who had been stricken during any previous comparable period. "It may be," he admitted before he dragged himself off to his own apartment to take his obligatory bath before tumbling into bed for a brief rest, "it just may be that we're going to beat this thing."

His colleagues were encouraged, too, when he passed the word to them the following day, and to his surprise they cheered him. A spirit of comradeship had arisen during this crisis period, and now, for the first time, Matthew realized that all animosity had been drained from his relations with the younger Chinese physicians. His ways and theirs remained vastly different, but somehow they had gained a mutual understanding and respect as they fought the plague shoulder to shoulder.

The end of the infestation came so suddenly that no one knew what had happened until forty-eight hours had passed. The transformation took place shortly before sundown one afternoon when an unexpected storm howled across the vast Manchurian plains from the high mountains to the northeast. Snow fell steadily for about two hours, driven by blistering, ferocious winds. It was the winds that caused the greatest discomfort and were responsible for the sharp drop in temperature. One moment Peking was enjoying a typical crisp autumn afternoon, and in almost no time the temperature plunged far below freezing.

The storm caught the city unprepared, thanks in part to the plague and partly because cold had not been anticipated at this early a date. Most householders had not yet gathered the firewood that was so vitally essential to keeping their small homes warm and habitable. Even the cavernous imperial palace suffered, and the temperature was icy, so much so that when Matthew returned from his day's rounds late that night, he had to use all his willpower to force himself to take the bath he had prescribed as essential to all workers.

The next day he was surprised, as were his colleagues, to find that no new cases of the plague had developed. Not until yet another twenty-four hours passed, however, did it finally dawn on Matthew that the plague had finally come to an end. For the first time in more weeks than he could recall, he and Wu-ling, although they traveled indefatigably from house to house, found no new patients to attend.

Dazed by their good fortune, they returned to the Forbidden City. As luck would have it, other physicians had brought the good word ahead of them, so it was general knowledge that the plague had come to an end. The mood in the palace was wildly celebratory, and special dishes were prepared in honor of the occasion.

Matthew and Wu-ling dined on chrysanthemum soup, a dish made with chicken stock, slivered chicken meat, and petals from fresh, large white chrysanthemums. As was customary at meals of consequence in the nation's capital, they were served roast duck with oyster sauce, and quail that had been prepared with minced ginger root and minced, dried tangerine peel. There was far more food than they could possibly consume, including Mongolian lamb prepared with chili oil, and stir-fried pork, with asparagus that had been cooked in rice wine. They drank quantities of rice wine with their meal as well, the first time in weeks that they had touched an alcoholic beverage, and that was their undoing. The wine made them so sleepy they could scarcely hold up their heads, and sitting side by side on a divan in front of a low table in the living room of Wu-ling's suite, they could not resist the impulse to sleep. Neither recalled dropping off, and they slept soundly, so soundly that they failed to hear the palace servants come in and remove the platters and dishes.

When Matthew awakened, the first rays of dawn were slanting in through the window, and a charcoal fire was burning in a brazier a few feet away, taking the chill off the air. He had no idea where he was until, inexplicably, he found his arms folded around Wu-ling. She stirred in his embrace, opened her eyes, and made herself more comfortable before she dozed off again.

Matthew had no idea how she had happened to be in his arms and couldn't, for the moment at least, recall having dropped off to sleep in her apartment, but that didn't matter.

He knew that the plague had come to an end and that there was no need to haul himself awake and start making more of his interminable rounds. So his hold on Wu-ling tightened, and he, too, dropped off again.

It seemed only natural and right when they awakened, more or less simultaneously several hours later, to make love. In all the months they had been together they had never before engaged in any intimacies, but that did not matter. They had been spending so much time in each other's company that a bond had sprung up between them, and although they hadn't recognized it previously, they knew now that their embrace was normal and natural. They moved closer, and a sense of peace and propriety took hold of them as their lips met.

Then their lovemaking became more insistent. They both were highly aroused now, and they kissed passionately as their hands roamed and their bodies became entwined. In a miraculous fashion that neither could understand, much less describe, they had cast inhibitions aside. That which they were doing together was a part of their mutual regard, and it seemed to be completely right.

Neither was experienced, in the real meaning of the word. Wu-ling had never before taken a lover, and Matthew had known only a very few women, but they behaved together with abandon, at the same time not losing their natural dignity. Their passion mounted ever higher as they removed their clothing and ultimately became one. They found great gratification in their mutual release, and they sank back on the divan, completely satisfied.

It seemed only natural, too, that they should drift off to sleep again, and it was almost noon when they finally awakened.

They bathed together in a tub of hot water filled by a serving maid, and a servant hurried to another wing of the palace to obtain clean clothes for Matthew. Soon rested and refreshed, as they had not been in many weeks, the couple sat opposite each other at the low table. They were served with what Matthew decided was one of the great luxuries available to him in the Forbidden City, a Western breakfast of scrambled eggs, ham, and muffins. The palace cooks had tried infinite variations on the basic dish but finally had given in to his desire to have it served his way.

Wu-ling found nothing out of the ordinary with the meal, which was similar to innumerable breakfasts that she had eaten in America and England, and she demonstrated that she was ravenous.

He looked across the table at her and grinned. "Just for your information," he said, "I think you should know that I don't make it my practice to go to bed with my assistants. This is the first time in my life that I've ever had an assistant, and it's the first time that I've ever done anything like this."

"I shall have to keep watch on the people whose services you utilize as your helpers from now on," she replied with a smile.

He nodded solemnly. "That's a splendid idea. I might add, though, that you'll need a certain measure of authority if you're going to intervene. Without it, a new assistant of mine could simply tell you to go to the devil."

She appeared to be somewhat perplexed by his observation.

"It does constitute a problem," Matthew said, "but it isn't really insurmountable. The best way to get around it will be for you to marry me."

Comprehension dawned, and she suddenly became very shy, very reticent.

He appeared not to notice. "It's by far the best way to handle the problem, don't you agree?" he asked.

"I don't know," she murmured.

"Well, I'm so thoroughly convinced of it, I refuse to take no, or even maybe, for an answer. How does one go about being married here?"

Wu-ling giggled. "If we were ordinary citizens living in the city," she said, "we would go to a marriage broker, who would make all the arrangements for us. For people in our position, I honestly don't know. Perhaps we should go to a temple and ask one of the imperial priests, or we might get the necessary information from the corps of eunuchs. They know just about everything."

He reached across the table for her small hand. "One way or another," he assured her, "we'll manage."

The implications of his proposal and her acceptance sank in at last, and Wu-ling looked at him in something of a daze. She had been working so hard, under such great pressures, that she had taken their relationship for granted. Now, however, she was able to sort out her own thinking, and she couldn't quite believe what was happening. "Are you quite sure you wish to marry me?" she demanded.

"I'm as certain of it," he replied, "as I've ever been of anything in my entire life. What about you?"

"It feels so right and good and natural," she said, "that it must be the right thing to do."

They sat beaming at each other, and neither heard a tapping at the door until it was repeated.

Wu-ling roused herself and called, "Come in."

Princess An Mien entered the living room, followed by her brother, the Tao Kuang Emperor, who, as always, shuffled his feet as he walked and looked distracted.

Matthew rose to his feet instantly, and Wu-ling, following his example, had to fight a tendency to lower herself to the floor in a kowtow to the Celestial Emperor. Since he was making one of his "nonappearances," he had to be humored, and she ignored his presence.

An Mien beamed at the couple. "I've been waiting all morning to speak to you both," she said, "but you deserved your rest far more, so a visit from me could wait."

Obviously she knew they had spent the night together, and Matthew could feel color rising in his face. Wu-ling looked dreadfully embarrassed, too.

The princess laughed. "I have not questioned your morals, and I certainly don't question them now."

"We're going to be married, Your Highness," Wu-ling blurted. "We just decided five minutes ago that we would do it."

The princess looked pleased, and her brother nodded as he

rubbed his hands together and grinned. "That is good," the Tao Kuang Emperor declared heartily. "Now Melton Matthew will be certain to remain in the Middle Kingdom and practice his medicine here. I was afraid he would wish to return to his own home and stay there. He is free to go whenever he wishes, and to visit as long as he likes, of course, but he has no idea how relieved I am that he has ties that will keep him in Cathay."

Matthew responded vigorously, though he continued to observe the fiction that the emperor was not present. "It is my hope," he said, "to spend my entire career here. I will want to go home to America every five years, perhaps, to learn of new developments in medicine that have taken place during my absence, but I have learned during the terrible plague that my place is here, and even if Wu-ling were not to become my bride, I would not be satisfied to go elsewhere."

An Mien spoke gravely. "It was a wonderful day for Cathay when Rakehell Jonathan sent you to us. You have proved your worth a thousand times over, and your conduct during the plague has ended the resistance of your Chinese colleagues to your methods. From now on, I'm sure there will be a constant exchange of opinions and advice and information between you and them."

"I sincerely hope so," he said. "Illness knows no national boundaries and no color lines."

An Mien studied Wu-ling. "Has your betrothed given you a ring or a necklace as a token of his regard?"

The young woman shook her head.

Matthew cut in swiftly. "I proposed and was accepted so suddenly, Your Highness, that I've had no chance as yet to go to a jeweler and obtain a suitable bauble."

An Mien smiled and then swiftly removed from her finger a sapphire ring, the size of a large robin's egg, surrounded by diamonds. She dropped the ring lightly into Matthew's hand. "Perhaps this will make a visit to the court jeweler unnecessary," she said.

Wu-ling was so overcome that she could only gasp. Matthew lost his composure and stammered his thanks.

"Nonsense!" the princess said briskly. "You both deserve this ring and more—a great deal more."

The Tao Kuang Emperor cleared his throat, wandered to the windows, and stood there with his back to the others as he looked down into the courtyard. "It is not easy," he said, "to express to the doctor from the West the gratitude of all of the Middle Kingdom for what he has done. His courage was even greater than his skill, and he set an example that all physicians in the Middle Kingdom will find it difficult to follow."

Matthew was embarrassed by the praise and was uncertain how to respond.

But the Tao Kuang Emperor gave him no opportunity. "If he were one of my subjects," he said, sounding slightly plaintive, "I would have no problem at all. I could award him the Order of the Chrysanthemum, second class, the highest decoration that may be given to a civilian under the law, and that would take care of that. But there is no provision under the law for making such an award to a foreigner. I had my law counselor look in the books written by the great mandarins of the law, and his reply was very plain. I am not allowed to hold a ceremony in which I make such an award to one who is not a subject, who refuses to kowtow to me because he regards it as a matter of principle, and whose skin is a different color than the skins of my people."

He made the problem sound very difficult and very complex. But An Mien was in no way perturbed and nodded encouragingly as she looked first at Matthew and then at Wu-ling. The emperor, his face still concealed, spoke more cheerfully. "But I am allowed to do what I wish when I wish it because there is no one in the realm who can raise a hand to me and say, 'You shall not do this, and you shall not do that.' " He turned slowly and beamed at Matthew.

There was no question that the American was now being addressed directly by the highest authority in Cathay.

The emperor fumbled in the pocket of his long shapeless robe and looked stricken. His sister remained calm, however. "You put it into your right-hand pocket, Kuang," she told him. "I took particular note of that fact."

The emperor plunged his free hand into his right pocket, and a look of great relief spread across his face. "If you kowtowed to me," he said to Matthew, speaking with the utmost severity, "you would have made my task much easier and would have saved me a great deal of bother. On the other hand, I wouldn't have had the respect that I now feel for you as a man of principle, so I suppose it's just as well that you're stubborn." He removed an object from his pocket, breathed on it absently, and shined it on the dusty cotton of his robe.

Wu-ling had to struggle hard to curb an insane desire to giggle aloud. The Celestial Emperor looped a gold chain around Matthew's neck and then took a single step backward and studied the American in satisfaction. Matthew was stunned. Reposing on his chest was a sunburst of yellow diamonds fashioned to represent a chrysanthemum. The petals were represented by perfectly formed yellow diamonds and in the center was a huge, clear diamond of perfect color and formation. He reflected dizzily that this decoration of the Order of the Chrysanthemum had to be equal to at least ten to twenty years' pay. Never could he afford such gems, just as he could never afford the ring that Princess An Mien had presented to Wu-ling.

"You're now a full-fledged member of the Order of the Chrysanthemum," the emperor said. "All sentries in the army and navy will salute you wherever you may go, and you will be entertained on the highest level. You are now a member of the elite in the Middle Kingdom."

"That is certainly true," added the Princess An Mien. "Of all the millions of people in this land, there are no more than twenty-five who have been awarded the Order of the Chrysanthemum, second class. You are now in very special company."

"I don't quite know what to say," Matthew replied, "except that I don't really feel that I deserve such an honor."

"Nonsense," the Tao Kuang Emperor told him. "I'm making it plain to my entire court that, hereafter, I am regarding you as my exclusive, personal physician. I will expect you to attend me whenever I feel poorly. You'll have to come to my quarters in private, of course, since your refusal to kowtow could set an unfortunate precedent for my own subjects.'' The Tao Kuang Emperor paused for a moment, looked at his sister, and then continued. ''Now to another matter. I can only tell you what I tell my own children when they are adults and take husbands and wives. Those who marry should live under their own roof.''

The princess nodded heartily.

Matthew was nonplussed. ''But how would it be possible for us to—''

The Celestial Emperor gestured impatiently for silence. ''We will arrange that you are given one of the private domiciles in the Forbidden City to use as your own. You and Wu-ling are our principal links to the outer world, and nothing is too good for you!''

The young couple lived in a daze in the weeks that followed. Wu-ling had neglected her translations when she had been helping Matthew combat the plague, and had to make up for lost time. As for her betrothed, he had to go over the reports on the plague accumulated by the corps of eunuchs, and then write his own monograph for the American Medical Association, tasks that took up time. His popularity at the court was vastly improved, too, and a steady stream of patients visited him from early morning until he closed his office at sundown. At his own insistence, he also took the time to travel into the city itself, to help the sick there.

So neither he nor Wu-ling had time to make adequate preparations for their new life after they were married. Since the house into which they were moving was not only handsome but was completely furnished, there was nothing that they needed. At the insistence of An Mien, imperial dressmakers made a dozen new gowns for the bride, and as a wedding present An Mien insisted that they spend their ten-day honeymoon at the so-called Summer Palace outside Peking. This magnificent edifice, sitting beside an artificial lake, was little used by the Tao Kuang Emperor, who found it too confining for his personal tastes, so the princess sent a full staff of servants to take care of the honeymoon couple, and they were to be driven out in an imperial carriage immediately following the ceremony.

The wedding was held in a pagoda directly adjacent to the imperial palace in the Forbidden City, the ceremony was conducted by a high priest on the staff of the emperor himself, and the smell of incense mingled with the odors of fresh-cut flowers, artfully arranged in the vases placed in the temple earlier in the day. The simple structure was filled to capacity because the bride and groom were known to be imperial favorites. Most of the guests were the younger imperial physicians and members of the corps of eunuchs who had worked side by side with Matthew and Wu-ling to fight the ravages of the plague. Only a moment before the ceremony began, a side door slid open part of the way, and a couple slipped unobtrusively into the temple and stood partly hidden by banks of flowers.

Everyone in the edifice recognized the Princess An Mien, who made no attempt to disguise herself, but no one dared to stare too hard at the man who stood behind her. Familiar with his ways, the members of the court knew all too well that the Tao Kuang Emperor had chosen to honor the bride and groom with his unofficial appearance, and they dutifully pretended not to see him.

The bride, as was customary, wore a gown of flaming red silk. Matthew was the only person present in Western attire, and he was amused to discover that he actually felt slightly out of place as a result. The ceremony was brief, simple, and to the point: the couple were married in the sight of their ancestors, who were asked to watch over them and guide them through the many pitfalls of marriage. Wu-ling already wore the magnificent ring that An Mien had given her, and Matthew vowed, when they made their first visit to America, to present her with another ring that was equally precious, the thin gold wedding band that had been his mother's. Only Westerners wore such a symbolic ring, which was unknown in the Middle Kingdom, but he knew Wu-ling would wear it proudly when her bridegroom placed it on her finger.

The bridal couple did not exchange a kiss in public, but after the ceremony they adjourned immediately to a reception hall in the palace, where *dim sum* were served, along with vast quantities of rice wine. The couple accepted the good wishes of more friends than either knew they had made at the imperial court, and at last they went out to the exceptionally handsome but uncomfortable imperial carriage that awaited them. The coach was pulled by a matched team of four strong horses, and as the coach itself, completely lacking springs or padded seats, bounced on the hard, rutted roads of the city, the bridal couple clung to each other and to the straps on the sides of the carriage provided for the purpose. At last they came to the extensive grounds of the palace, surrounded by a high wall, and the sentries on duty there saluted smartly the instant they saw Matthew's Order of the Chrysanthemum on his chest. They rode past formal gardens and came at last to the entrance, where a majordomo and at least fifty staff members greeted them.

Although the New Englander had been living in the shadow of royalty ever since he had arrived in China, he was unaccustomed to such opulence. Wu-ling, remembering her impoverished childhood in Canton, was equally overwhelmed.

They stood together, somewhat stunned by the obsequiousness of the servants who bowed low to them. Then Matthew managed to put the experience into its proper perspective. Although he was halfway around the world from his own people and customs, he was married to the woman he loved, and that was what mattered. For the next ten days they had no reason to think of anything but each other. He had no patients to see; she had no books or articles to translate.

Matthew turned to her with a grin and said quietly, "There's one custom of my country that I insist we observe." Giving her no chance to protest, he picked her up and carried her into the palace. The servants, shocked by the Westerner's boldness, tittered nervously, but Wu-ling accepted the gesture in the spirit that Matthew meant it. Their faces were close together, and before either of them quite realized it, their lips met in a prolonged kiss as he carried her into the exquisitely furnished imperial living room.

There, propped against a Ming vase, was a large square of parchment bearing the imperial seal. Wu-ling glanced at the calligraphy on the outside and was surprised. "It's addressed to us," she said, and when Matthew set her on her feet, she hurriedly retrieved the parchment and opened it. She glanced through it rapidly, and then read it slowly a second time, smiling to herself as she savored every word.

Matthew exercised great patience and waited until she was ready to reveal the contents to him.

"This," she said, "is written in the Princess An Mien's own hand. She and her brother wish us long lives and great prosperity. In order to insure our future, they have made a gift to us of a house on the grounds of the imperial palace in the Forbidden City. Furthermore, they are going to construct a hospital-clinic directly behind the house, according to your specifications. The architects have already been told to take their instructions from you, and will await our return to Peking for that purpose."

Matthew was stunned; the news was almost too good to be true. His future and that of Western medicine were guaranteed now in the Middle Kingdom. The mere presence of a hospital and clinic so close to the imperial palace was a way of making certain that the high officials of the realm cooperated in every way with the foreign doctor.

"I think I'm dreaming," Matthew murmured, and reached for his bride. Then, as they kissed and embraced, he added blissfully, "Now I know I am dreaming."

# II

The residents of Macao, most of them Chinese, with a substantial minority of Portuguese, poured into the amphitheater located on the grounds of the governor's palace, soon filling it to capacity. They were in a festive mood and were looking forward to being entertained.

Erika von Klausner sat in the governor-general's private box on the ground level and felt ill at ease. She was conspicuous in a daring, figure-molding gown of yellow silk, and the mere fact that she occupied the box told everyone who saw her that she was intimate with the Marquês de Braga. She disliked such advertising, which she ordinarily shunned, much preferring to operate quietly behind the scenes.

But Dom Manuel had insisted that she attend this function, since, by mutual consent, this was her last day in Macao. This occasion, which he had not bothered to explain to her, was in honor of her, a little parting token of his esteem for her.

So far he had signed still one more commercial contract with the von Eberling shipping company, and what she had been forced to do to get those precious words on paper made her shudder. She had subjected herself to his most warped desires, and she had never yearned so fervently for normal relations with a normal man. Well, she had come to this ceremony, or whatever it was, at his specific request, but this was her final gesture to please him. She had obtained everything from the Marquês de Braga that could be expected, and she was scheduled to leave Macao later today on board a junk that flew the Portuguese flag.

Beside her, stolid and unmoving, his face masklike, Reinhardt Braun sat inconspicuously awaiting the entertainment. He was obviously less patient than Erika, and one foot tapped incessantly on the pebbled flooring of the amphitheater.

"Why was it so important that we come here?" he muttered.

Erika shrugged prettily. "All I know is that it's some kind of a farewell celebration." She was about to say more, but broke off when Dom Manuel arrived at the amphitheater, escorted by about fifty troops of his household guards.

The crowd fell respectfully silent as he was escorted to his box. There he smiled broadly at the young German woman, and inclined his head a fraction of an inch in a curt nod to Braun as he took his seat.

"Today," he said, "in honor of your imminent leave-taking, you are going to witness the administration of Eastern-style Portuguese justice. Recently a plot against my government and against my own person was discovered. A trial was held at which I acted as the principal judge, and thirty plotters were condemned to death." He stood and raised a hand in a signal.

The crowd stirred as thirty men, some of them Portuguese, some Chinese, all naked to the waist and barefoot, were led into the amphitheater, their ankles shackled, and their hands manacled behind their backs. The men were connected by a long rope looped around the neck of each, and as the crowd watched, they were taken to small tablelike contraptions and were made to kneel beside them, placing their heads on the tops of the tables.

Erika sensed an electricity in the atmosphere.

Chuckling quietly to himself, his eyes gleaming, Dom Manuel signaled again. The huge throng fell silent.

The silence was shattered by a primitive, trumpetlike call.

Erika and Braun appeared to be the only people in the amphitheater who were surprised, and stared in openmouthed wonder as a huge elephant was escorted into a center arena by his keeper, who was armed with a short, sharp prod. The great beast was visibly agitated: his trunk swayed, he shuffled his enormous feet, and the small eyes that peered out at the crowd seemed to glitter. An officer of the household guard appeared at the far end of the arena, and making certain that he kept a considerable distance between the elephant and himself, he read the charges against the defendants. All had been found guilty of treason and had been sentenced to death. The governor-general, in his infinite mercy, the officer declared, had determined that Siroso would be the executioner.

Erika gleaned that the elephant was Siroso, and she was horrified. Her blood ran cold, and she caught her breath as the elephant trumpeted and then raised a front foot and brought it down on the head of the first of the guilty men. The victim's skull was smashed, and blood spurted onto the ground.

Erika felt sick to her stomach, though Reinhardt Braun watched the spectacle closely, his eyes narrowed as he nodded in slow approval. The executions demonstrated imagination, and manifestly were much to his liking.

Siroso disposed of a second traitor, then of a third. The bloodthirsty citizens who had taken advantage of the governor-general's generosity to share in watching the grisly spectacle cheered wildly.

Erika could tolerate no more. Afraid that she would become sick, she rose to her feet. "I'm leaving now," she said. "Good-bye, Your Excellency."

The Marquês de Braga feigned surprise. "You don't care for the little entertainment being held in your honor, my dear?" he inquired softly.

"I think it's disgusting," Erika replied, and fled from the amphitheater.

The floating, mocking laughter of Dom Manuel followed her as she rushed into the palace to collect her belongings and leave by carriage for the waterfront. Erika had never felt such loathing for any individual, and she was glad she was putting Dom Manuel and Macao behind her. She had done her duty here, and had obtained four reasonably good contracts for the von Eberling company, so her employers could find no fault with her. But she was determined not to return to Macao if it could be avoided.

Braun, however, was still impressed by what he had seen. "The Marquês de Braga is a man with an inventive mind and a lively imagination," he said. "I like him."

Erika shuddered and refrained from commenting.

The junk on which she sailed reached Hong Kong in a half-day, and Erika went straight to the office of Rakehell and Boynton, where she presented to Molinda a letter of introduction that Jonathan had given her when she had left New London. The two women chatted for a time, and Molinda shrewdly took note that the young German baroness had already visited Djakarta and Macao. It was clear that she was not traveling through the Far East for pleasure.

Lo Fang, who remained unobtrusively in the background, did not take his eyes off the woman or Braun.

Molinda made it clear to the new arrivals that although there were now two hotels for transient guests in Hong Kong, no lady of substance could stay at either of them because she would be inviting advances from countless men in a community where ladies were a rare commodity. Extending herself, Molinda revealed that she knew of a house, recently built for an English couple whose arrival had been delayed. With her help, Erika was able to rent the place, and there would be quarters for her companion, Braun, as well.

The introduction of Erika von Klausner into Hong Kong society was accomplished with ease, and her presence in the town created an immediate sensation.

Erika made it her business to charm Lord Williamson, paying special attention to his wife, and the approval of the governor-general and his lady opened every door to her. Molinda had remained firm in her refusal to resume her relationship with Sir Cedric Poole, so he was free to devote himself to Erika, and he escorted her everywhere. The colonel commanding the regiment of Royal Army troops stationed in the Crown Colony, and the commodore in command of the Royal Navy stationed there, both of them bachelors, immediately vied for her attention, and so did a number of representatives of commercial enterprises, including bachelors and married men whose families had remained behind in England.

Molinda was an interested bystander and watched Erika's success complacently. She was herself too beautiful and had won too many social triumphs to feel jealous of the newcomer, and she was absorbed by the drama she saw unfolding. What she could not figure out was why the baroness from Hamburg, a great, natural beauty, had elected to travel so far from home to the Orient. There had to be some reason that had been responsible for her long journey.

Although Molinda did not consider Lo Fang a social arbiter, she nevertheless regarded him as a sound judge of character, so she was curious regarding his reaction to the German woman. One evening, when Molinda had returned home from work and was spending an hour in her cool garden, she sat on a stone bench and beckoned Lo Fang to come closer. Her bodyguard had been carefully keeping watch over her from a short distance away, and now at her summons, he moved slowly toward her.

"I've just been thinking," she said, "about the Baroness von Klausner. She's certainly become vastly popular in Hong Kong."

Lo Fang smiled. "It is always this way in any place where a woman who is judged to be attractive suddenly appears. In the palace of the viceroy at Canton there was much preening among the men of high rank when a pretty girl came to visit the viceroy. All thought she was his niece, but when it was revealed that she was a concubine, the atmosphere changed very quickly."

Molinda laughed. "Are you suggesting, by any chance, that there is a relationship between Erika von Klausner and a concubine?"

The majordomo's face remained wooden. "In the Middle Kingdom," he said, "a woman wears clothes that show her body and she flirts openly with all men only when she is a concubine or a prostitute."

"That is so in the West, too, or so I understand," Molinda said. "I find it difficult to evaluate the baroness. Not that I have anything against her, you understand. On the contrary, she was introduced to me by Jonathan, whose judgment I trust in all things, and she has been very pleasant to me in every respect since our first meeting."

"She has good reason to be pleasant to you," Lo Fang said delicately. "You have done her many favors. You found a house for her; you launched her in the society of this place by introducing her to people of substance. She is in your debt."

Molinda shrugged. "At best, it's a very minor debt, then. I was wondering what you think of her, and unless I'm mistaken, you have none too good an opinion of the lady."

Lo Fang answered in a voice as expressionless as his face. "Does the lady Molinda know the fable of the great cave birds of Honan?" he asked guilelessly.

She shook her head.

"Once," he said, "long ago when the Middle Kingdom was very young, there lived in Honan Province a proud father who had four beautiful daughters. The father was poor, but the daughters were his legacy, and he knew that wealthy men would pay him large sums to take them as wives or concubines. He lived only for the day when they would be taken from him and he would be given vast sums of gold in return.

"But it so happens that there lived in Honan also a great bird who was larger than the largest house in the town, larger even than the great pagoda in which the people worshiped. The bird lived in a hidden cave in the mountains and came out only at night, because he knew that people would be too frightened of his size and his ferocious appearance if they saw him. He was very lonely, and one night when he was flying over the house of the poor father, he saw the four daughters and fell in love with them.

"So, beginning the following night, he returned every night for four nights in a row, and each night he picked up one of the daughters and carried her off to his cave. The father knew that his daughters had been kidnapped, and he aroused the whole town. The countryside was scoured, but none thought to look in the great caves in the mountains, so the secret of the bird was safe, and he kept the daughters captive, living happily with them for many years." He paused and smiled significantly.

Molinda knew that such stories always had an emphatic point. "What is the moral of this tale?" she wanted to know.

"If the father had kept his eyes open instead of having them blinded by greed, he would have found his daughters and could have rescued them. There are none so blind as those who close their eyes to reality and truth."

"Is that what I've done?" she asked with a half-smile.

Lo Fang did not reply directly. "Lady Molinda," he said, "has been watching the progress of the red-haired visitor. Has she also taken note of him who is the companion of the baroness?"

Molinda remembered meeting Reinhardt Braun and seeing him on occasion, but she had not paid too much attention to the man and was surprised that anyone should regard him as significant. "I believe," she said, "he serves her as a majordomo."

"No," Lo Fang replied with great dignity, "he lacks the broad knowledge necessary for such a post. His function is to guard the red-haired lady when she appears in public without a social escort. When she has such an escort, the man Braun does not stand guard over her."

Whatever the point he was trying to establish, he had not yet made it. "Go on," Molinda prompted.

"Braun always is heavily armed," Lo Fang declared. "He owns several pistols of varying calibers, and he has a large collection of knives. There are always two or three on his person when he goes out in public."

Molinda nodded.

"While the red-haired lady has been entertained by the colonel of the regiment and the commodore of the fleet and by Sir Cedric Poole," Lo Fang said, "the man Braun has not been idle. He has sought his own entertainment, and he found his level in the Tavern of the Seven Seas."

Her interest immediately sharpened. The tavern was a

waterfront establishment in the harbor district frequented by ships' officers and by the owners of the various Hong Kong warehouses. While ostensibly a reputable place, catering to the higher class of seafaring men, the owners had, in fact, acquired a highly questionable reputation in a short time. There were rumors to the effect that anyone wanting to smuggle contraband in or out of Hong Kong could make the necessary arrangements at the Seven Seas, and other equally unsavory deals could be set up there. Such talk, as Molinda well knew, was hearsay, and no hard evidence was available. Nevertheless, the fact that the man who had come to the Royal Crown Colony with Erika von Klausner frequented the Seven Seas was of considerable interest. She did not look like the kind of woman who would lend herself to chicanery.

"Braun goes to this place every evening while the woman is busy with her social life," he said. "He talks with some of the more disreputable characters there, and I think he is just looking for trouble."

Molinda stared at her majordomo, her eyes narrowing and her mouth setting in a straight, firm line. She didn't know why the baroness would associate herself with such an unsavory little man.

Lo Fang seemed to read her mind. "There is no need for the lady Molinda to worry," he said. "Everywhere that the man Braun goes, he is watched, and a full report is given to me. Everything the red-haired woman does is also watched and reported. We will make certain they are always on their very best behavior."

It was a regular event at the Southwark shipyard of Rakehell and Boynton, but that in no way detracted from the drama. A clipper was setting sail for a long voyage to the Middle Kingdom, and a crowd collected at the dockyard to watch her make the initial run of her journey under the tutelage of a River Thames pilot. There was excitement in the air, as always, because there was the opportunity on every voyage that the speed record for such journeys would be shattered.

As it happened, speed was far from the minds of those who

were making the voyage. Charles Boynton was burdened by the heavy responsibilities that he carried, and he thought of his final conversation with his father, who he hoped would be well enough to carry on in London without him. Somehow, Charles knew, a new, vital source of income had to be found in the near future.

His wife, Ruth, certainly was not thinking in terms of speed records, either. Filled with excitement because she was making her first trip to the Orient, she knew that she, at last, was being given the opportunity to experience a rare adventure. She would share in the world that Charles relished, the world in which David had been born, and she was grateful for the opportunity. Surely this journey could only solidify her marriage.

David Boynton was too excited to think clearly. He knew that after he reached Djakarta he would be reunited with his cousin Julian. In addition, his father had promised him that further lessons in navigation and seamanship would begin tomorrow, the second day of the voyage. Papa would take charge of his lessons and would act as his tutor himself for a time, and then David would be turned over to the bosun for further instruction. The day was not too far distant, the little boy thought, when he would stand on his own quarterdeck and command his own ship.

Standing on the dock, holding her husband's arm and waving to the trio on the deck with her free hand, Jessica Boynton spoke wistfully. "You'd think after all the sailings I've attended that I'd begin to regard them as routine," she said. "But they're not. Every one is individual, and this one is special."

Sir Alan looked pale and haggard in the watery, early winter sunlight. "How so?" he demanded.

His wife's tone was gently chiding. "The next two generations are on board that clipper," she said. "Our hopes for the entire future are riding with them as they sail to the East."

Elizabeth Boynton visited the Rakehells in New London for ten days before sailing with Jonathan and his children for the

411

Far East on board the *Lai-tse lu*. Everything augured well for the momentous voyage. Kai, who was accompanying the family, had firm though unexpressed ideas of his own regarding Jonathan's future, and it was plain that he heartily approved of the tall, blond young lady who would be making the journey with them. Certainly it did no harm that Jeremiah and Missy Sarah, particularly the latter, also approved of her. Kai could tell it in the way they treated her, and although Elizabeth did not know it, he had already vowed to keep watch over her once they reached the Far East.

She was badly—if temporarily—thrown when she discovered that the master of the ship would be Josiah Dowling. She had been intimate with him only months earlier, but to her infinite relief he appeared to be a total stranger now. That was partly due to his own sense of restraint: Josiah noted that she was traveling with Jonathan Rakehell, the active head of the shipping company, and he needed no instructions to guide him. He was polite and respectful to her, as she was to him, and that was the extent of their involvement.

When sailing time came, Kai went on board first, taking Harmony with him, and the chow dog responded to the solemnity of the occasion by walking up the gangplank with great dignity and not breaking into a run when he reached the open deck. He was, as several of the seamen later commented, a true shipowner's dog.

While Jonathan engaged in a last-minute conversation with his father and brother-in-law, Elizabeth and the children said good-bye to Missy Sarah. "Behave yourselves in the Middle Kingdom," she said. "Remember your manners and all you've been taught. Speak only in the Mandarin dialect in the presence of your equals and better, and never, never pile too much food on your chopsticks."

"Yes, Grandma," Julian and Jade replied in chorus. They knew Missy Sarah had lived in Cathay for many years, and consequently they were in awe of her.

The woman turned to Elizabeth. "Good luck," she said. "I wish you all that you wish yourself."

The young woman flushed faintly. "I've learned," she

said, "that people gain what they deserve in this world. I just hope that I will be able to earn the right to the happiness that I seek."

The Ellison family stood nearby, bidding farewell to young Brad, who looked smart in his uniform of an officer-in-training, and his mother, being a Rakehell, blinked back the tears that came to her eyes when she realized that she would not see the boy again for approximately one year. "I'll keep an eye on him for you," Elizabeth said to Judith.

The boy's mother nodded. "Thank you, my dear; I'm sure you will." Elizabeth had certainly changed in recent years, Judith thought, growing from an insecure adolescent, overly conscious of her own beauty, into a totally reliable, mature young woman. Knowing nothing of the abortion and other distressing experiences responsible for Elizabeth's maturation, Judith could only appreciate the person she had become.

Josiah Dowling signaled discreetly to Jonathan from the quarterdeck. Jonathan knew that this meant the tide would assist the sailing if he moved promptly, so he saw to it that the rest of the party went on board. "Brad," he said, "get to your duty post. You, too, Julian," he added to his son, who would come under the care of Oliver, the *Lai-tse lu*'s boatswain, as soon as he stepped on board. Both boys scurried off and boarded the ship. Jade was angry because she was not allowed to accompany her brother and cousin, and Elizabeth promptly distracted and comforted her by picking her up and carrying her onto the ship, speaking to her in an undertone all the while.

The Stars and Stripes were run up to the masthead, and so was the Rakehell and Boynton Tree of Life banner, which rested just below the American flag. The boatswain shouted orders, and the great clipper began to move downstream. Seamen appeared in the lines, as great clouds of canvas were slowly unfurled, and by the time the *Lai-tse lu* reached the entrance to Long Island Sound, she was already under full sail, skimming majestically through the waves and behaving like the great lady she was.

"No voyage on board a clipper ship is ever inconsequential,'' Jonathan told Elizabeth at dinner in the ship's saloon that evening, and she soon understood the significance of his words.

Certainly there was a difference in the spirit of the ship's crew with Jonathan, rather than Charles, occupying the owner's cabin. Commands were given and obeyed sharply, and Elizabeth had the feeling that every officer, every crewman was doing his utmost to create a good impression on Jonathan, a master seaman.

Somewhat to Elizabeth's surprise, the time passed quickly. For Jade's sake, she accompanied the little girl to daily seamanship and navigation lessons given to all the youngsters by Jonathan, and she was privately impressed by the depth of his knowledge and the clarity of his teaching. He not only told them what to do but explained in infinite detail why they were doing it.

She also spent time with the cook in his galley each day, and once the man learned that she wasn't interfering but was trying to be helpful, he began to confide in her. Elizabeth had her own lifetime of experience on board ships behind her, and had learned a great deal about the preparation of meals. That fact soon became evident: the quality of the meals served, although previously adequate, improved sharply, and even Captain Dowling was moved to comment on the dramatic improvement.

Life on shipboard was confining for an animal, but Harmony did not suffer, thanks to the care exercised on his behalf by Elizabeth. She romped with him on deck every morning and again in the afternoons, with Jade usually helping her. For a time Elizabeth was fearful that, in her excitement, Jade might fall overboard, but she soon learned that Harmony kept an ever-watchful eye on the little girl and was determined to let no harm befall her. Therefore, Elizabeth was able to relax, and she enjoyed the outings tremendously. She often spent an hour or more reading in the late afternoons and was prepared to read again after dinner at night. But Jonathan soon developed the habit of relaxing and chatting with her over coffee and the pencil-thin West Indian *cigarros* that he favored. These times

414

of day became precious to Elizabeth, and she enjoyed a camaraderie and intimacy with Jonathan that had existed previously only in her imagination.

For reasons that he himself did not understand, he was able to relax with her now, and felt completely at home in her company. He talked to her at length about the subject that was foremost in his mind, the financial difficulties of Rakehell and Boynton, and his conviction that if a way out of them could be found, the company would be saved in the long run by placing a greater reliance on clipper ships and by a heavier reliance on large, long-range steamships.

Although Elizabeth had often heard Charles and Papa discussing business at length at home, she gained for the first time a true understanding of the problems that Rakehell and Boynton faced.

She also was able to hold up her end of the conversations, Jonathan was surprised to discover. She had been shaped by Jessica Rakehell Boynton most of her life, and the effects of that training showed. Her questions were sharp and to the point, and the opinions she expressed were sound. Jonathan made mental notes of several of her thoughts, including a new way to pack cargo that promised to save space.

Oddly, Jonathan did not think of Elizabeth as beautiful. Although he failed to recognize the reasons for it, he took her appearance for granted, having seen her develop all through childhood into womanhood. Then, suddenly, his attitude changed. They stood together on the aft deck one afternoon when a stiff breeze was blowing, sending the young woman's hair streaming behind her and pressing her clothes close to her body. Jonathan observed that several seamen who were aloft in the rigging were eyeing Elizabeth, and that the second mate, who had the watch, a rather dashing young bachelor, kept his eyes riveted on her.

A spasm of totally unexpected jealousy racked him, and he examined his companion intently, seeing her as an adult woman for the first time. She was lovely, he had to admit, and he wondered how he could have been so blind for all these years.

Little by little the rapport between the couple grew. As Elizabeth lost her self-consciousness in Jonathan's presence, she abandoned all flirtatious games and behaved with complete naturalness in his company. This enabled her charms to shine, and the attraction that he felt became still stronger.

Jonathan found a great deal in Elizabeth to admire. Certainly her attitudes toward the sea and sun were heartening. Most ladies avoided sunlight like the plague, and appeared on deck wearing broad-brimmed hats and shawls that completely covered their shoulders and chests and arms. Elizabeth, however, did not care, and absorbed sun readily, her skin tanning and emphasizing her blond hair all the more.

No part of life on board ship was alien to her. One day, after Julian had completed his daily duties, she was fishing with the children off the fantail rail, when a strong tug at Julian's line told the boy that he had a major strike. He could not hold his pole himself, so strong was the tug, so Elizabeth grasped it and helped him, hauling in the line little by little. At last, she caught a glimpse of the fish at the other end of the line.

"Good heavens! I believe you've hooked a shark, Julian!"

"Really?" The boy became wildly excited.

"It's just a baby shark, from the looks of him, but it's a shark nevertheless."

"Should I fetch Kai—or Papa?"

Elizabeth shook her head. "I think we can manage ourselves without either of them," she replied. Jade, who was watching the struggle between the woman and the fish with fascination, shouted her approval of Elizabeth's decision. For the next half-hour or longer, Elizabeth fought the fish, giving the young shark yards of line and then hauling it in again. She repeated this process so often that she lost count of the number of times. Her arms ached, and she thought they would drop out of their sockets. Her back was sore, too, but she refused to admit defeat and continued to fight grimly. At last, she appeared to win the battle, and she began to pull in the line hand over hand.

Harmony began to bark furiously. Jade jumped up and

down in excitement, and Julian manfully helped manage the line as the young shark was brought onto the open deck. Elizabeth stared in fascination at the ugly creature, which was about four feet long but was fully developed, with a powerful jaw and a full set of razor-sharp teeth.

All at once an Indonesian knife landed in the shark's head, followed by a second and then a third, and the beast went limp. Jonathan hurriedly joined Elizabeth and his children, uncertain whether to laugh or to become very angry. "I can't believe you landed this creature all by yourself!" he exclaimed as he removed the throwing knives and, wiping them on a cloth, returned them to his belt.

"Julian helped," Elizabeth replied uncertainly, proud of her achievement yet somehow feeling uneasy.

"Obviously," Jonathan said, glowering first at her, then at his son, "neither of you had the good sense to know that a live shark is a danger to man. Had you gone near him, either of you, you could have lost an arm or a leg."

Julian tried to control a gasp but failed.

"I'm so sorry," Elizabeth said miserably. "I honestly didn't know, or I wouldn't have subjected the children to possible danger."

"Or yourself, either, I sincerely hope," Jonathan said, and grinned. "Well, there's no harm done, really. I was watching your struggle with the fish from a distance, and I was as proud as you were when you landed him. I intervened only when it became necessary."

"I thank you for that," Elizabeth said primly.

Tears came to Jade's eyes. "There, there, dear," Elizabeth said. "No harm's been done, you know." She picked up the child and hugged her.

Jonathan grinned at her approvingly. He ruffled Julian's hair and kissed Jade soothingly and then, somewhat to his own amazement, found himself kissing Elizabeth, too.

But what was intended as a light gesture of affection didn't turn out that way. His lips met hers and lingered there, and he was badly shaken when he drew back. He noted that Elizabeth also appeared to be upset.

He wanted to apologize to her, but a sixth sense told him that would be making an even worse mistake. So he changed the subject instead. "I wonder if the chef knows how to cook a shark?" he asked.

Elizabeth recovered her aplomb. "If not, I daresay I can advise him. I know Mama's simple recipe for preparing shark meat, and the results are delicious. As for the fins, however, I realize they're considered something of a delicacy in the Middle Kingdom, but I am afraid that Kai will have to instruct us in their preparation. I haven't the least idea of whether they're to be boiled or fried or roasted."

That night they ate shark steaks for dinner in the saloon, and as Elizabeth had predicted, the food was indeed delicious. The taste of the meat was all the sweeter when she realized that she had caught the shark herself.

As the *Lai-tse lu* sailed serenely through the West Indian Ocean, putting into St. Croix and Guadeloupe and Curaçao for various supplies of fruit, vegetables, and water, the weather grew very warm. Elizabeth did not seem to mind the heat, however, and appeared in sleeveless dresses with her hair tied in a ribbon. She looked again like the young girl she had been.

The winds died away when they reached the doldrums, and Captain Dowling announced that they were becalmed. Elizabeth accepted the news serenely.

"You don't appear to be troubled by our predicament," Jonathan remarked to her at supper that night.

"I'm not in the least upset," she replied. "Why should I be? This is your ship, and with your experience, I know that we'll be just fine."

The following morning a breeze appeared out of nowhere and saw them safely across the equator.

They put into Rio de Janeiro, intending to go ashore for twenty-four hours, but the local customs authorities advised them against it. An insurrection was in progress.

Julian and Jade, who had been looking forward to an outing, were bitterly disappointed, and Jonathan was afraid that there would be a storm of tears. But Elizabeth spoke

418

quietly to the children at length, and before their astonished father could believe his eyes, they were laughing and playing with Harmony on deck, their shore excursion completely forgotten. Elizabeth, he reflected, was a woman of rare talents.

Ultimately they came to the Strait of Magellan, a scenic waterway about three hundred and thirty miles long and varying in width from two and a half to fifteen miles. This channel separated South America from Tierra del Fuego and a number of smaller islands south of the continent of South America. It enabled a ship to pass between the Atlantic and Pacific oceans, and was particularly difficult to navigate because the waters at either end were agitated by almost never-ending storms. Such a storm lashed the *Lai-tse lu* as she approached the Strait off the uninhabited shores at the southern tip of Argentina, and for a time it appeared that the clipper would have to put into a sheltered harbor and wait for the gale to subside. It was not uncommon for a vessel to be forced to wait a full month or even longer before passing through the Strait.

On this occasion, however, the gale let up somewhat in intensity, and when Captain Dowling said that he felt certain that he could navigate safely, Jonathan told him to go ahead. The clipper edged out of the harbor in which she had been resting, her sail reduced, and it felt as though all hell had broken loose. Winds shrieked through her rigging, and she pitched and rocked simultaneously in what the seamen of later generations would come to call "a corkscrew motion." Every timber in the *Lai-tse lu* seemed to groan in protest, and to the amateur it felt as though the sturdily built ship would surely fall apart.

Jade had been in a number of storms in her young life, although she didn't remember them any too clearly. On this occasion, though, she became terrified. Her father was standing on the quarterdeck beside Josiah Dowling, making himself available for any counsel that the captain wanted, or that he himself deemed necessary to give. He heard the wailing of his daughter above the storm and peered through the rain and the saltwater spray that was cast up on deck by the cutting of the ship through violent waves.

Jade stood outside a hatch, clutching Elizabeth's hand and looking forlorn. There was nothing that Jonathan could do to mollify or quiet the frightened child.

There was nothing that he had to do, as he quickly learned. Elizabeth scooped up the little girl into her arms and spoke softly, earnestly, her lips only an inch or two from the child's ear. Gradually Jade became calm again and, to her father's astonishment, actually enjoyed the storm. He long remembered Elizabeth and his daughter, their arms around each other, laughing merrily as the clipper fought the gale.

Then, Jade's fear having been conquered, Elizabeth wisely took her below again, and the hatch covering was closed after they disappeared below deck.

Jonathan had to put the scene out of his mind in order to concentrate on the maneuvering of the *Lai-tse lu* as she made her way into the Strait of Magellan and crawled slowly westward through a dense fog.

Only later, after reaching the Pacific, where the storm finally abated, was he able to dwell again in his mind on the scene he had witnessed. He knew that Jade would never again be afraid of inclement weather on board a sailing ship.

That night when he and Elizabeth were alone in the saloon after dinner, he tried to thank her for her efforts on the little girl's behalf.

A mischievous expression appeared in Elizabeth's blue eyes. "Please don't thank me," she said. "Actually I'm quite indebted to Jade, you know."

"You are?" he asked, falling into the trap.

"Of course," she said with a laugh. "I was frightened half to death myself, and the only way I could grow calmer was by telling Jade that there was nothing in the world to fear. I talked her into believing me, and talked myself into it, too."

It was after the clipper reached the Pacific and headed for the Sandwich Islands for her one stop before going on to Hong Kong that the truth of Jonathan's relation with Elizabeth finally dawned on him. First he knew that he had to control

420

himself and curb a desire to kiss her. Then he realized that he wanted her. This was the first time since Lai-tse lu had died that he had wanted a woman for more than physical reasons. He had wanted Molinda, just as he had subsequently wanted Erika von Klausner, but he hadn't gone beyond the physical in his yearnings. Now, however, there was far more involved. He felt a strong urge to protect and shield Elizabeth, and feelings of great tenderness for her sometimes threatened to overwhelm him. He exercised rigid self-discipline, and only his remarkable self-control prevented him from revealing the way that he felt and making advances to her.

Their union, he told himself repeatedly, would be all wrong, a dreadful mistake. Elizabeth was scarcely into her twenties, on the threshold of adult life and experience. It would be a mistake to saddle her with a widower in his mid-thirties, with a son almost ten years old and a daughter approaching six. He could not, in good conscience, ask Elizabeth to accept such burdens or to sacrifice herself for him. If he was in love with her, and he was uncertain whether his feelings ran that deep, he could not permit her to ruin the rest of her days for his sake. In the meantime, to be sure, there was no escape for him. The *Lai-tse lu* was a tiny dot in the vast Pacific Ocean, and they were thrown into each other's company day and night—every day and every night. Jonathan had no idea where the drama would end, but he felt deep misgivings over the future.

He would have been startled had he become privy to Elizabeth's thoughts. She watched his growing involvement with her and was elated beyond measure. In all the years she had loved him, she now dared to hope that her dreams would come true.

The clipper carrying Charles Boynton and his family put into Bombay and into Columbo, Ceylon, for trade purposes, and at Charles's instigation took on a load of tea when they reached Calcutta.

"I see no reason why we shouldn't turn a profit on this voyage," he told Ruth.

They sailed on to the Dutch East Indies and put into Djakarta, which was recovering from a monsoon. Trees had been uprooted, and whole houses had been leveled. Ruth, accompanying her husband and child in the carriage that took them out to the Fat Dutchman's estate, marveled that any storm could be so powerful. The cities and nations of the East, she thought, seemed much closer to nature and the elements than did the cities and towns of America.

Nothing that Charles had told her prepared her for her first sight of the Fat Dutchman, sitting in his oversized wicker chair, surrounded by a dozen of his half-naked slave girls. Ruth felt very far from her upbringing in puritanical New England, and farther still from the rigidly observed proprieties of life in Belgravia. She tried not to show her feelings as, clutching David's hand, she walked beside Charles and felt the Dutchman's cold, pale eyes examining her with great care. She was aware, too, that his girls, most of them dark-skinned and bare-breasted, were examining her with great curiosity. They were neither being hostile nor insolent, however; she realized that she was one of the few white women that they had ever seen, so they were curious about her. The Dutchman boomed a welcome and extended a hand to Charles without rising from his chair.

Concealing his nervousness, Charles presented the Dutchman to his wife.

Acting on sudden impulse, Ruth leaned forward and planted a firm kiss on the Dutchman's fat cheek. The gesture was unpremeditated, and was an indication of the way she felt at that moment.

The Dutchman looked at her searchingly. "My dear Mrs. Boynton," he said, "I shall remember your greeting as long as I live. Heh-heh."

She wondered if the husky note that crept into his voice was sincere.

Then he reached for David, whom he hauled onto his lap and hugged. "You've grown since the last time I've seen you, son," he boomed. "How is your aim?"

"I think it's fairly good, sir," David replied with quiet confidence.

"Oh, we shall soon see." The Dutchman gestured, and one of his grinning security guards came forward, removing a throwing knife from his belt and handing it to the boy. The Dutchman pointed toward the trunk of a royal palm.

In order to hit it, David would be obliged to come close to several of the girls who were lolling on the ground nearby, and Ruth wanted to call a halt to the proceedings.

Charles divined her intention and shook his head, his expression indicating that the boy could take care of himself.

Ruth did not share her husband's feeling of certainty. David, after all, was not yet nine years of age, and it was a mistake, she thought, to ask too much of him. On this occasion, however, she felt compelled to defer to his father. It wouldn't do to make a scene in front of someone as important to them as the Dutchman so soon after meeting him.

David fingered the long bone-handled knife, then he gestured in the direction of the trunk of the royal palm. The little boy carefully measured his distance from the target.

Several of the girls giggled in nervousness and embarrassment. Paying no attention to them, and, indeed, eliminating everyone present from his consciousness, David concentrated on the immediate task awaiting him. Then, his face set in unusually stern lines, he let fly with the knife. Several of the guards who were watching nodded in surprised pleasure. The child was throwing the knife in the approved manner, placing his right foot forward as he released the blade, stiff-armed, with his right hand.

The knife penetrated deeply into the trunk of the palm tree. Some of the girls began to applaud.

Charles silenced them with a curt gesture, which his son was quick to imitate. Then David further delighted the guards by addressing them in their own tongue, using some of the words his father had taught him. "If you please," he asked, "may I have the use of several more knives?"

They complied with his request immediately and handed him a half-dozen of the throwing knives.

He placed them on the ground beside him and then picked them up one by one and threw them at the target. Every blade, without exception, landed in the trunk of the tree.

This time Charles and a vastly relieved, proud Ruth joined in the applause. The Fat Dutchman's florid moon-shaped face was wreathed in a broad smile. "You throw very well, boy," he said. "I shall give you a set of knives for your very own."

The boy was ecstatic.

"Provided, to be sure," the Dutchman continued, "that your mother approves."

Ruth was enormously grateful to him for granting her the privilege of exerting maternal authority. "David has worked diligently," she said, "and he deserves the prize you have offered him, sir. Indeed I do approve."

The little boy hurried to her side and hugged her.

A young woman served refreshments, and Ruth happily accepted a tall, frosted glass that contained bits of exotic, tropical fruits and fruit juices. The mixture was delicious, and she couldn't recall enjoying a cold drink so much.

But one of the girls seated near her leaned toward her and murmured in broken English. "You be careful," she half whispered, "plenty-much liquor in drink."

Ruth had been unaware that the beverage contained any alcohol whatsoever, and now she consumed it warily and slowly.

The Dutchman and Charles were already launched into a complex, intricate discussion of business matters, and her mind wandering, Ruth surreptitiously examined the young women who made up such a major portion of the Dutchman's "court." All were young, in their late teens or early twenties, and all undeniably had beautiful faces and exciting bodies. Some were Chinese, others were Javanese, and still others, as she would learn later, were pure Malaysians. There were also two girls taller than the rest who appeared at first glance to be white but on closer examination had somewhat Oriental features. All were completely lacking in self-consciousness and were in no way embarrassed by the exposure of their nude breasts and, when they sat, their long legs.

It dawned on Ruth slowly that these young women were present for the pleasure of those with whom the Dutchman did business. There was an air of complacency about them, of quiet, cheerful acceptance of their lot in life.

Ultimately the party adjourned to the dining room, where Ruth had her initial experience with *rijsttafel*. The number of dishes and the bewildering variety of foods that were served were little short of astonishing. She counted seventy-five dishes before she abandoned her enumeration, and she guessed that there had to be a total of one hundred to one hundred and fifty dishes that were served. Occasionally she recognized various meats, fish, and vegetables, but many of the dishes contained highly spiced combinations of foods that left her wondering what she was eating. No matter; the meal was delicious.

She continued to observe the young women, and what struck her most forcefully about them was the impersonal pleasantness they demonstrated toward Charles. Gradually the realization dawned on Ruth that when her husband had been unfaithful to her, he had engaged in affairs with girls such as these, in the employ of the Fat Dutchman.

It was small wonder that these relationships had meant so little to him and had left him emotionally untouched. He had commented to her, she remembered, that such an affair was like eating a large and satisfying dinner. She hadn't been able to grasp his meaning at the time, but now, suddenly, the whole picture jelled and came together for her.

She had been wrong, perhaps, to place as much emphasis as she had on his affairs. They truly had meant little to him, and she knew she had erred when she had given them more significance than was their due.

Something in the Dutchman's tone of voice brought Ruth back to the present conversation he was holding with Charles.

"I can well understand your need for more and more cash, Charles," he said. "You and Jonathan embark on a very broad and daring expansionist program."

"Well," Charles replied modestly, "we do aim rather high. We realize we'll never be as large or as influential as

425

the British East India Company, but if our plans work out, we won't be too far behind them."

"I approve of your aims and your methods as well," the Dutchman said heartily.

"That's quite heartening," Charles replied, and his wife thought she detected a hint of wariness or caution in his tone.

"You know, of course, that you can always come to me for any financial assistance you may need," the Dutchman declared.

Ruth felt greatly relieved but was puzzled that her husband didn't seem particularly pleased by the offer. In fact, his expression remained unchanged.

"That's kind of you," he said, "and both Jonnie and I appreciate it greatly, as I'm sure you know, but we prefer to do our own financing wherever possible. That's been a family tradition for a long time."

The Dutchman seemed unconcerned by the rejection of his offer. "I understand perfectly," he declared, "and I admire your motives and sympathize with them. You might just tuck one thought away in the backs of your minds. If you should decide anywhere along the way that you want or need outside help, feel free to come to me whenever you wish. I would very much enjoy becoming a limited partner in Rakehell and Boynton."

"I shall certainly keep it in mind," Charles told him, and then concentrated his full attention on the box of *cigarros* offered to him by one of the Dutchman's young women.

After the meal ended, it was customary for everyone to take an afternoon nap, and one of the girls conducted Charles, Ruth, and David to their suite. There the little boy was sent to rest on his bed, and husband and wife were able to converse once they were alone.

"This place and its people are utterly fascinating," Ruth said. "It's like a storybook suddenly coming alive."

"The Dutchman is a very complicated character, as well as an enormously wealthy and powerful man," Charles replied. "You heard him offering to put money into the company in order to ease our financial burden?"

"I certainly did," she replied. "But you didn't seem particularly pleased by his offer."

Charles smiled ruefully. "I anticipated it—and at the same time dreaded it. The Dutchman is no altruist, you know. Let him get his fat hands on Rakehell and Boynton, and he'll soon become a major stockholder and principal partner in the company. Jonnie and I would have to be utterly desperate before we'd even consider his offer."

"I see," Ruth said, and was silent for a time. "I begin to grasp now what you once told me about the East. Nothing is what it appears to be, is what you told me, and you're right. There are so many subtle layers of understanding to everything."

Charles nodded. "That's perspicacious of you, Ruth," he said. "There are people who never grasp that truth about the Orient, and are incapable of doing business here. The values aren't the same as those we use as weights and measures at home."

Ruth took a deep breath. "For the first time in the years that have passed since I learned of your infidelity to me," she said, "I can understand it. I thought you were speaking pure gibberish when you told me that your passing affairs had no connection with me or your love for me. Now, seeing the young women in this place, it's easy to imagine one of them having been sent to accompany you after finishing a meal. I can see at last how intimacy with one of them could be no more significant than eating that delicious dessert of coconut and banana and goodness only knows what other fruits."

Charles grinned at her. "You're generous to me, Ruth," he said.. "Far more so than I deserve. I could have shown self-discipline and abstained when the Dutchman offered me one of his women. As I've told you, I was weak." He took a deep breath and regarded her soberly. "It takes some men a very long time to grow up," he said, "and I appear to be one of them. I'd like to tell you something that I have no way to prove; you will simply have to take my word for it. If I were making this trip without you, the Dutchman would have offered me a woman as a matter of course. Believe this or not as you see fit, but I would have turned him down."

She was surprised but saw no reason to doubt his word.

"I've learned my lesson," he said. "I'm conscious of my marriage vows, and I'm determined not to transgress again."

Tears came to her eyes, and she was incapable of speaking.

"Here, now," Charles said brusquely, "the weather is too hot to weep." He went to her and kissed her gently.

Ruth clung to him. "I shall remember this place," she said. "I shall remember it always."

The growth of Hong Kong was phenomenal, Jonathan thought, as he inspected the city through his glass from the quarterdeck of his clipper as the great ship made her way slowly through the harbor crowded with other clippers, windjammers, junks, and sampans.

He would not have recognized the capital city of Victoria, where there were countless new homes, warehouses, and public buildings. Kowloon, too, had been transformed, and although there was more room for expansion there than on the island, the Chinese who resided there in large numbers followed their usual custom of crowding their dwellings together. He gazed at the sampans and junks, looked at the crowded streets, and suddenly was glad that he had come home. The Orient truly was home to him, and not only because the final resting place of Lai-tse lu was here; it was the place where he belonged, even more than his native New London. As the ship edged toward the quays owned by Rakehell and Boynton, where two other clippers already were berthed, he was joined by Elizabeth, Kai, and the increasingly excited children.

"I'm not going to touch a knife or a fork or a spoon here," Julian said. "I'm only going to use my chopsticks."

"Me, too," Jade added fiercely, "and I'm going to speak only in Chinese. Do I use Mandarin or Cantonese dialect, Kai?" she asked, having forgotten Missy Sarah's injunction about the use of languages.

Kai shrugged apologetically. "Hong Kong," he said, "looks as though it has been here for many years, but it is a new city and I don't know what dialect the Chinese residents speak."

Jonathan grinned. "Since you're far more familiar with Cantonese than you are with Mandarin, I suggest that you speak it and perfect your Mandarin before you try it. I think you'll find that most people will understand you once they have overcome the shock of hearing you speaking their language in the first place. Ah," he added, "there's Molinda."

Elizabeth politely asked to borrow his glass. "She's standing alone on the dock," he said. "The lady with long blue-black hair who is wearing a gown of pale gray silk."

Elizabeth inspected the Balinese woman carefully. "She's much younger than I expected," she said, "and far prettier."

"Yes," he agreed complacently. "She is young, and a great beauty as well. But she's extraordinarily competent, and we're very fortunate to have her in our employ."

Elizabeth lowered the glass and glanced at him obliquely. A sixth sense told her that Jonathan had engaged in an affair with Molinda at some time in the past. But scrutinizing him closely, she hastily concluded that the Balinese girl was no rival for his affections. Whatever their intimacies, they belonged to the past, not the present. She took care, all the same, to check her own hair, cosmetics, and dress in her cabin mirror before reappearing on deck to go ashore.

Lo Fang stood behind Molinda when the travelers came ashore, and the children hurled themselves first at Molinda and then at him. Harmony demonstrated his own favoritism by racing straight to Lo Fang and wagging his tail furiously. Molinda disentangled herself sufficiently from Julian and Jade to greet Jonathan cordially and then extended her hand, Western-fashion, to Elizabeth.

Silently, the two young women took each other's measure, and each liked what she saw in the other.

"Charles and his family will be arriving from Djakarta in the next two days," Molinda told Jonathan. "His meetings with the Dutchman have gone well."

"Has the Dutchman bought us out yet?" Jonathan asked with a slightly harsh laugh.

"No," Molinda answered smiling, "but it's no thanks to

him that he hasn't. He's very anxious to obtain an interest in the company."

"That's precisely what I predicted to you in my last letter before I left New England," he said.

Jonathan quickly toured the Rakehell and Boynton offices and warehouses, which had more than trebled in space since he had last visited Hong Kong, and then the entire party traveled by carriage to Molinda's house on the Peak. The dwelling actually was the property of the company, so, rightly speaking, it belonged to Jonathan. He immediately became aware of a space problem. "I don't think there's room for all of us here," he said.

"Oh, but there is," Molinda replied. "If Elizabeth doesn't mind sharing my bedroom with me."

"Of course I don't mind," Elizabeth replied promptly, "and it's very generous of you."

"There, that settles it," Molinda replied briskly. "There's a bedroom for you, Jonathan, and another for the children, and Kai can move into Lo Fang's quarters."

"That's all very well," Jonathan said, "but what do we do when Charles and his family arrive?"

"Oh, dear," Molinda replied.

"Do I gather that the hotels of Hong Kong are still unsuitable for ladies?"

Molinda nodded. "Under no circumstances could any lady be asked to stay in one of them."

"In that case," Jonathan said, "either the *Lai-tse lu* or the clipper that's bringing the Boyntons here will have to be used as hotel space for a time."

Molinda frowned. "That won't be any too easy," she said. "We're going to be getting rid of cargoes and taking on completely new cargoes, and the ships will be beehives of activity. They certainly won't be very attractive living quarters."

"I see." Jonathan as usual thought swiftly, in practical terms. "In that case," he said, "I think we'll ask Ruth and Elizabeth to go on with the children to Canton, under Kai's guidance, of course, and with a number of additional guards to make certain they're secure."

"What is in Canton?" Elizabeth wanted to know.

"That is my real home, my first home in the Middle Kingdom," Jonathan told her. "The old Soong Chao estate has been maintained just as it was when he and Lai-tse lu were still alive and Missy Sarah kept house for them. Their graves are there now, and we've expanded the offices substantially."

Molinda nodded. "That's right," she said, "we've four or five permanent employees stationed there, but there's ample room for everyone—far more room than you'll find here. One of the handicaps of Hong Kong is that it's so dreadfully crowded."

"Charles and I will join you in Canton ultimately," Jonathan told Elizabeth, "and I imagine Molinda will come with us. In that way we can continue our business discussions there as easily as we can hold them here."

That night, at Molinda's table, Elizabeth ate her first truly Chinese meal. The dinner featured chicken which had been boiled and then smoked and then was served with green onion, ginger root, anise, cinnamon, and soy sauce, and was combined with a mixture of brown sugar, rice, and black tea leaves. There was another main dish, barbequed pork served with a sweet lobster sauce and a sour oyster sauce. Among the more exotic side dishes were steamed spare ribs with fermented bean cake, and duckling baked in peppercorns, as well as stir-fried fish fillet with broccoli, and steamed fish poached in rice wine and peanut oil.

Everyone else at the table used chopsticks, so Elizabeth insisted on employing them as well. To the surprise of Jonathan and Molinda and to the delight of the children, she handled them with ease. She refrained from telling them that she had practiced from time to time with ivory chopsticks that Charles had brought home to England. That was her own business, and it was enough that Jonathan was impressed with her prowess.

The following morning she accompanied Jonathan and Molinda on a detailed tour of the Rakehell and Boynton warehouses, and she marveled at the exotic silks, the exquisite porcelains, and the many varieties of tea that awaited export to the United States and Great Britain. She had been on the fringes of the business all her life, but for the first time she was beginning to realize the extent of the Rakehell and Boynton operation.

Later in the day the clipper from Djakarta put into port, having made unexpectedly good time on its voyage, so the Rakehells and Boyntons were reunited. David, of course, was as pleased to see Julian and Jade as they were delighted to welcome him.

Rather than provide temporary quarters on board a ship for the newcomers, it was decided that Ruth and Elizabeth, accompanied by the children, Kai, and several other guards supplied by Lo Fang, would leave on the midnight tide for Canton. They enjoyed a reunion dinner at Molinda's house, and then the women departed on board the Siamese junk that was the most luxurious of the firm's coastal vessels.

The sailing was so late that the children went to sleep immediately, and Ruth and Elizabeth were left on deck, where they conversed quietly, aware of the stars that filled the sky overhead.

"I'm so glad for you," Elizabeth said, leaning against the rail. "You and Charles look so happy together."

"Does it show as plainly as all that?" Ruth demanded with a self-conscious laugh.

"As plainly as all that," Elizabeth replied, also laughing, and hugged her.

Ruth eyed her carefully. "How are things going with Jonathan?"

"I'm making considerable progress, thanks," Elizabeth said politely. "I won't say that he's falling all over me as yet, but he's certainly become very much aware of me as a woman, and I think that in time I'll be obliged to show great surprise when he proposes to me."

Ruth laughed.

"But I don't want to sound smug," Elizabeth added hastily. "I won't believe really that he's truly interested in me until he actually does propose." She was silent for a few moments. "Do you suppose it's safe to leave him with Molinda? She's enormously attractive."

"Yes, she is," Ruth replied, "but she has her own understanding with Jonnie and with Charles, too. I've made it an inviolable rule never to interfere in business relationships, and I think you'd be very wise to do the same."

Elizabeth nodded, realizing the advice was sound. She would be wise if she allowed nature to take its own course. She had no way of knowing, however, that the course of nature was about to be interrupted.

The arrival of Jonathan Rakehell and Charles Boynton in Hong Kong became common knowledge in the community within twenty-four hours, and it was inevitable that Erika von Klausner should hear the news. Elizabeth, who had successfully put Erika out of her mind, would have been sorely distressed to know that her old school chum had long been awaiting this day and was wasting no time. Erika immediately sent Jonathan a note, inviting him to dine that evening at her house. The note was delivered to him at the Rakehell and Boynton office while he, Molinda, and Charles were making a close scrutiny of the financial aspects of their Far Eastern business. He opened the communication, breaking the seal, and was more than pleased by the contents. The thought of seeing this stunning redhead again filled him with delightful anticipation, and he said, "If you two don't mind, I'll be busy for supper this evening." He handed them the note.

Charles read it and chuckled indulgently. Molinda, however, chose to regard the situation far more seriously. "We have reason to believe," she said, "that the intentions of the Baroness von Klausner are questionable." She went on to explain what Lo Fang had learned about Braun's association with unsavory characters. "We don't yet know what the baroness herself is up to, but at the very least she may be a fortune hunter."

"Then she's doing her hunting in the wrong place, to be sure," Jonathan replied with a grin. "As the three of us know only too well, I have almost no cash to spare."

"We know the facts of the matter," Molinda said stubbornly,

"but Erika von Klausner does not. If I were you, I'd beware of her, Jonnie."

He refused to take the warning seriously. "Don't tell me you believe the old Chinese myth about fire-eating female dragons?" he said.

"I'm not so certain," Molinda replied, "that the dragons of today necessarily eat fire. They disguise themselves as human beings now, and they're doubly dangerous as a result."

The smile faded from Charles's face. "You'd be wise to listen to Molinda, Jonathan. She has a far greater knowledge than either of us in matters of this sort, and besides, I trust her feminine instincts."

"With all due respect, Molinda," Jonathan said, "I'm not decrying your instincts, nor am I placing too little value on your opinions, but I believe I'm fairly well acquainted with Erika, and I don't see her as being dangerous to me in any way."

"That is because you're shortsighted and see only what you want to see," Molinda replied, refusing to yield ground to him. "Have you stopped to ask yourself why a baroness would travel halfway around the world from her own home and take up residence in a city like this? You'll be interested to learn that she obtained some contracts from the Dutchman in Djakarta and others from that loathsome Marquês de Braga in Macao. They're not major contracts, but they do give von Eberling a firm foothold in the Far Eastern trade."

"Ah," Jonathan said, brightening, "so she works for von Eberling. That's interesting." He thought for a moment or two and then shook his head. "I cannot for the life of me envision von Eberling as a serious competitor of Rakehell and Boynton in the Eastern markets," he said. "We're able to muster a dozen clippers and another dozen of the older, more standard ships here. I very much doubt if von Eberling could get together more than three or four very small vessels, so more power to Erika, and if she's conniving, let her do her damndest, I say." He removed his watch from the fob pocket of his waistcoat pocket. "We've done about all the business we can accomplish for today," he said, "so if you'll excuse me I'll leave now for my dinner engagement."

Molinda frowned as he left the office, and Charles seemed somewhat perturbed, too. "Do you really think that Erika is all that dangerous?" he wanted to know.

"Indeed she is," Molinda replied vehemently. "Largely because Jonnie is so vulnerable. He's lonelier than he realizes, and any attractive woman can snare him if she sets her mind to it."

Jonathan felt no misgivings as he rode a horse from the company stable to Erika's rented house on the Peak. She was an exceptionally attractive young woman, and he was flattered by her interest in him. It was that simple a situation, he told himself, and he reflected that Molinda might be motivated by a sense of personal jealousy. It was difficult to know such things about women.

Erika came to the front door herself in response to his summons, having seen him approach up the road. She feigned surprise, which changed quickly to delight, and with seeming impulsiveness, she embraced and kissed him, then quickly disengaged herself and stood back. "Oh, dear," she said, "now you'll think me forward. I shouldn't have given in to my impulse."

"I'm very glad you did," he told her, and there was substance as well as gallantry behind his words.

Erika had applied her makeup with consummate artistry, and wore a deceptively simple gown of black satin that revealed every curve and every line of her voluptuous body. All her experience, all the skill she had acquired had been a preparation for this meeting, and she did not waste a moment of her time, a breath, or a gesture. Flirting expertly as she prepared him a drink of Scotch whisky, she chatted about her experiences in the East. Knowing that he would learn that she represented von Eberling, she made a virtue of necessity and revealed that fact to him herself, telling him her impressions of the Fat Dutchman, whom she claimed she liked, and of the Marquês de Braga, for whom she made no secret of her dislike.

Jonathan, conscious of her beauty and of his own desire for her, was dazzled by her. It was difficult for him to think clearly when he was being subjected to such a concentrated barrage of subtle and seductive flattery, and the women who had made a play for him in the past, had they seen him now, would have realized their mistake. Erika's pursuit was relentless, ruthless, and she did not grant him a moment's respite. After he had consumed two substantial drinks of whisky, she conducted him to the table, and there she plied him with fresh beefsteak and a number of fresh vegetables, knowing that such a menu would be especially appealing to a man who had spent the past three months at sea.

Jonathan appeared to be putty in her hands.

Erika went too far, however, in her eagerness to persuade him to propose marriage to her. After dinner, as they returned to her living room for coffee and liqueurs, she contrived to stand very close to him, her body barely grazing his as she looked up at him. She was so close to him that he could feel her breath on his cheek.

Almost any man would have succumbed without a further struggle to someone as lovely and as appealing as Erika. But Jonathan Rakehell was no ordinary mortal. He had accomplished great things in the shipping industry because he was endowed with iron self-discipline, with a self-control that few others could match. He was on the verge of yielding to his desire for the beautiful red-haired woman, but a voice of caution whispered to him from the far recesses of his mind. If he gave in now, if he allowed himself to fall in love with her, she might become the mother of his children, and in time would become the matriarch of the house of Rakehell. He knew too little about her for that. He was in no way denying her appeal, nor was he questioning her eligibility as a wife. But he knew all the same that, based on their past relationship, events were moving far too swiftly for comfort. He needed time to stand back, weigh his relationship with Erika, and then make a dispassionate judgment on how he should or should not proceed. All of this went through his mind swiftly, and with it there was another thought that intruded. He had grown wonderfully close to Elizabeth Boynton on the long voyage to Hong Kong from New London. He had even begun to imagine what sort of lives they and the children would lead if they were married. He believed that Elizabeth was interested in him and cared for him, but that was not the issue. With her as prominent as she had become in his mind and in his desires, he could not take another woman with a clear conscience.

So, without further ado, he reacted to Erika's gesture by taking a backward step and increasing the air space between them.

Instantly aware of the rebuff, she knew she had gone too far, too fast, and had frightened him. She was annoyed with herself because she had not taken too many other factors into consideration. Principal among them, in her opinion, was the availability of Molinda to him. Not knowing anything about the deepening relationship between Jonathan and Elizabeth, Erika had measured the Balinese girl's beauty, brains, and charm and knew she would be a formidable opponent for the affections of any man. Furthermore, Jonathan had come here to this house after spending his entire day with Molinda.

Revealing none of her thoughts, she continued to chat amiably, and was her most charming self. She concealed her annoyance until Jonathan departed for the night after accepting another invitation from her, which she forced him to do by maneuvering him into a corner from which there was no graceful escape.

After Jonathan's departure, Erika reviewed her situation calmly and clearly. She had come within an eyelash of achieving the success she craved. Now she had to do two things. First she would be obliged to get rid of Molinda as her rival, having convinced herself that the woman was Jonathan's mistress. Then, when the field was clear, she would move swiftly and surely, and when she became Mrs. Jonathan Rakehell, her problems would be behind her for all time.

# III

Jonathan was very much present in the mind of another Hong Kong resident, Owen Bruce. It seemed to Bruce that it was almost too good to be true that his mortal enemy had returned to the British Crown Colony, and he was determined to put Jonathan out of the way once and for all. Having failed time and again to deter Molinda, he was sure that the death of the man largely responsible for the success of Rakehell and Boynton would mean the collapse of the firm. Then Bruce, of all people in Hong Kong, would be able to salvage much of the operation for himself. His own business surely would quadruple within a brief period of time once he eliminated Jonathan Rakehell, and Bruce would no longer have to bow and scrape to the tyrannical Marquês de Braga.

It was true that Rakehell had evaded death far too often in the past and seemed to lead a charmed life. Bruce saw no point in reviewing the various plots he had concocted, but he recalled all too vividly the fight they had once been involved in at Whampoa. On that occasion Rakehell had proved by far the better fighter, and Bruce had been fortunate to escape with his life. Now he had to plan with greater cunning than he had ever before utilized.

The scheme he envisaged was so simple that he was delighted with it. He would invent an occasion to be "insulted" by Rakehell in the immediate future, and would challenge him to a duel. As an honorable man, he knew that Jonathan would not refuse an affair of honor.

But Bruce had no intention of actually meeting him in combat with either pistols or swords. He would say that the governor-general of the Crown Colony frowned severely on dueling, which was true, and that those who engaged in such combat were expelled from the colony, which also was true. He would propose, therefore, that the duel take place in the fishing village of Aberdeen, founded by Scottish fishermen on the coast of Hong Kong Island, opposite from Victoria City. The road to Aberdeen led through an untamed tropical wilderness, and it would be a simple matter to have Rakehell attacked and killed there by supposed thugs. That would be the end of him, and it would be unnecessary for Bruce to lift his hand in actual combat. The plan seemed foolproof.

So it happened that the day after Jonathan had dined with Erika, he encountered Bruce abruptly on the street as he left his warehouse and the Scotsman presumably was approaching his. Although Jonathan ordinarily was careful of where he walked, he crashed headlong into the burly figure of Bruce.

The Scotsman feigned great indignation. "Ah," he said angrily, "so it's you, is it? I knew there would be trouble the minute I learned you were back in town."

Jonathan made no attempt to conceal his intense dislike for the man. "I assure you, Mr. Bruce, that colliding with you was the last intention in my mind. I vastly prefer to avoid you—at all costs. However, I'll gladly apologize to you in order to terminate this conversation with you. So there's an end to the matter." He stepped aside and started off down the street.

But Bruce reached out, caught hold of his shoulder, and spun him around. "Not so fast, Rakehell," he cried. "I say that you insulted me on purpose, and I demand satisfaction."

In spite of Jonathan's self-control, his temper surged. "You have gone too far, Bruce," he said, his voice deadly, his manner cold. "I'd thrash you within an inch of your life, but I prefer not to soil my hands with you. Let your seconds call on mine at their convenience, provided they're quick about it.

You've asked for a lesson, and you shall have it!" Still furious, he stamped off down the street.

Owen Bruce smiled without humor as he watched the American hurrying away. He had set his scheme in motion, and he was secretly delighted.

The indignant Jonathan related the incident to Molinda and Charles, and the beautiful Balinese woman was openly worried. "I don't like this in the least," she said.

"He'll have good cause to regret his attitude," Jonathan said. "I just hope that he goes through with the duel and sends a second here. You'll represent me, of course, Charles."

"Naturally," Charles replied grimly.

They did not have long to wait. Within an hour a Scotsman appeared at the Rakehell and Boynton office and introduced himself as Owen Bruce's second.

Charles went into conference with him at once, and they agreed that because of the governor-general's opposition to dueling, the fight should be private. Bruce's representative suggested Aberdeen as the site for the engagement, and Charles, who was less familiar with the geography of the area, nevertheless found the plan a good one and agreed to it. They set a date for two mornings later, and they agreed that sabers would be used to settle the affair of honor.

Molinda remained deeply concerned. "Bruce is a terrible trickster," she said, "and I wouldn't put it past him to have invented some diabolical scheme against you."

Jonathan shrugged. "There's very little he can do," he said. "I'm a fair enough swordsman, and you can be sure I'll give him a run for his money."

Others were interested in the coming duel as the news spread quickly in Hong Kong, and no one was more upset than Erika von Klausner. "You've met Bruce on a few occasions at that awful seaman's tavern you frequent," she said to Reinhardt Braun. "What do you make of all this?"

"I know only that Bruce has an obsession about Rakehell, and would sell his own soul to the devil in order to see him dead."

"Then you think he intends trickery of some sort in this duel?"

The German shrugged. "Certainly it is possible," he said. "I might even go so far as to say it's quite probable."

Erika's long fingernails tapped an impatient tattoo on a lacquered tabletop. She had good reason for her concern. Convinced that she was making substantial progress in her campaign to become Mrs. Jonathan Rakehell, she could envisage her entire plan being ruined by Owen Bruce's machinations. He had to be stopped at all costs.

"Are you familiar with the more subtle means that one uses in the East to dispose of one's enemies?" she demanded.

Braun laughed joylessly. "There are many such means," he said, and peering at her, was able to read her mind. "One of the best I have discovered is snake venom. I don't know the identity of the snakes whose venom is milked, but that's really irrelevant. I've been told on good authority that a slight scratch with a knife that's been dipped in venom will guarantee the death of an individual in less than one minute. The man who was telling me about it is an old hand in the Orient, and I have every reason to believe that he was not exaggerating."

"Can you obtain a quantity of this venom?" Erika demanded.

Braun hesitated for a moment before he replied. "Yes, I'm sure I can get some, but it's expensive. One hundred guineas in gold for one ounce of the substance."

Erika was reasonably certain he had quoted her a far higher price than he would actually have to pay for the snake venom because he saw an opportunity to line his own pocket. But she was in no mood to quibble with him. The results she sought were far too important.

She went into her bedchamber and returned with the sum of one hundred guineas in gold, which she handed to him. "Make sure that the seller of the poison remains discreet," she said. "Go at once to Jonathan Rakehell, and offer him your services as a second in the duel. Tell him I sent you as a favor to him."

Braun frowned. "One ordinarily chooses a close friend or

associate as a second," he said. "I'm scarcely acquainted with Herr Rakehell."

"That doesn't matter in the least," Erika said impatiently. "Make it plain that I've sent you to him because you are an expert with pistols and knives, and having become familiar with Hong Kong, you can offer him protection on his journey to Aberdeen."

He weighed the idea, shrugged, and accepted it reluctantly. "It might work," he said. "What then?"

"I have witnessed only one duel in my life," Erika said, "but as I recall it, the second can inspect the weapons that are to be used. Surely you could find an opportunity to paint the tip of Jonathan Rakehell's sword with poison while you're examining it. Does that seem like too great a task for you?"

He became disdainful, which was precisely her intention. "I could handle such a matter with the greatest of ease," he said.

"Then see to it that you follow my orders precisely, and I shall arrange with the von Eberling interests for you to receive a commendation and a bonus."

Braun regarded her curiously. "You appear to be most anxious that Herr Rakehell wins this engagement," he said thoughtfully.

She nodded. "It is important to me that he wins and that he emerges unharmed from the ordeal. It is also a matter of supreme indifference to me whether Herr Bruce lives or dies."

Her casual remark sealed Owen Bruce's doom. Reinhardt Braun removed the small wooden doll he carried from a jacket pocket, then opened his jackknife. Chuckling dryly, he cut a small incision in the tiny figure's wooden cheek.

Obeying Erika's orders to the letter, he first went to Jonathan, to whom he offered his services at the request of the baroness. Molinda and Lo Fang were dubious, but Jonathan was grateful for the offer, especially after Braun demonstrated his prowess with pistols in the yard outside the warehouses. "You're quite right, Mr. Braun," he said. "My cousin is already acting as my second, to be sure, but there is no reason I shouldn't be represented by two seconds, so I'll be very pleased and honored to have you with me, also. And my thanks to the baroness.''

Braun had established a solid base and went on to obtain the snake venom. As Erika had rightly suspected, he had doubled the price, so he stashed a considerable sum in his own wallet when he purchased the deadly poison.

The following morning, Molinda was awake long before dawn and had a pot of hot tea waiting for Jonathan and Charles when they joined her briefly in the dining room. ''I wish I could talk you out of this madness,'' she said. ''I still don't like it.''

''Some things in this world are necessary, whether we like them or not,'' Jonathan replied. ''Bruce has been a thorn in my side for years, and the time has come to put him permanently in his place.''

While they were drinking their tea, Reinhardt Braun arrived. He was very much the outsider, but he was greeted cordially, even by Molinda and Lo Fang, who now believed the man's intentions were honorable. Braun, too, had a cup of tea before the men departed.

Molinda watched in silence as Jonathan strapped on a belt to which were attached his Indonesian throwing knives and then transferred her attention to Charles, who was checking a brace of pistols to make certain they were loaded. ''Are you anticipating trouble?'' she wanted to know.

''We're hoping to avoid it,'' Charles replied. ''We understand that we'll be riding through some desolate stretches on our way to the village of Aberdeen, and it's best not to take any unnecessary risks. I don't know if any of the pirates who prey on Hong Kong shipping make their headquarters in the area, but it pays to take no chances.''

''It does indeed, Herr Boynton,'' Braun agreed, and checked his own pistols.

Molinda hesitated. ''Perhaps it would be wise if Lo Fang were to accompany you,'' she suggested.

Jonathan smiled and shook his head. ''That won't be in the

least necessary," he told her. "There are three of us going on the road, all heavily armed. Anyone foolish enough to attack us will have ample cause to regret it. Let Lo Fang attend to his normal duties; he's needed far more to watch over you."

She relented, and when they left the house to go to the stable for their horses, she kissed Jonathan lightly as she wished him good luck.

The first streaks of dawn appeared in the sky to the East above the South China Sea as the trio set out for Aberdeen. It was quiet, almost abnormally quiet; Hong Kong was not yet stirring. They rode in silence around the base of the Peak and took to the road that followed the shore to the opposite end of Hong Kong Island. None had ever before visited this part of the Royal Crown Colony, but it was impossible to lose one's way. The single road was the only path that would take the trio to their destination. They made their way up and down hills and across little valleys, sometimes seeing and hearing the crash of the surf off to their right and sometimes conscious of the chattering of birds at daybreak in the miniature forests through which they passed.

They rode silently. Jonathan and Charles were inhibited by the presence of Braun, whom they regarded as a well-meaning stranger, and he, ill-at-ease in their presence, had nothing to say, either. Here and there they passed a large estate, some owned by enterprising Englishmen, some by wealthy Chinese from the mainland. In the main, however, this portion of the island was virtually uninhabited and was still in its primitive state.

According to rumors that had never been substantiated, pirates who preyed on shipping in the island's waters often landed in this section of the island and lingered here for a few days at a time. Jonathan and Charles were expert seamen, and both were appreciative of the many small coves and sheltered harbors that they passed. The coastline was ideal for anyone trying to avoid a Royal Navy patrol.

Aberdeen, they had been told, was approximately a three-hour horseback ride from Hong Kong. The journey was quiet, unmarred by any incident for approximately an hour and a

445

half. Then, when they were riding single file through a grove of trees and bamboo thickets, they suddenly heard the neighing of strange horses and muffled shouts.

Jonathan, who was in the lead, halted and raised his hand. Braun, who brought up the rear, was the first to realize they were being approached on three sides—from the front, the left, and the right. "It is a trap!" he shouted. "We are being ambushed!"

Jonathan instinctively reached for two of the knives in his belt. At virtually the same instant Charles, who had halted his own gelding, drew both of his pistols.

Braun drew even with Charles so he would not be isolated in the rear, and he, too, reached for his firearms.

Men, on foot, with bandannas wrapped around the lower halves of their faces to conceal their identities, were approaching boldly but cautiously, brandishing the curved double-edged swords of ancient China.

As nearly as Jonathan could determine, the assailants were Oriental. They wore hats above their facial coverings to further conceal their identities, but their eyes revealed their race. He had no idea why he and his companions should be subjected to such an onslaught, but he wasted no time in idle speculation. Taking careful aim, he flipped the knife he held in his right hand, then threw that which he drew with his left.

Charles and Braun fired their pistols simultaneously, and the whole of the little forest reverberated with the sound.

The attackers appeared confused, and with good reason. Although Jonathan and his companions had no way of knowing the true situation, the brigands had been told that a white man was going to appear on the trail this morning heading toward Aberdeen, and they had received fifty percent of a generous payment to take his life. The odds of six to one had made them believe they were invincible.

Now, however, they found three white men, rather than one, on the trail, and all three were resisting strenuously. The two who wielded pistols obviously were experts in the handling of firearms, and every time a trigger was pulled, one of the assailants was hit. The tall, lean man in the lead was even more to be feared. He carried a number of lightweight bone-handled knives, similar to those used by Maylays and Indonesians, and he handled them with the expertise of a native Javanese.

Before the brigands quite knew what was happening to them, all six had suffered wounds from the defenders' knives and pistols. No fee was large enough for them to risk their lives, and they fled from the scene, throwing down their cumbersome Chinese swords as they hurried from the field of combat.

The one-sided fight was ended almost before it had begun.

Jonathan made certain that the assailants were in full retreat. Then he dismounted and retrieved the throwing knives he had hurled at the brigands. Charles stared off at the clumps of bamboo shoots and listened to the sounds of the retreating gang as they gradually died away. "It seems to me," he said, "that they were lying in wait for us and attacked us deliberately."

"So it appears," Jonathan replied, and then grinned. "Well, we managed to give them better than we received, I'll say that much for us. Congratulations, Braun; you were a big help."

The German nodded in embarrassment, unaccustomed to being praised for his skill with a pistol. He knew well that the attack had been deliberate, and it didn't require too much use of his imagination for him to figure out that Owen Bruce had been responsible, hiring the band of thugs and instructing them to do away with Jonathan. Well, he and his two unlikely allies had sent the brigands packing, and he was somewhat relieved. It had bothered him a trifle that he had been instructed to kill Bruce, who had bought him a few drinks at the seaman's tavern and whom Braun had regarded as his friend, but the knowledge that the Scotsman had been responsible for the attack relieved his conscience. Now he could smear poison on the tip of Jonathan's sword with a clear mind.

Scarcely delayed by the incident, the trio came at last to a hill that rose above the fishing village of Aberdeen. Looking at the town in the early light of morning, they saw clusters of houses, and in the large, sheltered harbor beyond the shore they made out a number of sampans riding at anchor. This was the fleet of fishermen who claimed that the waters off the coast were the richest anywhere in the South China Sea.

Someone hailed them softly, and a black-clad Scotsman sat his mount some yards away and beckoned to them. They followed him to an isolated cove around a bend in the coast from Aberdeen, and they knew that Owen Bruce had shown great foresight in choosing his location for the duel. No dwellings and no sampans could be seen from here, there was no sign of human habitation anywhere, and the area was deserted, as were the other islands of the British chain that stood farther off the shore of the mainland.

Owen Bruce and another aide were awaiting the arrival of Jonathan and his party, as were a doctor and the referee, a shipping man with whom Charles was slightly acquainted. Owen Bruce gave no sign that he recognized the arrival of the newcomers, but his eyes widened somewhat when he saw Braun acting as a second to his foe. He had no previous knowledge that they were even acquainted.

But his mind was too full to concern himself with the doings of Reinhardt Braun at the moment. The mere fact that Rakehell had arrived for the duel on time and unharmed meant that the plan to waylay him and kill him somehow had misfired. For whatever their reason, the brigands had failed, and now as a consequence it would be necessary for Bruce to fight him.

Very well. If that was what was necessary, Bruce would perform the deed himself and dispose of Rakehell once and for all.

The referee did his duty, and inquired whether the dispute could be settled by peaceful means. Jonathan stared off into space, remaining silent and making no move, while Bruce shook his head vehemently. It was apparent there could be no reconciliation.

"In the event that either of you has forgotten the fundamentals of the duel, let me refresh your memories regarding them," the referee said. "It is not necessary to kill your opponent in order to satisfy your honor. On the contrary, gentlemen. Killing is now regarded as bad form. It is sufficient to draw blood. In other words, it will be my duty to halt the duel and declare honor satisfied the moment that one of you inflicts as much as a scratch that draws blood. I trust my meaning is clear.''

Jonathan nodded. Owen Bruce seemed vaguely aware of what was being said.

The matched sabers were produced, and as Jonathan had been the challenged party, technically speaking, his seconds were given the choice of weapons. There was little or no difference between the weapons, so Charles selected one and then handed it to Braun, who seemed eager to inspect it more closely.

Jonathan and Bruce were sent from the arena and walked to opposite sides of it. Neither had acknowledged the other's presence.

It was an almost absurdly simple matter for Reinhardt Braun to coat Jonathan's saber with deadly snake venom. He removed the stopper from the small vial in his pocket, and while ostensibly holding the blade up to the light in order to study the sharpness of its point, he poured the liquid first over one side, and then over the other. He swished the blade experimentally, supposedly testing the balance, and was relieved when he saw the liquid drying on the steel. Returning the empty vial to his pocket and replacing the stopper, he knew that the only task still awaiting him was that of getting rid of the now-empty snake venom container.

Charles took the saber and presented it to his principal. "Don't waste any time with the surly brute, Jonnie," he said in a low voice. "Wound him quickly, and end this farce. I don't trust him, and I want to get out of here as fast as we can."

Jonathan nodded and looked complacent. Even Reinhardt Braun had to admire his cool demeanor. He had heard that Rakehell was one of those rare men who, instead of losing their heads in a time of crisis, actually thought and acted with deliberate precision. Apparently the stories were true.

The referee called the principals into the center of the ring, and the seconds standing at opposite sides of the arena gripped their own swords more firmly. If necessary, they were prepared to intervene, but no one could remember when seconds had been called upon to participate in a duel.

The referee again reminded the principals that honor would be satisfied the instant one of them drew blood. Then he extended his own sword between them and they ranged themselves on either side of it.

"*En garde*, gentlemen!" he called. "You may begin!"

Steel clashed against steel, and the duel was under way. Bruce instantly assumed the offensive and pressed his opponent hard.

Jonathan, forced from the outset to assume a defensive posture, quickly realized that his opponent had no intention of obeying the referee's instructions. Owen Bruce sought more than a scratch, and was determined to kill the man who had defeated him so often and in so many ways on the waterfronts of Whampoa and Hong Kong. Meeting thrust after thrust with delicate ripostes, Jonathan retreated slowly, carefully, as he made his way around the arena. He was aware of Charles's concern, which verged on alarm, and he was somehow pleased and mollified when he noted that Reinhardt Braun looked far less worried than did his principal second. Braun might be a stranger, he thought, but at least he was confident that his principal would ultimately achieve the victory.

Bruce made no secret of his intentions. His dark eyes gleaming, his thick lips set grimly, he tried to make every lunge the final blow of the duel. His own seconds and the referee recognized his intention, as did the mild-mannered English physician who had been half cajoled, half coerced into crossing the island from Hong Kong in order to be present for the duel.

Never had Jonathan encountered such concentrated, vicious hatred. He knew now beyond doubt that Molinda had been right. He had been drawn into this fight against his better judgment, and it had been his foe's intention from the outset to destroy him.

His mind remained calm, however, and his arm remained steady. Certainly he was aware of his own limitations as a swordsman. He was competent enough, but he was in no way superior, and an experienced foe could have defeated him handily. He lacked the smooth expertise with a sword that came so naturally to him when he fired a pistol or when he threw one of his Indonesian knives. He well knew that if he hoped to survive this engagement, he would have to score first. If he remained on the defensive, it would not be too difficult for Bruce to find a way to get past his guard.

In order to shift from the defensive to the offensive, he had to take a risk, and assumed it without hesitation, leaving himself open temporarily while he first parried a blow and then delivered a thrust of his own.

His sudden switch to a more aggressive posture surprised Bruce, who momentarily lost the rhythm of the duel. As Jonathan well knew, in swordplay, as in so many forms of individual combat, the maintenance of rhythm was essential. He who kept it held a slim advantage, while he who lost it could lose far more. In the instant that Bruce faltered momentarily, Jonathan saw his opportunity, and the tip of his blade creased his foe's cheek. A thin line of scarlet appeared, and with his free hand, Owen Bruce reached up and touched it. His fingertips were wet when he withdrew his hand.

The referee intervened instantly, precisely as he had said he would. His own sword was lowered sharply, separating the combatants, and he shouted an order to them. "Cease and desist at once!"

Jonathan obeyed obligingly, taking a single backward step and lowering his blade.

In so doing he almost lost his life. Bruce lunged at him for a last time, and the blow barely missed his mark, his blade passing through the inner sleeve of Jonathan's shirt but leaving him unscathed.

In the meantime, however, the snake venom was working swiftly and effectively. Bruce suddenly stood upright, and his sword fell to the ground as a perplexed expression crossed his face. He appeared to be in no pain, no distress, but all at once he collapsed onto the ground. The physician promptly knelt beside him and began to examine him.

"Good Lord!" the doctor murmured. "He's dead."

The others were too shocked to respond. Jonathan knew only that his blow could not have been responsible for the death of Owen Bruce.

The physician conducted a more thorough but necessarily hasty examination. "The scratch on the cheek inflicted by Mr. Rakehell," he said, "caused a loss of a few drops of blood and certainly gives the victory in the duel to Mr. Rakehell. Bruce must have had a far weaker heart than any of us suspected. He displays all the symptoms of having suffered a heart attack."

Reinhardt Braun remained expressionless, and his hand closed around the empty vial of deadly poison. He would get rid of it when they walked back to the spot where they had left their horses; he knew just the place. They would walk close to a cliff overlooking the sea, and he would throw the container into the water far below. Years might pass before anyone would discover the remains.

Braun had committed too many murders in the past to feel any sense of elation at having completed his mission so successfully. He had done what had been expected of him, and Herr Rakehell was still alive, for whatever the reason the baroness had for wanting him alive. What pleased the little German man the most was that he had made himself the appreciable sum of fifty guineas in gold in return for a simple task, simply performed.

The house in London's Belgravia was more than a half-world away from the vantage point of the splendid old Soong Chao estate in Canton. The London dwelling and all that it represented seemed to be part of another world.

The children were completely at home in Canton, and Elizabeth was amazed at how Julian and Jade and David flourished. They addressed the staff in the Cantonese dialect and conversed fluently with the cooks and gardeners, housemaids, and security guards. They knew the rules of the establishment and were careful not to break them; they never went beyond the high walls of the estate unless they were accompanied by guards and Kai had given his personal permission for them to go. They treated their elders with a gravity and respect that seemed so natural to youngsters in the Middle Kingdom and so alien to Anglo-Saxons. They ate heartily, but their manners were so polished that neither Ruth nor Elizabeth was obliged to deliver as much as a single lecture to them.

Elizabeth discovered that she, too, was changed. Perhaps, she reflected, living in the house in which Lai-tse lu had grown to womanhood was responsible. Sitting in the extensive floral gardens and looking at the massive banks of flowers, at the miniature bridges and lily pads in the ponds, she could begin to understand the inner serenity that had been so much a part of the character of Jonathan's wife. One afternoon, while the children were resting in their rooms after a hearty lunch, Elizabeth tried to explain to her sister-in-law how she felt.

"Whenever I saw Lai-tse lu," she said, "I wondered how a woman so beautiful and so full of life could also appear so tranquil. I've discovered the secret of her tranquillity here, and I feel much closer to her now than I ever have before. Living here on her property so close to her mausoleum has given me a new understanding of her childhood and womanhood."

Ruth nodded. "I know what you mean," she said. "There's a sense of continuity here that I find nowhere else on earth. Even the children feel it. Did you hear them talking at lunch today about what they're going to do and not do when they take over the operations of Rakehell and Boynton?"

"Yes," Elizabeth said with a smile, "and I realized why the future is so much on their minds."

"Why do you think?" Ruth asked.

"Because the *past* is everywhere. We never knew Lai-tse lu's father, Soong Chao, yet I feel as though I know him. The furnishings of the pavilions here, the scrolls and statues and porcelain vases were all selected by him. I almost feel as though he stands beside me when I look out at the hills of Canton spread out below us. It's an uncanny sensation.''

Ruth looked at her and slowly shook her head. "I wrote a letter to Charles in Hong Kong this morning that Kai assured me would be delivered by tonight,'' she said. "In it I said that both of us owe you a great apology, so consider that I'm now apologizing on Charles's behalf as well as my own.''

Elizabeth was somewhat bewildered. "Why should you or Charles apologize to me, for goodness sake?''

"We misjudged you badly,'' Ruth told her. "In fact, we couldn't have been more wrong about you. For years—ever since you were a child really—you've spoken of your love for Jonathan and your determination to become his wife. We laughed at you, just as your parents laughed. Then, when you became adult and persisted in dreaming your dream, we became concerned for you. For my part, I thought you were all wrong for Jonathan and that he would be all wrong for you. Well, I was mistaken. In my opinion, you were too beautiful for your own good, too headstrong, too spoiled, and too insensitive. You're none of those things. I think you're going to be the perfect wife for Jonathan.''

Elizabeth forced a laugh. "You're assuming that he's going to propose to me, but that may be too great an assumption.''

"I think not,'' Ruth replied with a smile. "You've been marvelously patient. Just be that same way a little longer, and everything will be just fine.''

Later that afternoon, however, there was some news that badly upset Elizabeth's sense of tranquillity and well-being. Charles had written to say that Jonathan had been involved in a duel, though he had emerged victorious and unharmed. The fact that Jonathan was exposed to such dangers in Hong Kong gave Elizabeth enough to worry about, but then Charles's other news was equally devastating. He mentioned that Elizabeth's old school friend, Erika von Klausner, was also living on Hong Kong Island, and had even entertained Jonathan at her house.

"It looks as if my worst fears have come to pass,''

Elizabeth said glumly as she and Ruth were drinking their afternoon tea. "The news that Erika von Klausner is in Hong Kong is terribly disturbing, to say the least. And then there's Jonathan living under the same roof with that lovely Molinda. If I were a man, I'd choose her as opposed to me in a twinkling."

"Molinda has been associated with Jonnie for a long time, and he has no romantic involvement with her, so you can put that out of your mind. As for Erika—well, every man is entitled to make a fool of himself once in a lifetime, and I daresay that Jonathan can afford that luxury."

"Provided he doesn't become too deeply involved with her," Elizabeth replied. "That's my one fear."

"You've got to allow him his freedom, you know," Ruth said. "You can't tie a man up and chain him to your side. I learned that in my own dealings with Charles."

"It's all well and good to talk as you do," Elizabeth said. "You and Charles are married. But I'm still obliged to sit and twiddle my thumbs until Jonathan comes to Canton. If he shouldn't propose after he gets here, I'm afraid I shall lose all patience and will have a fit of screaming hysteria."

Ruth laughed. "You'll do no such thing," she said. "If I know you, you'll continue to carry on quietly, and you'll be available when Jonnie finally sees the light."

"I hope I am," Elizabeth said with a deep sigh. "I've loved him for so long and I've waited so many years for him that I'm becoming exhausted. I'm restless, I'm afraid, and there's no way of getting rid of the feeling short of attaining the goals that I've sought all these years."

# IV

"You did well, I must admit, in the case of Owen Bruce," Erika von Klausner said crisply. "I have offered you my felicitations, and I have written a letter to Hamburg filled with your praises. Now I have a somewhat more difficult task for you to perform."

Braun looked at her, a contemptuous half-smile on his face.

"This," Erika said, "concerns the Far Eastern manager for Rakehell and Boynton—Molinda."

Braun's composure was momentarily shaken. "You don't wish me to poison her too, surely?" he said.

Erika smiled sweetly. "As a matter of fact, Molinda must be eliminated. Poison is hardly suitable, though."

"So?" Braun asked.

"I was making great progress in promoting greater intimacy with Jonathan Rakehell," Erika said, choosing not to reveal that her actual goal was marriage to Jonathan. "Suddenly, however, he grew cooler and drew back from me. I am certain that the woman called Molinda is responsible. She is very attractive—if one is drawn to her type—and she is very shrewd. I have no doubt in my mind whatsoever that she has serious designs on him herself. In her position, she sees him throughout the business day, and as he is living under her roof, she sees him at meals and in the evenings as well. I do not admit defeat easily, but even I have my limitations, and I

457

cannot compete with a woman who has such unlimited access to him. Therefore, she must be put out of the way permanently."

Braun studied his fingernails. "You're suggesting a hunting accident, perhaps, or a catastrophe at sea?"

Erika shook her head impatiently. "Such schemes would be far too cumbersome," she said. "The woman is engaged in business in Hong Kong and never goes hunting. As for an accident at sea, there is too much that could happen on board a clipper ship or junk, too much that could go wrong. I prefer a far simpler approach."

"You obviously have something specific in mind," he said.

"Indeed I do," she said. "Do you remember when we were visiting the Fat Dutchman in Djakarta, he took great pride one day in showing us his menagerie?"

Braun shrugged. "I didn't pay too much attention, I must say. I'm not particularly interested in animals."

"Nor am I," Erika replied. "But I was fascinated by his poisonous snakes. You will recall the little creatures about eighteen to twenty inches long and about as big around as my little finger? They were an exotic variety of coral snake, or something of the sort, because they have the ability to turn various shades of pink and green and even blue."

"What about them?" Braun demanded brusquely.

"Very simply," Erika told him, "the Dutchman has more of them than he needs. I distinctly recall he had five or six such creatures in his snake house. I'm going to send you to the Dutchman carrying some messages, and he is so hospitable that I'm sure you will be invited to spend the night with him. When you leave the following day, I trust you will have one of the deadly coral snakes in your possession. I don't know if such snakes are known to Hong Kong, but the climate is much like that of Djakarta, so it shouldn't be too hard to introduce one into Molinda's house and then let nature take its own course without anyone being able to point a finger at us." She smiled complacently.

Braun made no move. The thought of returning to the Dutchman's estate after the humiliating treatment he had received did not entirely please him, but he was willing to do anything for the right price. "Let us suppose," he said, "that I am able to accomplish everything that you have outlined for me. I am not paid by my masters in Hamburg for such functions, and I would require the sum of one hundred marks in gold, payable in advance."

"You'll get half in advance," she told him, "and the other half when you've returned here with the snake and have put it where it will be certain to dispose of Molinda."

It was significant, he thought, that she did not quibble over the sum of money that he demanded. "Very well," he said. "I agree to the arrangement, and I shall be on my way to Djakarta as soon as you give me the documents you wish delivered to the Dutchman."

Early the following morning, Braun sailed for Djakarta on a commercial junk, carrying with him a number of papers that Erika had hastily assembled for delivery to the Dutchman. He arrived in the capital of the Dutch East Indies without incident, and had himself driven without delay to the Dutchman's estate.

There he was received cordially, his earlier offense with the serving maid overlooked, if not totally forgotten. If the Dutchman thought it odd that a personal messenger should have been sent with the documents that Erika had dispatched to him, he kept his views to himself. It was by far preferable, he had learned, not to comment on such matters but to sit back and observe, and ultimately the reasons for human behavior usually revealed themselves.

Braun had obtained his return passage for the following day, and it was unnecessary for him to even ask if he could remain overnight. The Dutchman, generous as always indispensing hospitality, insisted that the German stay as his guest.

The girls were the first to notice a difference in Reinhardt Braun. On his first visit, he had ogled them unceasingly, but now he appeared only mildly interested in them. He further surprised them at dinner by inquiring about the Dutchman's zoo, and was promptly invited to tour it after the meal. This he did, with one of the girls acting as his guide, and he professed a greater interest in the monkeys than he felt. He paid virtually no attention to the occupants of the snake house. That night, however, after everyone had retired, he removed from his luggage a gallon container made of glass. Over the opening he had secured a wire mesh that would prevent the escape of anything inside, but would permit air to enter the container.

Long after midnight, when he was sure the entire estate had bedded down for the night, he made his way alone back to the zoo and carefully placed the glass container inside the entrance to the snake house. Inside the container was a small lizard he had caught, and he was hoping it would be sufficient bait for his purposes. He opened the cage containing the coral snakes, and then stood back. His luck was good, and a small serpent about eighteen to twenty-four inches long and no larger in circumference than his little finger noticed the presence of the lizard. Slithering quickly into the jar in search of food, the snake was promptly made prisoner when Braun replaced the wire mesh stopper over the opening. Closing up the snake cage again, he gingerly carried his captive back to his own quarters. There, after punching holes in a valise in order to admit air into it, he slept soundly for the rest of the night. In the morning, after a pleasant breakfast with the Dutchman and members of his entourage, he took his leave and returned to the docks in Djakarta.

A scant seventy-two hours later he returned to Hong Kong, and went to Erika with the concrete results of his journey.

She glanced at the snake, shuddered slightly, and said, "This is perfect. Now all you need to do is to hide it somewhere in Molinda's quarters, perhaps in her bed or clothes closet, where it will be sure to attack her."

He smiled sourly. "That is far easier said than done," he said. "Her majordomo, who has eyes in the back of his head, watches everyone who comes to her house, and I know of no way to sneak this snake in when the big Chinaman is watching me."

Erika shook her head contemptuously. "When will you

learn to think ahead and to plan accordingly? I made it my business to find out that since Jonathan Rakehell and Charles Boynton have been here, they and Molinda leave for the office at an early hour, and they don't return to the house until about an hour after sunset. The majordomo, of course, goes where Molinda goes. So that means that no one is in the house all day but the Chinese servants, who, after they clean the place, confine themselves either to the kitchen or to their own quarters. So you have virtually the whole day to place our small friend where he will do the most good.''

Braun looked very dubious, and Erika took a heavy bag of coins from her purse and jangled it. Then, smiling, she gave her retainer no opportunity to say anything more as she pressed the purse into his hand.

By accepting it, he committed himself to do as she wished.

Early that evening, as Erika came into her living room, she found Braun making himself at home there, drinking some schnapps she had been given by a local admirer.

He grinned without humor and raised his glass to her. "The Balinese woman," he told her, "is as good as dead."

"Oh? Where did you place the snake—"

"Never mind," he said, cutting her off. "This is one of those instances where a lack of knowledge won't hurt you."

As it happened, Molinda, Jonathan, and Charles carried over their business discussion of the day into the evening. As soon as they returned to Molinda's house just after sunset, the three of them sat in the living room drinking glasses of predinner sack, continuing the discussion they had held in the office. Their search for funds was thorough, and they were leaving no corner unexplored. Jonathan said, "I'm wondering how much the Dutchman is willing to invest in our company?"

"A great deal, I daresay," Charles replied.

Molinda nodded somberly. "He will invest whatever is necessary, and he has vast sums at his command, so you'd be wise if you'd keep in mind that money is no object to him."

Jonathan was struck by the ominous note in her tone. "You don't approve?"

"I do not!" she replied emphatically. "You know the

Dutchman as a friend and as a genial host. I know him first and foremost as a man of business, and I tell you flatly that he stops at nothing to gain his ends. He sees an opportunity currently to gain control of Rakehell and Boynton. Do you realize what this means to him? He would have entry to the markets of America and Great Britain. He would be transformed from a Dutch shipper in the Far East to an international figure of vast importance. Don't underestimate his vanity or his ruthlessness. If you give him the chance, he will ride roughshod over you in order to gain his ends."

The cousins looked at each other and smiled wanly. "That's just what Charles and I thought," Jonathan said, "but we wanted to see what you had to say. So then we're in agreement: under no circumstances should we go to the Dutchman for as much as a penny."

"Agreed," she replied. "You'll obligate yourselves to him, and you can be certain that he'll use every opening he can to pry still more from you, a great deal more."

They continued their discussion all through dinner and into the late evening. They were no nearer a solution as midnight approached, and after hours of the intense discussion, Molinda grew sleepy. She excused herself, and they continued their discussion with Charles pouring himself a stiff drink of whisky for energy. Both were determined to examine every possible approach.

Molinda went upstairs to her own quarters, where she applied a coconut lotion to remove the cosmetics from her face, and then she undressed, wrapping herself only in a Balinese skirt, which was her customary night attire. She went to her bed, carrying some notes she wanted to glance through before she dropped off to sleep. Her mind still on the discussion in which she had participated downstairs, she climbed into bed, noting that one foot brushed against something rough and cool. She glanced down, then froze. Coiled near the foot of the bed was a snake, which she recognized instantly as venomous in the extreme.

Her lifetime of training came to her aid, and she froze, not daring to move a muscle.

The snake was very much aware of her presence, however, and slowly raised its head higher.

Unable to curb her wild terror any longer, Molinda screamed loudly.

The sound was still echoing through the house when Jonathan burst into the room, with Charles at his heels and Lo Fang only a pace or two behind them.

Molinda was so badly frightened she could neither move nor speak. Finally she managed to point to the snake at the foot of the bed, only inches from her bare leg.

Jonathan took in the situation at a glance, and, as always, he remained cool in the emergency, his mind continuing to function. He knew he had to act quickly because the little serpent was preparing to strike, and he had no idea whether its poison was lethal.

A pistol would have suited his purposes best, but he carried no weapons in the house except his belt that contained his Indonesian throwing knives. He reached for a knife, and as his fingers closed around the bone handle, he felt a surge of confidence. Molinda was not out of danger yet, not by a long shot, but at least he had a chance to save her. He drew the knife, and both Charles and Lo Fang watched him, apparently confident of his ability to end the menace. He took careful aim, and just as the snake was about to shoot its head forward, he let fly with the blade.

The throw was deceptively easy and seemed to float through the air, but the thin, razor-sharp blade neatly severed the snake's head from its body.

Although it was no longer living and could harm no one now, the body continued to thrash convulsively.

Jonathan reached for Molinda, pulled her rapidly to her feet, and held her protectively in his arms. She shuddered, and began to weep silently.

Charles exhaled slowly. "My God, that was close," he murmured. "I must congratulate you, Jonnie; your aim was perfect."

"It had to be," Jonathan replied grimly.

The poker-faced Lo Fang went to the bed and picked up the

body of the snake with one hand and the head with the other. He examined the creature at length and then said softly, "This snake does not come from the Middle Kingdom."

"What do you mean?" Jonathan demanded.

Lo Fang was patient. "There are many snakes in Cathay," he said, "and of these, many are poisonous. But this snake, which was hiding in the bed of Molinda, is not native to Hong Kong or Kowloon or any other place in the Middle Kingdom."

Charles looked at him blankly. "Then how in the devil did it get here?" he demanded.

Lo Fang shrugged. "That remains to be seen," he said. "If I can, I will find out."

The significance of Lo Fang's remark struck Jonathan, who was still trying to comfort and quiet the badly disturbed woman. "Are you suggesting that this snake was left here in a deliberate attempt to harm Molinda?"

Lo Fang shrugged. "Anything is possible in Hong Kong, now," he said, and shrugging, he stalked out, still holding the two parts of the snake in his hands.

Charles hastened back to the living room to fetch a drink for Molinda, and Jonathan further calmed her by conducting a minute search of her room, which revealed no other hidden dangers. "I think you can sleep now with a clear mind," he told her. "You won't be harmed tonight."

"If need be," Charles added, "we'll stand guard over you ourselves."

Molinda smiled wanly and thanked them. Ultimately they left her. It was useless to speculate on the identity of a possible murderer, but Lo Fang made progress in his own quiet investigation. Learning that the snake was indigenous to the interior of the Dutch Island of Java gave him the clue that he needed, and he immediately got in touch with the major-domo for the Fat Dutchman's principal representative in Hong Kong.

The short, slender, brown-skinned Maylay stared in fascination at the snake with the severed head. "This is a most unusual specimen," he declared. "Only in the zoo at the estate of the Dutchman have I seen its equal."

Lo Fang placed the remains of the snake in its box. "By all means," he said, "send this to the Dutchman, because I think it may be of interest to him." His tone was friendly, but his eyes remained cold.

Less than a week later invitations arrived for Molinda, Charles, and Jonathan, asking them to come to Djakarta on board one of the Dutchman's more palatial junks for a conference with him. Certain that he wanted to make them an offer of a partnership in their company, they nevertheless could not insult him by refusing his invitation. So Jonathan hastily scribbled a note to Elizabeth in Canton, telling her that he and Charles would be delayed in their arrival there.

When they went to the dock area and boarded the Dutchman's junk, they were astonished to find Erika von Klausner and Reinhardt Braun already on board. Erika was equally astonished, both at finding Molinda alive and well and at seeing Jonathan. But she concealed her feelings, and trying to take advantage of the opportunity offered her, she flirted gently but insistently with Jonathan on the voyage.

Only when she was alone with Braun did she show her contempt for him. "Bungler!"

He was truly bewildered. "I don't understand it," he said, "I don't understand it at all."

When they arrived in Djakarta, a small carriage awaited Molinda and Erika to take them to the Dutchman's estate, and mounts were provided for the men. The Dutchman did them the rare honor of coming to the front gate of his establishment to greet them. He embraced and kissed Molinda, and it was obvious that he was very fond of her. He greeted the others with equal cordiality, and as they started off toward the house he nodded almost imperceptibly in Braun's direction.

Two of his concubines immediately escorted the German to his own quarters, and when his traveling companions met again at a sumptuous *rijsttafel* dinner a short time later, Reinhardt Braun did not appear.

# V

Dom Manuel Sebastian was in a rage. Everything he had done to foil Rakehell and Boynton had gone awry, and his only satisfaction at all was the news of Owen Bruce's death. Perhaps now that the bungling Scotsman was out of the way, the governor's plans could succeed. And he had a new plan—the most cunning and treacherous yet.

He had been following with great interest the visit of Jonathan Rakehell to the British Crown Colony. Rakehell was his implacable enemy, the man who had married Lai-tse lu, the only woman the marquês had ever wanted and lost. The destruction of Jonathan Rakehell was all that he wanted now.

Dom Manuel knew that it was too much to hope that Rakehell would pay a visit to Macao. The American was far too intelligent to go to territory controlled by his foe, and it was too much to hope that he might change his mind. After a great deal of thought, however, the Marquês de Braga came up with a scheme: to invite Elizabeth Boynton to Macao. He had received many reports on the young Englishwoman since her arrival in the Orient, and he had been intrigued by the tales of her rare, porcelainlike beauty. He had also been extremely interested in the information that she well might become Jonathan Rakehell's wife.

The scheme was simple, but as the marquês well realized, it was far from foolproof. Even if, as Dom Manuel suspected, Elizabeth Boynton knew nothing about the enmity between the governor-general and Jonathan Rakehell, there would still be her Oriental bodyguards, who no doubt would forbid her to visit Macao. Dom Manuel could only hope that his invitation would sound so tempting, and that Elizabeth Boynton would be so willingly disposed, that she would somehow avoid her guards and come to his palace.

Dom Manuel was quite positive, at least in his own mind, that she would provide the perfect bait that would bring Jonathan Rakehell to Macao. When Rakehell learned that the girl had accepted the invitation and was the guest of the governor-general, he would—in all probability—hurry to the Portuguese colony in order to rescue her from the man whom he had good cause to mistrust and hate.

Actually, de Braga intended no harm to Elizabeth. In fact, he knew it would be a far too dangerous matter for him to tamper in any way with her safety. She was the daughter of prominent aristocrats, and the family was said to be influential in royal circles. Portugal was Great Britain's ally, and if anything untoward happened to the young lady, there would be repercussions in Lisbon that could be extremely dangerous to the marquês.

Rakehell himself was a different matter. The disappearance of the American shipper might create a tempest in Hong Kong for a brief time, but Dom Manuel could not imagine Washington locking horns with Lisbon over the matter. So he put his plan into operation as soon as he heard that Rakehell had gone off to Djakarta, and he hoped for the best.

As it turned out, luck was with him. A crisis had arisen in the hills outside Canton, and a rebellion had broken out. With a population that was growing ever larger, the Middle Kingdom was experiencing more and more insurrections, as the recent rebellion not far from Peking had made clear, and in the rural sections of the provinces there was often great destruction and loss of life. The Society of Oxen were called into action to help the peasants who were the unwitting victims of the rebellious factions, and Kai, as a leading member of the Oxen, was summoned, too. Leaving the children, Ruth, and Elizabeth in the care of the guards Jonathan had sent along from Hong Kong, the redoubtable Chinese man went out into the countryside to do what he could to help his people.

Thus the one individual in Canton who could have warned Elizabeth about the Marquês de Braga was not present at the estate when Dom Manuel's invitation arrived, and Elizabeth marveled when she showed it to Ruth. "I can't imagine how the governor-general of Macao even knew I was here, and I can't imagine how he gleaned my identity."

Ruth smiled. "I don't find it so mysterious," she said. "There are very few ladies from England who visit this part of the world, and I think he means exactly what he says. He'd like the opportunity to entertain you in Macao."

"Then why did he invite just me?" Elizabeth demanded. "Why haven't you received an invitation, too?"

Ruth shrugged. "I don't know the gentleman," she said, "but I guess, offhand, that the reason you were invited and I was not is because I'm married."

"Oh, I see," Elizabeth said. "Am I going to have trouble with the fellow? It would be embarrassing having him chasing me all over the palace."

They both laughed at the idea, and Ruth suggested they check with Chen Mei, the man whom Kai had left in charge in his place.

The substitute majordomo, unlike Kai, knew nothing of the treachery of Dom Manuel, having only recently arrived in Kwangtung Province from Szechwan. All Chen Mei knew about the governor-general was that he was the foremost representative of Portugal in the Orient, and was the highest-ranking official in the colony of Macao.

The ladies absorbed this information and Ruth said, "If I were you, Elizabeth, I'd go."

"What about the children?" Elizabeth asked. "I don't want Julian and Jade to think that I've deserted them."

"Hardly that!" Ruth replied. "I'll be here to look after them, and so will Chen Mei—not to mention more servants than either you or I have ever seen in our lives. I think that Julian and Jade can manage for a few days while you go off to Macao."

"I suppose you're right," Elizabeth said a trifle dubiously. "Do you suppose Jonathan would approve?"

"Of course," Ruth replied heartily. "I can't imagine any reason why he wouldn't. The Marquês de Braga is a high-ranking Portuguese nobleman, and he holds a position of great authority and responsibility. He's a Westerner, as we are, so you'd be visiting him in accordance with our own standards, not with alien ways that are unfamiliar to us."

Elizabeth was lost in thought for a few moments. "Then I will accept," she said finally. "Frankly, I'm at my wit's end just waiting here for Jonathan to come to Canton. If our own future were truly settled now, as I hope it will be, I'm sure I could relax somewhat, but the tensions keep mounting, and I'm nearly beside myself thinking of Jonathan keeping company with Molinda and Erika. Perhaps the change of scene will help to take my mind off myself for a few days and speed up the passage of time until Jonnie gets here."

"Good!" Ruth said. "Go, and have a marvelous time!"

So Elizabeth wrote a brief note in response to the Marquês de Braga's invitation, accepting his kind offer and telling him she would be ready to leave in two more days. At that time, as the governor-general had explained in his invitation, he would provide a Portuguese warship to take her from Whampoa to glorious, exotic Macao.

Thus began the most incredible and dangerous adventure yet in the life of the young Englishwoman. Her trunks were packed, she was carried in a sedan chair to the waterfront, and she was escorted by a number of the household guards, who left her in the care of the governor-general's highly efficient staff. They carried her luggage on board the impressive Portuguese frigate waiting to take her to Macao, and meanwhile a small welcoming committee made up of Portuguese dignitaries and headed by the captain of the ship was on hand to greet her. Though it was only a short journey to Macao, she was given a suite of rooms on board ship the likes of which she had never seen, even in the most extravagant homes in Belgravia. The furnishings were exquisite, and everywhere there were vases filled with fresh flowers. Along the far wall were enormous glass windows leading out to a covered balcony directly above the water. It was like a fantastic storybook adventure come true, and as Elizabeth stood outside on the balcony at the stern of the ship, watching as the docks of Whampoa receded behind her, she was filled with wonder and awe.

She would have been astonished, however, to learn what her host, Dom Manuel Sebastian, had been doing since he had received word of the acceptance of his invitation. For the last two days, he had been pacing about his palace, occasionally smiling to himself, or else breaking into loud laughter as he clenched his fists and said aloud, to no one in particular, "I've got you, Rakehell! At last I've got you!"

While the Fat Dutchman entertained his other guests at an elaborate *rijsttafel* banquet that lasted many hours, a group of his specially selected concubines were treating Reinhardt Braun to entertainment of a different sort.

One by one they tempted him, goading him into making love to them, and he needed little urging, greedily taking one, then another of the lovely girls. They fed him when he was hungry, and held a full cup to his lips when he was thirsty. He soon discovered, however, that they had no intention of allowing him to sleep. His exertions made him drowsy, but whenever he wanted to drop off, the girls immediately pounced on him, tickling him and, becoming far more vehement, pinching him and even pulling his hair and poking him with pointed knives in order to keep him awake. When he protested at the treatment, they struck provocative poses and began to make love to him again. Unable to resist, he yielded repeatedly.

As the hours passed, however, and his exertions did not lessen, his need for sleep became much greater. But it was impossible for him to drop off. The girls saw to it that he remained wide awake at all times.

Ultimately Braun became short-tempered and ordered the

girls to leave him in peace. They giggled but seemed hard-of-hearing, and continued to use every means at their disposal to keep him awake. When he lost his temper with them, as many as a half-dozen of them took hold of his arms and legs and tickled him into further submission. Gradually a great weariness overcame him, but still they wouldn't leave him. In his bleary-eyed state, he realized that the girls who had been with him when he had first come into the quarters he was occupying had now been replaced by others. It did not cross his mind that he was being subjected to the "gentle torture" devised by an Oriental thousands of years earlier, who had found that any man could be bent to his will if subjected to such treatment for a long enough period. For a day, a night, and the better part of another day, the concubines, working in platoons, kept Reinhardt Braun busy. He became so tired he could no longer make love to a girl, so the girls made love to him. When he became too weary to eat, they forced food and drink into his mouth, and whenever he tried to sleep, they prodded and poked and tickled and, in one way and another, kept him awake. He was reduced to a gibbering shadow of his former self, his pleas to be left in peace fell on deaf ears, and the torment to which he was subjected seemed unending. The delight of the experience vanished, and in its place was a never-ending nightmare.

Suddenly, inexplicably, the girls vanished, and focusing with difficulty, Braun saw that the Fat Dutchman, armed with a steel-pointed prod, had taken their place. "For God's sake, let me sleep," Braun begged him. "I don't know why you're doing this to me, but I ask you in the name of all that's merciful, please let me rest."

"You shall have ample rest if you answer my questions," the Dutchman told him. "You visited me very recently, and I've since received information that led me to check on the population of my zoo. I made the discovery that a snake vanished from my snake house at the conclusion of your visit. Can you explain this phenomenon to me?"

Braun would have laughed at such a question, had it been directed to him when he'd been hearty and in his right mind.

In his present and weakened state, however, he could think of only the sleep that had been promised to him if he answered a few simple questions. Se he began to babble.

The Dutchman, interrupting occasionally to stop Braun from rambling, managed to gain the full story from him on the theft of the snake and the reasons of it. In addition, the Dutchman was surprised when Braun confessed to another crime, the poisoning of Owen Bruce in his duel with Jonathan Rakehell.

When Braun, so hoarse that his voice was barely intelligible, finished his recital, streams of perspiration poured down his face unheeded. The Dutchman had learned all that he had wanted to know. "Thank you for your cooperation," he said courteously, "you may sleep now."

By the time he left the room, Reinhardt Braun was already unconscious, breathing deeply.

There was no need to drug him, as the Dutchman had planned to do. He was so tired that he continued to sleep, even when he was placed in a metal cage that had come from the Dutchman's zoo. The cage was covered, then it was conveyed to the wharves of Djakarta and carried on board the deck of a junk that set sail for Macao.

Two wiry brown-skinned Javanese were in charge of the captive, and one of them carried a letter written to Dom Manuel Sebastian, informing him that in the cage was the murderer of his partner, Owen Bruce.

Nothing in the Fat Dutchman's jovial manner even hinted at the harsh punishment he had meted out to Reinhardt Braun. That evening at dinner, one of his concubines poured glasses of the most expensive French champagne, and the Dutchman rose and offered a toast. "I drink to the continuing success of Rakehell and Boynton," he said, "and to my indissoluble friendship with its principals."

The others, smiling broadly, raised their glasses in return.

"I have offered previously," he said, "to buy a portion of your firm and become your partner. I renew that offer now."

His listeners knew they would be treading on delicate

ground, and Jonathan replied carefully. "We shall give every consideration to your offer, and I assure you, my good friend, that if we admitted anyone outside the family to the firm you would be the very first."

His reply seemed to satisfy the Dutchman, who turned to Erika. "Do you suppose, Fräulein," he asked, "that the von Eberling interests would be willing to invest also in Rakehell and Boynton?"

The issue was beyond the German woman's authority, and she left no doubt as to where she herself stood. "Certainly I would recommend it as a very sound investment," she said, "but only our directors have the authority to make such an offer."

"You might wish to write to them accordingly," the Dutchman replied casually. "There's no rush about this matter." Neither Erika nor any of the others realized that he had made his suggestion deliberately in order to justify Erika's presence under his roof.

Charles now explained that the junk that had brought them to Djakarta had been ordered to make ready for an early departure the following morning.

"I shall be sorry, as always, when you leave," the Dutchman said, "but, fortunately, I'll see you at breakfast before you go."

As they rose from their chairs and bade him good night, he indicated with a gesture to Erika von Klausner that he wished her to remain. So she stayed in her chair while Jonathan, Charles, and Molinda took their leave.

At last she was alone with the Dutchman, and he smiled blandly at her. "I note," he said, "that you are exceptionally friendly with Jonathan Rakehell, and that you would become far friendlier if you could."

Since there was no point in denying the obvious, she merely nodded in confirmation.

The Dutchman's tone remained pleasant and conversational. "I would say," he declared, "that you have gone to rather extreme limits to make certain that he will marry you."

Erika was startled and didn't know what to reply.

"You were responsible for the death of Owen Bruce when he fought a duel with Rakehell," he continued with a smile, "and not satisfied with these efforts, you sent your man, Braun, here to steal a snake from my zoo in order to murder Molinda."

She was astonished that he knew so much, and wanted to deny the charges but was too stunned to move, much less to speak.

"Braun is paying for his perfidy," the Dutchman told her, "and now, my dear, it is your turn."

Cold, unreasoning fear gripped Erika, and she half rose, but the Dutchman waved her back to her seat, and she saw that three of his security guards, all of them wiry brown-skinned men, all of them armed with throwing knives and swords with wavy blades known as *kris*, had come into the room and were standing behind her. They were prepared to do the Dutchman's bidding, and she realized that she was powerless to oppose him, so she sank weakly back into her chair.

"I am fond—very fond—of Molinda," he said, "and I would have grieved had she died. I am delighted that your plan misfired."

It was impossible for him to prove anything against her, so she decided to bluster. "I don't know where you get your misinformation, sir," she said boldly, "and I don't know what you're talking about, but—"

The Dutchman gestured impatiently as he cut in. "Quiet," he said. "I've heard quite enough, and I don't intend to listen to any of your lies or evasions. You plotted against someone who is very dear to me, and now you shall pay the penalty."

She sat ramrod straight, and replied proudly, "I am a citizen of the free city of Hamburg and—"

"You are, for all practical purposes, my prisoner, Fraülein von Klausner, and you'll oblige me by being good enough not to forget it. I prefer not to order my retainers to teach you a lesson, but if it should be necessary, they will bind you hand and foot and gag you, and then you shall hear what I have to say."

She gathered her shattered dignity as best she could. "That will be unnecessary," she replied stiffly.

He nodded companionably. "I'm glad you're being so sensible," he said. "Now, my dear, I give you a choice." He picked up a tiny silver bell that sat on the table close to his hand, and rang it.

A slave girl came into the room carrying a glass, which she handled with great caution.

Erika looked at it curiously as it was placed in front of her, and saw that it contained a clear liquid that was odorless.

"That," the Dutchman told her with a chuckle, "is venom that has been milked from a snake similar to the one that your retainer, Braun, stole from me. You first choice is to drink the liquid. The smallest sip will suffice, I assure you, and it will kill you instantly."

Erika was no coward, but she shuddered involuntarily.

"The second choice, heh-heh," the Dutchman continued, "is to join my harem and become a full-fledged member of my entourage."

She stared at him, unable to believe that she had heard him correctly. He returned her gaze without blinking. His heavy lips were parted in a smile, but his pale eyes were cold and remorseless.

"You—you must be joking," she murmured, badly shaken.

"Not at all," he replied. "I give you the choice of death or life."

"You—you can't do this," she protested. "My employers surely will wonder what has become of me and will come looking for me."

"I do not think so," the Fat Dutchman said calmly. "Not after they receive a letter that I will write personally, explaining that you were killed, quite tragically, in a boating accident. Now," he repeated, "which do you choose?"

She stared at him proudly. "I choose life."

"Very well." He gestured, and one of the security guards removed the glass of snake venom. Then he rang the bell again and the slave girl returned carrying a jar of ink, a quill pen, and a sheet of parchment, which she placed in front of Erika and then withdrew.

"Be good enough," the Dutchman declared, "to write a note of farewell to Jonathan Rakehell, Charles, and Molinda. Tell them that you are staying to hold further business discussions with me at my invitation. Heh-heh."

She wanted to retort but thought better of it and hastily scribbled a note. There was no sound in the room but the scratching of her pen.

When she was finished, the Dutchman picked it up, read what she had written, and nodded in approval. "That will do nicely," he said, and rang the silver bell sharply.

A woman dressed like the concubines in a wraparound skirt came into the room with a short, ugly whip in her right hand. She was somewhat older than the girls of the harem.

"This is Erika, your new charge. Heh-heh," the Dutchman told her. "You'll know what to do with her." He nodded in dismissal.

The whip flicked out and missed Erika's face by no more than an inch. She looked in startled dismay at the woman, who indicated with a sharp gesture that she was to rise and follow her.

Erika was slow in gaining her feet, and the whip sang out a second time, landing in the middle of her back and causing an excruciating pain to spread through her entire body. The point, she gathered, was that the slave mistress demanded instant obedience. Erika followed her in a daze.

What followed was a nightmare. She was taken into a large chamber, where a half-dozen or more of the concubines lolled, obviously awaiting her arrival. They stripped her, placed her in a tub which they filled with warm, perfumed water, and after they had bathed her, they painted the soles of her feet and the palms of her hands with henna. She had never noticed before, but all of them were similarly adorned. Then they gave her a single garment, a skirt which they wrapped around her, and treating her as though she were a doll, proceeded to apply cosmetics heavily to her face. Never had she worn so much makeup, and they finished the task by placing a cluster of white gardenias in her hair. Then, to her annoyance, they rouged her nipples, but she did not dare protest because she saw the slave mistress was standing a few feet away, the whip still in her hand, prepared to use it at the first sign of rebellion.

Erika was not permitted to sleep for many hours. The girls taught her how to sit, how to stretch, and how to walk in her long, tight-fitting skirt, and she discovered that these feats required considerable dexterity. Then they showed her how to kowtow, and were not satisfied until she could go from a standing position to a cross-legged, sitting one and then bend forward until she touched the floor with her forehead.

Her instructions were almost finished, and only one more remained. The slave mistress said something to her in a language she didn't understand, and she didn't know how to respond. The whip cracked, and as the leather thong came in contact with the bare skin of her stomach, she was in agony.

"That," the slave mistress told her in English, "is to teach you to learn the tongue of Java quickly. We have no time to waste on you, girl. You may sleep now," she added as she took her departure. The other concubines lowered themselves to the floor and touched their foreheads to it as she departed, and Erika hastened to make a similar obeisance. She was taking no chances on being struck again with the whip.

After the slave mistress had departed, the girls showed her a cotton pallet that would serve as her bed, and as she lowered herself to it wearily, she caught a glimpse of her reflection in a full-length mirror that occupied the better part of one wall. She was astonished to see that she looked remarkably like the others, and differed from them only in the color of her skin and hair and in the cast of her features. Never had she felt so forlorn, so lonely and heartsick, but she already knew that no escape was possible.

The Marquês de Braga was charming, and Macao seemed to Elizabeth to be an enchanted land, remote from all the rest of the world and a realm unto itself. She was enjoying herself and wasn't worrying about Jonathan and the possibility that he might be with Molinda or Erika at this time. She sat on the governor-general's right at dinner, at which some of the more prominent Portuguese residents of the colony also were present, and the conversation flowed without a pause. For her sake, everyone present spoke English, and the talk was as cosmopolitan as any she had ever heard in London's high society.

It was surprising to her that she could follow the conversation so easily and hold her own in it. Having been raised in the shipping business, she found nothing out of the ordinary in the talk of trade and cargo and ships' schedules that swirled around the table. Only the names of ports and the destinations of vessels were strange to her.

The closed society of Macao was starved for newcomers, and the appearance of the exceptionally attractive and personable young Englishwoman was greeted with great enthusiasm. Elizabeth was inundated with invitations to dinner and supper, to which the governor-general escorted her, and the scheduling of which he arranged. She became familiar with performances of Chinese opera, which she found unique and strange, unlike any theatrical performances she had ever seen in the West. She also heard many *fado* singers who, in the true Portuguese tradition, told stories in their songs, usually tales of unrequited love.

She was invited, too, to picnics, and on one occasion was asked to join a fishing party that set out on a junk. In all, she enjoyed herself enormously.

The Marquês de Braga played his cards carefully. He was a perfect host and a complete gentleman. The concubines in his harem were kept out of sight, and at no time did he make either verbal or physical advances to Elizabeth. He was much taken with her beauty, to be sure, and hoped the opportunity would arise that he could capitalize on her presence in Macao, but he kept constantly in mind the fact that she was a member of a prominent family of English aristocrats, and, even more important, that she was the magnet through whom he intended to bring Jonathan Rakehell to Macao.

Only one aspect of her visit struck Elizabeth as strange.

The suite she occupied in the palace was luxuriously comfortable, but it was a constant source of distress to her to find armed, uniformed sentinels outside the entrance at all times. She was free to wander where she pleased on the palace grounds, but an officer and two sentries inevitably followed her and stayed close behind her.

The thought flicked through her mind that she was being treated like a prisoner, that Dom Manuel could call a halt to her comings and goings at any time that he pleased. Then, however, she chided herself for being overly imaginative. He was a gentleman in all ways at all times, and he had given her no cause for concern.

Contributing to her lack of ease, however, was a brief conversation she held with the marquês on the subject. "I'm having a lovely time here, Your Excellency," she told him, "but I must think of returning to Canton."

"Put all such thoughts out of your mind," he said jovially but firmly. "Your visit to Macao is just beginning."

It was not easy for Elizabeth to acclimate to the ways of the Portuguese colony, and one habit she could not form was that of taking a *siesta* after noon dinner. Granted that the temperature was at its height at that hour and that it was sensible, perhaps, to go to bed and sleep until cooler breezes blew in from the sea, but her lifetime habits prevailed, and she remained wide awake.

So it happened that, one afternoon, she heard a strange, eerie sound she had never heard before, that of an elephant trumpeting. The sound was repeated, and was even louder and wilder. Impelled by curiosity, Elizabeth left her suite and walked to some windows overlooking the large inner courtyard of the palace. She realized that the sentries outside her door were watching her, but she paid no attention to them. She saw a large male elephant, its trunk raised, thundering around the enclosure, and she looked at the beast as it trumpeted loudly for a third time. Suddenly her blood froze. Bound hand and foot, with his head on a block of wood, was a man, and he was unable to flee from the beast, unable to move. As she stared at him hard, she thought she recognized him, and all at once she knew him. He was Reinhardt Braun, who had been Erika von Klausner's servant, and she had seen him both in London and in New England. What he was doing in Macao was beyond her, but she knew he was in mortal danger.

Suddenly the elephant charged toward the man and, halting only inches in front of him, raised a front foot and brought it down deliberately on Braun's head.

Feeling ill, Elizabeth tore her gaze away and staggered back to her own suite, sickened by the murder she had just witnessed.

For several hours she felt faint and was in an inner turmoil. There was no doubt in her mind that the killing of Reinhardt Braun had been deliberate, and she was in no doubt, either, that the Marquês de Braga knew of the gruesome incident.

This knowledge changed the entire complexion of her visit. Dom Manuel might be charming, but he was also ruthlessly cold-blooded. Her own visit took on a new significance. Why was she here? Why had he resisted and demurred when she had mentioned returning to Canton? Was she being held prisoner because Dom Manuel had some hidden motive?

Her head spinning, Elizabeth knew only that for reasons beyond her ability to fathom, she was in grave danger, but she could not reveal her fear to her host. Somehow she had to dissemble with him and, for the sake of her safety, pretend that all was well.

When Erika awakened late in the morning, several of the other girls indicated to her in sign language that she was expected to bathe in water to which oil had been added in order to make her skin glisten. Then she applied a heavy coat of cosmetics to her face, and affixed a fresh flower to her hair. She donned another skirt of flimsy silk, and before she quite knew what was happening, she and a number of the girls were herded into the Dutchman's dining room, where a business dinner was in progress. A half-dozen men were seated at the table smoking *cigarros* and drinking Dutch gin. The girls had been summoned as part of the routine hospitality of the establishment.

The concubines lowered themselves to a sitting position, then touched their foreheads to the floor, and Erika, although deeply embarrassed, followed the example of her new colleagues. When she raised her head she discovered that because of her pale skin and red hair, she was the center of interest.

No one stared at her harder than did a balding middle-aged man, obviously a native of the Dutch East Indies. He was brown-skinned and pudgy, his teeth were yellow with tobacco stains, and his eyes were small and hard. The way his eyes bored into her sent shivers of apprehension up and down her bare spine.

Various men at the table were selecting the girls of their choice, and the middle-aged man beckoned imperiously to Erika.

She had no choice but to go to him, and she forced a smile to her lips, then halted when she reached him and kowtowed deeply. The gesture was humiliating in the extreme to her. She who had considered herself superior to people of other races was abasing herself before an Oriental. The man pulled her to her feet, hauled her onto his lap, and saying something to his companions in a language she did not understand, reached out and pinched her nipples.

The men roared with laughter, and even the Dutchman, watching with half-closed eyes from his end of the table, seemed amused.

Erika wanted to pick up a knife from the table and drive it into the brown-skinned man's heart, but she knew what was expected of her, so she squirmed on his lap and simulated delight. He was becoming aroused now and began to fondle her breasts in earnest.

She was afraid that he intended to take her then and there, in the presence of his business acquaintances and the other girls, and she felt a momentary relief when he rose to his feet hastily, spilling her off his lap.

She regained her balance just in time. Snapping his fingers imperiously, he beckoned her, and she was obliged to follow him, pretending all the while that she was thrilled by his conquest.

As she well knew, her ordeal was just beginning. She was acquainted with her brown-skinned lover's type. He was crass, crude, and would enjoy humbling her. Well, she had no pride left, and she knew that her going to bed with him was just the start of the hell on earth she would be forced to endure for as long as the Dutchman chose to keep her in torment. She was almost sorry now that she had not swallowed the poison and ended her life swiftly. It would have been far better that way, perhaps, than to die a little at a time, to be forced to suffer endless humiliations as she paid the supreme penalty for her transgressions.

# VI

Jonathan was bemused by the note Erika had left him, and which he received as they left the Fat Dutchman's estate. Clearly, Molinda and Lo Fang had not been too far off in their estimations: the baroness and her manservant were conniving opportunists, looking out only for their own interests. Needless to say, if he had known what had really happened to Erika and Braun, he would have been aghast.

Instead of returning to Hong Kong, Jonathan, Charles, and Molinda sailed in their junk directly to Whampoa and then went by horseback to the familiar Soong Chao estate in Canton. There a shock awaited them.

Jonathan scarcely could believe he was hearing correctly when Ruth told him that Elizabeth had gone to visit the Marquês de Braga in Macao, at his invitation. Lo Fang also was badly shaken, and held a hurried consultation with Kai, who had only just returned to the estate himself, and now felt fully responsible for Elizabeth's departure, even though his mission to help the Chinese people had been vitally important. Chen Mei, Kai's replacement while he was gone, begged to commit suicide, but Jonathan would hear nothing of this.

"There's only one way to undo the potential damage," Jonathan said flatly. "I must go to Macao at once and bring Elizabeth back here."

"That is precisely what you must not do," Molinda told

485

him, and Charles agreed. "It stands to reason," Molinda said thoughtfully, "that Dom Manuel is using Elizabeth as bait to attract you to Macao. If you go there, you might never leave the colony alive."

"I have no intention of allowing the Marquês de Braga to injure me," Jonathan replied grimly, "any more than I intend to let Elizabeth remain under his roof for one moment longer than is absolutely necessary."

Refusing to listen to the pleas of those who were so deeply concerned for his welfare, he insisted on sailing on the afternoon tide that same day on board the junk that had brought them from Djakarta. Never had Charles seen him so determined or so stubborn. Lo Fang, accompanied by an abashed Kai, sought an immediate audience with Jonathan. "We will sail with you ourselves," Lo Fang said. "It is the least we can do for our brother."

Jonathan tried to dissuade them from accompanying him. "If I'm going to be in danger," he said, "there's no point in subjecting you to unnecessary hazards too."

Kai looked angry as he replied, "We will go. It is our duty to go."

So with the head of the Society of Oxen and his oldest companion in the Middle Kingdom accompanying him, Jonathan returned to the Rakehell and Boynton docks in Whampoa and boarded the junk without further ado. To his annoyance, Lo Fang—usually the most reliable of men—disappeared from sight, and although Jonathan would have sailed without him, the Chinese captain of the junk refused to depart until the head of the Society of Oxen finally showed up.

As Jonathan saw the situation, every minute that Elizabeth spent in Macao she was in jeopardy, and he scowled at Lo Fang as he came on board the ship.

But the majordomo remained unperturbed. "I was delayed," he said, "because I visited the Elephant Man."

His remark made no sense, and Jonathan was about to retort sharply when suddenly he recalled that his brother-in-law had been put to death by a trained elephant in Macao.

"My friend," Lo Fang said, sounding strangely vague, "is a very old man who lived for many years in the island of Ceylon. He knows all there is to know about elephants. I thought it wise to see him before we sailed to Macao."

Jonathan restrained himself, and knew his annoyance was caused, at least in part, by the fact that he had not taken the time to pray at Lai-tse lu's tomb before hurrying back to Whampoa.

"It is said," Lo Fang declared, "that he who rules Macao for the Portuguese keeps killer elephants in his stables there. It is not wise to go near the palace unless one has protection from these elephants."

Jonathan nodded, and knew he would have to be polite if Lo Fang presented him with some sort of a magic token to protect him from harm. The Chinese were a remarkably superstitious people, and he didn't want to hurt the feelings of an old comrade.

Lo Fang reached into a pocket of his tunic and withdrew three glass vials. One he kept, and he presented the others to Jonathan and to Kai. "In this is a special liquid," he said. "It is an essence made from herbs which the Elephant Man himself has collected and mixed with new wine. It is given to male elephants before they mate."

Jonathan began to change his mind about the supposed superstitions of Lo Fang. Apparently there was more substance to his protective device than the New Englander had assumed.

"When the male elephant smells or drinks this substance, which is known as *musth*, there is no power on earth that can prevent him from taking a female elephant who is anywhere near him. The word '*musth*' comes from the Hindi tongue, and it means 'lustful.' It has a special quality, however. When no female elephant is near at hand, the male goes berserk after he has smelled or consumed the substance. He becomes a rogue killer until the *musth* wears off. No matter how well trained he has become, he will obey no man and will heed the voice of no master. The Elephant Man has suggested that if any of the Marquês de Braga's killer elephants are seen, the vial of *musth* should be opened at once and thrown at his feet. Then he will go mad, and will not obey an order to murder us."

Jonathan nodded somberly as he carefully placed the small glass vial in his inside coat pocket. The means of protecting himself were unorthodox, but he was deeply grateful for Lo Fang's intervention.

Another unorthodox procedure was in store as the entire original crew of the junk was replaced with silent, black-clad Chinese men. These were the members of the Society of Oxen who had returned with Kai from his mission in the Canton countryside and whom Lo Fang had rounded up to accompany them on this, an entirely different mission.

As the junk drew nearer to Macao, Jonathan sat down with Lo Fang to plan their strategy. "The entire crew of this junk," Lo Fang said, "is now made up of members of the Society of Oxen. If there is trouble in Macao, we can cause much trouble in return."

"I'm glad to hear it," Jonathan told him, "but I very much prefer to take no action when we first land. I want to see if it isn't possible to extricate Elizabeth Boynton by peaceful means, so there's no risk of any danger to her. We'll resort to firmer means only if and when it should become necessary."

Lo Fang nodded, and the chastened Kai also agreed.

"When we dock," Jonathan said, "I'll go alone to the palace and will request to see the governor-general. He will be unable to refuse, and with any luck, I will be reunited with Elizabeth Boynton. I will then try to leave with her, and I'll ask for your help only if we're threatened and are unable to get out. In that event, I'll see to it that a handkerchief is hung from one of the windows in the palace."

Lo Fang solemnly nodded. "We will have men watching every window," he said. "But if we do not receive a sign from you within one hour, we will know you and the young woman are in danger, and we will come after you."

Jonathan nodded in agreement as the Chinese man handed him a neatly folded red bandanna handkerchief, which Jonathan carefully stuffed into his hip pocket. The plans were simple, but it was best not to go into too much detail and to allow room for improvisation and maneuver. He had worked with the Society of Oxen for many months during the Opium War, and they and he knew each other well, so he trusted in their ability to meet the coming crisis.

When the junk was tied up at a commercial dock, Jonathan, already wearing his knife belt and carrying a sword, took a brace of pistols as an added precaution and walked alone up the hill toward the governor-general's palace. Nothing in his manner or in the demeanor of his comrades aboard ship suggested that more than a dozen members of the Society of Oxen were waiting on board, alerted to danger.

Jonathan gave his name to the officer of the watch at the palace, and as he had anticipated, he was soon granted permission to enter. His hunch that Elizabeth had been used as bait to lure him to Macao seemed to be confirmed, and he anticipated trouble at any moment as he was escorted through the high-ceilinged corridors of the palace. He suspected that he was being brought directly to the Marquês de Braga. He had no idea what the governor-general had planned for him, but his own plans were to demand to leave the palace at once with Elizabeth.

Two soldiers armed with rifles and bayonets were standing sentry duty outside a door, and the officer who was escorting Jonathan stopped politely in the anteroom. "If you please, sir, be good enough to surrender your weapons to me, and they'll be returned to you when you leave. No man is permitted to carry arms of any kind beyond this point in the palace."

Jonathan hesitated. He was afraid that if he objected he would not be permitted to go any farther and would never find Elizabeth, so he gave in to the request with great reluctance. The young officer placed his sword, pistols, and the belt containing his throwing knives on a table in the corner of the reception room, and laboriously wrote out a receipt for him. Then he tapped at the door, and when it opened, the officer motioned for Jonathan to enter. He walked in, and he was astonished to see Elizabeth Boynton in the living room of a suite. Radiantly beautiful in a pastel-colored gown, she was equally astonished to see him, and before Jonathan could stop himself, he was so overcome by emotion that he embraced and kissed her.

All she knew was that her lifelong dream seemed to be coming true, and her joy was unconfined.

"Thank God you're safe," he said as he released her. He hastily explained the situation to her, telling her that the Marquês de Braga was his enemy, who had used her as bait to get him to come to Macao.

She raised a hand to her throat as she listened to his brief recital. Her worst fears were confirmed, and she knew now that they both were in the gravest of danger.

"I think," Jonathan said, "that pretty soon we're going to be paid a visit by the Marquês de Braga, now that he has me where he wants me." Wasting no time, Jonathan hurriedly took the bandanna handkerchief out of his pocket and gave it to Elizabeth. "I want you to have this in the event there's any trouble or we're separated. Tie the handkerchief to any window sash, and help will be on its way to you. I can tell you no more than that, but trust me."

"I do," she replied, "as I've never trusted anyone else."

Before she could say anything more, the door opened, and the exulting Dom Manuel Sebastian stood in the frame. "Welcome to Macao, Rakehell," he said. "Our meeting has been delayed for too many years."

Jonathan bowed stiffly. "I was expecting you, Your Excellency, but I won't take up much of your time, you may be sure," he said. "The lady and I will take our departure immediately."

Dom Manuel smiled as he shook his head. "You seem to forget, sir," he said, "you thwarted me years ago when I intended to marry Soong Lai-tse lu. You thwarted my efforts in more trade and financial dealings than I could possibly count. You have built the success of Rakehell and Boynton on the ruins of my own trade, and you have done great damage to my own purse. As to the lady," he said, smiling at

Elizabeth, "I shall discuss her disposition with her later, at an appropriate time. As for you, Rakehell, perhaps you'll be good enough to accompany me now."

"Accompany you where?" Jonathan demanded, making no secret of his contempt for the Portuguese official.

"I believe that the lady is distressed at the aura of conflict that surrounds us," the Marquês de Braga said smoothly, "so I suggest that we absent ourselves from her presence and settle our disputes in our own way, as gentlemen."

As he had hoped, his appeal was effective, and Jonathan followed him warily as they went out into the corridor and walked rapidly down a flight of stairs. Jonathan realized that, without weapons, he was powerless to refuse the marquês's request, that he would have to play for time and rely on his cunning and wit in order to avoid Dom Manuel's treachery. In the meantime, he was vastly relieved that he had given the bandanna to Elizabeth, for he knew that if she was in any danger, or if he didn't soon reappear, she would be able to get help from the Oxen immediately, before the hour time limit was up.

Before Jonathan quite realized where he was, a door closed behind him, and he found himself in an inner courtyard of the palace. To his astonishment, the door had no handle on it.

"I have waited a long time for this day, Rakehell," the Marquês de Braga said, venom creeping into his voice, "and I shall treasure the memory as long as I shall live." He turned to the far end of the courtyard and called, "Send in Siroso."

Jonathan was surprised when a large white elephant lumbered slowly into the yard. This, undoubtedly, had to be one of the governor-general's feared killer elephants.

"Siroso," Dom Manuel said, "allow me to present your latest victim. You may do with him as you please."

The elephant began to advance slowly, warily, its trunk raised, its tread heavy on the tiles of the courtyard. Jonathan knew now why his weapons had been taken from him; the Marquês de Braga had prepared for his death with great cunning.

Thankfully, however, he still had the container of *musth*

that the Elephant Man of Ceylon had given to Lo Fang, and he reached into the inner pocket of his coat for it. All was not yet lost.

Dom Manuel, who had been alert to trickery of some sort, immediately saw the glass vial. "What have you got there?" he demanded. "Give it to me." He lunged for Jonathan's wrist.

Jonathan snatched his hand away and sidestepped.

The elephant, sensing the excitement and the mounting tension between the two men, increased its pace. Dom Manuel Sebastian was in no physical condition for a fight with Jonathan Rakehell. Overweight and badly out of condition, he could have been easily subdued by a man in as good trim as Jonathan. But his anxiety made him desperate, and he lunged a second time at Jonathan's wrist, caught hold of it, and with his free hand, clawed for the vial of the substance that was known in Hindi as "lustful."

Jonathan knew his life depended on the essence contained in the vial and struggled to keep it. In the course of the brief battle, the cork came loose. Just at that moment, Dom Manuel pulled with all his might, and the liquid spilled down his shirt and waistcoat. Both men were startled when Siroso raised his trunk and uttered a long, wild call.

The sound, that of the jungle, was so primitive that Jonathan's blood froze. Siroso's small eyes gleamed, and the beast looked drunk. He staggered slightly, straightened, and trumpeted again.

Inside the palace, Elizabeth heard the trumpeting sound and needed no explanation of it. She knew that Jonathan's life was being threatened by the killer elephant she had seen murder Reinhardt Braun. She hastily tied the bandanna handkerchief to the window sash, then she rushed past the two startled Portuguese soldiers, who were so taken aback that they were unable to halt her. Racing to the staircase, she descended as rapidly as she could to the ground floor.

The officer in charge of the detail caught a glimpse of her and ordered her to halt. She paid no attention to him, however, and instead increased her speed. He started in pursuit of her.

In the meantime, Siroso lived up to the Elephant Man's predictions and went berserk in the courtyard. He raced madly around the enclosure, at one point hurling himself into a wall which, although made of stone, seemed as though it would surely crumble under the impact.

The Marquês de Braga had never seen Siroso so completely out of control. Heretofore, even when trampling a victim to death, the elephant had remained disciplined and had responded to orders. Now, however, he was in a wild frenzy.

Dom Manuel shouted repeatedly, first in Portuguese, then in Hindi, but the great beast paid no attention to the sound of his voice. The essence of *musth* that had spilled onto the Marquês de Braga had attracted the full attention of the elephant, however. He lowered his head, stomped, and thundered toward the terrified governor-general.

Elizabeth stumbled, lost her footing, and started to plunge headlong down the half-flight of stairs. She caught hold of the bannister just in time to right herself, and discovered that she had already covered most of the remaining distance. She could hear the Portuguese officer, his spurs jangling, coming down the stairs behind her, however, and her sense of panic increased. She reached the ground-floor level, saw the heavy door that opened onto the courtyard, and hurried to it. Raising the latch, she pulled hard, but it would not budge.

Straining every muscle, she tugged still harder, afraid that the Portuguese officer would arrive at any moment and stop her.

In the courtyard Jonathan realized that Dom Manuel, not he, was the primary object of the elephant's wrath. The *musth* was an enormously powerful magnet, and Jonathan was able to edge away, but he was still in grave danger. The wildly stomping creature, his trunk swaying from side to side as he snorted and occasionally trumpeted, was not in its right mind, and anything could happen to a man unfortunate enough to be in the beast's path.

To Elizabeth's infinite relief, the door opened an inch, then another inch. In the arena Jonathan saw the door opening and thought he was imagining things. Then he caught a glimpse of a silk pastel dress and knew that Elizabeth had come to his aid. He immediately pushed on the door, just enough so that he could slide inside, and reaching safety, he slammed it shut and bolted it behind him.

Elizabeth looked at him in wonder and breathed a sigh of relief. He was safe, and that was all that mattered to her. Jonathan was trembling so badly that he leaned against the door as he recovered his strength.

Elizabeth looked out the window and saw a sight she would never forget as long as she lived. Dom Manuel Sebastian tried to flee from the mad elephant, but Siroso, still attracted by the pungent odor of *musth,* thundered after him, and a heavy foot crashed into the Marquês de Braga, knocking him to the ground.

The elephant's bloodlust demanded satiation. Siroso raised his head high, and his trumpet call sounded throughout the governor-general's palace and beyond it as the elephant raised his left front foot, then his right, again and again, in endless succession as he trampled the Marquês de Braga to death. Dom Manuel, who had ordered the cruel execution of so many, now was killed himself in precisely the manner that he had prescribed for his victims. Scarcely able to believe that she had witnessed such brutality, Elizabeth covered her eyes with her hands.

The Portuguese officer saw her standing at the base of the stairs as he hurtled down toward her. He completely missed seeing Jonathan, who stood against the door several yards to his right. The officer reached the bottom of the stairs and took hold of the girl's shoulders. ''Where's the Marquês de Braga? What have you done to the Marquês de Braga?'' he demanded.

Elizabeth was incapable of speech and pointed out the window.

Jonathan lost no time and hurled himself at the Portuguese officer, both fists flailing. He landed a solid blow against the man's cheekbone, another caught him in the solar plexus, and another bone-crushing punch in the pit of the stomach doubled him over.

As the officer slid groggily to the floor, Jonathan bent over him and drew his sword. "Come along," he ordered, and with one arm protectively encircling Elizabeth's waist, he started up the stairs. The bewildered sentries stood outside the suite, but not even the sight of the stranger carrying the sword moved them to action. They obeyed orders automatically but were incapable of thinking for themselves, and they stared blankly at the pair who hurried into Elizabeth's suite and quickly closed the outer door behind them. Jonathan's weapons were where the officer had left them on the anteroom table, and he hastily retrieved them. "Did you give the signal?" he asked tersely.

Elizabeth nodded. "The bandanna handkerchief? Yes," she said, "I attached it to the sash and opened the window."

Jonathan opened the door to the living room of the suite, motioned her inside, and following her, hurried to the window.

What he saw encouraged him. In the distance he could make out the twin giants, Lo Fang and Kai, curved swords in their hands, making their way along the guard-tower walk on the wall that surrounded the palace. Behind them, all in black, came the other members of the Society of Oxen.

This was like old times, Jonathan thought, and leaning out of the window, he cupped his hands and gave a creditable imitation of an owl hooting. The approaching Society of Oxen men halted, and Lo Fang returned the signal. There was a drop of about fifteen feet from the open window to the wall, as Jonathan estimated the distance, and he hastily ran into the adjoining bedchamber and began to rip up sheets, which he tied together to make a rope. Returning quickly to the living room, he tied one end of his makeshift rope around the legs of a grand piano and tugged hard to make sure that the line held fast. "I'm going down to the wall," he said, "then you let yourself down hand over hand. Don't worry about falling, because I'll be there to catch you."

There had been times in the past when Elizabeth could not

have imagined engaging in such an athletic feat, but she was prepared to trust Jonathan implicitly in all things, and she was ready to follow his orders to the letter. He stood on the windowsill, waved to the Society of Oxen men, and climbed to the parapet below. "Hurry," he called to Elizabeth. "Climb down. Quickly!"

Had she hesitated, she would have been too terrified to obey, but the sound of his voice galvanized her into action, and she began the difficult task of climbing down the make-shift rope of sheets. She felt dizzy, and her arms felt as though they were being wrenched from their sockets, but she clung grimly to the sheets as she perilously, slowly, lowered herself hand over hand.

Then Jonathan's strong hands reached up and closed around her waist, and he lifted her gently to the safety of the parapet.

"So far, so good," he told her. "We're on our way."

Things were happening with such bewildering speed that she found it difficult to grasp the situation fully. "Who are those men?" she asked as the group of Chinese approached them.

"They're friends," he assured her.

At the same moment she recognized Kai and felt infinite relief. How Jonathan had managed to plan this move to extricate her from the palace of the governor-general of Macao was beyond her comprehension, but with his arm firmly encircling her, she felt safe, ready for anything that might transpire. Lo Fang approached, and he and Jonathan conferred rapidly in Cantonese.

Elizabeth had no idea what he was saying, of course, as he told Lo Fang that the Marquês de Braga had been killed by the elephant and that they had to make good their escape, or certainly they would be charged with his murder.

Lo Fang was quietly confident. "There are fifty soldiers stationed there at the main gate," he said. "There are steps that lead down from the wall near the gate, so that is the easiest way to remove the lady. I think we can handle fifty Portuguese soldiers without too much trouble."

Jonathan weighed the matter briefly, and decided that Lo

Fang was right. The troops had little or nothing in their favor except their numbers. Their rifles were old-fashioned and, at best, were inaccurate when fired. Most important, with Dom Manuel Sebastian dead, there was no one strong man to direct the activities of the troops. Their officers, perhaps, were competent, but had no idea what was afoot, and Jonathan relied on their confusion. "We'll chance it," he said. "Come along."

Elizabeth suddenly found herself surrounded by the impassive-faced men in black pajamas. They made their way silently down the length of the wall toward the stairs that led to the front gate, and all of them, she noted, were carrying the new Colt revolvers that had appeared in the United States a few years earlier. Obviously Jonathan had supplied arms to the Society of Oxen. All at once the thought occurred to Elizabeth that she was leaving a number of her dresses and other belongings behind. The thought struck her as ludicrous, when she could lose her life at any moment, and she laughed aloud.

Not knowing the cause of her laughter, Jonathan thought she was enjoying the adventure and nodded approvingly. As long as her spirits remained high, their chances of escape were better. Lo Fang and Kai were pleased, too, and grinned. They should have known, as they told each other without words, that any woman in whom Rakehell Jonathan was interested was certain to be courageous.

Peering at the watchtowers on either side and peering at the ground below, Jonathan was relieved beyond measure to see that the sentries were paying literally no attention to the group. Incredible though it seemed, the Portuguese officers and men were far more interested in the quiet that enabled them to take naps.

"Walk toward the stairs slowly," he ordered, speaking in Cantonese. "Keep your weapons concealed, and under no circumstances fire, unless we're fired upon. Make it appear as though we're a convivial group seeing the sights." He set an example by laughing heartily himself as he put an arm around Elizabeth's shoulders.

The Society of Oxen members chuckled appreciatively and seemed completely relaxed.

Elizabeth saw no humor in the situation, but when she smiled tentatively, Jonathan nodded encouragement. "That's better," he said. "Pretend you're having a grand time, and don't appear tense."

They came to the staircase and strolled down to the ground level, then still moving in a body, forming a protective cordon around Jonathan and Elizabeth, they moved to the entrance gate. There a Portuguese officer and several of his men were stationed, and Jonathan knew the period of quiet was about to be shattered. The officer's duty required him to obtain identification from everyone who passed in and out of the gate.

"Keep moving until we no longer have any choice," Jonathan directed in Cantonese. "The closer we are to the gates, the less far we'll be obliged to run."

Only experienced members of a secret society that had fought a long, grueling war against superior forces could have acted so boldly and decisively. The Society of Oxen men pressed toward the gate and ignored two orders from the Portuguese officer to halt. Only when he instructed his subordinates to shoot if he was not obeyed did the Chinese finally halt. Jonathan took the initiative and addressed the officer, uncertain whether the man would understand English. "You recognize the lady, I'm sure, Captain," he said. "She's been a guest of the Marquês de Braga."

The young Portuguese officer did indeed comprehend. He peered at the girl, recognized her, and was satisfied as to her identity, but many questions continued to crowd his mind.

Jonathan spoke quickly and glibly. "I am an official of Hong Kong," he said, "and I have been directed by the governor-general of that colony to escort the young lady to him. These Chinese gentlemen have been assigned to us as bodyguards because we understand there's been trouble lately with brigands in the Pearl River Basin."

Not waiting for the officer to act, he waved the members of his party through the gate. He'd spoken gibberish, as Kai and Lo Fang realized, but they gave the Portuguese officer no opportunity to analyze Jonathan's words. They promptly set their men in motion again, and a gentle pressure from Jonathan's hand instructed Elizabeth to go, too. She smiled brightly at the officer as though to reassure him, and within moments the entire party was outside the palace wall.

If Elizabeth expected her deliverers to relax now, she was badly mistaken. They needed no directive, as with one accord, they started toward the Macao waterfront. It was only a question of time before the colonel in charge of the palace guard connected the Marquês de Braga's death with the disappearance of his English guest and of the American who had come to call on him this very day.

Events were taking place so quickly that Elizabeth had no chance to reflect on what was happening. All she knew was that she appeared to be safe and that Jonathan seemed very much in charge. They reached the junk, where four crew members had been left as a guard, and Elizabeth felt a surge of joy when she saw the Tree of Life banner flying from the masthead.

But the ordeal was not yet ended.

Jonathan assumed the command as soon as he set foot on the ship. "Cut the anchors loose and raise your sails," he told Lo Fang. "The sooner we get away from here, the better."

Within moments the cumbersome vessel began to move slowly toward the entrance to the harbor.

Jonathan stood on the quarterdeck, studying the two small forts that stood at either side of the harbor entrance, and he obviously didn't care for what he found there. "Crowd on all the sail that you can carry," he told Lo Fang and Kai, "and give your entire sailing crew the duty. We may be required to use some evasive tactics."

For Elizabeth's sake, he did not explain, as he had no wish to frighten her.

But the reasons for his precautions became evident as soon as the junk came within hailing distance of the starboard fort. A Portuguese naval officer called out an order for the vessel to return at once to the harbor.

Jonathan ignored the order and commanded the junk to tack abruptly.

Suddenly Elizabeth saw the ship was sailing on an erratic, zigzagging course, lurching unexpectedly to port and then to starboard. The reason for the unorthodox maneuver soon became evident. A cannon was fired from the starboard fort, and an iron ball capable of wreaking great destruction fell harmlessly into the sea about one hundred feet behind the vessel. Then the two batteries in the portside fort spoke. Thereafter the cannonading was continuous.

But the Society of Oxen seamen responded to the emergency as one man, obeying Jonathan's rapid-fire commands to the precise letter, and the ship seemed to lead a charmed existence. The artillerymen manning the guns in the forts were skilled at their trade, but they were no match for the New Englander, who kept well ahead of the steady stream of destructive iron balls that fell harmlessly into the waters of the South China Sea. Junks were built for their safety, comfort, and cargo capacity rather than speed, but Jonathan utilized every trick of seamanship at his command, and his vessel remained unscathed. If the Portuguese had possessed any sloops of war, these sleek, fast vessels undoubtedly could have overtaken the junk. But the one Portuguese naval squadron in Far Eastern waters was at sea, rather than in port, and there were no ships that could be sent in pursuit. So, as the distance between the forts and their quarry lengthened, Jonathan eventually breathed more easily.

"I congratulate all hands," he called at last. "We're safe now."

Although he spoke in Cantonese, the reaction of the Chinese crew to his words was so emphatic that Elizabeth needed no translation.

At last Jonathan could devote his whole attention to her. "You behaved well throughout the crisis," he said, "and I owe you my life. If you hadn't opened the courtyard door when you did, the rogue elephant would have trampled me to death, just as he killed the Marquês de Braga."

"I don't like to think about such matters," Elizabeth replied as she shuddered. "We're both safe now, and the nightmare is ended."

"We can look forward to the future now," Jonathan told her. "A joint future." Ignoring the presence of the Chinese on deck, he grasped her hand. "In all of the furor," he said, "I don't believe I've had an opportunity to tell you that I love you. I do, with my whole heart."

She looked up at him, her eyes shining. "I've never loved anyone else," she replied.

He embraced and kissed her, and the world spun madly for both of them.

When they drew apart, Jonathan realized that the Tree of Life medallion hanging from his neck had remained cool to the touch. The spirit of Lai-tse lu, he knew, approved of his union with Elizabeth.


Ruth and Charles Boynton were relieved beyond measure that Jonathan had succeeded in his mission to rescue Elizabeth from Macao, and they were delighted by the swift and climactic development of the couple's romance.

"How soon will you marry?" Ruth wanted to know.

Jonathan frowned and shook his head. "That's difficult to say," he replied. "I don't think it's fair to start married life under a cloud, and I'm insisting that we wait until we solve the company's financial problem."

Elizabeth sighed gently. "I've tried to make him understand that there's no connection between our marriage and the company's situation, but he's just being a stubborn Rakehell, and I can't budge him."

"Well," Charles said, "I'm going to visit the treaty ports in the immediate future—taking Ruth and David with me, of course—but I don't expect any trade miracles to occur at any of them."

"I must visit the Tao Kuang Emperor and the Princess An Mien," Jonathan said. "I have several packing cases of books and Western tools for them, and I'm anxious, too, to have them meet Elizabeth, so we'll go to Peking while you're visiting the treaty ports. Then, I daresay, we'll be ready to return home."

"I very much doubt that anything miraculous has happened either in New England or in London," Charles said.

"It seems to me," Elizabeth said a trifle plaintively, "that my wedding is going to have to wait indefinitely." She refrained from mentioning that her one hope was that Jonathan's father and Missy Sarah would be able to persuade him to set a date in the immediate future after they arrived in New London.

Before they left Canton, Jonathan paid a final visit to his late wife's tomb, and Elizabeth quietly joined him there. They knelt side by side in silent prayer, and Jonathan felt at peace within himself as he rose and they walked out of the incense-laden pagoda into the bright sunlight of Canton. "Do you think she approves?" Elizabeth asked.

"I know she does," Jonathan replied. "I can't tell you how, but I'm sure of it."

"I know I can never take her place," Elizabeth said, "and frankly, I don't intend to try. She has a special place in your affections, and I hope I will have my own."

"You already have it," he assured her.

She smiled gently. "That's all I'll ever ask," she murmured.

Charles and his family were already at sea, and Jonathan and Elizabeth bade farewell to Molinda and Lo Fang. "I shall keep in touch with you, as I've always done," Molinda said, "and I know you can count on a steady but undramatic increase in our trade with the Middle Kingdom."

"Thanks to you, yes," Jonathan said, and kissed her fondly.

Molinda and Elizabeth embraced. "You have a wonderful man, my dear," Molinda said. "Take care of him, for your own sake, for his children's sake, and for all of us."

"I shall do my best," Elizabeth promised her.

They set sail that same day on board the *Lai-tse lu* for Tientsin, accompanied by Julian, Jade, the ever-present Harmony, and Kai. On the voyage northward along the coast,

Elizabeth and Jonathan spent many hours together on deck, she telling him all about her past—about her indiscretions but also about her constant love for him. He merely took her hand and smiled, his expression showing that he had no misgivings, that he loved her.

"You must know this," she went on. "I am no longer able to bear children. After the operation, I—I—"

He silenced her with a kiss. "When we marry, we'll have children—Julian and Jade. And we'll have each other."

When they arrived in Tientsin, the usual interminable messages were exchanged between the quarterdeck of the clipper and the huge fort guarding the harbor. The identity of every passenger was duly noted, and only when the garrison commander discovered that Rakehell Jonathan was listed in his records as a favorite of the emperor, was the vessel permitted to enter the harbor. A strong military escort was summoned, and the customary three-day journey to Peking began. Julian and Jade were veterans of the overland trip, but Elizabeth was fascinated by the topography and people of northern Cathay, who were so different from those of the south. The Cantonese and most of the Chinese in Hong Kong were short, slender, and wiry. Those of the north were tall and rugged, and the cast of their features suggested that they numbered Mongol conquerors as well as Chinese among their ancestors.

On the third day, they approached Peking, and drew to a halt when a party of horsemen traveling in the opposite direction hailed them. Jonathan was delighted when he recognized Matthew Melton and Wu-ling, who had heard of his arrival and had come to the city gates in order to escort him to the Forbidden City.

Although they had written him their news, he had not yet received their letter, and was highly pleased to learn that they had married.

"I can only hope for you," Wu-ling told Elizabeth, "that you and Jonathan will find happiness to equal Matthew's and mine."

They rode slowly through the streets of outer Peking and

the Imperial City, coming at last to the Forbidden City, where they would be the guests of the Meltons, who would not hear of them staying in quarters usually reserved for foreigners. Jonathan sent word of his arrival to the emperor and the Princess An Mien, and, as he confided to Elizabeth, he expected that he would be received in a private audience the following day. The visitors had their own extensive suite in the Melton house and were left to themselves to rest for several hours before dinner. Julian and Jade were too excited to sleep, however, and went out into the yard to play, taking their dog with them; and Jonathan stood at a window in the living room of the suite, pointing out various parts of the imperial palace to Elizabeth. There was a tap at the door behind them, and before he could reply, Princess An Mien came into the room. She greeted Jonathan warmly, and he was proud to present Elizabeth to her.

Then he heard Harmony barking and, to his utter dismay, saw the dog racing into the room ahead of a man in a pearl cap and a dusty black robe. He was carrying Jade on one shoulder, and Julian skipped beside him, holding his other hand. To treat the Tao Kuang Emperor so informally was unheard of, and Jonathan wanted to snatch his children away and lecture them severely, but the emperor seemed to be enjoying himself thoroughly.

"Papa, Papa!" Jade exclaimed. "Here's the nice man who gave us presents the last time we came to Peking."

Elizabeth knew at once that this man was none other than the Celestial Emperor himself. Uncertain whether to curtsy as she would to Queen Victoria, she glanced at Jonathan. He knew at once what was in her mind and shook his head. This was no time to explain to her that the Tao Kuang Emperor chose to make himself invisible when it suited his purposes. It also suited his purposes at the moment to speak bluntly.

"So this is the lady whom Rakehell Jonathan has chosen to marry," he said, speaking in heavily accented but good English. "She is very lovely."

"Very," his sister added pointedly.

The embarrassed Elizabeth did not know what to reply.

504

Jonathan bowed his head in acknowledgment of the compliment, then he hurried to the door and instructed Kai to have the packing boxes of gifts for the royal couple brought into the room at once.

As this task was performed by members of the imperial household staff, the emperor saved the need for ceremony by walking to a window and staring out it, with his back to the room.

Jonathan carefully enumerated his gifts, telling the emperor and his sister the nature of the various books he had brought them, and the purposes of the various items of machinery, all of which he felt certain could be duplicated in the Middle Kingdom and would help propel the backward nation into the nineteenth century.

When he had presented the last of his gifts and they had been removed and carried off to the imperial quarters in the main building of the palace, the Tao Kuang Emperor exchanged a significant glance with his sister. "As always," he said, "the Middle Kingdom is in the debt of Rakehell Jonathan."

"This man," An Mien said to Elizabeth, "has done more than anyone else to modernize our country. We can never repay our debt to him."

"But we can try," the Tao Kuang Emperor said, and gestured sharply.

Kai immediately entered, followed by several servants in yellow uniforms who laid what looked like greased metal tracks. Julian and Jade were curious, but Elizabeth warned them not to get too close.

The Tao Kuang Emperor offered no explanation of the reason for the laying of the tracks.

"My sister and I," he said, "have the right to be very angry with Rakehell Jonathan. It has been called forcibly to our attention that he is in financial need, largely because of his great generosity in giving a large fortune to the poor of the Middle Kingdom. How does it happen that you told us nothing about this need?"

Jonathan realized that it was wrong to reply directly to a

question asked by the Tao Kuang Emperor because such a gesture would destroy the myth of his supposed nonpresence, but under the circumstances a direct answer could not be avoided.

"The Tao Kuang Emperor," he said, "has many problems. He must deal with the welfare and guide the lives of many millions of people. Surely it would be wrong to burden him with one man's problems."

The emperor frowned, and his manner became chiding. "When that man is Rakehell Jonathan, everything that concerns him is of interest to the emperor and his sister. How else can they begin to discharge their debts to him?"

He did not wait for an answer, but snapped his fingers as a signal to the imperial household servants.

They sprang into action immediately, and pushed two very heavy metal cases into the room. Now the reason for the greased tracks became evident. The cases were so unwieldy that the only way they could be moved was to slide them into the chamber on top of the tracks. "This," the emperor said, pointing to one metal box, "is my gift, and the other is my sister's."

Jonathan stood uncertainly as the children clamored for the right to open the lids and see what was inside.

A half-smile lighted Princess An Mien's face as she replied to Julian and Jade. "The lids are too heavy for you children to lift," she said. "I think you'd best leave that task to your father."

Jonathan knew now that he was expected to open the boxes, so he went to them and raised the lids.

There was no sound in the room but Elizabeth's gasp of utter astonishment.

Jonathan could only stare at the boxes. Both of them were filled with gold yuan, and the realization dawned on him that, between them, the two containers held a vast fortune.

"Your financial problems are solved now, I believe," the emperor said.

Jonathan shook his head in disbelief. The fortune contained in the two cases was so great that it would solve the financial difficulties of Rakehell and Boynton for all time. By accepting the money, he would propel the company into the ranks of the foremost shipbuilding and trading companies on the face of the earth.

But there was a snag that appeared to him to be insurmountable. "I am deeply touched," he said, "more so than Your Imperial Majesty and Your Imperial Highness will ever know, but I cannot accept a gift of such magnitude."

The Tao Kuang Emperor looked hurt. "Why not?" he demanded.

"Because there is no way I can repay you for your great generosity! Ever!" Jonathan exclaimed.

The emperor ignored him and addressed himself exclusively to Elizabeth. "It will be your duty," he said, "as it was that of Lai-tse lu, to pound sense into the head of your husband. He is capable of incredible stupidity."

The Princess An Mien appeared to be equally indignant. "How do you measure all that Rakehell Jonathan has done for the Middle Kingdom?" she demanded. "How many lives were saved by Dr. Melton, whom Rakehell Jonathan sent to us, when the plague descended on Peking? How many of our farmers now use the cotton gin that Rakehell Jonathan first brought to Cathay, and how many thousands upon thousands of our subjects are now gainfully employed in manufacturing useful items that benefit all our people, using machinery that Rakehell Jonathan introduced into the Middle Kingdom."

"Our debt to him, Mistress Boynton, is endless. If he does not accept this gift," the emperor added, "he will be condemned to spend the rest of his days confined to an underground dungeon."

Jade was so startled that she burst into tears.

The Princess An Mien was quick to reassure the child. "Never fear," she said, "that will not happen, because this lovely lady, whom your father will marry, will persuade him it is in his best interests to accept our gift."

Elizabeth found her voice at last. "Of course he will accept the gift," she said. "He is overwhelmed by your magnificent gesture, and it has paralyzed his mind temporarily. But you

507

are right. I've been finding out all that he has done for this country, and I think that he has more than earned this reward. Even if he were to continue to refuse it, I assure you that I would nevertheless accept it on his behalf.''

The Tao Kuang Emperor chuckled, and the Princess An Mien smiled. ''You are a young lady who has a mind of her own and uses it,'' she said. ''I like that. May I ask why you're so positive?''

''Because we cannot marry, according to Jonathan, until the company's financial crisis is solved, and, frankly, I'm tired of waiting.''

The emperor roared with laughter, and Princess An Mien turned to Julian and Jade. ''Do you wish to see your father married to this lady?''

''Yes! Yes!'' they shouted, and Jade threw herself at Elizabeth and planted a wet kiss on her cheek.

The Tao Kuang Emperor pulled his pearl cap down more firmly onto his head. ''Your days of waiting have come to an end,'' he told her.

He kept his word, and both Jonathan and Elizabeth were startled by the speed with which their wedding developed. A high priest was ordered to marry them, and the delighted Matthew and Wu-ling Melton were asked to be witnesses. The children stood in the temple, flanking Princess An Mien, and the Tao Kuang Emperor shattered custom by insisting that he give the bride away himself. He also provided her with a wide band of gold that had been in his family for hundreds of years. Before dinner was served that same evening, Jonathan and Elizabeth were husband and wife, intending also to be married in an Anglican ceremony when they returned to New London.

That night they slept together and truly became one. All that Elizabeth had suffered had not been in vain, and her wounds were healed as she held Jonathan tightly, and he held her.

Jonathan, loving her and being loved in return, knew he could never be lonely again. He was at peace within himself because the Tree of Life medallion remained cool to the touch, and he knew that Lai-tse lu believed, as he did, that he was doing the right thing, for himself, for Elizabeth, and for his children.

The next morning Wu-ling kept the children entertained so the honeymooners could sleep late, and when they finally appeared for a hearty breakfast of broiled fish, mung bean noodles, and a fiery soup dish, the bride was radiant and Jonathan had a permanent smile on his face. Immediately after breakfast, he announced that he had to send word of their extraordinary good fortune to Charles and Molinda. It was pointless to send letters to his father and Sir Alan Boynton, as well, because they would carry the news themselves more rapidly than a letter could travel on board any other ship. He arranged, too, to have the fortune in gold transported to the hold of the *Lai-tse lu,* and Kai arranged for the presence of a strong guard on board to keep watch on the fortune.

Then the bride and groom wandered hand in hand through the vast, dazzling imperial gardens. Never had they seen such a profusion of flowers, nor such artistry in their arrangement. There were marble statues of figures from Chinese mythology everywhere, and marble pagodas dotted the gardens, too. "I've heard it said," Jonathan told his bride, "that over one thousand men tend these gardens."

"I can well believe it," Elizabeth replied. "I can begin to understand now why you feel such a strong attachment to China. I feel it, too, and it goes far beyond the generous gift of the emperor and his sister that has solved all our financial problems. There's something in this country that appeals to me and that I can't define. It's a spirit, a feeling, a mystery, really."

Jonathan halted and pointed. Directly ahead of them, but not seeing them, Julian and Jade were at play. The boy sat astride a marble horse, which he was pretending to ride, while Jade stared at her reflection in a clear pool that was surrounded by hundreds of massed growing flowers. "There's your answer," he said. "The future belongs to them. All that we do is a preparation of the world they will know when they

509

inherit Rakehell and Boynton. They're learning already that their ultimate destiny lies in this strange, contradictory land where life seems so simple, yet is so terribly complex.''

Harmony became aware of their proximity and ran to greet them, his tail wagging furiously. They bent down simultaneously to pat him, and as they straightened again, their lips met. The sun rose higher over the ornamental roof of a pagoda and bathed them in its light. The good they could do for Cathay and the benefits they would reap in return were endless, a stream that would never stop flowing, just as the great rivers of China flowed endlessly into the sea.

# ESPECIALLY FOR YOU
# FROM WARNER

**BOLD BREATHLESS LOVE**
*by Valerie Sherwood*                                    *(D30-310, $3.50)*
The surging saga of Imogene, a goddess of grace with riotous golden
curls—and Verholst Van Rappard, her elegant idolator. They marry and he
carries her off to America—not knowing that Imogene pines for a copper-
haired Englishman who made her his on a distant isle and promised to
return to her on the wings of love.

**THE OFFICERS' WIVES**
*by Thomas Fleming*                                      *(A90-920, $3.95)*
This is a book you will never forget. It is about the U.S. Army, the huge
unwieldy organism on which much of the nation's survival depends. It is
about Americans trying to live personal lives, to cling to touchstones of
faith and hope in the grip of the blind, blunderous history of the last 25
years. It is about marriage, the illusions and hopes that people bring to it,
the struggle to maintain and renew commitment.

To order, use the coupon below. If you prefer to use your
own stationery, please include complete title as well as
book number and price. Allow 4 weeks for delivery.